PENGUIN BOOKS

THE MANTICORE

The son of a journalist, Robertson Davies was born in 1913 in
Thamesville, Ontario, and educated at Queen's University and
at Oxford. He became a journalist himself, and his first book,
The Table Talk of Samuel Marchbanks, had its origin in an
editorial column. Davies was also, for a while, a professional
actor, studying at the Old Vic Drama School, where he met his
wife, and serving as Sir Tyrone Guthrie's literary assistant. His
own plays, characterized by superb epigrammatic wit, are
widely performed in Canada. It is as a fiction writer, however,
that Davies, now Master of Massey College in Toronto, has
achieved international recognition with such novels as *A Mixture of Frailties, Leaven of Malice,* and especially his major
work, the trilogy composed of *Fifth Business, The Manticore,*
and *World of Wonders.*

BY THE SAME AUTHOR

NOVELS

Tempest-Tost

Leaven of Malice

A Mixture of Frailties

Fifth Business

World of Wonders

CRITICISM

A Voice from the Attic

THE
MANTICORE

Robertson Davies

PENGUIN BOOKS

Penguin Books Ltd, Harmondsworth,
Middlesex, England
Penguin Books, 40 West 23rd Street,
New York, New York 10010, U.S.A.
Penguin Books Australia Ltd, Ringwood,
Victoria, Australia
Penguin Books Canada Limited, 2801 John Street,
Markham, Ontario, Canada L3R 1B4
Penguin Books (N.Z.) Ltd, 182–190 Wairau Road,
Auckland 10, New Zealand

First published in the United States of America by The Viking Press 1972
Published in Canada by The Macmillan Company of Canada Limited 1972
Published in Penguin Books 1976
Reprinted 1977, 1978, 1979, 1980, 1981, 1982 (twice), 1983

LIBRARY OF CONGRESS CATALOGING IN PUBLICATION DATA
Davies, William Robertson, 1913—
The manticore.
The second of three linked novels,
the first being Fifth business (1970),
and the third being World of wonders (c1975).
Reprint of the 1972 ed. published by The Viking Press, New York.
I. Title.
[PZ4.D258MAN6] [PR9199.3.D3]   813'.5'4
ISBN 0 14 00.4388 8   76-43018

Printed in the United States of America by
Offset Paperback Mfrs., Inc., Dallas, Pennsylvania
Set in Linotype Garamond No. 3

Contents

I   Why I Went to Zürich   3

II   David Against the Trolls   75

III   My Sorgenfrei Diary   265

THE MANTICORE

· I ·

Why I Went to Zürich

(1)

WHEN DID YOU decide you should come to Zürich, Mr. Staunton?

"When I heard myself shouting in the theatre."

"You decided at that moment?"

"I think so. Of course I put myself through the usual examination afterward to be quite sure. But I could say that the decision was made as soon as I heard my own voice shouting."

"The usual examination? Could you tell me a little more about that, please."

"Certainly. I mean the sort of examination one always makes to determine the nature of anyone's conduct, his degree of responsibility, and all that. It was perfectly clear. I was no longer in command of my actions. Something had to be done, and I must do it before others had to do it on my behalf."

"Please tell me again about this incident when you shouted. With a little more detail, please."

"It was the day before yesterday, that is to say November ninth, at about ten forty-five p.m. in the Royal Alexandra Theatre in Toronto, which is my home. I was sitting in a bad seat in the top gallery. That in itself was unusual. The performance was something rather grandiosely called *The Soirée of Illusions*—a magic show, given by a conjuror called Magnus Eisengrim. He is well known, I understand, to people who like that kind of thing. He had an act which he called *The Brazen Head of Friar Bacon*. A large head that looked like brass, but was made of some almost transparent material, seemed to float in the middle of the stage; you couldn't see how it was done—wires of some sort, I suppose. The Head gave what purported to be advice to people in the audience. That was what infuriated me. It was imprudent, silly stuff hinting at scandal —adulteries, little bits of gossip, silly, spicy rubbish—and I felt irritation growing in me that people should be concerned about such trash. It was an unwarranted invasion of privacy, you understand, by this conjuror fellow whose confident assumption of superiority—just a charlatan, you know, seeming to patronize serious people! I knew I was fidgeting in my seat, but it wasn't until I heard my own voice that I realized I was standing up, shouting at the stage."

"And you shouted—?"

"Well, what would you expect me to shout? I shouted, as loud as I could—and that's very loud, because I have some experience of shouting—I shouted, 'Who killed Boy Staunton?' And then all hell broke loose!"

"There was a furore in the theatre?"

"Yes. A man standing in a box gave a cry and fell down. A lot of people were murmuring and some stood up to see who had shouted. But they quieted down immediately the Brazen Head began to speak."

"What did it say?"

"There are several opinions. The broadcast news reported that the Head suggested he had been killed by a gang. All I heard was something about 'the woman he knew—the woman he did not know,' which, of course, could only mean my stepmother. But I was getting away as fast as I could. It is a very steep climb up to the doors in that balcony, and I was in a state of excitement and shame at what I had done, so I didn't really hear well. I wanted to get out before I was recognized."

"Because you are Boy Staunton?"

"No, no, no; Boy Staunton was my father."

"And was he killed?"

"Of course he was killed! Didn't you read about it? It wasn't just some local murder where a miser in a slum is killed for a few hundred dollars. My father was a very important man. It's no exaggeration to say it was international news."

"I see. I am very sorry not to have known. Now, shall we go over some of your story again?"

And we did. It was long, and often painful for me, but he was an intelligent examiner, and at times I was conscious of being an unsatisfactory witness, assuming he knew things I hadn't told him, or that he couldn't know. I was ashamed of saying "of course" so often, as if I were offering direct evidence instead of stuff that was at best presumptive—something I would never tolerate in a witness myself. I was embarrassed to be such a fool in a situation that I had told myself and other people countless times I would never submit to—talking to a psychiatrist, ostensibly seeking help, but without any confidence that he could give it. I have never believed these people can do anything for an intelligent man he can't do for himself. I have known many people who leaned on psychiatrists, and every one of them was a leaner by nature, who would have leaned on a priest if he had lived in an age of faith, or leaned on a teacup-reader or an astrologer if he had not had enough money to afford the higher hokum. But here I was, and there was nothing to do now but go through with it.

It had its amusing side. I had not known what to expect,

but I rather thought I would be put on a couch and asked about sex, which would have been a waste of time, as I have no sex to tell about. But here, in the office of the Director of the Jung Institute, 27 Gemeindestrasse, Zürich, there was no couch—nothing but a desk and two chairs and a lamp or two and some pictures of a generally Oriental appearance. And Dr. Tschudi. And Dr. Tschudi's big Alsatian, whose stare of polite, watchful curiosity was uncannily like the doctor's own.

"Your bodyguard?" I had said when I entered the room.

"Ha ha," laughed Dr. Tschudi in a manner I came to be well acquainted with in Switzerland; it is the manner which acknowledges politely that a joke has been made, without in any way encouraging further jokiness. But I received the impression—I am rather good at receiving impressions—that the doctor met some queer customers in that very Swiss little room, and the dog might be useful as more than a companion.

The atmosphere of the whole Jung Institute, so far as I saw it, puzzled me. It was one of those tall Zürich houses with a look that is neither domestic nor professional, but has a smack of both. I had had to ring the bell several times to be admitted through the door, the leaded glass of which made it impossible to see if anyone was coming; the secretary who let me in looked like a doctor herself, and had no eager public-relations grin; to reach Dr. Tschudi I had to climb a tall flight of stairs, which echoed and suggested my sister's old school. I was not prepared for any of this; I think I expected something that would combine the feeling of a clinic with the spookiness of a madhouse in a bad film. But this was—well, it was Swiss. Very Swiss, for though there was nothing of the cuckoo-clock, or the bank, or milk chocolate about it, it had a sort of domesticity shorn of coziness, a matter-of-factness within which one could not be quite sure of its facts, that put me at a disadvantage. And though when visiting a psychiatrist

I had expected to lose something of my professional privilege of always being at an advantage, I could not be expected to like it when I encountered it.

I was an hour with the Director, and a few important things emerged. First, that he thought I might benefit by some exploratory sessions with an analyst. Second, that the analyst would not be himself, but someone he would recommend who was free to accept another patient at this time and to whom he would send a report; third, that before that I must undergo a thorough physical examination to make sure that analysis, rather than some physical treatment, was appropriate for me. Dr. Tschudi rose and shook me by the hand. I offered also to shake the paw of the Alsatian, but it scorned my jocosity, and the Director's smile was wintry.

I found myself once again in Gemeindestrasse, feeling a fool. Next morning, at my hotel, I received a note giving directions as to where my medical examination would take place. I was also instructed to call at ten o'clock in the morning, three days hence, on Dr. J. von Haller, who would be expecting me.

(2)

The clinic was thorough beyond anything I had ever experienced. As well as the familiar humiliations—hanging about half-naked in the company of half-naked strangers, urinating in bottles and handing them warm and steamy to very young nurses, coughing at the behest of a physician who was prodding at the back of my scrotum, answering intimate questions while the same physician thrust a long finger up my rectum and tried to catch my prostate in some irregularity, trudging up and down a set of steps while the physician counted; gasping, puffing, gagging, sticking out my tongue, rolling my eyes, and doing all the other silly tricks which reveal so much to the doctor while making the patient feel a fool—I underwent a few things that were new to me. Quite a lot of blood was taken from me at various points—much more than the usual tiny bit removed from the ear lobe. I drank a glass of a chocolate-flavoured mixture and was then, every hour for six hours, stood on my head on a movable X-ray table to which I had been strapped, as pictures were taken to see how the mess was getting through my tripes. A variety of wires was attached to me whose purpose I could only guess, but as my chair was whirled and tilted I suppose it had something to do with my nervous system, sense of balance, hearing, and all that. Countless questions, too, about how long my grandparents and parents had lived, and of what they had died. When I gave the cause of my father's death as "Murder" the clinician blinked slightly, and I was glad to have disturbed his Swiss phlegm, even for an instant. I had not been feeling well when I came to Zürich, and after two days of medical rough-house I was tired and dispirited and in a mood to go—not home, most certainly not—somewhere else. But I thought I ought to see Dr. J. von Haller at least once, if only for the pleasure of a good row with him.

Why was I so hostile toward a course of action I had undertaken of my own will? There was no single answer to that. As I told the Director, I made the decision on a basis of reason, and I would stick with it. Netty had always told me that when something unpleasant must be done—medicine taken, an apology made for bad behaviour, owning up to something that would bring a beating from my father—I had to be "a little soldier." Little soldiers, I understood, never hesitated; they did what was right without question. So I must be a little soldier and visit Dr. J. von Haller at least once.

Ah, but did little soldiers ever have to go to the psychiatrist? They visited the dentist often, and many a time I had shouldered my little invisible musket and marched off in that direction. Was this so very different? Yes, it was.

I could understand the use of a dentist. He could grind and dig and refill, and now and then he could yank. But what could psychiatrists do? Those I had seen in court contradicted each other, threw up clouds of dust, talked a jargon which, in cross-examination, I could usually discredit. I never used them as witnesses if I could avoid it. Still, there was a widespread belief in their usefulness in cases like mine. I had to do whatever seemed best, whether I personally approved or not. To stay in Toronto and go mad simply would not do.

Why had I come to Zürich? The Director accepted it as perfectly in order for me to do so, but what did he know about my situation? Nothing would have got me to a psychiatrist in Toronto; such treatment is always supposed to be confidential, but everybody seems to know who is going regularly to certain doctors, and everybody is ready to give a guess at the reason. It is generally assumed to be homosexuality. I could have gone to New York, but everyone who did so seemed to be with a Freudian, and I was not impressed by what happened to them. Of course, it need not have been the Freudians' fault, for as I said, these people were leaners, and I don't suppose Freud himself could have done much with them. Nothing will make an empty bag stand up, as my grandfather often said. Of the Jungians I knew nothing, except that the Freudians disliked them, and one of my acquaintances who was in a Freudian analysis had once said something snide about people who went to Zürich to—

> hear sermons
> From mystical Germans
> Who preach from ten till four.

But with a perversity that often overtakes me when I have a personal decision to make, I had decided to give it a try. The Jungians had two negative recommendations: the Freudians hated them, and Zürich was a long way from Toronto.

(3)

It was a sharp jolt to find that Dr. J. von Haller was a woman. I have nothing against women; it had simply never occurred to me that I might talk about the very intimate things that had brought me to Zürich with one of them. During the physical examination two of the physicians I encountered were women and I felt no qualm. They were as welcome to peep into my inside as any man that ever lived. My mind, however, was a different matter. Would a woman—could a woman—understand what was wrong? There used to be a widespread idea that women are very sensitive. My experience of them as clients, witnesses, and professional opponents had dispelled any illusions I might have had of that kind. Some women are sensitive, doubtless, but I have met with nothing to persuade me that they are, on the whole, more likely to be sensitive than men. I thought I needed delicate handling. Was Dr. J. von Haller up to the work? I had never heard of a woman psychiatrist except as someone dealing with children. My troubles were decidedly not those of a child.

Here I was, however, and there was she in a situation that seemed more social than professional. I was in what appeared to be her sitting-room, and the arrangement of chairs was so unprofessional that it was I who sat in the shadow, while the full light from the window fell on her face. There was no couch.

Dr. von Haller looked younger than I; about thirty-eight,

I judged, for though her expression was youthful there was a little gray in her hair. Fine face; rather big features but not coarse. Excellent nose, aquiline if one wished to be complimentary but verging on the hooky if not. Large mouth and nice teeth, white but not American-white. Beautiful eyes, brown to go with her hair. Pleasant, low voice and a not quite perfect command of colloquial English. Slight accent. Clothes unremarkable, neither fashionable nor dowdy, in the manner Caroline calls "classic." Altogether a person to inspire confidence. But then, so am I, and I know all the professional tricks of how that is done. Keep quiet and let the client do all the talking; don't make suggestions—let the client unburden himself; watch him for revealing fidgets. She was doing all these things, but so was I. The result was a very stilted conversation, for a while.

"And it was the murder of your father that decided you to come here for treatment?"

"Doesn't it seem enough?"

"The death of his father is always a critical moment in a man's life, but usually he has time to make psychological preparation for it. The father grows old, relinquishes his claims on life, is manifestly preparing for death. A violent death is certainly a severe shock. But then, you knew your father must die sometime, didn't you?"

"I suppose so. I don't remember ever thinking about it."

"How old was he?"

"Seventy."

"Hardly a premature death. The psalmist's span."

"But this was murder."

"Who murdered him?"

"I don't know. Nobody knows. He was driven, or drove himself, off a dock in Toronto harbour. When his car was raised he was found clutching the steering-wheel so tightly that they had to pry his hands from it. His eyes were wide open, and there was a stone in his mouth."

"A stone?"

"Yes. This stone."

I held it out to her, lying on the silk handkerchief in which I carried it. Exhibit A in the case of the murder of Boy Staunton: a piece of Canadian pink granite about the size and shape of a hen's egg.

She examined it carefully. Then, slowly, she pushed it into her own mouth, and looked solemnly at me. Or was it solemnly? Was there a glint in her eye? I don't know. I was far too startled by what she had done to tell. Then she took it out, wiped it very carefully on her handkerchief, and gave it back.

"Yes; it could be done," she said.

"You're a cool customer," said I.

"Yes. This is a very cool profession, Mr. Staunton. Tell me, did no one suggest that your father might have committed suicide?"

"Certainly not. Utterly unlike him. Anyhow, why does your mind turn immediately to that? I told you he was murdered."

"But no evidence of murder was found."

"How do you know?"

"I had Dr. Tschudi's report about you, and I asked the librarian at our *Neue Zürcher Zeitung* to check their archive. They did report your father's death, you know; he had connections with several Swiss banks. The report was necessarily discreet and brief, but it seemed that suicide was the generally accepted explanation."

"He was murdered."

"Tschudi's report suggests you think your stepmother had something to do with it."

"Yes, yes; but not directly. She destroyed him. She made him unhappy and unlike himself. I never suggested she drove him off the dock. She murdered him psychologically—"

"Really? I had the impression you didn't think much of psychology, Mr. Staunton."

"Psychology plays a great part in my profession. I am rather a well-known criminal lawyer—or have you checked that, too? I have to know something about the way people function. Without a pretty shrewd psychological sense I couldn't do what I do, which is to worm things out of people they don't want to tell. That's your job, too, isn't it?"

"No. My job is to listen to people say things they very badly want to tell but are afraid nobody else will understand. You use psychology as an offensive weapon in the interest of justice. I use it as a cure. So keen a lawyer as yourself will appreciate the difference. You have shown you do. You think your stepmother murdered your father psychologically, but you don't think that would be enough to drive him to suicide. Well—I have known of such things. But if she was not the real murderer, who do you think it might have been?"

"Whoever put the stone in his mouth."

"Oh, come, Mr. Staunton, nobody could put that stone in a man's mouth against his will without breaking his teeth and creating great evidence of violence. I have tried it. Have you? No, I thought you hadn't. Your father must have put it there himself."

"Why?"

"Perhaps somebody told him to do it. Somebody he could not or did not wish to disobey."

"Ridiculous. Nobody could make Father do anything he didn't want to do."

"Perhaps he wanted to do this. Perhaps he wanted to die. People do, you know."

"He loved life. He was the most vital person I have ever known."

"Even after your stepmother had murdered him psychologically?"

I was losing ground. This was humiliating. I am a fine cross-examiner and yet here I was, caught off balance time and again by this woman doctor. Well, the remedy lay in my own hands.

"I don't think this line of discussion profitable, or likely to lead to anything that could help me," I said. "If you will be good enough to tell me your fee for the consultation, we shall close it now."

"As you wish," said Dr. von Haller. "But I should tell you that many people do not like the first consultation and want to run away. But they come back. You are a man of more than ordinary intelligence. Wouldn't it simplify things if you skipped the preliminary flight and continued? I am sure you are much too reasonable to have expected this kind of treatment to be painless. It is always difficult in the beginning for everyone, and especially people of your general type."

"So you have typed me already?"

"I beg your pardon; it would be impertinent to pretend anything of the kind. I meant only that intelligent people of wealth, who are used to having their own way, are often hostile and prickly at the beginning of analytical treatment."

"So you suggest that I bite the bullet and go on."

"Go on, certainly. But let us have no bullet-biting. I think you have bitten too many bullets recently. Suppose we proceed a little more gently."

"Do you consider it gentle to imply that my father killed himself when I tell you he was murdered?"

"I was telling you only what was most discreetly implied in the news report. I am sure you have heard the implication before. And I know how unwelcome such an implication usually is. But let us change our ground. Do you dream much?"

"Ah, so we have reached dreams already? No, I don't dream much. Or perhaps I should say that I don't pay much attention to the dreams I have."

"Have you had any dreams lately? Since you decided to come to Zürich? Since you arrived?"

Should I tell her? Well, this was costing me money. I might as well have the full show, whatever it might be.

"Yes. I had a dream last night."

"So?"

"Quite a vivid dream, for me. Usually my dreams are just scraps—fragmentary things that don't linger. This was of quite a different order."

"Was it in colour?"

"Yes. As a matter of fact, it was full of colour."

"And what was the general tone of the dream? I mean, did you enjoy it? Was it pleasant?"

"Pleasant. Yes, I would say it was pleasant."

"Tell me what you dreamed."

"I was in a building that was familiar, though it was nowhere known to me. But it was somehow associated with me, and I was somebody of importance there. Perhaps I should say I was surrounded by a building, because it was like a college—like some of the colleges at Oxford—and I was hurrying through the quadrangle because I was leaving by the back gate. As I went under the arch of the gate two men on duty there—porters, or policemen, functionaries and guardians of some kind—saluted me and smiled as if they knew me, and I waved to them. Then I was in a street. Not a Canadian street. Much more like a street in some pretty town in England or in Europe; you know, with trees on either side and very pleasant buildings like houses, though there seemed to be one or two shops, and a bus with people on it passed by me. But I was hurrying because I was going somewhere, and I turned quickly to the left and walked out into the country. I was on a road, with the town behind me, and I seemed to be walking beside a field in which I could see excavations going on, and I knew that some ruins were being turned up. I went through the field to the little makeshift hut that was the centre of the archaeological work—because I knew that was what it was—and went in the door. The hut was very different inside from what I had expected, because as I said it looked like a temporary shelter for tools and plans and things of that kind, but inside it was Gothic; the ceiling was low, but beautifully groined in stone, and the whole affair was a stone structure. There were a couple of young men in there, commonplace-looking fellows in their twenties, I would say, who were talking at the top of what I knew was a circular staircase that led down into the earth. I wanted to go down, and I asked these fellows to let me pass, but they wouldn't listen, and though they didn't speak to me and kept on talking to one another, I could tell that they thought I was simply a nosey intruder, and had no right to go down, and probably didn't want to go down in any serious way. So I left the hut, and walked to the road, and turned back toward the town, when I met a woman. She was a strange person, like a gypsy, but not a dressed-up showy gypsy; she wore old-fashioned, ragged clothes that seemed to have been faded by sun and rain, and she had on a wide-brimmed, battered black velvet hat with some gaudy feathers in it. She seemed to have something important to say to me, and kept pestering me, but I couldn't understand anything she said. She spoke in a foreign language; Romany, I presumed. She wasn't begging, but she wanted something, all the same. I thought, 'Well, well; every country gets the foreigners it deserves'—which is a stupid remark, when you analyse it. But I had a sense that time was running short, so I hurried back to town, turned sharp to the right, this time, and almost ran into the college gate. One of the guardians called to me, 'You can just make it, sir. You won't be fined this time.' And next thing I knew I was sitting at the head of a table in my barrister's robes, presiding over a meeting. And that was it."

"A very good dream. Perhaps you are a better dreamer than you think."

"Are you going to tell me that it means something?"

"All dreams mean something."

"For Joseph and Pharaoh, or Pilate's wife, perhaps. You will have to work very hard to convince me that they mean anything here and now."

"I am sure I shall have to work hard. But just for the moment, tell me without thinking too carefully about it if you recognized any of the people in your dream."

"Nobody."

"Do you think they might be people you have not yet seen? Or had not seen yesterday?"

"Doctor von Haller, you are the only person I have seen whom I did not know yesterday."

"I thought that might be so. Could I have been anybody in your dream?"

"You are going too fast for me. Are you suggesting that I could have dreamed of you before I knew you?"

"That would certainly seem absurd, wouldn't it? Still—I asked if I could have been anybody in your dream?"

"There was nobody in the dream who could possibly have been you. Unless you are hinting that you were the incomprehensible gypsy. And you won't get me to swallow that."

"I am sure nobody could get a very able lawyer like you to swallow anything that was ridiculous, Mr. Staunton. But it is odd, don't you think, that you should dream of meeting a female figure of a sort quite outside your experience, who was trying to tell you something important that you couldn't understand, and didn't want to understand, because you were so eager to get back to your enclosed, pleasant surroundings, and your barrister's robes, and presiding over something?"

"Doctor von Haller, I have no wish to be rude, but I think you are spinning an ingenious interpretation out of nothing. You must know that until I came here today I had no idea that J. von Haller was a woman. So even if I had dreamed of coming to an analyst in this very fanciful way, I couldn't have got that fact right, could I?"

"It is not a fact, except insofar as all coincidences are facts. You met a woman in your dream, and I am a woman. But not necessarily that woman. I assure you it is nothing uncommon for a new patient to have an important and revealing dream before treatment begins—before he has met his doctor. We always ask, just in case. But an anticipatory dream containing an unknown fact is a rarity. Still, we need not pursue it now. There will be time for that later."

"Will there be any later? If I understand the dream, I cannot make head or tale of the gypsy woman with the incomprehensible conversation, and go back to my familiar world. What do you deduce from that?"

"Dreams do not foretell the future. They reveal states of mind in which the future may be implicit. Your state of mind at present is very much that of a man who wants no conversation with incomprehensible women. But your state of mind may change. Don't you think so?"

"I really don't know. Frankly, it seems to me that this meeting has been a dogfight, a grappling for advantage. Would the treatment go on like this?"

"For a time, perhaps. But it could not achieve anything on that level. Now—our hour is nearly over, so I must cut some corners and speak frankly. If I am to help you, you will have to speak to me from your best self, honestly and with trust; if you continue to speak always from your inferior, suspicious self, trying to catch me out in some charlatanism, I shall not be able to do anything for you, and in a few sessions you will break off your treatment. Perhaps that is what you want to do now. We have one minute, Mr. Staunton. Shall I see you at our next appointment, or not? Please do not think I shall be offended if you decide not to continue, for there are many patients who wish to see me, and if you knew them they would assure you that I am no charlatan, but a serious, experienced doctor. Which is it to be?"

I have always hated being put on the spot. I was very angry. But as I reached for my hat, I saw that my hand was shaking, and she saw it, too. Something had to be done about that tremor.

"I shall come at the appointed time," I said.

"Good. Five minutes before your hour, if you please. I keep a very close schedule."

And there I was, out in the street, furious with myself, and Dr. von Haller. But in a quiet corner of my mind I was not displeased that I should be seeing her again.

(4)

Two days passed before my next appointment, during which I changed my mind several times, but when the hour came, I was there. I had chewed over everything that had been said and had thought of a number of good things that I would have said myself if I had thought of them at the proper time. The fact that the doctor was a woman had put me out more than I cared to admit. I have my own reasons for not liking to be instructed by a woman, and by no means all of them are associated with that intolerable old afreet Netty Quelch, who has ridden me with whip and spur for as long as I can remember. Nor did I like the dream-interpretation game, which contradicted every rule of evidence known to me; the discovery of truth is one of the principal functions of the law, to which I have given the best that is in me; is truth to be found in the vapours of dreams? Nor had I liked the doctor's brusque manner of telling me to make up my mind, not to waste her time, and to be punctual. I had been made to feel like a stupid witness, which is as ridiculous an estimate of my character as anybody could contrive. But I would not retreat before Dr. Johanna von Haller without at least one return engagement, and perhaps more than that.

A directory had told me her name was Johanna. Beyond that, and that she was a Prof. Dr. med. und spezialarzt für Psychiatrie, I could find out nothing about her.

Ah well, there was the tremor of my hand. No sense in making a lot of that. Nerves, and no wonder. But was it not because of my nerves I had come to Zürich?

This time we did not meet in the sitting-room but in Dr. von Haller's study, which was rather dark and filled with books, and a few pieces of modern statuary that looked pretty good, though I could not examine them closely. Also, there was a piece of old stained glass suspended in the window, which was fine in itself, but displeased me because it seemed affected. Prominent on the desk was a signed photograph of Dr. Jung himself. Dr. von Haller did not sit behind the desk, but in a chair near my own; I knew this trick, which is supposed to inspire confidence because it sets aside the natural barrier—the desk of the professional person. I had my eye on the doctor this time, and did not mean to let her get away with anything.

She was all smiles.

"No dogfight this time, I hope, Mr. Staunton?"

"I hope not. But it is entirely up to you."

"Entirely? Very well. Before we go further, the report has come from the clinic. You seem to be in depleted general health and a little—nervous, shall we say? What used to be called neurasthenic. And some neuritic pain. Rather under-weight. Occasional marked tremor of the hands."

"Recently, yes. I have been under great stress."

"Never before?"

"Now and then, when my professional work was heavy."

"How much have you had to drink this morning?"

"A good sharp snort for breakfast, and another before coming here."

"Is that usual?"

"It is what I usually take on a day when I am to appear in court."

"Do you regard this as appearing in court?"

"Certainly not. But as I have already told you several times, I have been under heavy stress, and that is my way of coping with stress. Doubtless you think it a bad way. I think other-wise."

"I am sure you know all the objections to excessive use of alcohol?"

"I could give you an excellent temperance lecture right now. Indeed, I am a firm believer in temperance for the kind of people who benefit from temperance. I am not one of them. Temperance is a middle-class virtue, and it is not my fate, or good fortune if you like that better, to be middle-class. On the contrary, I am rich and in our time wealth takes a man out of the middle class, unless he made all the money himself. I am the third generation of money in my family. To be rich is to be a special kind of person. Are you rich?"

"By no means."

"Quick to deny it, I observe. Yet you seem to live in a good professional style, which would be riches to most people in the world. Well—I *am* rich, though not so rich as people imagine. If you are rich you have to discover your own truths and make a great many of your own rules. The middle-class ethic will not serve you, and if you devote yourself to it, it will trip you up and make a fool of you."

"What do you mean by rich?"

"I mean good hard coin, Doctor. I don't mean the riches of the mind or the wealth of the spirit, or any of that pompous crap. I mean money. Specifically, I count a man rich if he has an annual income of over a hundred thousand dollars *before* taxes. If he has that he has plenty of other evidences of wealth, as well. I have considerably more than a hundred thousand a year, and I make much of it by being at the top of my profession, which is the law. I am what used to be called 'an eminent advocate.' And if being rich and being an eminent advocate also requires a drink before breakfast, I am prepared to pay the price. But to assure you that I am not wholly unmindful of my grandparents, who hated liquor as the prime work of the Devil, I always have my first drink of the day with a raw egg in it. That is my breakfast."

"How much in a day?"

"Call it a bottle, more or less. More at present, because as I keep telling you, I have been under stress."

"What made you think you needed an analyst, instead of a cure for alcoholics?"

"Because I do not think of myself as an alcoholic. To be an alcoholic is a middle-class predicament. My reputation in the country where I live is such that I would cut an absurd figure in Alcoholics Anonymous; if a couple of the brethren came to minister to me, they would be afraid of me; anyhow I don't go on the rampage or pass out or make a notable jackass of myself—I just drink a good deal and talk rather frankly. If I were to go out with another A.A. to cope with some fellow who was on the bottle, the sight of me would terrify him; he would think he had done something dreadful in his cups, and that I was his lawyer and the police were coming with the wagon. Nor would I be any good in group therapy; I took a look at that, once; I am not an intellectual snob, Doctor—at least, that is my story at present—but group therapy is too chummy for me. I lack the confessional spirit; I prefer to encourage it in others, preferably when they are in the witness-box. No, I am not an alcoholic, for alcoholism is not my disease, but my symptom."

"Then what do you call your disease?"

"If I knew, I would tell you. Instead, I hope you can tell me."

"Such a definition might not help us much at present. Let us call it stress following your father's death. Shall we begin talking about that?"

"Don't we start with childhood? Don't you want to hear about my toilet-training?"

"I want to hear about your trouble now. Suppose we begin with the moment you heard of your father's death."

"It was about three o'clock in the morning on November 4 last. I was wakened by my housekeeper, who said the police wanted to talk to me on the telephone. It was an inspector I knew who said I should come to the dock area at once as there had been an accident involving my father's car. He didn't want to say much, and I didn't want to say anything that would arouse the interest of my housekeeper, who was hovering to hear whatever she could, so I called a taxi and went to the docks. Everything there seemed to be in confusion, but in fact it was all as orderly as the situation permitted. There was a diver in a frog-man outfit, who had been down to the car first; the Fire Department had brought a crane mounted on a truck, which was raising the car; there were police cars and a truck with floodlights. I found the inspector, and he said it was my father's car for a certainty and there was a body at the wheel. So far as they could determine, the car had been driven off the end of a pier at a speed of about forty miles an hour; it had carried on some distance after getting into the water. A watchman put in an alarm as soon as he heard the splash, but by the time the police arrived it was difficult to find exactly where it was, and then all the diving, and getting the crane, and putting a chain on the front part of the frame, had taken over two hours, so that they had seen the licence plate only a matter of minutes before I was called; it was a car the police knew well. My father had a low, distinctive licence number.

"It was one of those wretched situations when you hope that something isn't true which common sense tells you is a certainty. Nobody else drove that car except my father. At last they got it on the pier, filthy and dripping. A couple of firemen opened the doors as slowly as the weight of water inside would allow, because the police didn't want anything to be washed out that might be of evidence. But it was quickly emptied, and there he sat, at the wheel.

"I think what shocked me most was the terrible dishevelment of his body. He was always such an elegant man. He was covered with mud and oil and harbour filth, but his eyes were wide open, and he was gripping the wheel. The firemen tried to get him out, and it was then we found that his grip was so tight nothing ordinary would dislodge it. Probably you know what emergencies are like; things are done that nobody would think of under ordinary circumstances; finally they got him free of the wheel, but his hands had been terribly distorted and afterward we found that most of the fingers had been broken in doing it. I didn't blame the firemen; they did what had to be done. They laid him on a tarpaulin and then everybody held back, and I knew they were waiting for me to do something. I knelt beside him and wiped his face with a handkerchief, and it was then we saw that there was something amiss about his mouth. The police surgeon came to help me, and when my father's jaws were pried open we found the stone I showed you. The stone you tried yourself because you doubted what I told you."

"I am sorry if I shocked you. But patients come with such strange stories. Go on, please."

"I know police procedure. They were as kind as possible, but they had to take the body to the morgue, make reports, and do all the routine things that follow the most bizarre accidents. They strained a point by letting me get away with the stone, though it was material evidence; they knew I would not withhold it if it should be necessary, I suppose. Even as it was, some reporter saw me do it, or tricked the doctor into an admission, and the stone played a big part in the news. But they all had work to do, and so had I, but I had nobody to help me with my work.

"So I did what had to be done. I went at once to my father's house and wakened Denyse (that's my stepmother) and told what had happened. I don't know what I expected. Hysterics, I suppose. But she took it with an icy self-control for which I was grateful, because if she had broken down I think I would have had some sort of collapse myself. But she was extremely wilful. 'I must go to him,' she said. I knew the police would be making their examination and tried to persuade her to wait till morning. Not a chance. Go she would, and at once. I didn't want her to drive, and it is years since I have driven a car myself, so that meant rousing the chauffeur and giving some sort of partial explanation to him.

Oh, for the good old days—if there ever were such days—when you could tell servants to do something without offering a lot of reasons and explanations! But at last we were at the central police station, and in the morgue, and then we had another hold-up because the police, out of sheer decency, wouldn't let her see the body until the doctor had finished and some not very efficient cleaning-up had been done. As a result, when she saw him he looked like a drunk who has been dragged in out of the rain. Then she did break down, and that was appalling for me, because you might as well know now that I heartily dislike the woman, and having to hold her and soothe her and speak comfort to her was torture, and it was then I began to taste the full horror of what had happened. The police doctor and everybody else who might have given me a hand were too respectful to intrude; wealth again, Dr. von Haller—even your grief takes on a special quality, and nobody quite likes to dry your golden tears. After a while I took her home, and called Netty to come and look after her.

"Netty is my housekeeper. My old nurse, really, and she has kept my apartment for me since my father's second marriage. Netty doesn't like my stepmother either, but she seemed the logical person to call, because she has unshakable character and authority.

"Or rather, that is what I thought. But when Netty got over to my father's house and I told her what had happened, she flew right off the handle. That is her own expression for being utterly unstrung, 'flying right off the handle.' She whooped and bellowed and made awful feminine roaring noises until I was extremely frightened. But I had to hold her and comfort her. I still don't know what ailed her. Of course my father was a very big figure in her life—as he was in the life of anybody who knew him well—but she was no kin, you know.

The upshot of it was that very soon my stepmother was attending to Netty, instead of the other way round, and as the chauffeur had roused all the other servants there was a spooky gathering of half-clad people in the drawing-room, staring and wondering as Netty made a holy show of herself. I got somebody to call my sister, Caroline, and quite soon afterward she and Beesty Bastable appeared, and I have never been so glad to see them in my life.

"Caroline was terribly shocked, but she behaved well. Rather a cold woman, but not a fool. And Beesty Bastable—her husband—is one of those puffing, goggle-eyed, fattish fellows who don't seem worth their keep, but who have sometimes a surprising touch with people. It was he, really, who got the servants busy making hot drinks—and got Netty to stop moaning, and kept Caroline and my stepmother from having a fight about nothing at all, or really because Caroline started in much too soon assuming that proprietorial attitude people take toward the recently bereaved, and my stepmother didn't like being told to go and lie down in her own house.

"I was grateful to Beesty because when things were sorted out he said, 'Now for one good drink, and then nothing until we've had some sleep, what?' Beesty says 'what?' a great deal, as a lot of Old Ontario people with money tend to do. I think it's an Edwardian affectation and they haven't found out yet that it's out of fashion. But Beesty kept me from drinking too much then, and he stuck to me like a burr for hours afterward, I suppose for the same reason. Anyhow, I went home at last to my apartment, which was blessedly free of Netty, and though I didn't sleep and Beesty very tactfully kept me away from the decanters, I did get a bath, and had two hours of quiet before Beesty stuck his head into my room at eight o'clock and said he'd fried some eggs. I didn't think I wanted fried eggs; I wanted an egg whipped up in brandy, but it was astonishing how good the fried eggs tasted. Don't you think it's rather humbling how hungry calamity makes one?

"As we ate, Beesty told me what had to be done. Odd, perhaps, because he's only a stockbroker and my father and I had always tended to write him off as a fool, though decent enough. But his family is prominent, and he'd managed quite a few funerals and knew the ropes. He even knew of a good undertaker. I wouldn't have known where to look for one. I mean, who's ever met an undertaker? It's like what people say about dead donkeys: who's ever seen one? He got on the telephone and arranged with his favourite undertaker to collect the body whenever the police were ready to release it. Then he said we must talk with Denyse to arrange details of the burial. He seemed to think she wouldn't want to see us until late in the morning, but when he called she was on the line at once and said she would see us at nine o'clock and not to be late because she had a lot to do.

"That was exactly like Denyse, whom as I told you I have never liked because of this very spirit she showed when Beesty called. Denyse is all business, and nobody can help her or do anything for her without being made a subordinate: she must always be the boss. Certainly she bossed my father far more than he knew, and he was not a man to subject himself to anybody. But women are like that. Aren't they?"

"Some women, certainly."

"In my experience, women are either bosses or leaners."

"Isn't that your experience of men, too?"

"Perhaps. But I can talk to men. I can't talk to my stepmother. From nine o'clock till ten, Denyse talked to us, and would probably have talked longer if the hairdresser had not been coming. She knew she would have to see a lot of people, and it was necessary for her hair to be dressed as she would have no opportunity later.

"And what she said! My hair almost stood on end. Denyse hadn't slept either: she had been planning. And I think this is the point, Doctor, when you will admit that I have cause to be nervous. I've told you my father was a very important man. Not just rich. Not just a philanthropist. He had been in politics, and during the greater part of the Second World War he had been our Minister of Food, and an extraordinarily able one. Then he had left active politics. It was the old story, not unlike Churchill's; the public hate a really capable man except when they can't get along without him. The decisive, red-tape-cutting qualities that made my father necessary in war got him into trouble with the little men as soon as the war was over, and they hounded him out of public life. But he was too big to be ignored and his public service entitled him to recognition, and he was to be the next Lieutenant-Governor of our Province. Do you know what a Lieutenant-Governor is?"

"Some sort of ceremonial personage, I suppose."

"Yes: a representative of the Crown in a Canadian province."

"A high honour?"

"Yes, but there are ten of them. My father might suitably have been Governor-General, which is top of the heap."

"Ah yes; very grand, I see."

"Silly people smile at these ceremonial offices because they don't understand them. You can't have a parliamentary system without these official figures who represent the state, the Crown, the whole body of government, as well as the elected fellows who represent their voters.

"He had not taken office. But he had received the official notice of his appointment from the Secretary of State, and the Queen's charge would have come at the proper time, which would have been in about a month. But Denyse wanted him to be given a state funeral, as if he were already in office.

"Well! As a lawyer, I knew that was absurd. There was a perfectly valid Lieutenant-Governor at the time we were discussing this crazy scheme. There was no way in the world my father could be given an official funeral. But that was what she wanted—soldiers in dress uniform, a cushion with his D.S.O. and his C.B.E. on it, a firing-party, a flag on the coffin, as many officials and politicians as could be mustered. I was flabbergasted. But whatever I said, she simply replied, 'I know what was owing to Boy even if you don't.'

"We had a blazing row. Things were said that had poor Beesty white with misery, and he kept mumbling, 'Oh come on, Denyse, come on, Davey; let's try to get along'—which was idiotic, but poor Beesty has no vocabulary suitable to large situations. Denyse dropped any pretence of liking me and let it rip. I was a cheap mouthpiece for crooks of the worst kind, I was a known drunk, I had always resented my father's superiority and tried to thwart him whenever I could, I had said inexcusable things about her and spied on her, but on this one occasion, by the living God, I would toe the line or she would expose me to unimaginable humiliations and disgraces. I said she had made a fool of my father since first she met him, reduced his stature before the public with her ridiculous, ignorant pretensions and stupidities, and wanted to turn his funeral into a circus in which she would ride the biggest elephant. It was plain speaking for a while, I can tell you. It was only when Beesty was near to tears—and I don't mean that metaphorically; he was sucking air noisily and mopping his eyes—and when Caroline turned up that we became a little quieter. Caroline has a scornful manner that exacts good behaviour from the humbler creation, even Denyse.

"So in the end Beesty and I were given our orders to go to the undertaker and choose a splendid coffin. Bronze would be the thing, she thought, because it would be possible to engrave directly upon it.

" 'Engrave what?' I asked. I will say for her that she had the grace to colour a little under her skilful make-up. 'The Staunton arms,' she said. 'But there aren't any——' I began, when Beesty pulled me away. 'Let her have it,' he whispered. 'But it's crooked,' I shouted. 'It's pretentious and absurd and crooked.' Caroline helped him to bustle me out of the room. 'Davey, you do it and shut up,' she said, and when I protested, 'Carol, you know as well as I do that it's illegal,' she said, 'Oh, *legal!*' with terrible feminine scorn."

(5)

At my next appointment, feeling rather like Scheherazade unfolding one of her never-ending, telescopic tales to King Schahriar, I took up where I had left off. Dr. von Haller had said nothing during my account of my father's death and what followed, except to check a point here and there, and she made no notes, which surprised me. Did she truly hold all the varied stories told by her patients in her head, and change from one to another every hour? Well, I did no less with the tales my clients told me.

We exchanged a few words of greeting, and I continued.

"After we had finished with the undertaker, Beesty and I had a great many details to attend to, some of them legal and some arising from the arrangement of funeral detail. I had to get in touch with Bishop Woodiwiss, who had known my father for over forty years, and listen to his well-meant condolences and go over the whole funeral routine. I went to the Diocesan House, and was a little surprised, I can't really say

why, that it was so businesslike, with secretaries drinking coffee, and air-conditioning and all the atmosphere of business
premises. I think I had expected crucifixes on the walls and
heavy carpets. There was one door that said 'Diocesan Chan-
cellery: Mortgages' that really astonished me. But the Bishop
knew how to do funerals, and there wasn't really much to it.
There were technicalities: our parish church was St. Simon's,
but Denyse wanted a cathedral ceremony, as more in keeping
with her notions of grandeur, and as well as the Bishop's, the
Dean's consent had to be sought. Woodiwiss said he would
take care of that. I still don't know why I was so touchy about
the good man's words of comfort; after all, he had known my
father before I was born, and had christened and confirmed
me, and he had his rights both as a friend and a priest. But
I felt very personally about the whole matter—"

"Possessively, would you say?"

"I suppose so. Certainly I was angry that Denyse was determined to take over and have everything her own way, especially when it was such a foolish, showy way. I was still furious
about that matter of engraving the coffin with heraldic doodads
that weren't ours, and couldn't ever be so, and which my
father had rejected himself, after a lot of heart-searching. I
want that to be perfectly clear to you; I have no quarrel with
heraldry, and people who legitimately possess it can use it as
they like, but the Staunton arms weren't ours. Do you want to
know why?"

"Later, I think. We'll come to it. Go on now about the
funeral."

"Very well. Beesty took over the job of seeing the people
from the papers, but it was snatched from him by Denyse,
who had prepared a handout with biographical details. Silly,
of course, because the papers had that already. But she achieved
one thing by it that made me furious: the only mention of my

mother in the whole obituary was a reference to 'an earlier marriage to Leola Crookshanks, who died in 1942.' Her name was Cruikshank, *not* Crookshanks, and she had been my father's wife since 1924 and the mother of his children, and a dear, sad, unhappy woman. Denyse knew that perfectly well, and nothing will convince me that the mistake wasn't the result of spite. And of course she dragged in a reference to her own wretched daughter, Lorene, who has nothing to do with the Staunton family—nothing at all.

"When was the funeral to be? That was the great question. I was for getting it over as quickly as possible, but the police did not release the body until late on Monday—and *that* took some arranging, I can assure you. Denyse wanted as much time as possible to arrange her semi-state funeral and assemble all the grandees she could bully, so it was decided to have it on Thursday.

"Where was he to be buried? Certainly not in Deptford, where he was born, though his parents had providently bought a six-holer in the cemetery there years ago, and were themselves the only occupants. But Deptford wouldn't do for Denyse, so a grave had to be bought in Toronto.

"Have you ever bought a grave? It's not unlike buying a house. First of all they show you the poor part of the cemetery, and you look at all the foreign tombstones with photographs imbedded in them under plastic covers, and the inscriptions in strange languages and queer alphabets, and burnt-out candles lying on the grass, and your heart sinks. You wonder, can this be death? How sordid! Because you aren't your best self, you know; you're a stinking snob; funerals bring out that sort of thing dreadfully. You've told yourself for years that it doesn't matter what happens to a corpse, and when cocktail parties became drunken-serious you've said that the Jews have the right idea, and the quickest, cheapest funeral is the best and philosophically the most decent. But when you get into the cemetery, it's quite different. And the cemetery people know it. So you move out of the working-class and ethnic district into the area of suburban comfiness, but the gravestones are really rather close together and the inscriptions are in bad prose, and you almost expect to see jocular inscriptions like 'Take-It-Aisy' and 'Dunroamin' on the stones along with 'Till the Day Breaks' and 'In the Everlasting Arms.' Then things begin to brighten; bigger plots, no crowding, an altogether classier type of headstone and—best of all—the names of families you know. On the Resurrection Morn, after all, one doesn't want to jostle up to the Throne with a pack of strangers. And that's where the deal is settled.

"Did you know, by the way, that somebody has to own a grave? Somebody, that is, other than the occupant. I own my father's grave. A strange thought."

"Who owns your mother's grave? And why was your father not buried near her?"

"I own her grave, because I inherited it as part of my father's estate. The only bit of real estate he left me, as a matter of fact. And because she died during the war, when my father was abroad, the funeral had to be arranged by a family friend, and he just bought one grave. A good one, but single. She lies in the same desirable area as my father, but not near. As in life.

"By Tuesday night the undertakers had finished their work, and the coffin was back in his house, at the end of the drawing-room, and we were all invited in to take a look. Difficult business, of course, because an undertaker—or at any rate his embalmer—is an artist of a kind, and when someone has died by violence it's a challenge to see how well they can make him look. I must say in justice they had done well by Father, for though it would be stupid to say he looked like himself, he didn't look as though he had been drowned. But you know how it is; an extremely vital, mercurial man, who has always had a play of expression and even of colour, doesn't look like himself with a mat complexion and that inflexible calm they produce for these occasions. I have had to see a lot of people in their coffins, and they always look to me as if they were under a malign enchantment and could hear what was said and would speak if the enchantment could be broken. But there it was, and somebody had to say a kind word or two to the undertakers, and it was Beesty who did it. I was always being amazed at the things he could do in this situation, because my father and I had never thought he could do anything except manage his damned bond business. The rest of us looked with formal solemnity, just as a few years before we had gathered to look at Caroline's wedding cake with formal pleasure; on both occasions we were doing it chiefly to give satisfaction to the people who had created the exhibit.

"That night people began to call. Paying their respects is the old-fashioned phrase for it. Beesty and Caroline and I hung around in the drawing-room and chatted with the visitors in subdued voices. 'So good of you to come. . . . Yes, a very great shock. . . . It's extremely kind of you to say so. . . .' Lots of that sort of thing. Top people from my father's business, the Alpha Corporation, doing the polite. Lesser people from the Alpha Corporation, seeing that everybody who came signed a book; a secretary specially detailed to keep track of telegrams and cables, and another to keep a list of the flowers.

"Oh, the flowers! Or, as just about everybody insisted on calling them, the 'floral tributes.' Being November, the florists were pretty well down to chrysanthemums, and there were forests of them. But of course the really rich had to express their regret with roses because they were particularly expensive at the time. The rich are always up against it, you see; they have to send the best, however much they may hate the costly flower of the moment, or somebody is sure to say they've been cheap. Denyse had heard somewhere of a coffin being covered with a blanket of roses, and she wanted one as her own special offering. It was Caroline who persuaded her to hold herself down to a decent bunch of white flowers. Or really, persuaded isn't the word; Caroline told me she was finally driven to saying, 'Are you trying to make us look like the Medici?' and that did it, because Denyse had never heard any good spoken of the Medici.

"This grisly business went on all day Wednesday. I was on duty in the morning, and received and made myself pleasant to the Mayor, the Chief of Police, the Fire Chief, a man from the Hydro-Electric Power Commission, and quite a crowd of dignitaries of one sort and another. There was a representative of the Bar Association, which called to mind the almost forgotten fact that my father's professional training had been as a lawyer; I knew this man quite well because he was a frequent associate of my own, but the others were people I knew only by name or from their pictures in the newspapers. There were bank presidents, naturally.

"Denyse, of course, did none of the receiving. It wouldn't have suited the role for which she had cast herself. Officially, she was too desolated to be on view, and only special people were taken to an upstairs room where she held state. I don't quarrel with that. Funerals are among the few ceremonial occasions left to us, and we assume our roles almost without thinking. I was the Only Son, who was bearing up splendidly, but who was also known not to be, and to have no expectation of ever being, the man his father was. Beesty was That Decent Fellow Bastable, who was doing everything he could under difficult circumstances. Caroline was the Only Daughter, stricken with grief, but of course not so catastrophically stricken as Denyse, who was the Widow and assumed to be prostrate under her affliction. Well—all right. That's the pattern, and we break patterns at our peril. After all, they became patterns because they conform to realities. I have been in favour of ceremonial and patterns all my life, and I have no desire to break the funeral pattern. But there was too much real feeling behind the pattern for me to be anything other than wretchedly overwrought, and the edicts Denyse issued from her chamber of affliction were the worst things I had to bear.

"Her edict that at all costs I was to be kept sober, for instance. Beesty was very good about that. Not hatefully tactful, you know, but he said plainly that I had to do a great many things that needed a level head and I'd better not drink much. He knew that for me not drinking much meant drinking what would be a good deal for him, but he gave me credit for some common sense. And Caroline was the same. 'Denyse is determined that you're going to get your paws in the sauce and disgrace us all. So for God's sake spite her and don't,' was the way she put it. Even Netty, after her first frightful outburst, behaved very well and didn't try to watch over me for my own good, though she lurked a good deal. Consequently, though I drank pretty steadily, I kept well within my own appointed bounds. But I hated Denyse for her edict.

"Nor was that her only edict. On Wednesday, before lunch, she called Beesty to her and told him to get me to look over my father's will that afternoon, and see her after I had done so. This was unwarrantable interference. I knew I was my father's principal executor, and I knew, being a lawyer, what had to be done. But it isn't considered quite the thing to get down to business with the will before the funeral is over. There's nothing against it, particularly if there is suspicion of anything that might prove troublesome in the will, but in my father's case that was out of the question. I didn't know what was in the will, but I was certain it was all in perfect order. I thought Denyse was rushing things in an unseemly way.

"I suppose if you are to do anything for me, Doctor, I must be as frank as possible. I didn't want to look at the will until it became absolutely necessary. There have been difficulties about wills in our family. My father had a shock when he read his own father's will, and he had spoken to me about it more than once. And relations between my father and myself had been strained since his marriage to Denyse. I thought there might be a nasty surprise for me in the will. So I put my foot down and said nothing could be done until Thursday afternoon.

"I don't know why I went to my father's house so early on Thursday, except that I woke with an itching feeling that there was a great deal to be settled, and I would find out what it was when I was on the spot. And I wanted to take farewell of my father. You understand? During the last forty-eight hours it had been impossible to be alone in the room with his body, and I thought if I were early I could certainly manage it. So I went to the drawing-room as softly as possible, not to attract attention, and found the doors shut. It was half-past seven, so there was nothing unusual about that.

"But from inside there were sounds of a man's voice and a woman's voice, apparently quarrelling, and I heard scuffling and thudding. I opened the door, and there was Denyse at the coffin, holding up my father's body by the shoulders, while a strange man appeared to be punching and slapping its face. You know what people say in books—'I was thunderstruck . . . my senses reeled.' "

"Yes. It is a perfectly accurate description of the sensation. It is caused by a temporary failure of circulation to the head. Go on."

"I shouted something. Denyse dropped the body, and the

man jumped backward as if he thought I might kill him. I knew him then. He was a friend of Denyse's, a dentist; I had met him once or twice and thought him a fool.

"The body had no face. It was entirely covered in some shiny pinkish material, so thickly that it was egglike in its featurelessness. It was this covering they were trying to remove.

"I didn't have to ask for an explanation. They were unnerved and altogether too anxious to talk. It was a story of unexampled idiocy.

"This dentist, like so many of Denyse's friends, was a dabbler in the arts. He had a tight, ill-developed little talent as a sculptor, and he had done a few heads of Chairmen of the Faculty of Dentistry at the University, and that sort of thing. Denyse had been visited by one of her dreadful inspirations, that this fellow should take a death-mask of my father, which could later be used as the basis for a bust or perhaps kept for itself. But he had never done a corpse before, and it is quite a different business from doing a living man. So, instead of using plaster, which is the proper thing if you know how to work it, he had the lunatic idea of trying some plastic mess used in his profession for taking moulds, because he thought he could get a greater amount of detail, and quicker. But the plastic wasn't for this sort of work, and he couldn't get it off!

"They were panic-stricken, as they had every right to be. The room was full of feeling. Do you know what I mean? The atmosphere was so alive with unusual currents that I swear I could feel them pressing on me, making my ears ring. Don't say it was all the whisky I had been drinking. I was far the most self-possessed of us three. I swear that all the tension seemed to emanate from the corpse, which was in an unseemly state of dishevelment, with coat and shirt off, hair awry, and half-tumbled out of that great expensive coffin.

"What should I have done? I have gone over that moment a thousand times since. Should I have seized the poker and killed the dentist, and forced Denyse's face down on that dreadful plastic head and throttled her, and then screamed for the world to come and look at the last scene of some sub-Shakespearean tragedy? What in fact I did was to order them both out of the room, lock it, telephone the undertakers to come at once, and then go into the downstairs men's room and vomit and gag and retch until I was on the floor with my head hanging into the toilet bowl, in a classic Skid Row mess.

"The undertakers came. They were angry, as they had every right to be, but they were fairly civil. If a mask was wanted, they asked, why had they not been told? They knew how to do it. But what did I expect of them now? I had pulled myself together, though I knew I looked like a drunken wreck, and I had to do whatever talking was done. Denyse was upstairs, having divorced herself in that wonderful feminine way from the consequences of her actions, and I am told the dentist left town for a week.

"It was a very bad situation. I heard one of the undertakers ask the butler if he could borrow a hammer, and I knew the worst. After a while I had my brief time beside my father's coffin; the undertakers did not spare me that. The face was very bad, some teeth had been broken; no eyebrows or lashes, and a good deal of the front hair was gone. Much worse than when he lay on the dock, covered in oil and filth, with that stone in his mouth.

"So of course we had what is called a closed-coffin funeral. I know they are common here, but in North America it is still usual to have the corpse on display until just before the burial service begins. I sometimes wonder if it is a hold-over from pioneer days, to assure everybody that there has been no foul play. That was certainly not the case this time. We had

had fool play. I didn't explain to Caroline and Beesty; simply said Denyse had decided she wanted it that way. I know Caroline smelled a rat, but I told her nothing because she might have done something dreadful to Denyse.

"There we all were, in the cathedral, with Denyse in the seat of the chief mourner, of course, and looking so smooth a louse would have slipped off her, as Grandfather Staunton used to say. And he would certainly have said I looked like the Wreck of the Hesperus; it was one of his few literary allusions.

"There was the coffin, so rich, so bronzey, so obviously the sarcophagus of somebody of the first rank. Right above where that pitifully misused face lay hidden was the engraving of the Staunton arms: Argent two chevrons sable within a bordure engrailed of the same. Crest, a fox statant proper. Motto, *En Dieu ma foy.*

"Bishop Woodiwiss might have been in on the imposture, so richly did he embroider the *En Dieu ma foy* theme. I have to give it to the old boy; he can't have seen that engraving until the body arrived at the cathedral door, but he seized on the motto and squeezed it like a bartender squeezing a lemon. It was the measure of our dear brother gone, he said, that the motto of his ancient family should have been this simple assertion of faith in Divine Power and Divine Grace, and that never, in all the years he had known Boy Staunton, had he heard him mention it. No: deeds, not words, was Boy Staunton's mode of life. A man of action; a man of great affairs; a man loving and tender in his personal life, open-handed and perceptive in his multitudinous public benefactions, and the author of countless unknown acts of simple generoᵤity. But no jewel of great price could be concealed forever, and here we saw, at last, the mainspring of Boy Staunton's great and—yes, he would say it, he would use the word, knowing that we would understand it in its true sense—his beautiful life. *En Dieu ma foy*. Let us all carry that last word from a great man away with us, and feel that truly, in this hour of mourning and desolation, we had found an imperishable truth. *En Dieu ma foy*.

"Without too much wriggling, I was able to look about me. The congregation was taking it with that stuporous receptivity which is common to Canadians awash in oratory. The man from the Prime Minister's department, sitting beside the almost identical man from the Secretary of State's department; the people from the provincial government; the civic officials; the Headmaster of Colborne School; the phalanx of rich business associates: not one of them looked as if he were about to leap up and shout, 'It's a God-damned lie; his lifelong motto wasn't *En Dieu ma foy* but *En moi-même ma foy* and that was his tragedy.' I don't suppose they knew. I don't suppose that even if they knew, they cared. Few of them could have explained the difference between the two faiths.

"My eye fell on one man who could have done it. Old Dunstan Ramsay, my father's lifelong friend and my old schoolmaster, was there, not in one of the best seats—Denyse can't stand him—but near a stained-glass window through which a patch of ruby light fell on his handsome ravaged old mug, and he looked like a devil hot from hell. He didn't know I was looking, and at one point, when Woodiwiss was saying *En Dieu ma foy* for the sixth or seventh time, he grinned and made that snapping motion with his mouth that some people have who wear ill-fitting false teeth.

"Is this hour nearly finished, by the way? I feel wretched."

"I am sure you do. Have you told anyone else about the death-mask?"

"Nobody."

"That was very good of you."

"Did I hear you correctly? I thought you analysts never expressed opinions."

"You will hear me express many opinions as we get deeper in. It is the Freudians who are so reserved. You have your schedule of appointments? No doubts about coming next time?"

"None."

(6)

Back again, after two days' respite. No: respite is not the word. I did not dread my appointment with Dr. von Haller, as one might dread a painful or depleting treatment of the physical kind. But my nature is a retentive, secretive one, and all this revelation went against the grain. At the same time, it was an enormous relief. But after all, what was there in it? Was it anything more than Confession, as Father Knopwood had explained it when I was confirmed? Penitence, Pardon, and Peace? Was I paying Dr. von Haller thirty dollars an hour for something the Church gave away, with Salvation thrown in for good measure? I had tried Confession in my very young days. Father Knopwood had not insisted that I kneel in a little box, while he listened behind a screen; he had modern ways, and he sat behind me, just out of sight, while I strove to describe my boyish sins. Of course I knelt while he gave me Absolution. But I had always left the two or three sessions when I tried that feeling a fool. Nevertheless, despite our eventual quarrel, I wouldn't knock Knopwood now, even to myself; he had been a good friend to me at a difficult time in my life—one of the succession of difficult times in my life —and if I had not been able to continue in his way, others had. Dr. von Haller now—had it something to do with her being a woman? Whatever it was, I looked forward to my next hour with her in a state of mind I could not clarify, but which was not wholly disagreeable.

"Let me see; we had finished your father's funeral. Or had we finished? Does anything else occur to you that you think significant?"

"No. After the Bishop's sermon, or eulogy or whatever it was, everything seemed to be much what one might have expected. He had so irrevocably transposed the whole thing into a key of fantasy, with his rhapsodizing on that irrelevant motto, that I went through the business at the cemetery without any real feeling, except wonderment. Then perhaps of the funeral people a hundred and seventy trooped back to the house for a final drink—a lot of drinking seems to go on at funerals—and stayed for a fork lunch, and when that was over I knew that all my time of grace had run out and I must get on with the job of the will.

"Beesty would have been glad to help me, I know, and Denyse was aching to see it, but she wasn't in a position to bargain with me after the horrors of the morning. So I picked up copies for everybody concerned from my father's solicitors, who were well known to me, and took them to my own office for a careful inspection. I knew I would be cross-examined by several people, and I wanted to have all the facts at my finger-tips before any family discussion.

"It was almost an anticlimax. There was nothing in the will I had not foreseen, in outline if not in detail. There was a great deal about his business interests, which were extensive, but as they boiled down to shares in a single controlling firm called Alpha Corporation it was easy, and his lawyers and the Alpha lawyers would navigate their way through all of that. There were no extensive personal or charity bequests, because he left the greatest part of his Alpha holdings to the Castor Foundation.

"That's a family affair, a charitable foundation that makes grants to a variety of good, or apparently good, causes. Such things are extremely popular with rich families in North America. Ours had a peculiar history, but it isn't important just now. Briefly, Grandfather Staunton set it up as a fund to assist temperance movements. But he left some loose ends, and he couldn't resist some fancy wording about 'assisting the public weal,' so when father took it over he gently eased all the preachers off the board and put a lot more money into it. Consequence: we now support the arts and the social sciences, in all their lunatic profusion. The name is odd. Means 'beaver' of course, and so it has Canadian relevance; but it also means a special type of sugar—do you know the expression castor-sugar, the kind that goes in shakers?—and my father's money was made in part from sugar. He began in sugar. The name was suggested years ago as a joke by my father's friend Dunstan Ramsay; but Father liked it, and used it when he created the Foundation. Or, rather, when he changed it from the peculiar thing it was when Grandfather Staunton left it.

"This large bequest to Castor ensured the continuance of all his charities and patronages. I was pleased, but not surprised, that he had given a strong hint in the will that he expected me to succeed him as Chairman of Castor. I already had a place on its Board. It's a very small Board—as small as the law will permit. So by this single act he had made me a man of importance in the world of benefactions, which is one of the very few remaining worlds where the rich are allowed to say what shall be done with the bulk of their money.

"But there was a flick of the whip for me in the latter part of the will, where the personal bequests were detailed.

"I told you that I am a rich man. I should say that I have a good deal of money, caused, if not intended, by a bequest from my grandfather, and I make a large income as a lawyer. But compared with my father I am inconsiderable—just 'well-to-do,' which was the phrase he used to dismiss people who were well above the poverty line but cut no figure in the important world of money. First-class surgeons and top lawyers and some architects were well-to-do, but they manipulated nothing and generated nothing in the world where my father trod like a king.

"So I wasn't looking for my bequest as something that would greatly change my way of life or deliver me from care. No, I wanted to know what my father had done about me in his will because I knew it would be the measure of what he thought of me as a man, and as his son. He obviously thought I could handle money, or he wouldn't have tipped me for the chairmanship of Castor. But what part of his money—and you must understand money meant his esteem and his love—did he think I was worth?

"Denyse was left very well off, but she got no capital—just a walloping good income for life or—this was Father speaking again—so long as she remained his widow. I am sure he thought he was protecting her against fortune-hunters; but he was also keeping fortune-hunters from getting their hands on anything that was, or had been, his.

"Then there was a bundle for 'my dear daughter, Caroline' which was to be hers outright and without conditions—because Beesty could have choked on a fishbone at his club any day and Caroline remarried at once and Father wouldn't have batted an eye.

"Then there was a really large capital sum in trust 'for my dear grandchildren, Caroline Elizabeth and Boyd Staunton Bastable, portions to be allotted *per stirpes* to any legitimate children of my son Edward David Staunton from the day of their birth.' There it was, you see."

"Your father was disappointed that you had no children?"

"Certainly that is how he would have expected it to be interpreted. But didn't you notice that I was simply his son, when all the others were his dear this and dear that? Very significant, in something carefully prepared by Father. It would be nearer the truth to say he was angry because I wouldn't marry—wouldn't have anything to do with women at all."

"I see. And why is that?"

"It's a very long and complicated story."

"Yes. It usually is."

"I'm not a homosexual, if that's what you are suggesting."

"I am not suggesting that. If there were easy and quick answers, psychiatry would not be very hard work."

"My father was extremely fond of women."

"Are you fond of women?"

"I have a very high regard for women."

"That is not what I asked."

"I like them well enough."

"Well enough for what?"

"To get along pleasantly with them. I know a lot of women."

"Have you any women friends?"

"Well—in a way. They aren't usually interested in the things I like to talk about."

"I see. Have you ever been in love?"

"In love? Oh, certainly."

"Deeply in love?"

"Yes."

"Have you had sexual intercourse with women?"

"With a woman."

"When last?"

"It would be—let me think for a moment—December 26, 1945."

"A very lawyer-like answer. But—nearly twenty-three years ago. How old were you?"

"Seventeen."

"Was it with the person with whom you were deeply in love?"

"No, no; certainly not!"

"With a prostitute?"

"Certainly not."

"We seem to be approaching a painful area. Your answers are very brief, and not up to your usual standard of phrasing."

"I am answering all your questions, I think."

"Yes, but your very full flow of explanation and detail has dried up. And our hour is drying up, as well. So there is just time to tell you that next day we should take another course. Until now we have been clearing the ground, so to speak. I have been trying to discover what kind of man you are, and I hope you have been discovering something of what I am, as well. We are not really launched on analysis, because I have said little and really have not helped you at all. If we are to go on—and the time is very close when you must make that decision—we shall have to go deeper, and if that works, we shall then go deeper still, but we shall not continue in this extemporaneous way. Just before you go, do you think that by leaving you nothing in his will except this possibility of money for your children, your father was punishing you—that in his own terms he was telling you he didn't love you?"

"Yes."

"And you care whether he loved you or not?"

"Must it be called love?"

"It was your own word."

"It's a very emotional term. I cared whether he thought

I was a worthy person—a man—a proper person to be his son."

"Isn't that love?"

"Love between father and son isn't something that comes into society nowadays. I mean, the estimate a man makes of his son is in masculine terms. This business of love between father and son sounds like something in the Bible."

"The patterns of human feeling do not change as much as many people suppose. King David's estimate of his rebellious son Absalom was certainly in masculine terms. But I suppose you recall David's lament when Absalom was slain?"

"I have been called Absalom before, and it isn't a comparison I like."

"Very well. There is no point in straining an historical comparison. But do you think your father might have meant something more than scoring a final blow in the contest between you when he arranged his will as he did?"

"He was an extremely direct man in most things, but in personal relationships he was subtle. He knew the will would be studied by many people and that they would know he had left me obligations suitable to a lawyer but nothing that recognized me as his child. Many of these people would know also that he had had great hopes of me at one time, and had named me after his hero, who had been Prince of Wales when I was born, and that therefore something had gone wrong and I had been a disappointment. It was a way of driving a wedge between me and Caroline, and it was a way of giving Denyse a stick to beat me with. We had had some scenes about this marriage and woman business, and I would never give in and I would never say why. But he knew why. And this was his last word on the subject: spite me if you dare; live a barren man and a eunuch; but don't think of yourself as my son. That's what it meant."

"How much does it mean to you to think of yourself as his son?"

"The alternative doesn't greatly attract me."

"What alternative is that?"

"To think that I am Dunstan Ramsay's son."

"The friend? The man who was grinning at the funeral?"

"Yes. It has been hinted. By Netty. And Netty might just have known what she was talking about."

"I see. Well, we shall certainly have much to talk about when next we meet. But now I must ask you to give way to my next patient."

I never saw these next patients or the ones who had been with the doctor before me because her room had two doors, one from the waiting-room but the other giving directly into the corridor. I was glad of this arrangement, for as I left I must have looked very queer. What had I been saying?

(7)

"Let me see; we had reached Friday in your bad week, had we not? Tell me about Friday."

"At ten o'clock, the beginning of the banking day, George Inglebright and I had to meet two men from the Treasury Department in the vault of the bank to go through my father's safety-deposit box. When somebody dies, you know, all his accounts are frozen and all his money goes into a kind of limbo until the tax people have had a full accounting of it. It's a queer situation because all of a sudden what has been secret becomes public business, and people you've never seen before outrank you in places where you have thought yourself important. Inglebright had warned me to be very quiet with the tax men. He's a senior man in my father's firm of lawyers, and of course he knows the ropes, but it was new to me.

"The tax men were unremarkable fellows, but I found it embarrassing to be locked up in one of the bank's little cubbyholes with them while we counted what was in the safetydeposit box. Not that I counted; I watched. They warned me not to touch anything, which annoyed me because it suggested I might snatch a bundle of brightly coloured stock certificates and make a run for it. What was in the box was purely personal, not related to Alpha or any of the companies my father controlled. It wasn't as personal as I feared, however; I've heard stories of safety-deposit boxes with locks of hair, and baby shoes, and women's garters, and God knows what in them. But there was nothing of that sort. Only shares and bonds amounting to a very large amount, which the tax men counted and inventoried carefully.

"One of the things that bothered me was that these men, obviously not paid much, were cataloguing what was in itself a considerable fortune: what did they think? Were they envious? Did they hate me? Were they glorying in their authority? Were they conscious of putting down the mighty from their seat and exalting the humble and meek? They looked crusty and non-committal, but what was going on in their heads?

"It took most of the morning and I had nothing whatever to do but watch, which I found exhausting because of the reflections it provoked. It was the kind of situation that leads one to trite philosophizing: here is what remains of a very large part of a life's effort—that kind of thing. Now and then I thought about the chairmanship of Castor, and a phrase I hadn't heard since my law-student days came into my head and wouldn't be driven out. *Damnosa hereditas;* a ruinous inheritance. It's a phrase from Roman Law; comes in Gaius's *Institutes,* and means exactly what it says. Castor could very

well be that to me because it is big already, and with what
will come into it from my father's estate it will be a very
large charitable foundation even by American standards, and
being the head of it will devour time and energy and could
very well be the end of the kind of career I have tried to make
for myself. *Damnosa hereditas.* Did he mean it that way?
Probably not. One must assume the best. Still—

"I gave George lunch, then marched off like a little soldier
to talk to Denyse and Caroline about the will. They had had
a chance to go over their own copies, and Beesty had explained most of it, but he isn't a lawyer and they had a lot
of points they wanted clarified. And of course there was a row,
because I think Denyse had expected some capital, and in
fairness I must say that she was within her rights to do so.
What really burned her, I think, was that there was nothing
for her daughter Lorene, though what she had been left for
herself would have been more than enough to take care of all
that. Lorene is soft in the head, you see, though Denyse pretends otherwise, and she will have to be looked after all her
life. Although Lorene's name was never mentioned, I could
sense her presence; she had called my father Daddy-Boy, and
Daddy-Boy hadn't lived up to expectation.

"Caroline is above fussing about inheritances. She is really a
very fine person, in her frosty way. But naturally she was
pleased to have been taken care of so handsomely, and Beesty
was openly delighted. After all, with the trust money and Caroline's personal fortune and what would come from himself
and his side of the family, his kids were in the way of being
rich even by my father's demanding standards. Both Caroline
and Beesty saw how I had been dealt with, but they were too
tactful to say anything about it in front of Denyse.

"Not so Denyse herself. 'This was Boy's last chance to get

you back on the rails, David,' said she, 'and for his sake I hope it works.'

" 'What particular rails are you talking about?' I said. I knew well enough, but I wanted to hear what she would say. And I will admit I led her on to put her foot in it because I wanted a chance to dislike her even more than I did already.

" 'To be utterly frank, dear, he wanted you to be married, and to have a family, and to cut down on your drinking. He knew what a balancing effect a wife and children have on a man of great talents. And of course everybody knows that you have great talents—potentially.' Denyse was not one to shrink from a challenge.

" 'So he has left me the toughest job in the family bundle, and some money for children I haven't got,' I said. 'Do you happen to know if he had anybody in mind that he wanted me to marry? I'd like to be sure of everything that is expected of me.'

"Beesty was wearing his toad-under-the-harrow expression, and Caroline's eyes were fierce. 'If you two are going to fight, I'm going home,' she said.

" 'There will be no fighting,' said Denyse. 'This is not the time or the place. David asked a straight question and I gave him a straight answer—as I have always done. And straight answers are something David doesn't like except in court, where he can ask the questions that will give him the answers he wants. Boy was very proud of David's success, so far as it went. But he wanted something from his only son that goes beyond a somewhat notorious reputation in the criminal courts. He wanted the continuance of the Staunton name. He would have thought it pretentious to talk of such a thing, but you know as well as I do that he wanted to establish a line.'

"Ah, that line. My father had not been nearly so reticent

about mentioning it as Denyse pretended. She has never understood what real reticence is. But I was sick of the fight already. I quickly tire of quarrelling with Denyse. Perhaps, as she says, I only like quarrelling in court. In court there are rules. Denyse makes up her rules as she goes along. As I must say women tend to do. So the talk shifted, not very easily, to other things.

"Denyse had two fine new bees in her bonnet. The death-mask idea had failed, and she knew I would not tell the others, so as far as she was concerned it had perished as though it had never been. She does not dwell on her failures.

"What she wanted now was a monument for my father, and she had decided that a large piece of sculpture by Henry Moore would be just the thing. Not to be given to the Art Gallery or the City, of course. To be put up in the cemetery. I hope that gives you the measure of Denyse. No sense of congruity; no sense of humour; no modesty. Just ostentation and gall working under the governance of a fashionable, belligerent, unappeasable ambition.

"Her second great plan was for a monument of another kind; she announced with satisfaction that my father's biography was to be written by Dunstan Ramsay. She had wanted Eric Roop to do it—Roop was one of her protégés and as a poet he was comparable to her dentist friend as a sculptor—but Roop had promised himself a fallow year if he could get a grant to see him through it. I knew this already, because Roop's fallow years were as familiar to Castor as Pharaoh's seven lean kine, and his demand that we stake him to another had been circulated to the Board, and I had seen it. The Ramsay plan had merit. Dunstan Ramsay was not only a schoolmaster but an author who had enjoyed a substantial success in a queer field: he wrote about saints—popular books for tourists, and at least one heavy-weight work that had brought him a reputation in the places where such things count.

"Furthermore, he wrote well. I knew because he had been my history master at school; he insisted on essays in what he called the Plain Style; it was, he said, much harder to get away with nonsense in the Plain Style than in a looser manner. In my legal work I had found this to be true and useful. But—what would we look like if a life of Boy Staunton appeared over the name of a man notable as a student of the lives of saints? There would be jokes, and one or two of them occurred to me immediately.

"On the other hand, Ramsay had known my father from boyhood. Had he agreed? Denyse said he had wavered a little when she put it to him, but she would see that he made up his mind. After all, his own little estate—which was supposed to be far beyond what a teacher and author could aspire to—was built on the advice my father had given him over the years. Ramsay had a nice little block of Alpha. The time had come for him to pay up in his own coin. And Denyse would work with him and see that the job was properly done and Ramsay's ironies kept under control.

"Neither Caroline nor I was very fond of Ramsay, who had been a sharp-tongued nuisance in our lives, and we were amused to think of a collaboration between him and our step-mother. So we made no demur, but determined to spike the Henry Moore plan.

"Caroline and Beesty got away as soon as they could, but I had to wait and hear Denyse talk about the letters of condolence she had been receiving in bulk. She graded them; some were Official, from public figures, and subdivided into Warm and Formal; some were from personal friends, and these she classified as Moving and Just Ordinary; and there were many from Admirers, and the best of these were graded Touching. Denyse has an orderly mind.

"We did not talk about a dozen or so hateful letters of abuse that had come unsigned. Nor did we say much about the newspaper pieces, some of which had been grudging and covertly offensive. We were both habituated to the Canadian spirit, to which generous appreciation is so alien.

"It had been a wearing afternoon, and I had completed all my immediate tasks, so I thought I would permit myself a few drinks after dinner. I dined at my club and had the few drinks, but to my surprise they did nothing to dull my wretchedness. I am not a man who is cheered by drink. I don't sing or make jokes or chase girls, nor do I stagger and speak thickly; I become remote—possibly somewhat glassy-eyed. But I do manage to blunt the edge of that heavy axe that seems always to be chopping away at the roots of my being. That night it was not so. I went home and began to drink seriously. Still the axe went right on with its destructive work. At last I went to bed and slept wretchedly.

"It is foolish to call it sleep. It was a long, miserable reverie, relieved by short spells of unconsciousness. I had a weeping fit, which frightened me because I haven't cried for thirty years; Netty and my father had no use for boys who cried. It was frightening because it was part of the destruction of my mind that was going on; I was being broken down to a very primitive level, and absurd kinds of feeling and crude, inexplicable emotions had taken charge of me.

"Imagine a man of forty crying because his father hadn't loved him! Particularly when it wasn't true, because he obviously had loved me, and I know I worried him dreadfully. I even sank so low that I wanted my mother, though I knew that if that poor woman could have come to me at that very time, she wouldn't have known what to say or do. She never really knew what was going on, poor soul. But I wanted something, and my mother was the nearest identification I could find for it. And this blubbering booby was Mr. David Staunton, Q.C., who had a dark reputation because the criminal world thought so highly of him, and who played up to the role, and who secretly fancied himself as a magician of the courtroom. But in the interest of justice, mind you; always in the constant and perpetual wish that everyone shall have his due.

"Next morning the axe was making great headway, and I began with the bottle at breakfast, to Netty's indignation and dismay. She didn't say anything, because once before when she had interfered I had given her a few sharp cuffs, which she afterward exaggerated into 'beating her up.' Netty hasn't seen some of the beatings-up I have observed in court or she wouldn't talk so loosely. She has never mastered the Plain Style. Of course I had been regretful for having struck her, and apologized in the Plain Style, but she understood afterward that she was not to interfere.

"So she locked herself in her room that Saturday morning, taking care to do it when I was near enough to hear what she was doing; she even pushed the bed against the door. I knew what I was up to; she wanted to be able to say to Caroline, 'When he's like that I just have to barricade myself in, because if he flew off the handle like he did that time, the Dear knows what could happen to me.' Netty liked to tell Caroline and Beesty that nobody knew what she went through. They had a pretty shrewd notion that most of what she went through was in her own hot imagination.

"I went back to my club for luncheon on Saturday, and although the barman was as slow as he could be when I wanted him, and absent from the bar as much as he could manage, I got through quite a lot of Scotch before I settled down to having a few drinks before dinner. A member I knew called Femister came in and I heard the barman mutter something to him about 'tying on a bun' and I knew he meant me.

"A bun! These people know nothing. When I bend to the work it is no trivial bun, but a whole baking of double loaves I tie on. Only this time nothing much seemed to be happening, except for a generalized remoteness of things, and the axe was chopping away as resolutely as ever. Femister is a good fellow, and he sat down by me and chatted. I chatted right back, clearly and coherently, though perhaps a little fancifully. He suggested we have dinner together, and I agreed. He ate a substantial club dinner, and I messed my food around on my plate and tried to take my mind off its smell, which I found oppressive. Femister was kindly, but my courteous *non sequiturs* were just as discouraging as I meant them to be, and after dinner it was clear that he had had all the Good Samaritan business he could stand.

" 'I've got an appointment now,' he said. 'What are you going to do? You certainly don't want to spend the evening all alone here, do you? Why don't you go to the theatre? Have you seen this chap at the Royal Alec? Marvellous! Magnus Eisengrim his name is, though it sounds unlikely, doesn't it? The show is terrific! I've never seen such a conjuror. And all the fortune-telling and answering questions and all that. Terrific! It would take you right out of yourself.'

" 'I can't imagine anywhere I'd rather be,' I said, slowly and deliberately. 'I'll go. Thank you very much for suggesting it. Now you run along, or you'll miss your appointment.'

"Off he went, grateful to have done something for me and to have escaped without trouble. He wasn't telling me anything I didn't already know. I had been to Eisengrim's *Soirée of Illusions* the week before, with my father and Denyse and Lorene, whose birthday it was. I was sucked into it at the last minute, and had not liked the show at all, though I could see that it was skilful. But I detested Magnus Eisengrim.

"Shall I tell you why? Because he was making fools of us

all, and so cleverly that most of us liked it; he was a con man of a special kind, exploiting just that element in human credulity that most arouses me—I mean the *desire* to be deceived. You know that maddening situation that lies behind so many criminal cases, where somebody is so besotted by somebody else that he lays himself open to all kinds of cheating and ill-usage, and sometimes to murder? It isn't love, usually; it's a kind of abject surrender, an abdication of common sense. I am a victim of it, now and then, when feeble clients decide that I am a wonder-worker and can do miracles in court. I imagine you get it, as an analyst, when people think you can unweave the folly of a lifetime. It's a powerful force in life, yet so far as I know it hasn't even a name—"

"Excuse me—yes, it has a name. We call it projection."

"Oh. I've never heard that. Well, whatever it is, it was going full steam ahead in that theatre, where Eisengrim was fooling about twelve hundred people, and they were delighted to be fooled and begging for more. I was disgusted, and most of all with the nonsense of the Brazen Head.

"It was second to the last illusion on his program. I never saw the show to the end. I believe it was some sexy piece of nonsense vaguely involving Dr. Faustus. But *The Brazen Head of Friar Bacon* was what had caused the most talk. It began in darkness, and slowly the light came up inside a big human head that floated in the middle of the stage, so that it glowed. It spoke, in a rather foreign voice. 'Time is,' it said, and there was a tremble of violins; 'Time was,' it said, and there was a chord of horns; 'Time's past,' it said, and there was a very quiet ruffle of drums, and the lights came up just enough for us to see Eisengrim—he wore evening clothes, but with knee-breeches, as if he were at Court—who told us the legend of the Head that could tell all things.

"He invited the audience to lend him objects, which his assistants sealed in envelopes and carried to the stage, where he mixed them up in a big glass bowl. He held up each envelope as he chose it by chance, and the Head identified the owner of the hidden object by the number of the seat in which he was sitting. Very clever, but it made me sick, because people were so delighted with what was, after all, just a very clever piece of co-operation by the magician's troupe.

"Then came the part the audience had been waiting for and that caused so much sensation through the city. Eisengrim said the Head would give personal advice to three people in the audience. This had always been sensational, and the night I was there with my father's theatre party the Head had said something that brought the house down, to a woman who was involved in a difficult legal case; it enraged me because it was virtually contempt of court—a naked interference in something that was private and under the most serious consideration our society provides. I had talked a great deal about it afterward, and Denyse had told me not to be a spoil-sport, and my father had suggested that I was ruining Lorene's party—because of course this sort of nonsense was just the kind of thing a fool like Lorene would think marvellous.

"So you see I wasn't in the best mood for the *Soirée of Illusions,* but some perversity compelled me to go, and I bought a seat in the top gallery, where I assumed nobody would know me. A lot of people had been going to this show two and even three times, and I didn't want anybody to say I had been among their number.

"The program was the same, but the flatness I had expected in a show I had seen before was notably missing, and that annoyed me. I didn't want Eisengrim to be as good as he was. I thought him dangerous and I grudged him the admiration the audience plainly felt for him. The show was very clever; I must admit that. It had real mystery, and beautiful girls very cleverly and tastefully displayed, and there was a quality of fantasy about it that I have never seen in any other magician's performance, and very rarely in the theatre.

"Have you ever seen the Habima Players do *The Dybbuk?* I did, long ago, and this had something of that quality about it, as if you were looking into a stranger and more splendid world than the one you know—almost a solemn joy. But I had not lost my grievance, and the better *The Soirée of Illusions* was, the more I wanted to wreck it.

"I suppose the drink was getting to me more than I knew, and I muttered two or three times until people shushed me. When *The Brazen Head of Friar Bacon* came, and the borrowed objects had been identified, and Eisengrim was promising his answers to secret questions, I suddenly heard myself shouting, 'Who killed Boy Staunton?' and I found I was on my feet, and there was a sensation in the theatre. People were staring at me. There was a crash in one of the boxes, and I had the impression that someone had fallen and knocked over some chairs. The Head began to glow, and I heard the foreign voice saying something that seemed to begin, 'He was killed by a gang . . .' then something about 'the woman he knew . . . the woman he did not know,' but really I can't be sure what I heard because I was dashing up the steps of the balcony as hard as I could go—they are very steep—and then pelting down two flights of stairs, though I don't think anybody was chasing me. I rushed into the street, jumped into one of the taxis that had begun to collect at the door, and got back to my apartment, very much shaken.

"But it was as I was leaving the theatre in such a sweat that the absolute certainty came over me that I had to do something about myself. That is why I am here."

"Yes, I see. I don't think there can be any doubt that it was a wise decision. But in the letter from Dr. Tschudi he said something about your having put yourself through what you called 'the usual examination.' What did you mean?"

"Ah—well. I'm a lawyer, as you know."

"Yes. Was it some sort of legal examination, then?"

"I am a thorough man. I think you might say a whole-hearted man. I believe in the law."

"And so—?"

"You know what the law is, I suppose? The procedures of law are much discussed, and people know about lawyers and courts and prisons and punishment and all that sort of thing, but that is just the apparatus through which the law works. And it works in the cause of justice. Now, justice is the constant and perpetual wish to render to everyone his due. Every law student has to learn that. A surprising number of them seem to forget it, but I have not forgotten it."

"Yes, I see. But what is 'the usual examination'?"

"Oh, it's just a rather personal thing."

"Of course, but clearly it is an important personal thing. I should like to hear about it."

"It is hard to describe."

"Is it so complex, then?"

"I wouldn't say it was complex, but I find it rather embarrassing."

"Why?"

"To someone else it would probably seem to be a kind of game."

"A game you play by yourself?"

"You might call it that, but it misrepresents what I do and the consequences of what I do."

"Then you must be sure I do not misunderstand. Is this game a kind of fantasy?"

"No, no; it is very serious."

"All real fantasy is serious. Only faked fantasy is not serious. That is why it is so wrong to impose faked fantasy on children. I shall not laugh at your fantasy. I promise. Now—please tell me what 'the usual examination' is."

"Very well, then. It's a way I have of looking at what I have done, or might do, to see what it is worth. I imagine a court, you see, all perfectly real and correct in every detail. I am the Judge, on the Bench. And I am the prosecuting lawyer, who presents whatever it is in the worst possible light—but within the rules of pleading. That means I may not express a purely personal opinion about the rights or wrongs of the case. But I am also the defence lawyer, and I put the best case I can for whatever is under examination—but again I mayn't be personal and load the pleading. I can even call myself into the witness-box and examine and cross-examine myself. And in the end Mr. Justice Staunton must make up his mind and give a decision. And there is no appeal from that decision."

"I see. A very complete fantasy."

"I suppose you must call it that. But I assure you it is extremely serious to me. This case I am telling you about took several hours. I was charged with creating a disturbance in a public place while under the influence of liquor, and there were grave special circumstances—creating a scandal that could seriously embarrass the Staunton family, for one."

"Surely that is a moral rather than a legal matter?"

"Not entirely. And anyhow, the law is, among other things, a codification of a very large part of public morality. It expresses the moral opinion of society on a great number of subjects. And in Mr. Justice Staunton's court, morality carries great weight. It's obvious."

"Truly? What makes it obvious?"

"Oh, just a difference in the Royal Arms."

"The Royal Arms?"

"Yes. Over the judge's head, where they are always displayed."

"And what is the difference? . . . Another of your pauses, Mr. Staunton. This must mean a great deal to you. Please describe the difference."

"It's nothing very much. Only that the animals are complete."

"The animals?"

"The supporters, they are called. The Lion and the Unicorn."

"And are they sometimes incomplete?"

"Almost always in Canada. They are shown without their privy parts. To be heraldically correct they should have distinct, rather saucy pizzles. But in Canada we geld everything, if we can, and dozens of times I have sat in court and looked at those pitifully deprived animals and thought how they exemplified our attitude toward justice. Everything that spoke of passion—and when you talk of passion you talk of morality in one way or another—was ruled out of order or disguised as something else. Only Reason was welcome. But in Mr. Justice Staunton's court the Lion and the Unicorn are complete, because morality and passion get their due there."

"I see. Well, how did the case go?"

"It hung, in the end, on the McNaghton Rule."

"You must tell me what that is."

"It is a formula for determining responsibility. It takes its name from a nineteenth-century murderer called McNaghton whose defence was insanity. He said he did it when he was not himself. This was the defence put forward for Staunton. The prosecution kept hammering away at Staunton to find out whether, when he shouted in the theatre, he fully understood the nature and quality of his act, and if he did, did he know it was wrong? The defence lawyer—Mr. David Staunton, a very eminent Q.C.—urged every possible extenuating circumstance: that the prisoner Staunton had been under severe stress for several days; that he had lost his father in a most grievous fashion, and that he had undergone severe psychological harassment because of that loss; that unusual responsibilities and burdens had been placed upon him; that his last hope of regaining the trust and approval of his late father had been crushed. But the prosecutor—Mr. David Staunton, Q.C., on behalf of the Crown—would not recognize any of that as exculpatory, and in the end he put the question that defence had been dreading all along. 'If a policeman had been standing at your elbow, would you have acted as you did? If a policeman had been in the seat next to you, would you have shouted your scandalous question at the stage?' And of course the prisoner Staunton broke down and wept and had to say, 'No,' and then, to all intents, the case was over. The Judge—Mr. Justice Staunton, known for his fairness but also for his sternness— didn't even leave the Bench. He found the prisoner Staunton guilty, and the sentence was that he should seek psychiatric help at once."

"Then what did you do?"

"It was seven o'clock on Sunday morning. I called the airport, booked a passage to Zürich, and twenty-four hours later I was here. Three hours after arrival I was sitting in Dr. Tschudi's office."

"Was the prisoner Staunton very much depressed by the outcome of the case?"

"It could hardly have been worse for him, because he has a very poor opinion of psychiatry."

"But he yielded?"

"Doctor von Haller, if a wounded soldier in the eighteenth century had been told he must have a battlefield amputation, he would know that his chances of recovery were slim, but he would have no choice. It would be: die of gangrene or die of the surgeon's knife. My choice in this instance was to go mad unattended or to go mad under the best obtainable auspices."

"Very frank. We are getting on much better already. You have begun to insult me. I think I may be able to do something for you, Prisoner Staunton."

"Do you thrive on insult?"

"No. I mean only that you have begun to feel enough about me to want to strike some fire out of me. That is not bad, that comparison between eighteenth-century battlefield surgery and modern psychiatry; this sort of curative work is still fairly young and in the way it is sometimes practised it can be brutal. But there were recoveries, even from eighteenth-century surgery, and as you point out, the alternative was an ugly one.

"Now let us get down to work. The decisions must be entirely yours. What do you expect of me? A cure for your drunkenness? You have told me that it is not your disease, but your symptom; symptoms cannot be cured—only alleviated. Illnesses can be cured when we know what they are and if circumstances are favourable. Then the symptoms abate. You have an illness. You have talked of nothing else. It seems very complicated, but all descriptions of symptoms are complicated. What did you expect when you came to Zürich?"

"I expected nothing at all. I have told you that I have seen many psychiatrists in court, and they are not impressive."

"That's nonsense. You wouldn't have come if you hadn't had some hope, however reluctant you were to admit it. If we are to achieve anything you must give up the luxury of easy despair. You are too old for that, though in certain ways you seem young for your age. You are forty. That is a critical age. Between thirty-five and forty-five everybody has to turn a corner in his life, or smash into a brick wall. If you are ever going to gain a measure of maturity, now is the time. And I must ask you not to judge psychiatrists on what you see in court. Legal evidence and psychological evidence are quite different things, and when you are on your native ground in court, with your gown on and everything going your way, you can make anybody look stupid, and you do—"

"And I suppose the converse is that when you have a lawyer in your consulting-room, and you are the doctor, you can make him look stupid and you do?"

"It is not my profession to make anyone look stupid. If we are to do any good here, we must be on terms that are much better than that; our relationship must go far beyond merely professional wrangling for trivial advantages."

"Do you mean that we must be friends?"

"Not at all. We must be on doctor-and-patient terms, with respect on both sides. You are free to dispute and argue anything I say if you must, but we shall not go far if you play the defence lawyer every minute of our time. If we go on, we shall be all kinds of things to each other, and I shall probably be your stepmother and your sister and your housekeeper and all sorts of people in the attitude you take toward me before we are through. But if your chief concern is to maintain your image of yourself as the brilliant, drunken counsel with a well-founded grudge against life, we shall take twice as long to do our work because that will have to be changed before anything else can be done. It will cost you much more money, and I don't think you like wasting money."

"True. But how did you know?"

"Call it a trade secret. No, that won't do. We must not deal with one another in that vein. Just recognize that I have had rich patients before, and some of them are great counters of their pennies. . . . Would you like a few days to consider what you are going to do?"

"No. I've already decided. I want to go ahead with the treatment."

"Why?"

"But surely you know why."

"Yes, but I must find out if you know why."

"You agree with me that the drinking business is a symptom, and not my disease?"

"Let us not speak of disease. A disease in your case would be a psychosis, which is what you fear and what of course is always possible. Though the rich are rarely mad. Did you know that? They may be neurotic and frequently they are. Psychotic, rarely. Let us say that you are in an unsatisfactory state of mind and you want to get out of it. Will that do?"

"It seems a little mild, for what has been happening to me."

"You mean, like your Netty, nobody knows what you are going through? I assure you that very large numbers of people go through much worse things."

"Aha, I see where we are going. This is to destroy my sense of uniqueness. I've had lots of that in life, I assure you."

"No, no. We do not work on the reductive plan, we of the Zürich School. Nobody wants to bring your life's troubles down to having been slapped because you did not do your business on the pot. Even though that might be quite important, it is not the mainspring of a life. You are certainly unique. Everyone is unique. Nobody has ever suffered quite like you before because nobody has ever been you before. But we are members of the human race, as well, and our unique quality has limits. Now—about treatment. There are a few simple things to begin with. You had better leave your hotel and take rooms somewhere. There are quite good pensions where you can be quiet, and that is important. You must have quiet and retirement, because you will have to do a good deal of work yourself between appointments with me, and you will find that tiring."

"I hate pensions. The food is usually awful."

"Yes, but they have no bars, and they are not pleased if guests drink very much in their rooms. It would be best if it were inconvenient, but not impossible, for you to drink very much. I think you should try to ration yourself. Don't stop. Just take it gently. Our Swiss wines are very nice."

"Oh God! Don't talk about *nice* wine."

"As you please. But be prudent. Much of your present attitude toward things comes from the exacerbations of heavy drinking. You say it doesn't affect you, but of course it does."

"I know people who drink just as much as I do and are none the worse."

"Yes. Everybody knows such people. But you are not one of them. After all, you would not be in that chair if you were."

"If we are not going to talk about my toilet-training, what is the process of your treatment? Bullying and lectures?"

"If necessary. But it isn't usually necessary, and when it is, that is only a small part of the treatment."

"Then what are you going to do?"

"I am not going to *do* anything to you. I am going to try to help you in the process of becoming yourself."

"My best self, I expected you to say. A good little boy."

"Your real self may not be a good little boy. It would be very unfortunate if that were so. Your real self may be something very disagreeable and unpleasant. This is not a game we are playing, Mr. Staunton. It can be dangerous. Part of my work is to see the dangers as they come and help you to get through them. But if the dangers are inescapable and possibly destructive, don't think I can help you to fly over them. There will be lions in the way. I cannot pull their teeth or tell them to make paddy-paws; I can only give you some useful tips about lion-taming."

"Now you're trying to scare me."

"I am warning you."

"What do we do to get to the lions?"

"We can start almost anywhere. But from what you have told me I think we would be best to stick to the usual course and begin at the beginning."

"Childhood recollections?"

"Yes, and recollections of your life up to now. Important things. Formative experiences. People who have meant much to you, whether good or bad."

"That sounds like the Freudians."

"We have no quarrel with the Freudians, but we do not put the same stress on sexual matters as they do. Sex is very important, but if it were the single most important thing in life it would all be much simpler, and I doubt if mankind would have worked so hard to live far beyond the age when sex is the greatest joy. It is a popular delusion, you know, that people who live very close to nature are great ones for sex. Not a bit. You live with primitives—I did it for three years, when I was younger and very interested in anthropology—and you find out the truth. People wander around naked and nobody cares —not even an erection or a wiggle of the hips. That is because their society does not give them the brandy of Romance, which is the great drug of our world. When sex is on the program they sometimes have to work themselves up with dances and ceremonies to get into the mood for it, and then of course they are very active. But their important daily concern is with food. You know, you can go for a lifetime without sex and come to no special harm. Hundreds of people do so. But you go for a day without food and the matter becomes imperative. In our society food is just a start for our craving. We want all kinds of things—money, a big place in the world, objects of beauty, learning, sainthood, oh, a very long list. So here in Zürich we try to give proper attention to these other things, as well.

"We generally begin with what we call *anamnesis*. Are you a classicist? Do you know any Greek? We look at your history, and meet some people there whom you may know or perhaps you don't, but who are portions of yourself. We take a look at what you remember, and at some things you thought you had forgotten. As that goes on we find we are going much deeper. And when that is satisfactorily explored, we decide whether to go deeper still, to that part of you which is beyond the unique, to the common heritage of mankind."

"How long does it take?"

"It varies. Sometimes long, sometimes surprisingly short, especially if you decide not to go beyond the personal realm. And though of course I give advice about that, the decision, like all the decisions in this sort of work, must be your own."

"So I should begin getting a few recollections together? I don't want to be North American about this, but I haven't unlimited time. I mean, three years or anything of that sort is out of the question. I'm the executor of my father's will. I can do quite a lot from here by telephone or by post but I can't be away forever. And there is the problem of Castor to be faced."

"I have always understood that it takes about three years to settle an estate. In civilized countries, that is; there are countries here in Europe where it can go on for ten if there is enough money to pay the costs. Does it impress you as interesting that to settle a dead man's affairs takes about the same length of time as settling a life's complications in a man of forty? Still, I see your difficulty. And that makes me wonder if a scheme I have been considering for you might not be worth a trial."

"What are you thinking of?"

"We do many things to start the stream of recollection flowing in a patient, and to bring forth and give clues to what is important for him. Some patients draw pictures, or paint, or model things in clay. There have even been patients who have danced and devised ceremonies that seemed relevant to their situation. It must be whatever is most congenial to the nature of the analysand."

"Analysand? Am I an analysand?"

"Horrid word, isn't it? I promise I shall never call you that. We shall stick to the Plain Style, shall we, in what we say to one another?"

"Ramsay always insisted that there was nothing that could not be expressed in the Plain Style if you knew what you were talking about. Everything else was Baroque Style, which he said was not for most people, or Jargon, which was the Devil's work."

"Very good. Though you must be patient, because English is not my cradle-tongue, and my work creates a lot of Jargon. But about you, and what you may do; I think you might create something, but not pictures or models. You are a lawyer, and you seem to be a great man for words: what would you say to writing a brief of your case?"

"I've digested hundreds of briefs in my time."

"Yes, and some of them were for cases pleaded before Mr. Justice Staunton."

"This would be for the case pleaded in the court of Mr. Justice von Haller."

"No, no; Mr. Justice Staunton still. You cannot get away from him, you know."

"I haven't often pleaded very successfully for the defendant Staunton in that court. The victories have usually gone to the prosecution. Are you sure we need to do it this way?"

"I think there is good reason to try. It is the heroic way, and you have found it without help from anyone else. That suggests that heroic measures appeal to you, and that you are not really afraid of them."

"But that was just a game."

"You played it with great seriousness. And it is not such an uncommon game. Do you know Ibsen's poem—

> To live is to battle with trolls
>   in the vaults of heart and brain.
> To write: that is to sit
>   in judgement over one's self.

I suggest that you make a beginning. Let it be a brief for the defence; you will inevitably prepare a brief for the prosecution as you do so, for that is the kind of court you are to appear in—the court of self-judgement. And Mr. Justice Staunton will hear all, and render judgement, perhaps more often than is usual."

"I see. And what are you in all this?"

"Oh, I am several things; an interested spectator, for one, and for another, I shall be a figure that appears only in military courts, called Prisoner's Friend. And I shall be an authority on precedents, and germane judgements, and I shall keep both the prosecutor and the defence counsel in check. I shall be custodian of that constant and perpetual wish to render to everyone his due. And if Mr. Justice Staunton should doze, as judges sometimes do—"

"Not Mr. Justice Staunton. He slumbers not, nor sleeps."

"We shall see if he is as implacable as you suppose. Even Mr. Justice Staunton might learn something. A judge is not supposed to be an enemy of the prisoner, and I think Mr. Justice Staunton sounds a little too eighteenth century in his out-look to be really good at his work. Perhaps we can lure him into modern times, and get him to see the law in a modern light. . . . And now—until Monday, isn't it?"

· II ·

David Against
the Trolls

(*This is my Zürich Notebook, containing notes and sum-
maries used by me in presenting my case to Dr. von
Haller; also memoranda of her opinions and interpretations as I made them after my hours with her. Without
being a verbatim report, this is the essence of what passed
between us.*)

(1)

IT IS NOT EASY to be the son of a very rich man.

This could stand as an epigraph for the whole case, for and
against myself, as I shall offer it. Living in the midst of great
wealth without being in any direct sense the possessor of it has
coloured every aspect of my life and determined the form of
all my experience.

Since I entered school at the age of seven I have been aware
that one of the inescapable needs of civilized man—the need
for money—showed itself in my life in a way that was different from the experience of all but a very few of my acquaintances. I knew the need for money. Simple people seem to think
that if a family has money, every member dips what he wants

out of some ever-replenished bag that hangs, perhaps, by the front door. Not so. I knew the need for money, as I shall demonstrate, with special acuteness because although as a boy I was known to be the son of a very rich man, I had in fact a smaller allowance than was usual in my school. I knew that my carefulness about buying snacks or a ticket to the movies was a source of amusement and some contempt among the other boys. They thought I was mean. But I knew that I was supposed to be learning to manage money wisely, and that this was a part of the great campaign to make a man of me. The other boys could usually get an extra dollar or two from their fathers, and were virtually certain to be able to raise as much again from their mothers; to them their allowance was a basic rather than an aggregate income. Their parents were good-natured and didn't seem to care whether, at the age of nine or ten, they could manage money or not. But with my dollar a week, of which ten cents was earmarked for Sunday-morning church, and much of which might be gobbled up by a sudden need for a pair of leather skate-laces or something of that sort, I had to be prudent.

My father had read somewhere that the Rockefeller family preserved and refined the financial genius of the Primal Rockefeller by giving their children tiny allowances with which they had learned, through stark necessity, to do financial miracles. It may have been fine for the Rockefellers, but it was no good for me. My sister Caroline usually had lots of money because she was under no necessity to become a man and had to have money always about her for unexplained reasons connected with protecting her virtue. Consequently I was always in debt to Caroline, and because she domineered over me about it I was always caught up in some new method of scrimping or cheese-paring. When I was no more than eight a boy at school told my friends that Staunton was so mean he would skin a louse for the hide and tallow. I was ashamed and hurt; I was not a mini-miser: I was simply, in terms of my situation, poor. I knew it; I hated it; I could not escape from it.

I am not asking for pity. That would be absurd. I lived among the trappings of wealth. Our chauffeur dropped me at school every morning from a limousine that was an object of wonder to car-minded little boys. I was not one of them; to me a car was, and still is, anything that—mysteriously and rather alarmingly—goes. In the evening, after games, he picked me up again, and as Netty was usually with him, ready to engulf me, it was impossible for me to offer car-fanciers a ride. At home we lived in what I now realize was luxury, and certainly in most ways it was less troublesome than real poverty, which I have since had some opportunities to examine. I was enviable, and if I had the power to cast curses, I should rank the curse of being enviable very high. It has extensive ramifications and subtle refinements. As people assured me from time to time, I had everything. If there was anything I wanted, I could get it by asking my father for it and convincing him that I really needed it and was not merely yielding to a childish whim. This was said to be a very simple matter, but in my experience it might have been simple for Cicero on one of his great days. My father would listen carefully, concealing his amusement as well as he could, and in the end he would knuckle my head affectionately and say: "Davey, I'll give you a piece of advice that will last you all your life: never buy anything unless you really need it; things you just *want* are usually junk."

I am sure he was right, and I have always wished I could live according to his advice. I have never managed it. Nor did he, as I gradually became aware, but somehow that was different. I needed to be made into a man, and he was fully and splendidly and obviously a man. Everybody knew it.

Lapped as I was in every comfort, and fortunate above other boys, how could I have thought I needed money?

What I did need, and very badly, was character. Manhood. The ability to stand on my own feet. My father left me in no doubt about these things, and as my father loved me very much there could be no question that he was right. Love, in a parent, carries with it extraordinary privileges and unquestionable insight. This was one of the things which was taken for granted in our family, and so it did not need to be said.

Was I then a poor little rich boy, wistful for the pleasures available to my humble friends, the sons of doctors and lawyers and architects, most of whom could not have passed even the hundred-thousand-a-year test? Not at all. Children do not question their destiny. Indeed, children do not live their lives; their lives, on the contrary, live them. I did not imagine myself to be the happiest of mortals because no such concept as happiness ever entered my head, though sometimes I was happy almost to the point of bursting. I was told I was fortunate. Indeed, Netty insisted that I thank God for it every night, on my knees. I believed it, but I wondered why I was thanking God when it was so obviously my father who was the giver of all good things. I considered myself and my family to be the norm of human existence, by which all other lives were to be measured. I knew I had troubles because I was short of pocket-money, but this was trivial compared with the greater trouble of not being sure I would ever be a man, and able to stand on my own two feet, and be worthy of my father's love and trust. I was told that everything that happened to me was for my good, and by what possible standard of judgement would I have reached a dissenting opinion?

So you must not imagine I have come here to whine and look for revenge on the dead; this retrospective spiting and birching of parents is one of the things that gets psychoanalysis a bad name. As a lawyer I know there is a statute of limitations on personal and spiritual wrongs as well as on legal ones, and that there is no court in the world that can provide a rescript on past griefs. But if some thoughtful consideration of my past can throw useful light on my present, I have the past neatly tucked away and can produce it on demand.

DR. VON HALLER: Yes, I think that would be best. You have got into your swing, and done all the proper lawyer-like things. So now let us get on.

MYSELF: What do you mean, exactly, by "the proper law-yer-like things?"

DR. VON HALLER: Expressing the highest regard for the person you are going to destroy. Declaring that you have no real feeling in the matter and are quite objective. Suggesting that something is cool and dry which by its nature is hot and steamy. Very good. Continue, please.

MYSELF: If you don't believe what I say, what is the point of continuing? I have said I am not here to blacken my father; I don't know what else I can do to convince you that I speak sincerely.

DR. VON HALLER: Very plainly you must go on, and convince me that way. But I am not here to help you preserve the *status quo*, and leave all your personal relationships exactly as you believe them to be now. Remember, among other things, I am Prisoner's Friend. You know what a friend is, I suppose?

MYSELF: Frankly, I'm not sure that I do.

DR. VON HALLER: Well—let us hope you will find out. About your early childhood—?

I was born on September 2, 1928, and christened Edward David because my father had been an aide-de-camp—and a friend, really—of the Prince of Wales during his 1927 tour of Canada. My father sometimes jokingly spoke of the Prince as my godfather, though he was nothing of the kind. My real godfathers were a club friend of Father's named Dorris and a stockbroker named Taylor, who moved out of our part of the world not long after my christening; I have no recollection of either of them. I think they had just been roped in to fill a gap, and Father had dropped them both by the time I was ready to take notice. But the Prince sent me a mug with his cipher on it, and I used to drink my milk from it; I still have it, and Netty keeps it polished.

I had a number of childhood diseases during my first two years, and became what is called "delicate." This made it hard to keep nurses, because I needed a lot of attention, and children's nurses are scarce in Canada and consequently don't have to stay in demanding places. I had English and Scots nurses to begin with, I believe, and later I used to hear stories of the splendid outfits they wore, which were the wonder of the part of Toronto where we lived. But none of them stuck, and it was my Grandmother Staunton who said that what I needed was not one of those stuck-up Dolly Vardens but a good sensible girl with her head screwed on straight who would do what she was told. That was how Netty Quelch turned up. Netty has been with us ever since.

Because I was delicate, life in the country was thought good for me, and for all of my early years I spent long summers with my grandparents in Deptford, the little village where they lived. My upbringing was a good deal dominated by my grandparents at that time because neither of my parents could stand Deptford, though they had both been born there, and referred to it between themselves as "that hole." So every May I was shipped off to Deptford, and stayed till the end of September, and my memories of it are happy. I suppose unless you are unlucky, anywhere you spend your summers as a child is an Arcadia forever. My grandmother couldn't bear the English nurses, and in my second year she told my mother to send her the baby and she would find a local girl to care for me. Indeed, she had such a girl in mind.

Grandmother was a placid, sweet woman whose great adoration was my father, her only son. She had been "a daughter of the parsonage," and in my scale of values as a child this was fully equivalent to being a friend of the Prince of Wales. I remember that when I was quite small—four or five—I used to pass the time before I went to sleep thinking what a fine thing it would be if the Prince and Grandmother Staunton could meet; they would certainly have some fine talks about me, and I could imagine the Prince deferring to Grandmother on most matters because of her superior age and experience of the world, although of course as a man he would have some pretty interesting things to say; it was likely that he would want me to take charge of Deptford and run it for him. Grandmother was not an active person; she liked sitting, and when she moved she was deliberate. Indeed, she was fat, though I quickly learned that "fat" was a rude word, to be thought but not spoken of older people. It was the job of the good sensible girl to be active, and Netty Quelch was furiously active.

Netty was one of Grandmother's good works. Her parents, Abel and Hannah Quelch, had been farmers, and were wiped out by one of those fires caused by an overheated stove which were such a common disaster in rural Ontario. They were good, decent folk, and had come as young people from the Isle of Man. Henrietta and her younger brother, Maitland, were left orphans and a responsibility of the neighbours because there was no orphanage nearby, and anyhow an orphanage was a place of last resort. A nearby farmer and his wife added them to their own six children and brought them up. And now Netty was sixteen and was to be launched on the world. Level-headed. A demon for work. Deserving. Just what Grand-mother Staunton wanted.

I have never known the world without Netty, so her per-sonal characteristics seemed to me for a long time to be ordained and not matters on which likes or dislikes had any bearing. She was, and is now, below medium height, so spare that all her tendons, strings, and muscles show when they are at work, noisy and clumsy as small people sometimes are, and of boundless overheated energy. Indeed, the impression you get from Netty is that there is a very hot fire burning inside her. Her skin is dry, her breath is hot and strong and suggests com-bustion, though it is not foul. She is hot to the touch, but not moist. Her complexion is a reddish-brown, as though scorched, and her hair is a dark, dry-red—not carroty but a withered auburn. Her responses are quick, and her gaze is a parched glare. Of course I am used to her, but people who meet her for the first time are sometimes alarmed and mistake the intensity of her personality for some furious, pent-up criticism of them-selves. Caroline and Beesty call her the Demon Queen. She is now my housekeeper, and considers herself my keeper.

Netty regards work as the natural state of man. Not to be doing something is, to her, to be either seriously unwell or bone idle, which ranks well below crime. I do not suppose it ever occurred to her when she took on the job of being my nurse that she was to have any time to herself or let me out of her sight, and that was how she functioned. I ate, prayed, defe-cated, and even slept in the closest proximity with her. Only when she was doing nursery laundry, which was every morn-ing after breakfast, could I escape her. She had a cot in my room, and sometimes when I was restless she took me into her bed to soothe me, which she did by stroking my spine. She could be gentle with a child, but oh—how hot she was! I lay beside her and fried, and when I opened my eyes hers were always open, goggling hotly at me, reflecting whatever light might be in the room.

She had been very helpful to her foster-parents, and they were good people who had done their best for her. She always speaks of them with affection and respect. There had been some babies after she joined the family, and Netty had learned all the elementary arts of child-raising. It was my grandmother who finished her education in that realm, and my grandfather who gave her what I suppose must be called post-doctoral instruction.

Grandfather Staunton was a physician by profession, though when I knew him his chief occupation was his business, which was raising sugar-beets on a large scale and manufacturing them into raw sugar. He was an awesome figure, tall, broad, and fat, with a big stomach that had got away from him, so that when he sat down it rested on his thighs almost like some familiar creature he was coddling. He looked, in fact, not unlike J. P. Morgan, and like Morgan he had a big strawberry nose. I know he liked me, but it was not his way to show affection, though on a few occasions he called me "boykin," an endearment nobody else used. He had great resources of dissatisfaction and disapproval, but he never vented them on me. However, so much of his conversation with my grandmother was rancorous about the government, or Deptford, or his employees, or his handful of remaining patients, that I felt him to be dangerous and never took liberties.

Netty held him in great awe because he was rich, and a doctor, and looked on life as a serious, desperate struggle. As I grew older, I found out more about him by snooping in his office. He had qualified as a physician in 1887, but before that he had done some work, under the old Upper Canada medical-apprentice system, with a Dr. Gamsby, who had been the first doctor in Deptford. He had retained all Doc Gamsby's professional equipment, for he was never a man to get rid of anything, and it lay in neglect and disorder in a couple of glass-fronted cases in his office, a fearful museum of rusty knives, hooks, probes, speculums, and even a wooden stethoscope like a little flageolet. And Doc Gamsby's books! When I could give Netty the slip—and she never thought of looking for me in Grandfather's consulting-room, which was holy ground to her—I would very quietly lift one out of the shelves and gloat over engravings of people swathed in elaborate bandages, or hiked up in slings for "luxations," or being cauterized, or—this was an eye-popper—being reamed out for fistula. There were pictures of amputations of all kinds, with large things like pincers for cutting off breasts, diggers for getting at polyps in the nose, and fierce saws for bone. Grandfather did not know I looked at his books, but once, when he met me in the hall outside his room, he beckoned me in and took something out of Doc Gamsby's cabinet.

"Look at this, David," he said. "Any idea what that might be?"

It was a flat metal plate about six inches by three, and perhaps three-quarters of an inch thick, and at one end of it was a round button.

"That's for rheumatism," he said. "People with rheumatism always tell the doctor they can't move. Seized right up so they can't budge. Now this thing here, Davey, is called a scarifier. Suppose a man has a bad back. Nothing helps him. Well, in the old days, they'd hold this thing here right tight up against where he was stiff, and then they'd press this button—"

Here he pressed the button, and from the surface of the metal plate leapt twelve tiny knife-points, perhaps an eighth of an inch long.

"Then he'd budge," said Grandfather, and laughed.

His laugh was one I have never heard in anyone else; he did not blow laughter out, he sucked it in, with a noise that sounded like snuk-snuk, snuk-snuk, snuk.

He put the scarifier away and took out a cigar and hooked the spittoon toward him with his foot, and I knew I was dismissed, having had my first practical lesson in medicine.

What he taught Netty was the craft of dealing with constipation. He had been trained in an era when this was a great and widespread evil, and in rural districts it was, as he himself said with unconscious humour, a corker. Farm people understandably dreaded their draughty privies in winter and cultivated their powers of retention to a point where, in my grandfather's opinion, they were inviting every human ill. During his more active days as a doctor he had warred against constipation, and he kept up the campaign at home. Was I delicate? Obviously I was full of poisons, and he knew what to do. On Friday nights I was given cascara sagrada, which rounded up the poisons as I slept, and on Saturday morning, before breakfast, I was given a glass of Epsom salts to drive them forth. On Sunday morning, therefore, I was ready for church as pure as the man from whom Paul drove forth the evil spirits. But I suppose I became habituated to these terrible weekly aids, and nothing happened in between. Was Doc Staunton beaten? He was not. I was a candidate for Dr. Tyrrell's Domestic Internal Bath.

This nasty device had been invented by some field-marshal in the war against auto-intoxication, and it was supposed to bring all the healing miracle of Spa or Aix-les-Bains to its possessor. It was a rubber bag of a disagreeable gray colour, on the upper side of which was fixed a hollow spike of some hard, black composition. It was filled with warm water until it was fat and ugly; I was impaled on the spike, which had been greased with Vaseline; a control stopcock was turned, and my bodily weight was supposed to force the water up inside me to seek out the offending substances. I was not quite heavy enough, so Netty helped by pushing downward on my shoulders. As I was dismayingly invaded below, her breath, like scorching beef, blew in my face. Oh, Calvary!

Grandfather had made a refinement of his own on the great invention of Dr. Tyrrell; he added slippery elm bark to the warm water, as he had a high opinion of its healing and purgative properties.

I hated all of this, and most of all the critical moment when I was lifted off the greasy spike and carried as fast as Netty could go to the seat of ease. I felt like an overfilled leather bottle, and was in dread lest I should spill. But I was a child, and my wise elders, led by all-knowing Grandfather Staunton, who was a doctor and could see right through you, had decreed this misery as necessary. Did Grandfather Staunton ever resort to the Domestic Internal Bath himself? I once asked timidly. He looked me in the eye and said solemnly that there had been a time when, he was convinced, he owed his life to its efficacy. There was no answer to that except the humblest acquiescence.

Was I therefore a spiritless child? I don't think so. But I seem to have been born with an unusual regard for authority and the power of reason, and I was too small to know how readily these qualities can be brought to the service of the wildest nonsense and cruelty.

Any comment?

DR. VON HALLER: Are you constipated now?

MYSELF: No. Not when I eat.

DR. VON HALLER: All of this is still only part of the childhood scene. We usually remember painful and humiliating things. But are they all of what we remember? What pleasant recollections of childhood have you? Would you say that on the whole you were happy?

MYSELF: I don't know about "on the whole." Sensations in childhood are so intense I can't pretend to recall their duration. When I was happy I was warmly, brimmingly happy, and when I was unhappy I was in hell.

DR. VON HALLER: What is the earliest recollection you can honestly vouch for?

MYSELF: Oh, that's easy. I was standing in my grandmother's garden, in warm sunlight, looking into a deep red peony. As I recall it, I wasn't much taller than the peony. It was a moment of very great—perhaps I shouldn't say happiness, because it was really an intense absorption. The whole world, the whole of life, and I myself, became a warm, rich peony-red.

DR. VON HALLER: Have you ever tried to recapture that feeling?

MYSELF: Never.

DR. VON HALLER: Well, shall we go on with your childhood?

MYSELF: Aren't you even interested in Netty and the Domestic Internal Bath? Nothing about homosexuality yet?

DR. VON HALLER: Have you ever subsequently felt drawn toward the passive role in sodomy?

MYSELF: Good God, no!

DR. VON HALLER: We shall keep everything in mind. But we need more material. Onward, please. What other happy recollections?

Church-going. It meant dressing up, which I liked. I was an observant child, so the difference between Toronto church and Deptford church kept me happy every Sunday. My parents were Anglicans, and I knew this was a sore touch with my grandparents, who belonged to the United Church of Canada, which was a sort of amalgam of Presbyterians and Methodists, and Congregationalists, too, wherever there happened to be any. Its spirit was evangelical and my grandmother, who was the child of the late Reverend Ira Boyd, a hell-fire Methodist, was evangelical; she had family prayers every morning, and Netty and I and the hired girl all had to be there; Grandfather wasn't able to make it very often, but the general feeling was that he didn't need it because of being a doctor. She read a chapter of the Bible every day of her life. And this was the 'thirties, mind you, not the reign of Queen Victoria. So I was put in the way of thinking a lot about God, and wondering what God thought about me. As with the Prince of Wales, I suspected that He thought rather well of me.

As for church, I liked to compare the two rituals to which I was exposed. The Uniteds didn't think they were ritualists, but that was not how it looked to me. I acquired some virtuosity in ritual. In the Anglican church I walked in smiling, bent my right knee just the proper amount—my father's amount—before going into the pew, and then knelt on the hassock, gazing with unnaturally wide-open eyes at the Cross on the altar. In the United Church, I put on a meek face, sat forward in my pew, and leaned downward, with my hand shielding my eyes, and inhaled the queer smell of the hymn-books in the rack in front of me. In the Anglican church I nodded my head, as if to say "Quite so," or (in the slang of the day) "Hot spit!" whenever Jesus was named in a hymn. But in the United Church if Jesus turned up I sang the name very low, and in the secret voice I used when talking to my grandmother about what my bowels were doing. And of course I was aware that the United minister wore a black robe, a great contrast to Canon Woodiwiss's splendid and various vestments, and that Communion at Deptford meant that everybody got a little dose of something in his pew, and there was no walking about and traffic control by the sidesmen, as at St. Simon Zelotes. It was a constant, delightful study, and I appreciated all its refinements. This won me a reputation outside the family as a pious child, and I think I was held up to lesser boys as an example. Imagine it—rich *and* pious! I suppose I bodied forth some ideal for a lot of people, as the plaster statues of the Infant Samuel at Prayer used to do in the nineteenth century.

Sunday was always a great day. Dressing up, my hobby of ritual study, and a full week to go before another assault on my uncooperative colon! But there were wonderful weekdays, too.

Sometimes my grandfather took me and Netty to what was called "the farm" but was really his huge sugar-beet plantation and the big mill at the centre of it. The country around Deptford is very flat, alluvial soil. So flat, indeed, that often Netty took me to the railway station, which she elegantly called "the deepo" just before noon, so that I could have the thrill of seeing a plume of smoke rising far down the track as the approaching train left Darnley, seven miles away. As we drove along the road Grandfather would sometimes say, "Davey, I own everything on both sides of this road for as far as you can see. Did you know that?" And I always pretended I didn't know it and was amazed, because that was what he wanted. A mile or more before we reached the mill its sweet smell was apparent, and when we drew nearer we could hear its queer noise. It was an oddly inefficient noise—a rattly, clattering noise—because the machinery used for chopping the beets and pressing them and boiling down their sweetness was all huge and powerful, rather than subtle. Grandfather would take me through the mill, and explain all the processes, and get the important man who managed the gauge on the boiler to show me how that worked and how he tested the boiling every few minutes to see that its texture was right.

Best of all was a tiny railway, like a toy, that pulled little carloads of beets from distant fields, puffing and occasionally tooting in a deeply satisfying way as it bustled along. My grandfather owned a railway! And—oh, joy beyond all telling!—he would sometimes tell the engine-driver, whose name was Elmo Pickard, to take me on one of his jaunts into the fields, riding in the little engine! Whether Grandfather wanted to give me a rest, or whether he simply thought women had no place near engines, I don't know, but he never allowed Netty to go with me, and she sat at the mill, fretting that I would get dirty, for the two hours it took to make a round trip. The little engine burned wood, and the wood was covered in a fine layer of atomized sugar syrup, like everything else near the mill, so its combustion was dirty and deliciously smelly.

Elmo and I chuffed and rattled through the fields, flat as Holland, which seemed to be filled with dwarves, for most of the workers were Belgian immigrants who worked on their knees with sawed-off hoes. Elmo scorned them and had only a vague notion where they came from. "Not a bad fella, fer an Eye-talian!" was the best he would say of the big hulking Flemings, who talked (Elmo said they "jabbered") in a language that was in itself like the fibrous crunching of chopped beets. But there were English-speaking foremen here and there on the line, and from their conversation with Elmo I learned much that would not have done for Netty's ears. When we had filled all the trucks, we hurtled back to the mill, doing ten miles an hour at the very least, and I was allowed to pull the whistle to tell the mill, and the frantic Netty, that we were approaching.

There were other expeditions. Once or twice every summer

Grandmother would say, "Do you want to go see the people down by the crick today?" I knew from her tone that no great enthusiasm would be welcome. The people down by the crick were my other grandparents, my mother's people, the Cruikshanks.

The Cruikshanks were poor. That was really all that was wrong with them. Ben Cruikshank was a self-employed carpenter, a small dour Scot, whose conversation was full of references to himself as "independent" and "self-respecting" and "owing nothing to no man." I realize now that he was talking at me, justifying himself for daring to be a grandfather without any money. I think the Cruikshanks were frightened of me because I was such a glossy little article and full of politeness which had a strong edge of sauce. Netty held them cheap; mere orphan though she was herself, she carried a commission from the great Doc Staunton. Well do I remember the day when my Cruikshank grandmother, who was making jam, offered me some of the frothy barm to eat as she skimmed it from the pot. "Davey isn't let eat off of an iron spoon," said Netty, and I saw tears in the inferior grandmother's eyes as she meekly found a spoon of some whiter metal (certainly not silver) for her pernickety grandson. She must have mentioned it to Ben, because later in the day he took me into his workshop and showed me his tools and all the things they could do, while talking in a strain I did not understand, and often in a kind of English I could not easily follow. I know now that he was quoting Burns.

> The rank is but the guinea stamp;
> The man's the gowd for a' that—

he said, and in strange words I could not follow I nevertheless knew he was getting at Grandfather Staunton—

> Ye see yon birkie, ca'd a lord
>   Wha struts and stares, and a' that:
> Tho' thousands worship at his word,
>   He's but a coof for a' that,
> For a' that, and a' that,
>   His riband, star and a' that,
> The man of independent mind
>   He looks and laughs at a' that.

But I was a child, and I suppose I was a hateful child, for I snickered at the repetitions of "for a' that" and the Lowland speech because I was on Grandfather Staunton's side. And in justice I suppose it must be said that poor Ben overdid it; he was as self-assertive in his humility as the Stauntons were in their pride, and both came to the same thing; nobody had any real charity or desire to understand himself or me. He just wanted to be on top, to be best, and I was a prize to be won rather than a fellow-creature to be respected.

God, I've seen the gross self-assertion of the rich in its most sickening forms, but I swear the orgulous self-esteem of the deserving poor is every bit as bad! Still, I wish I could apologize to Ben and his wife now. I behaved very, very badly, and it's no good saying that I was only a child. So far as I understood, and with the weapons I had at hand, I hurt them and behaved badly toward them. The people down by the crick . . .

(*Here I found I was weeping and could not go on.*)

It was at this point Dr. von Haller moved into a realm that was new in our relationship. She talked quite a long time about the Shadow, that side of oneself to which so many real but rarely admitted parts of one's personality must be assigned. My bad behaviour toward the Cruikshanks was certainly a reality, however much my Staunton grandparents might have allowed it to grow. If I had been a more loving child, I would not have behaved so. Lovingness had not been greatly encouraged in me; but had it shown itself as present for encouragement? Slowly, as we talked, a new concept of Staunton-as-Son-of-a-Bitch emerged, and for a few days he gave me the shivers. But there he was. He had to be faced, not only in this, but in a thousand instances, for if he were not understood, none of his good qualities could be redeemed.

Had he good qualities? Certainly. Was he not unusually observant, for a child, of social differences and other people's moods? At a time when so many children move through life without much awareness of anything but themselves and their wants, did he not see beyond, to what other people were and wanted? This was not just infant Machiavellianism; it was sensitivity.

I had never thought of myself as sensitive. Touchy, certainly, and resentful of slights. But were all the slights unreal? And were my antennae always used for negative purposes? Well, perhaps not. Sensitivity worked both in sunlight and shadow.

MYSELF: And I presume the notion is to make the sensitivity always work in a positive way.

DR. VON HALLER: If you manage that, you will be a very uncommon person. We are not working to banish your Shadow, you see, but only to understand it, and thereby to work a little more closely with it. To banish your Shadow would be of no psychological service to you. Can you imagine a man without a Shadow? Do you know Chamisso's story of Peter Schlemihl? No? He sold his shadow to the Devil, and he was miserable ever after. No, no; your Shadow is one of the things that keeps you in balance. But you must recognize him, you know, your Shadow. He is not such a terrible fellow if you know him. He is not lovable; he is quite ugly. But accepting this ugly creature is needful if you are really looking for psychological wholeness. When we were talking earlier I said I thought you saw yourself to some extent in the role of Sydney Carton, the gifted, misunderstood, drunken lawyer. These literary figures, you know, provide us with an excellent shorthand for talking about aspects of ourselves, and we all encompass several of them. You are aware of Sydney; now we are getting to know Mr. Hyde. Only he isn't Dr. Jekyll's gaudy monster, who trampled a child; he is just a proud little boy who hurt some humble people, and knew it and enjoyed it. You are the successor to that little boy. Shall we have some more about him?

Very well. I could pity the boy, but that would be a falsification because the boy never pitied himself. I was a little princeling in Deptford, and I liked it very much. Netty stood between me and everyone else. I didn't play with the other boys in the village because they weren't clean. Probably they did not wash often enough under their foreskins. Netty was very strong on that. I was bathed every day, and I dreaded Netty's assault, the culmination of the bath, when I stood up and she stripped back my foreskin and washed under it with soap. It tickled and it stang and I somehow felt it to be ignominious, but she never tired of saying, "If you're not clean under there, you're not clean anyplace; you let yourself get dirty under there, and you'll get an awful disease. I've seen it thousands of times." Not being clean in this special sense was as bad as spitting. I was not allowed to spit, which was a great deprivation in a village filled with accomplished spitters. But it was possible, Netty warned, to spit your brains out. Indeed, I remember seeing an old man in the village named Cece Athelstan, who was quite a well-known character; he had the staggering, high-stepping gait of a man well advanced in syphilis, but Netty assured me that he was certainly a victim of unchecked spitting.

My greatest moment as the young princeling of Deptford was certainly when I appeared as the Groom in a Tom Thumb Wedding at the United Church.

It was in late August, when I was eight years old, and it was an adjunct of the Fall Fair. This was a great Deptford occasion, and in addition to all the agricultural exhibits, the Indians from the nearby reservation offered handiwork for sale—fans, bead-work, sweet-grass boxes, carved walking-canes, and so forth—and there was a little collection of carnival games, including one called Hit the Nigger in the Eye! where, for twenty-five cents, you could throw three baseballs at a black man who stuck his head through a canvas and defied you to hit him. My grandfather bought three balls for me, and I threw one short, one wide, and one right over the canvas, to the noisy derision of some low boys who were watching and at whom the black man—obviously a subversive type—kept winking as I made a fool of myself. But I pitied their ignorance and despised them, because I knew that when night fell I would be the star of the Fair.

A Tom Thumb Wedding is a mock nuptial ceremony in which all the participants are children, and the delight of it is its miniature quality. The Ladies' Aid of the United Church had arranged one of these things to take place in the tent where, during the day, they had served meals to the fair-goers, and it was intended to offer a refined alternative to the coarse pleasures of the carnival shows. At half-past seven everything was ready. Quite a large audience was assembled, consisting chiefly of ladies who were congratulating themselves on having minds above sword-swallowing and the pickled foetuses of two-headed babies. The tent was hot, and the light from the red, white, and blue bulbs was wavering and rather sickly. At the appropriate moment the boy who played the part of the minister and my best man and I stepped forward to await the Bride.

This was a little girl who had been given the part for her virtue in Sunday School rather than for outward attractions, and although her name was Myrtle she was known to her contemporaries as Toad Wilson. A melodeon played the Wedding Chorus from *Lohengrin* and Toad, supported by six other little girls, walked toward us as slowly as she could, producing an effect rather of reluctance than ceremony.

Toad was dressed fit to kill in a wedding outfit over which her mother and nobody knows how many others had laboured for weeks; her figure was bunchy, but she lacked nothing in satin and lace, and was oppressed by her wreath and veil. She should have been the centre of attention, but my grandmother and Netty had taken care of that.

I was a figure of extraordinary elegance, for my grandmother had kept old Mrs. Clements, the local dressmaker, busy for a month. I wore black satin trousers, a tail-coat made of velvet, and a sash, or cummerbund, of red silk. With a satin shirt and a large flowing red bow tie I was a rich, if rather droopy, sight. Everybody agreed that a silk hat was what was wanted to crown my finery, but of course there was none of the right size; however, in one of the local stores, my grandmother had unearthed a bowler hat of a type fashionable perhaps in 1900, for it had a narrow flat brim and a very high crown, as if it might have been made for a man with a pointed skull. It fitted, when plenty of cotton wool had been pressed under the inner band. I wore this until the Bride approached, at which moment I swept it off and held it over my heart. This was my own idea, and I think it shows some histrionic flair, because it kept Toad from unfairly monopolizing everybody's attention.

The ceremony was intended to be funny, and the parson was

the clown of the evening. He had many things to say that were in a script some member of the Ladies' Aid must have kept since the heyday of Josh Billings—because these Tom Thumb Weddings were already old-fashioned in the 'thirties. "Do you, Myrtle, promise to get up early and serve a hot breakfast every day in the week?" was one of his great lines, and Toad piped up solemnly, "I do." And I recall that I had to promise not to chew tobacco in the house, or use my wife's best scissors to cut stovepipe wire.

All, however, led up to the culminating moment when I kissed the Bride. This had been carefully rehearsed, and it was meant to bring down the house, for I was to be so pressing, and kiss the Bride so often, that the parson, after feigning horror, had to part us. Sure-fire comedy, for it had just that spice of sanctified lewdness that the Ladies' Aid loved, the innocence of children giving it a special savour. But here again I had an improvement; I disliked being laughed at as a child, and I felt that being kissed by me was a serious matter and far too good for such a pie-face as Toad Wilson. I had been to the movies a few times, as a great treat, and had seen kissers of international renown at work. So I went along with the foolish ideas of the Ladies' Aid at rehearsals, but when the great moment arrived at the performance, I threw my hat to one side, knelt gracefully, and lifted Toad's unready paw to my lips. Then I rose, seized her around her nail-keg waist, and pressed a long and burning kiss upon her mouth, bending her backward at the same time as much as her thicky-thumpy body would allow. This, I thought, would show Deptford what romance could be in the hands of a master.

The effect was all I could have hoped. There were oohs and ahs, some of delight, some of disapproval. As Toad and I walked down the aisle to wheezy Mendelssohn it was I, and not the Bride, who held all eyes. Best of all, I heard one

woman murmur, with implications that I did not then understand, "That young one is Boy Staunton's son, all right." Toad
showed a tendency to shine up to me afterward, when we were
having ice-cream and cake at the Ladies' Aid expense, but I
was cold. When I have squeezed my orange, I throw it away;
that was my attitude at the time.

Netty was not pleased. "I suppose you thought you were
pretty smart, carrying on like that," was her comment as I was
going to bed, and this led to high words and tears. My grandmother thought I was overwrought by public performance, but
my chief sensation was disappointment because nobody
seemed to understand how remarkable I truly was.

(*It was not easy work, this dredging up what could be recovered of my childish past and displaying it before another
person. Quite a different thing from realizing, as everybody
does, that at some far-off time they have not behaved well.
It was at this period that I had a dream, or a vision between
waking and sleeping one night, that I was once again on that
pier, and was wiping filth and oil from the face of a drowned
figure; but as I worked I saw that it was not my father, but a
child who lay there, and that the child was myself.*)

(2)

Dreaming had become a common experience for me, though I
had never been a great dreamer. Dr. von Haller asked me to
recover some dreams from childhood, and although I was
doubtful, I found that I could do so. There was my dream from
my sixth year that I saw Jesus in the sky, floating upward as in
pictures of the Ascension; within His mantle, and it seemed to
me part of His very figure, was a globe of the world, which He

engulfed as though protecting it and displaying it to me, as I stood in the middle of the road down below. Had this been a dream, or a day-time vision? I could never satisfactorily decide, but it was brilliantly clear. And of course there was my recurrent dream, so often experienced, always in a somewhat different form but always the same in the quality of dread and terror that it brought. In this dream I was in a castle or fortress, closed against the outer world, and I was the keeper of a treasure—or sometimes it seemed to be a god or idol—the nature of which I never knew though its value was great in my mind. An Enemy was threatening it from without; this Enemy would run from window to window, looking for a way in, and I would pant from room to room to thwart it and keep it at bay. This dream had been attributed by Netty to my reading of a book called *The Little Lame Prince*, in which a lonely boy lived in a tower, and the book was arbitrarily forbidden; Netty liked to forbid books and always mistrusted them. But I knew perfectly well that I had had the dream long before I read the book and continued to have it long after the book had lost colour in my mind. The intensity of the dream and its sense of threat were of quite a different order from any book I knew.

Dr. von Haller and I worked for some time on this dream, trying to recover associations that would throw light on it. Although it seems plain enough to me now, it took several days for me to recognize that the tower was my life, and the treasure was what made it precious and worth defending against the Enemy. But who was this Enemy? Here we had quite a struggle because I insisted that the Enemy was external, whereas Dr. von Haller kept leading me back to some point at which I had to admit that the Enemy might be some portion of myself—some inadmissible entity in David which did not accept every circumstance of his life at face value, and which, if it beheld the treasure or the idol, might not agree about its superlative value. But at last, when I had swallowed that and admitted with some reluctance that it might be true, I was anxious to consider what the treasure might be, and it was here that the doctor showed reluctance. Better to wait, she said, and perhaps the answer would emerge of itself.

DR. VON HALLER: We do not want to use your grandfather's severe methods for getting at harmful things, do we? We must not press you down upon the hateful, invading spike. Let it alone, allow Nature to have her curative way, and all will be well.

MYSELF: I'm not afraid, you know. I'm willing to go straight ahead and get it over.

DR. VON HALLER: You have had quite enough of being a little soldier for the moment. Please accept my assurance that patience will bring better results here than force.

MYSELF: I don't want to go on stressing this, but I am not a stupid person. Haven't I been quick to accept—as an hypothesis anyhow—your ideas about dream interpretation?

DR. VON HALLER: Indeed, yes. But accepting an hypothesis is not facing psychological truth. We are not building up an intellectual system; we are attempting to recapture some forgotten things and arousing almost forgotten feelings in the hope that we may throw new light on them, but even more new light on the present. Remember what I have said so many times; this is not simply rummaging in the trash-heap of the past for its own sake. It is your present situation and your future that concern us. All of what we are talking about is gone and unchangeable; if it had no importance we could dismiss it. But it has importance, if we are to heal the present and ensure the future.

MYSELF: But you are holding me back. I am ready to accept all of what you say; I am ready and anxious to go ahead. I learn quickly. I am not stupid.

DR. VON HALLER: Excuse me, please. You *are* stupid. You can think and you can learn. You do these things like an educated modern man. But you cannot feel, except like a primitive. Your plight is quite a common one, especially in our day when thinking and learning have been given such absurd prominence, and we have thought and learned our way into world-wide messes. We must educate your feeling and persuade you to experience it like a man and not like a maimed, dull child. So you are not to gobble up your analysis greedily, and then say, "Aha, I understand that!" because understanding is not the point. Feeling is the point. Understanding and experiencing are not interchangeable. Any theologian understands martyrdom, but only the martyr experiences the fire.

I was not prepared to accept this, and we set off on a long discussion which it would be useless to record in detail, but it hung on the Platonic notion that man apprehends the world about him in four main ways. Here I thought I was at a considerable advantage, because I had studied *The Republic* pretty thoroughly in my Oxford days and had the Oxford man's idea that Plato had been an Oxford man before his time. Yes, I recalled Plato's theory of our fourfold means of apprehension, and could name them: Reason, Understanding, Opinion, and Conjecture. But Dr. von Haller, who had not been to Oxford, wanted to call them Thinking, Feeling, Sensation, and Intuition, and seemed to have some conviction that it was not possible for a rational man to make his choice or establish his priorities among these four, plumping naturally for Reason. We were born with a predisposition toward one of the four, and had to work from what we were given.

She did say—and I was pleased about this—that Thinking (which I preferred to call Reason) was the leading function in my character. She also thought I was not badly endowed with Sensation, which made me an accurate observer and not to be confused about matters of physical detail. She thought I might be visited from time to time by Intuition, and I knew better than she how true that was, for I have always had a certain ability to see through a brick wall at need and have treasured Jowett's rendering of Plato's word for that; he called it "perception of shadows." But Dr. von Haller gave me low marks for Feeling, because whenever I was confronted with a situation that demanded a careful weighing of values, rather than an accurate formulation of relevant ideas, I flew off the handle, as Netty would put it. "After all, it was because your feelings became unbearable that you decided to come to Zürich," said she.

MYSELF: But I told you; that was a rational decision, arrived at somewhat fancifully but nevertheless on the basis of a strict examination of the evidence, in Mr. Justice Staunton's court. I did everything in my power to keep Feeling out of the matter.

DR. VON HALLER: Precisely. But have you never heard that if you drive Nature out of the door with a pitchfork, she will creep around and climb in at the window? Feeling does that with you.

MYSELF: But wasn't the decision a right one? Am I not here? What more could Feeling have achieved than was brought about by Reason?

DR. VON HALLER: I cannot say, because we are talking about you, and not about some hypothetical person. So we must stick to what you are and what you have done. Feeling types have their own problems; they often think very badly, and it gets them into special messes of their own. But you should recognize this, Mr. Justice Staunton: your decision to come here was a cry for help, however carefully you may have disguised it as a decision based on reason or a sentence imposed on yourself by your intellect.

MYSELF: So I am to dethrone my Intellect and set Emotion in its place. Is that it?

DR. VON HALLER: There it is, you see! When your unsophisticated Feeling is aroused you talk like that. I wonder what woman inside you talks that way? Your mother, perhaps? Netty? We shall find out. No, you are not asked to set your Intellect aside, but to find out where it can serve you and where it betrays you. And to offer a little nourishment and polish to that poor Caliban who governs your Feeling at present.

(Of course it took much longer and demanded far more talk than what I have put down in these notes, and there were moments when I was angry enough to abandon the whole thing, pay off Dr. von Haller, and go out on a monumental toot. I have never been fond of swallowing myself, and one of my faults in the courtroom is that I cannot hide my chagrin and sense of humiliation when a judge decides against me. However, my hatred of losing has played a big part in making me win. So at last we went on.)

If Deptford was my Arcadia, Toronto was a place of no such comfort. We lived in an old, fashionable part of the city, in a big house in which the servants outnumbered the family. There were four Stauntons, but the houseman (who was now and then sufficiently good at his job to be called a butler), the cook, the parlourmaid, the laundry maid, the chauffeur, and of course Netty were the majority and dominated. Not that any-

body wanted it that way, but my poor mother had no gift of
dealing with them that could prevent it.

People who have no servants often have a quaint notion
that it would be delightful to have people always around to do
one's bidding. Perhaps so, though I have never known a house
where that happened, and certainly our household was not a
characteristic one. Servants came and went, sometimes bewil-
deringly. Housemen drank or seduced the women-servants;
cooks stole or had terrible tempers; laundry maids ruined expensive clothes or put crooked creases in the front of my father's trousers; housemaids would do no upstairs work and
hadn't enough to do downstairs; the chauffeur was absent
when he was wanted or borrowed the cars for joy-riding. The
only fixed and abiding star in our household firmament was
Netty, and she tattled on all the others and grew in course of
time to want the absolute control of a housekeeper, and so was
always in a complicated war with the butler. Some servants
were foreign and talked among themselves in languages that
Netty assumed must conceal dishonest intentions; some were
English and Netty knew they were patronizing her. Children
always live closer to the servants than their elders, and Caroline and I never knew where we stood with anybody, and
sometimes found ourselves hostages in dark, below-stairs in-
trigues.

The reason, of course, was that my poor mother, who had
never had a servant in her life before her marriage (unless you
count Grandmother Cruikshank, who seemed to fear her
daughter and defer to her and I suppose had always done so)
had no notion how to manage such a household. She was naturally kind, and somewhat fearful, and haunted by dread that
she would not come up to the standards the servants expected.
She courted their favour, asked their opinions, and I suppose it
must be said that she was more familiar with them than was

prudent. If the housemaid were near her own age she would invite her views on dress; my father knew this, and disapproved, and sometimes said Mother dressed like a housemaid on her day out. Mother knew nothing about the kind of food professional cooks prepare, and let them have their head, so that Father complained that the same few dishes appeared in a pattern. Mother did not like being driven by a chauffeur, so she had a car of her own which she drove, and the chauffeur had not enough to do. She did not insist that the servants speak of my sister and myself as Miss Caroline and Mr. David, which was what my father wanted. I suppose there must have been good servants somewhere—other people seemed to find them, and keep them—but we never found any except Netty, and Netty was a nuisance.

There were two major things wrong with Netty. She was in love with my father, and she had known my mother before her marriage and subsequent wealth. It was not until my mother's death that I recognized this, but Caroline was quick to spot it, and it was she who opened my eyes. Netty loved Father abjectly and wordlessly. I doubt if it ever entered her head that her love might be requited in any lasting way—certainly not in any physical way. All she wanted was an occasional good word, or one of his wonderful smiles. As for my mother, I think if Netty had ever clarified her thoughts she would have recognized my mother as a beautiful toy, but without real substance or importance as a wife, and it was not in Netty's nature to recognize any justice in the position my mother had achieved because of her beauty. She had been aware of Mother as the most beautiful girl in Deptford—no, better than that, for Mother was the most beautiful woman I have ever seen— but she had known Mother as the daughter of the people down by the crick. And beauty excepted, what set somebody from down by the crick above Netty herself?

My mother could not have known anything of the spirit that drove my father on and sometimes made him behave in a way that very few people—perhaps nobody but myself— understood. People saw only his present success; they knew nothing of his great dreams and his discontentment with things as they were. He was rich, certainly, and he had made his money by his own efforts. Grandfather Staunton was quite content to be the local rich man in Deptford, and his ventures in beet sugar had been shrewd. But it was my father who saw that the trifling million and a half pounds of beet sugar produced every year in Canada was nothing compared to what might be done by a man who moved boldly but intelligently into the importation and refining of cane sugar. People eat about a hundred pounds of sugar a year in one form or another. Father supplied eighty-five pounds of it. And certainly it was Father who saw that much of what had been thought of as waste from the refining process could be used as mineral supplement to poultry and stock foods. So it was not very long before Father was heavily involved in all kinds of bakeries and candy-making and soft drinks and scientifically prepared animal foods, which were managed from a single central agency called the Alpha Corporation. But to look on that as the guiding element in his life was to misunderstand him completely.

His deepest ambition was to be somebody remarkable, to live a fully realized life, to leave nothing undone that came within the range of his desires. He hated people who slouched and slummocked through life, getting nowhere and being nothing. He used to quote a line from a Browning poem he had studied at school about "the unlit lamp and the ungirt loin." His lamp was always blazing and his loins were girded as tight as they could be. I suppose that according to the rigmarole about types to which Dr. von Haller was introducing me (and which I was inclined to take with a pinch of salt) he would be called a Sensation man, because his sense of the real, the actual and tangible, was so strong. But he was sometimes mistaken about people, and I am much afraid he was mistaken about my mother.

She was a great beauty, but not in the classical style. Hers was the sort of beauty people admired so much in the 'twenties, when girls were supposed to have boyish figures and marvellous big eyes and pretty pouting mouths and above all a great air of vitality. Mother could have been a success in the movies. Or perhaps not, because although she had the looks she was not in the least a performer. I think Father saw in her something that wasn't really there. He thought that a girl with such stunning looks couldn't be just a Deptford girl; I think he supposed that her association with the people down by the crick was not one of parents-and-child, but a fairy-tale arrangement where a princess has been confided to the care of simple cottage folk. It was just a matter of lots of fine clothes and lots of dancing and travelling abroad and unlimited lessons at tennis and bridge, and the princess would stand revealed as what she truly was.

Poor Mother! I always feel guilty about her because I should have loved her more and supported her more than I did, but I was under my father's spell, and I understand now that I sensed his disappointment, and anyone who disappointed him could not have my love. I took all his ambitions and desires for my own and had as much as I could do to endure the fact which became so plain as I grew older, that I was a disappointment myself.

During my work with Dr. von Haller I was astonished when one night Felix came to me in a dream. Felix had been my great comfort and solace when I was about four years old, but I had forgotten him.

Felix was a large stuffed bear. He had come to me at a very

bitter time, when I had disappointed my father by playing with a doll. Not a girl doll, but a doll dressed like a Highlander that somebody had given me—I cannot recall who it was because I tore all details of the affair out of my mind. It made no difference to Father that it was a soldier doll; what he saw was that I had wrapped it up in a doll's blanket belonging to Caroline and taken it to bed. He smashed the doll against the wall and demanded of Netty in a terrible voice if she was bringing his son up to be a sissy, and if that were so, what further plans had she? Dresses, perhaps? Was she encouraging me to urinate sitting down, so that I could use the ladies' room in hotels when I grew up? I was desolate, and Netty was stricken but tearless, and it was a dreadful bedtime which took unlimited cocoa to alleviate. Only my mother stood up for me, but all she could say was, "Boy, don't be so *silly!*" and this merely succeeded in drawing his anger on herself.

However, she must have made some compromise with him, for next day she brought Felix to me and said he was a very strong, brave bear for a very strong, brave boy, and we would have lots of daring adventures together. Felix was large, as nursery bears go, and a rich golden-brown, to begin with, and he had an expression of thoughtful determination. He had been made in France, and that was how he came to be named Felix; my mother thought of all the French names for boys that she knew, which were Jules and Felix, and Jules was rejected as not being so fully masculine as we desired and not fitting the character of this brave bear. So Felix he was, and he was the first of a large brotherhood of bears which I took to bed every night. There was a time when there were nine bears of various sizes in my bed, and not much room left for me.

My father knew about the bears, or at least about Felix, but he raised no objection, and from one or two remarks he let drop I know why. He had been impressed by what he had heard of Winnie-the-Pooh, and he felt that a bear was a proper toy for an upper-class little English boy; he had a great admiration for whatever was English and upper class. So Felix and I led an untroubled life together even after I had begun to go to school.

My father's admiration for whatever was English was one aspect of the ambiguous relationship between Canada and England. I suppose unkind people would say it was evidence of a colonial quality of mind, but I think it was the form taken by his romanticism. There was something terribly stuffy about Canada in my boyhood—a want of daring and great dimension, a second-handedness in cultural matters, a frowsy old-woman quality—that got on his nerves. You could make money, certainly, and he was doing that as fast as he could. But living the kind of life he wanted was very difficult and in many respects impossible. Father knew what was wrong. It was the Prime Minister.

The Right Honourable William Lyon Mackenzie King was undoubtedly an odd man, but subsequent study has led me to the conclusion that he was a political genius of an extraordinary order. To Father, however, he was the embodiment of several hateful qualities; Mr. King's mistrust of England and his desire for greater autonomy for Canada seemed to my father simply a perverse preferring of a lesser to a greater thing; Mr. King's conjuror-like ability to do something distracting with his right hand while preparing the denouement of his trick unobtrusively with his left hand had not the dash and flair my father thought he saw in British statesmanship; but the astonishing disparity between Mr. King's public and his personal character was what really made my father boil.

"He talks about reason and necessity on the platform, while all the time he is living by superstition and the worst kind of voodoo," he would roar. "Do you realize that man never calls an election without getting a fortune-teller in Kingston to name a lucky day? Do you realize that he goes in for automatic writing? And decides important things—nationally important things—by opening his Bible and stabbing at a verse with a paper-knife, while his eyes are shut? And that he sits with the portrait of his mother and communes—*communes* for God's sake!—with her spirit and gets her advice? Am I being taxed almost out of business because of something that has been said by Mackenzie King's mother's ghost? And this is the man who postures as a national leader!"

He was talking to his old friend Dunstan Ramsay, and I was not supposed to be listening. But I remember Ramsay saying, "You'd better face it, Boy; Mackenzie King rules Canada because he himself is the embodiment of Canada—cold and cautious on the outside, dowdy and pussy in every overt action, but inside a mass of intuition and dark intimations. King is Destiny's child. He will probably always do the right thing for the wrong reasons."

That was certainly not the way to reconcile Father to Mackenzie King.

Especially was this so when, around 1936, things began to go wrong in England in a way that touched my father nearly.

(3)

I never really understood Father's relationship with the Prince of Wales, because I had included the Prince as a very special and powerful character in my childish daydreams, and the truth and the fantasy were impossible to disentangle. But children hear far more than people think, and understand much, if not everything. So it began to be clear to me in the autumn of 1936 that the Prince was being harassed by some evil men, whose general character was like that of Mackenzie King. It had to do with a lady the Prince loved, and these bad men—a Prime Minister and an Archbishop—wanted to thwart them both. Father talked a great deal—not to me, but within my hearing—about what every decent man ought to do to show who was boss, and what principles were to prevail. He lectured my mother on this theme with an intensity I could not understand but which seemed to oppress her. It was as if he could think of nothing else. And when the actual Abdication came about he ordered the flag on the Alpha building to fly at half-staff, and was utterly miserable. Of course we were miserable with him, because it seemed to Caroline and me that terrible misfortune had overtaken our household and the world, and that nothing could ever be right again.

Christmas of that year brought one of the great upheavals that influenced my life. My father and mother had some sort of dreadful quarrel, and he left the house; as it proved, he did not come back for several days. Dunstan Ramsay, the family friend I have mentioned so often, was there, and he was as kind to Caroline and me as he knew how to be—but he had no touch with children and when our father was angry and in pain we wanted nothing to do with any other man—and he seemed to be very kind and affectionate toward Mother. Netty was out for the day, but Ramsay sent us children up to our own quarters, saying he would look in later; we went, but kept in close touch with what was going on downstairs. Ramsay talked for a long time to our weeping mother; we could hear his deep voice and her sobs. At last she went to her bedroom, and after some rather confused discussion, Carol and I thought we would go along and see her; we didn't know what we would do when we were with her, but we desperately wanted to be with somebody loving and comforting, and we had always counted on her for that. But if she were crying? This was terrible, and we were not sure we could face it. On the other hand we couldn't possibly stay away. We were lonely and frightened. So we crept silently into the passage, and were tiptoeing toward her door when it opened and Ramsay came out, and his face was as we had never seen it before, because he was grinning, but he was also quite clearly angry. He had an alarming face for children, all eyebrows and big nose and lantern jaws, and although he was genial toward us we were always a little frightened by him.

But far worse than this we heard Mother's voice, strange with grief, crying, "You don't love me!" It was in no tone we had ever heard from her before, and we were terribly alarmed. Ramsay did not see us, because we were some distance away, and when he had thumped downstairs—he has a wooden leg from the First Great War—we scuttled back to our nursery in misery.

What was wrong? Caroline was only six and all she could think of was that Ramsay was hateful not to love Mother and make her cry. But I was eight—a thinking eight—and I had all kinds of emotions I could not understand. Why should Ramsay love Mother? That was what Father did. What was Ramsay doing in Mother's room? I had seen movies and knew that men did not go to bedrooms just to make conversation; something special went on there, though I had no clear idea what it was. And Mother so wretched when Father had inexplicably gone away! Bad things were going on in the world; wicked men were interfering between people who loved each other; what mischief might Ramsay be making between my parents? Did this in some way connect with the misfortunes of the Prince? I thought about it till I had a headache, and I was cross with Caroline, who was not inclined to put up with that from me and made a terrible fuss.

At last Netty came home. She had been spending Christmas

with her brother Maitland and his fiancée's family, and she was loaded down with things they had given her. But when she wanted to show them to us we would have none of it. Mother was crying and had gone to bed, and Mr. Ramsay had been in her room, and she had called those strange words after him in that strange voice. Netty became very grave and went to Mother's room, Caroline and I close on her heels. Mother was not in her bed. The bathroom door was slightly ajar, and Netty tapped on it. No answer. Netty peeped around the door. And shrieked. Then she turned at once and drove us from the room with instructions to go to the nursery and not dare to budge out of it till she came.

She came at last, and though she was not inclined to yield to our demands to see our mother she must have seen that it was the only way to keep us from further hysteria, so we were allowed to go to her room and very quietly creep up to the bed and kiss her. Mother was apparently asleep, pale as we had never seen her, and her arms lay stiffly on the counterpane, wrapped in bandages. She roused herself enough to smile faintly at us, but Netty forbade any talk and quickly led us away.

But out of the corner of my eye, in an instant as I passed, I saw the horror in the bathroom, and what seemed to be a tub filled with blood. I did not cry out, but cold terror seized me, and it was quite a long time before I could tell Caroline. Not, indeed, until Mother was dying.

Children do not give way to emotional stresses as adults do; they do not sit and mope or go to bed. We went back to the nursery and Caroline played with a doll, wrapping and unwrapping its wrists with a handkerchief and murmuring comfort; I held a book I was not able to read. We were trying to cling to normality; we were even trying to get some advantage out of being up much later than was proper. So we knew that

Dunstan Ramsay came back and thumped up the stairs to the room he had left four hours ago, and a doctor came, and Netty did a great deal of running about. Then the doctor came to see us and suggested that we each have some warm milk with a few drops of rum in it to make us sleep. Netty was horrified by the suggestion of rum, so we had crushed aspirin, and at last we slept.

And that was the Christmas of the Abdication for us.

After that, home was never really a secure place. Mother was not the same, and we supposed it was because of whatever happened on Christmas night. The vitality of the 'twenties girl never returned, and her looks changed. I shall never say that she was anything but beautiful, but she had always seemed to have even more energy than her children, which is one of the great fascinations in adults, and after that terrible night she had it no longer, and Netty kept telling us not to tire her.

I see now that this milestone in our family history meant a great advance in power for Netty, because she was the only person who knew what had happened. She had a secret, and a secret is an invaluable adjunct of power.

Her power was not exercised for her own direct advantage. I am sure that all of Netty's world and range of ambition was confined to what went on in our house. Later, when I was studying history, I saw a great deal of the feudal age in terms of Netty. She was loyal to the household and never betrayed it to any outside power. But within the household she was not to be thought of as a paid servant who could be discharged with two weeks' notice, nor do I think it ever crossed her mind that she was free to leave on the same terms. She was somebody. She was Netty. And because of who she was and what she felt, she was free to express opinions and take independent lines that lay far outside the compass of a servant in the ordinary sense. My father once told me that in all the years of their association Netty never asked him for a raise in pay; she assumed that he would give her what was fair and that in emergency she could call upon him with complete certainty of her right to do so. I recall years later some friend of Caroline's questioning the strange relationship between Don Giovanni and Leporello in the opera; if Leporello didn't like the way the Don lived, why didn't he leave him? "Because he was a Netty," said Caroline, and although the friend, who was very much of this age, didn't understand, it seemed to me to be an entirely satisfactory answer. "Though he slay me, yet will I trust in him," expressed half of Netty's attitude toward the Staunton family; the remainder was to be found in the rest of that verse—"but I will maintain mine own ways before him." Netty knew about Deptford; she knew about the people down by the crick; she knew what happened on Abdication Christmas. But it was not for lesser folk to know these things.

Did all of this make Netty dear to us? No, it made her a holy terror. People who prate about loyal old servants rarely know the hard-won coin of the spirit in which their real wages are paid. Netty's terrible silences about things that were foremost in our minds oppressed Caroline and me and were a great part of what seemed to us to be the darkness that was falling over our home.

DR. VON HALLER: Did you never ask Netty what happened on Christmas night?

MYSELF: I cannot recall whether I did, but Caroline asked the next day and got Netty's maddening answer, "Ask no questions and you'll be told no lies." When Caroline insisted, "But I want to know," there came another predictable answer, "Then Want will have to be your master."

DR. VON HALLER: And you never asked your mother?

MYSELF: How could we? You know how it is with children; they know there are forbidden areas, charged with intense feeling. They don't know that most of them are concerned with sex, but they suspect something in the world that would open up terrifying things and threaten their ideas about their parents; half of them wants to know, and half dreads to know.

DR. VON HALLER: Did you know nothing of sex, then?

MYSELF: Odds and ends. There was Netty's insistence about washing "under there," which conveyed something special. And in Grandfather Staunton's office I had found a curious students' aid called Philips' Popular Manikin, which was a cardboard man who opened up to show his insides, and who had very discreet privy parts like my own. There was also a Popular Manikin (Female) who was partly flayed so that her breasts could only be guessed at, but who had a kind of imperforate bald triangle where the gentleman had ornaments. From some neat spy-work when Caroline was being dressed I knew that Philips had not told the whole story, and as soon as I went to school I was deluged with fanciful and disgusting information, none of which threw much light on anything and which I never dreamed of associating with my mother. I don't think I was as curious about sex as most boys. I wanted to keep things—meaning the state of my own knowledge—pretty much as it was. I suppose I had an intuition that more knowledge would mean greater complications.

DR. VON HALLER: Were you happy at school?

It was a good school, and on the whole I liked it there. Happiness was not associated with it because my real life was with my home and family. I was not bad at lessons and managed well enough at games not to be in trouble, though I never excelled. Until I was twelve I went to the preparatory part of the school by the day, but when I was twelve Father decided I should be a boarder and come home only at weekends. That was in 1940, and the war was getting into its stride, and he had to be away a great deal and thought I ought to have masculine influences in my life that Netty certainly could not have provided and my fading mother didn't know about.

Father became very important during the war because one of our jobs in Canada was to provide as much food as we could for Britain. Getting it there was a Navy job, but providing as much as possible of the right things was a big task of organization and expert management, and that was Father's great line. Quite soon he was asked to take on the Ministry of Food, and after warm assurances from the hated Prime Minister that he could have things his own way, Father decided that Mr. King had great executive abilities and that anyhow personal differences had to be set aside in an emergency. So he was away for months at a time, in Ottawa and often abroad, and home became a very feminine place.

I see now that one of the effects of this was to make Dunstan Ramsay a much bigger figure in my life. He was the chief history master at my school, Colborne College, and because he was a bachelor and lived a queer kind of inward life, he was one of the masters who was resident in the school and supervised the boarders. Indeed he was Acting Headmaster for most of the war years, because the real Headmaster had gone into the Army Education Service. But he still taught a good many classes, and he always taught history to the boys who were fresh from the Prep, because he wanted them to get a good grounding in what history was; he caught up with them afterward when they were in the top classes and gave them a final polishing and pushed them for university scholarships. So I saw Ramsay nearly every day.

Like so many good schoolmasters, he was an oddity, and the boys liked him and dreaded him and jeered at him. His nickname was Old Buggerlugs, because he had a trick of jabbing his little finger into his ear and rooting with it, as if he were scratching his brain. The other masters called him Corky because of his artificial leg, and they thought we did so too, but it was Buggerlugs when the boys were by themselves.

The bee in his bonnet was that history and myth are two aspects of a kind of grand pattern in human destiny: history is the mass of observable or recorded fact, but myth is the abstract or essence of it. He used to dredge up extraordinary myths that none of us had ever heard of and demonstrate—in a fascinating way, I must admit—how they contained some truth that was applicable to widely divergent historical situations.

He had another bee, too, and it was this one that made him a somewhat suspect figure to a lot of parents and consequently to their sons—for the school always had a substantial anti-Ramsay party among the boys. This was his interest in saints. The study of history, he said, was in part a study of the myths and legends that mankind has woven around extraordinary figures like Alexander the Great or Julius Caesar or Charlemagne or Napoleon; they were mortal men, and when the fact could be checked against the legend it was wonderful to see what hero-worshippers had attributed to them. He used to show us a popular nineteenth-century picture of Napoleon during the retreat from Moscow, slumped tragically in his sleigh, defeat and a sense of romantic doom written on his face and on those of the officers about him: then he would read us Stendhal's account of the retreat, recording how chirpy Napoleon was and how he would look out of the windows of his travelling carriage—no open sleigh for him, you can bet—saying, "Wouldn't those people be amazed if they knew who was so near to them!" Napoleon was one of Ramsay's star turns. He would show us the famous picture of Napoleon on Elba, in full uniform, sitting on a rock and brooding on past greatness. Then he would read us reports of daily life on Elba, when the chief concern was the condition of the great exile's pylorus, and the best possible news was a bulletin posted by his doctors, saying, "This morning, at 11.22 a.m., the Emperor passed a well-formed stool."

But why, Ramsay would ask, do we confine our study to great political and military figures to whom the generality of mankind has attributed extraordinary, almost superhuman qualities, and leave out the whole world of saints, to whom mankind has attributed phenomenal virtue? It is trivial to say that power, or even vice, are more interesting than virtue, and people say so only when they have not troubled to take a look at virtue and see how amazing, and sometimes inhuman and unlikable, it really is. The saints also belong among the heroes, and the spirit of Ignatius Loyola is not so far from the spirit of Napoleon as uninformed people suppose.

Ramsay was by way of being an authority on saints, and had written some books about them, though I have not seen them. You can imagine what an uncomfortable figure he could be in a school that admitted boys of every creed and kind but which was essentially devoted to a modernized version of a nine-teenth-century Protestant attitude toward life. And of course our parents were embarrassed by real concern about spiritual things and suspicious of anybody who treated the spirit as an ever-present reality, as Ramsay did. He loved to make us un-comfortable intellectually and goad us on to find contradic-tions or illogicalities in what he said. "But logic is like cricket," he would warn, "it is admirable so long as you are playing according to the rules. But what happens to your game of cricket when somebody suddenly decides to bowl with a foot-ball or bat with a hockey-stick? Because that is what is contin-ually happening in life."

The war was a field-day for Ramsay as an historian. The legends that clustered around Hitler and Mussolini were victuals and drink to him. "The Führer is inspired by voices—as was St. Joan: Il Duce feels no pain in the dentist's chair—neither did St. Appollonia of Tyana when her teeth were wrenched out by infidels. These are the attributes of the great; and I say attributes advisedly, because it is we who attribute these supernormal qualities to them. Only after his death did it leak out that Napoleon was afraid of cats."

I liked Ramsay, then. He worked us hard, but he was endlessly diverting and made some pretty good jokes in class. They were repeated around the school as Buggerlugs' Nifties.

My feelings about him underwent a wretched change when my mother died.

(4)

That was in the late autumn of 1942, when I was in my fifteenth year. She had had pneumonia, and was recovering, but I don't think she had much will to live. Whatever it was, she was convalescent and was supposed to rest every afternoon. The doctor had given instructions that she was on no account to take a chill, but she hated heavy coverings and always lay on her bed under a light rug. One day there was a driving storm, turning toward snow, and her bedroom windows were open, although they certainly should have been shut. We assumed that she had opened them herself. A chill, and in a few days she was dead.

Ramsay called me to his room at school and told me. He was kind in the right way. Didn't commiserate too much, or say anything that would break me down. But he kept me close to him during the next two or three days, and arranged the funeral because Father had to be in London and had cabled to ask him to do it. The funeral was terrible. Caroline didn't come because it was still thought by Netty and the Headmistress of her school that girls didn't go to funerals, so I went with Ramsay. There was a small group, but the people from down by the crick were there, and I tried to talk to them; of course they hardly knew me and what could anybody say? Both my Staunton grandparents were dead, so I suppose if there was a Chief Mourner—the undertakers asked who it was and Ramsay dealt with that tactfully—I was the one. My only feeling was a kind of desolated relief, because without ever quite forming the thought in my mind, I knew my mother had not been happy for some years, and I supposed it was because she felt she had failed Father in some way.

I recall saying to Ramsay that I thought perhaps Mother was better off, because she had been so miserable of late; I meant it as an attempt at grown-up conversation, but he looked queer when he heard it.

Much more significant to me than my mother's actual death and funeral—for, as I have said, she seemed to be taking farewell of us for quite a long time—was the family dinner on the Saturday night following. Caroline had been at home all week, under Netty's care, and I went home from school for the weekend. There was a perceptible lightening of spirits, and an odd atmosphere, for Father was away and Caroline and I were free of the house as we had never been. What I would have done about this I don't know; I suppose I should have swanked about a little and perhaps drunk a glass of beer to show my emancipation. But Caroline had different ideas.

She was always the daring one. When she was eight and I was ten she had cut one of Father's cigars in two and dared me to a smoke-down; we were to light up and puff away while soaring and descending rhythmically on the see-saw in the garden. She won. She had a reputation at her school, Bishop Cairncross's, as a practical joker, and had once captured a beetle and painted it gaily before offering it to the nature mistress for identification. The nature mistress, who was up to that one, got off the traditional remark in such circumstances. "This is known as the *nonsensicus impudens,* or Impudent Humbug, Caroline," she had said, and gained great face among her pupils as a wit. But when Mother died, Caroline was twelve, and in that queer time between childhood and nubile girlhood, when some girls seem to be wise without experience, and perhaps more clear-headed than they will be again until after their menopause. She took a high line with me on this particular Saturday and said I was to make myself especially tidy for dinner.

Sherry beforehand! We had never been allowed that before, but Caroline had it set out in the drawing-room, and Netty was taken unaware and did not get her objection in until we had glasses. Netty took none herself; she was fiercely T.T. But Caroline had asked her to dine with us, and Netty must have been shaken by that, because it had never occurred to her that she would do otherwise. She had put on some ceremonial garments instead of her nurse's uniform, and Caroline was in her best and had even put on a dab of lipstick. But this was merely a soft prelude to what was to follow.

There were three places at table and it was clear enough that I was to have Father's chair, but when Netty was guided by Caroline to the other chair of state—my mother's—I wondered what was up. Netty demurred, but Caroline insisted that she take this seat of honour, while she herself sat at my right. It did not occur to me that Caroline was pulling Netty's teeth; she was exalting her as a guest, only to cast her down as a figure of authority. Netty was confused, and missed her cue when the houseman brought in wine and poured a drop for me to approve; she barely recovered in time to turn her own glass upside down. We had had wine before; on great occasions my father gave us wine diluted with water, which he said was the right way to introduce children to one of the great pleasures of life; but undiluted wine, and me giving the nod of approval to the houseman, and glasses refilled under Netty's popping eyes —this was a new and heady experience.

Heady indeed, because the wine, following the sherry, was strong within me, and I knew my voice was becoming loud and assertive and that I was nodding agreement to things that needed no assent.

Not Caroline. She hardly touched her wine—the sneak!— but she was very busy guiding the conversation. We all missed Mother dreadfully, but we had to bear up and go on with life. That was what Mother would have wanted. She had been such a gay person; the last thing she would wish would be prolonged mourning. That is, she had been gay until five or six years ago. What had happened? Did Netty know? Mother had trusted Netty so, and of course she knew things that we were not thought old enough to know—certainly not when we had been quite small children, really. But that was long ago. We were older now.

Netty was not to be drawn.

Daddy was away so much. He couldn't avoid it, really, and the country needed him. Mummy must have felt the loneliness. Odd that she seemed to see so little of her friends during the last two or three years. The house had been gloomy. Netty must have felt it. Nobody came, really, except Dunstan Ramsay. But he was a very old friend, wasn't he? Hadn't Daddy and Mummy known him since before they were married?

Netty was a little more forthcoming. Yes, Mr. Ramsay had

been a Deptford boy. Much older than Netty, of course, but she heard a few things about him as she grew up. Always a queer one.

Oh? Queer in what way? We had always remembered him coming to the house, so perhaps we didn't notice the queerness. Daddy always said he was deep and clever.

I felt that as host I should get into this conversation—which was really more like a monologue by Caroline, punctuated with occasional grunts from Netty. So I told a few stories about Ramsay as a schoolmaster, and confided that his nickname was Buggerlugs.

Netty said I should be ashamed to use a word like that in front of my sister.

Caroline put on a face of modesty, and then said she thought Mr. Ramsay was handsome in a kind of scary way, like Mr. Rochester in *Jane Eyre,* and she had always wondered why he never married.

Maybe he couldn't get the girl he wanted, said Netty.

Really? Caroline had never thought of that. Did Netty know any more? It sounded romantic.

Netty said it had seemed romantic to some people who had nothing better to do than fret about it.

Oh, Netty, don't tease! Who was it?

Netty underwent some sort of struggle, and then said if anybody had wanted to know they had only to use their eyes.

Caroline thought it must all have been terribly romantic when Daddy was young and just back from the war, and Mummy so lovely, and Daddy so handsome—as he still was, didn't Netty think so?

The handsomest man she had ever seen, said Netty, with vehemence.

Had Netty ever seen him in those days?

Well, said Netty, she had been too young to pay much heed

to such things when the war ended. After all, she wasn't exactly Methuselah. But when Boy Staunton married Leola
Cruikshank in 1924 she had been ten, and everybody knew it
was a great love-match, and they were the handsomest pair
Deptford had ever seen or was ever likely to see. Nobody had
eyes for anyone but the bride, and she guessed Ramsay was
like all the rest. After all, he had been Father's best man.

Here Caroline pounced. Did Netty mean Mr. Ramsay had
been in love with Mother?

Netty was torn between her natural discretion and the
equally natural desire to tell what she knew. Well, there had
been those that said as much.

So that was why he was always around our house! And why
he had taken so much care of Mother when Father had to be
away on war business. He was heart-broken but faithful. Caroline had never heard of anything so romantic. She thought Mr.
Ramsay was sweet.

This word affected Netty and me in different ways. Old
Buggerlugs sweet! I laughed much louder and longer than I
would have done if I had not had two glasses of Burgundy. But
Netty snorted with disdain, and there was that in her burning
eyes that showed what she thought of such sweetness.

"Oh, but you'd never admit any man was attractive except
Daddy," said Caroline. She even leaned over and put her hand
on Netty's wrist.

What did Caroline mean by that, she demanded.

"It sticks out a mile. You adore him."

Netty said she hoped she knew her place. It was a simple
remark, but extremely old-fashioned for 1942, and if ever I
have seen a woman ruffled and shaken, it was Netty as she said
it.

Caroline let things simmer down. Of course everybody
adored Daddy. It was inescapable. He was so handsome, and

attractive, and clever, and wonderful in every way that no woman could resist him. Didn't Netty think so?

Netty guessed that was about the size of it.

Later Caroline brought up another theme. Wasn't it extraordinary that Mother had taken that chill, when everybody knew it was the worst possible thing for her? How could those windows have been open on such a miserable day?

Netty thought nobody would ever know.

Did Netty mean Mother had opened them herself, asked Caroline, all innocence. But—she laid down her knife and fork—that would be suicide! And suicide was a mortal sin! Everybody at Bishop Cairncross's—yes, and at St. Simon Zelotes, where we went to church—was certain of that. If Mother had committed a mortal sin, were we to think that now—? That would be horrible! I swear that Caroline's eyes filled with tears.

Netty was rattled. No, of course she meant nothing of the kind. Anyway that about mortal sins was just Anglican guff and she had never held with it. Never.

But then, how did Mother's windows come to be open?

Somebody must have opened them by mistake, said Netty. We'd never know. There was no sense going on about it. But her baby girl wasn't to think about awful things like suicide.

Caroline said she couldn't bear it, because it wasn't just Anglican guff, and everybody knew suicides went straight to Hell. And to think of Mummy—!

Netty never wept, that I know of. But there was, on very rare occasions, a look of distress on her face which in another woman would have been accompanied by tears. This was such a time.

Caroline leapt up and ran to Netty and buried her face in her shoulder. Netty took her out of the room and I was left amid the ruins of the feast. I thought another glass of Burgundy would be just the thing at that moment, but the butler had removed it, and I had not quite the brass to ring the bell, so I took another apple from the dessert plate and ate it reflectively all by myself. I could not make head or tail of what had been going on. When the apple was finished, I went to the drawing-room and sat down to listen to a hockey-game on the radio. But I soon fell asleep on the sofa.

When I woke, the game was over and some dreary war news was being broadcast. I had a headache. As I went upstairs I saw a light under Caroline's door, and went in. She was in pyjamas, carefully painting her toe-nails red.

"You'd better not let Netty catch you at that."

"Thank you for your invaluable, unsought advice. Netty is no longer a problem in my life."

"What have you two been hatching up?"

"We have been reaching an understanding. Netty doesn't fully comprehend it yet, but I do."

"What about?"

"Dope! Weren't you listening at dinner? No, you weren't, of course. You were too busy stuffing your face and guzzling booze to know what was happening."

"I saw everything that happened. What didn't I see? Don't pretend to be so smart."

"Netty opened up and made a few damaging admissions. That's what happened."

"I didn't hear any damaging admissions. What are you talking about?"

"If you didn't hear it was because you were drinking too much. Booze will be your downfall. Many a good man has gone to hell by the booze route, as Grandfather used to say. Didn't you hear Netty admit that she loves Father?"

"What? She never said that!"

"Not in so many words. But it was plain enough."

"Well! She certainly has a crust!"

"For loving Father? How refreshingly innocent you are! One of these days, if you remind me, I'll give you my little talk about the relation of the sexes. It's a lot more complicated than your low schoolboy mind can comprehend."

"Oh, shut up! I'm older than you are. I know things you've never even heard of."

"You probably mean about fairies. Old stuff, my poor boy!"

"Carol, I'm going to have to swat you."

"Putting me to silence by brute strength? Okay, Tarzan. Then you'll never hear the rest—which is also the best."

"What?"

"Do you acknowledge me as the superior mind?"

"No. What do you know that makes you so superior?"

"Just the shameful secret of your birth, that's all."

"What!"

"I have every reason to believe that you are the son of Dunstan Ramsay."

"Me!"

"You. Now I take a good look, in the light of my new information, you are quite a bit like him."

"I am not! Listen, Carol, you just explain what you've said or I'll kill you!"

"Lay a finger on me, dear brother, and I'll clam up and leave you forever in torturing doubt."

"Is that what Netty said?"

"Not in so many words. But you know my methods, Watson. Apply them. Now, attend very carefully. Daddy took Mummy away from Dunstan Ramsay and married her. Dunstan Ramsay went right on visiting this house as Trusted Friend. If you read more widely and intelligently you would know the role that Trusted Friend plays in all these affairs. Cast your mind back six years, to that awful Christmas. A quarrel. Daddy sweeps out in a rage. Ramsay remains. We are sent upstairs. Later we see Ramsay leave Mummy's bedroom, where she is in her nightie. We hear her call out, 'You don't love me.' A few hours later, Mummy tries to kill herself. You remember all that blood, that you couldn't keep your mouth shut about. Daddy isn't around home nearly so much after that, but Ramsay keeps coming. The obvious—the only—conclusion is that Daddy discovered Ramsay was Mummy's lover and couldn't bear it."

"Carol, you turd! You utter, vile, maggoty, stinking turd! How can you say that about Mother?"

"I don't enjoy saying it, fathead. But Mummy was a very beautiful, attractive woman. Being rather in that line myself I understand the situation, and her feelings, as you never will. I know how passion drives people on. And I accept it. To know all is to forgive all."

"You'll never get me to believe it."

"Don't, then. I can't help what you believe. But if you don't believe that you certainly won't believe what came of it."

"What?"

"What's the good of my telling you, if you don't want to hear?"

"You've got to tell me. You can't just tell me part. I'm a member of this family too, you know. Come on. If you don't I'll get hold of Father next time he's home and tell him what you just said."

"No you won't. That is one thing you will never do. Admit yourself to be Ramsay's son! Daddy would probably disinherit you. You'd have to go and live with Ramsay. You'd be branded as a bastard, a love-child, a merry-begot—"

"Stop milking the dictionary, and tell me."

"Okay. I am in a kindly mood, and I won't torture you. Netty killed Mummy."

I must have looked very queer, for Caroline dropped her Torquemada manner and went on.

"This is deduction, you understand, but deduction of a very superior kind. Consider: the orders were strict against Mummy getting a chill, so we must accept either that Mummy opened those windows herself or somebody else opened them, and the only person around who could have done it was Netty. If Mummy did it, she killed herself knowingly, and that would be suicide, and forgetting all that Netty so rightly calls Anglican guff are you ready to believe Mummy killed herself?"

"But why would Netty do it?"

"Love, dumb-bell. That tempest of passion of which you still know nothing. Netty loves Daddy. Netty has a very fierce, loyal nature. Mummy had deceived Daddy. Listen, do you know what she said to me, after we had left you hogging the wine? We talked a long time about Mummy, and she said, 'Everything considered, I think your mother's better out of it.' "

"But that isn't admitting she killed anybody."

"I am not simple. I put the question directly—or as directly as seemed possible in the rather emotional situation. I said, 'Netty, tell me truly, who opened the windows? Netty, darling, I'll never breathe it to a soul—did you do it, out of loyalty to Daddy?' She gave me the very queerest look she's ever given me—and there have been some dillies—and said, 'Caroline don't you ever breathe or hint any such terrible thing again!' "

"Well, then, there you have it. She said she didn't."

"She said no such thing! If she didn't, who did? Things make sense, Davey. There is nothing without an explanation. And that is the only explanation possible. She didn't say she hadn't done it. She chose her words carefully."

"God! What a mess."

"But fascinating, don't you think? We are children of a fated house."

"Oh, bullshit! But look—you've jumped to a lot of conclusions. I mean, about us being Ramsay's children—"

"About you being Ramsay's child. I don't come into that part."

"Why me?"

"Well, look at me; I am unmistakably Boy Staunton's daughter. Everybody says so. I look very much like him. Do you?"

"That doesn't prove anything."

"I can quite understand you don't want to think so."

"I think this is all something you've made up to amuse yourself. And I think it's damn nasty—throwing dirt on Mother and making me out to be a bastard. And all this crap about love. What do you know about love? You're just a kid! You haven't even got your monthlies yet!"

"So what, Havelock Ellis? I've got my full quota of intelligence and that's more than you can say."

"Intelligence! You're just a nasty-minded, mischief-making kid!"

"Oh, go and pee up a tree!" said my sister, who picked up a lot of coarse language at Bishop Cairncross's.

I took my headache, which was now much worse, to my own room. I looked in the mirror. Caroline was crazy. There was nothing in my face to suggest Dunstan Ramsay. Or was there? If you put my beautiful mother and old Buggerlugs together, would you produce anything like me? Caroline had such certainty. Of course she was a greedy novel-reader and romancer, but she was no fool. I didn't look in the least like my father, or the Stauntons, or the Cruikshanks. But—?

I went to bed disheartened but could not sleep. I wanted something, and it took me a long time to admit to myself what

I wanted. It was Felix. This was terrible. At my age, wanting a
toy bear! It must be the drink. I would never touch a drop of
that awful stuff again.

Next day, with elaborate casualness, I asked Netty what had
happened to Felix.

"I threw him out years ago," she said. "What would you
want with an old thing like that? He'd only breed moths."

DR. VON HALLER: Your sister sounds very interesting.
Is she still like that?

MYSELF: In an adult way, yes, she is. A great manager.
And quite a mischief-maker.

DR. VON HALLER: She sounds like a very advanced
Feeling Type.

MYSELF: Was it Feeling to sow a doubt in my mind that
I have never completely settled since?

DR. VON HALLER: Oh, certainly. The Feeling Type understands feeling; that does not mean that such people always
share feeling or use it tenderly. They are very good at evoking
and managing feeling in others. As your sister did with you.

MYSELF: She caught me off balance.

DR. VON HALLER: At fourteen, you were no match for a
girl of twelve who was an advanced Feeling Type. You were
trying to think your way out of an extremely emotional situation. She was just interested in stirring things up and getting
Netty under her thumb. Probably it never occurred to her that
you would take seriously what she said about your parentage,
and would have laughed at you for being foolish if she knew
that you did so.

MYSELF: She planted terrible doubts in my mind.

DR. VON HALLER: Yes, but she woke you up. You must
be grateful to her for that. She made you think of who you
were. And she put your beautiful mother in a different per-

spective, as somebody over whom men might quarrel, and whom another woman might think it worth-while to murder.

MYSELF: I don't see the good of that.

DR. VON HALLER: Very few sons ever do. But it is hard on women to be looked on as mothers only. You North American men are especially guilty of casting your mothers in a cramping, minor role. It is bad for men to look back toward their mothers without recognizing that they were also people —people who might be loved, or possibly murdered.

MYSELF: My mother knew great unhappiness.

DR. VON HALLER: You have said that many times. You have even said it about periods when you were too young to have known anything of the sort. It is a kind of refrain in your story. These refrains are always significant. Suppose you tell me what genuine reasons you have for thinking of your mother as an unhappy woman. Reasons that Mr. Justice Staunton would admit as evidence in his strict court.

MYSELF: Direct evidence? Does a woman ever tell her children she is unhappy? A neurotic woman, perhaps, who is trying to get some special response out of them by saying so. My mother was not neurotic. She was a very simple person, really.

DR. VON HALLER: What indirect evidence, then?

MYSELF: The way she faded after that terrible Abdication Christmas. She seemed to be more confused than before. She was losing her hold on life.

DR. VON HALLER: She had been confused before, then?

MYSELF: She had problems. My father's high expectations. He wanted a brilliant wife, and she tried to be one, but she wasn't cut out for it.

DR. VON HALLER: You observed this before her death? Or did you think of it afterward? Or did somebody tell you it was so?

MYSELF: You're worse than Caroline! My father told me so. He gave me some advice one time: Never marry your childhood sweetheart, he said; the reasons that make you choose her will all turn into reasons why you should have rejected her.

DR. VON HALLER: He was talking of your mother?

MYSELF: He was really talking about a girl I was in love with. But he mentioned Mother. He said she hadn't grown.

DR. VON HALLER: And did you think she had grown?

MYSELF: Why would I care whether she had grown or not? She was my mother.

DR. VON HALLER: Until you were fourteen. At that age one is not intellectually demanding. If she were alive now, do you think that you and she would have much to say to one another?

MYSELF: That is not the kind of question that is admitted in Mr. Justice Staunton's court.

DR. VON HALLER: Was she a woman of any education? Had she any mind?

MYSELF: Does it matter? I suppose not, really.

DR. VON HALLER: Were you angry with your father because of what he said?

MYSELF: I thought it was a hell of a thing to say to a boy about his mother, and I thought it was an unforgivable thing to say about the woman who had been his wife.

DR. VON HALLER: I see. Suppose we take a short cut. I wish you would take some time during the next few days to sort out why you think your father must always be impeccable in conduct and opinion, but that very much must be forgiven your mother.

MYSELF: She did try to commit suicide, remember. Doesn't that speak of unhappiness? Doesn't that call for pity?

DR. VON HALLER: So far we do not know why she

made that attempt. Your sister could be right, don't you see? It could have been because of Ramsay.

MYSELF: That's nonsense! You've never seen Ramsay.

DR. VON HALLER: Only through your eyes. As I have seen your parents. But I have seen many women with lovers, and it is not always Venus and Adonis, I assure you. But let us leave this theme until we have done more work, and you have had time to do some private investigation of your feelings about your mother. See what you can do to form an opinion of her as a woman—as a person you might meet. . . . But now I should like to talk for a moment about Felix. You tell me he has been appearing in your dreams? What does he do there?

MYSELF: He doesn't do anything. He's just there.

DR. VON HALLER: Alive?

MYSELF: Alive as he was when I knew him. He seemed to have a personality, you know. Rather puzzled and considering, and I did all the talking. And he usually agreed. Sometimes he was doubtful and said no. But his attention seemed to lend something to whatever I had talked about or decided. Do I make any sense?

DR. VON HALLER: Oh, yes; excellent sense. These figures we have in our deep selves, you know, have a way of being both external and internal. That one we talked of—the Shadow—he was inward, wasn't he? And yet as we talked, it appeared that so many of the things you disliked so strongly about him were also to be found in people you knew. You were particularly vehement about Netty's brother, Maitland Quelch—

MYSELF: Yes, but I should have made it clear that I very rarely met him. I just heard about him from Netty. He was so deserving and he had his way to make in the world single-handed, and he would have been so glad of some of the chances I hardly seemed to notice, and all that sort of thing.

Matey's struggle to qualify as a Chartered Accountant pretty much paralleled my own studies for the Bar, but of course in Netty's eyes everything had been made easy for me, whereas he did it the hard way. Meritorious Matey! But when I met him, which was as seldom as decency allowed, I always thought he was a loathsome little squirt—

DR. VON HALLER: I know. We went into that quite extensively. But in the end we agreed, I think, that you simply read into Matey's character things you disliked, and these proved after some more investigation to be things which were not wholly absent from your own character. Isn't that so?

MYSELF: It's difficult for me to be objective about Matey. When I talk about him I feel myself becoming waspish, and I can't help describing him as if he were some sort of Dickensian freak. But is it my fault he has damp hands and a bad breath and shows his gums when he smiles and calls me Ted, which nobody else on God's green earth does, and exudes democratic forgiveness of my wealth and success—

DR. VON HALLER: Yes, yes: we were through all that, and at last you admitted that Matey was your scapegoat—a type of all you disliked and feared might come to the surface in yourself—please, one moment—not in these physical characteristics but in the character of the Deserving Person, ill rewarded and ill understood by a careless world. The Orphan of the Storm: the Battered Baby. You don't have to blush for harbouring something of this in your most secret image of yourself. The important thing is to know what you are doing. That tends to defuse it, you understand. I was not trying during those difficult hours to make you like Matey. I was trying to persuade you to examine a dark corner of yourself.

MYSELF: It was humiliating, but I suppose it must be true.

DR. VON HALLER: The truth will grow as we work.

That is what we are looking for. The truth, or some part of it.

MYSELF: But although I admit I projected some of the least admirable things in my own character on Matey—you notice how I am picking up words like "projected" from you— I have a hunch that there is something fishy about him. He's too good to be true.

DR. VON HALLER: I am not surprised. Unless one is very naïve, one does not project one's own evil on people who are especially good. As I have said, if psychiatry worked by rules, every policeman would be a psychiatrist. But let us get back to Felix.

MYSELF: Does his appearance now mean some sort of reversion to childhood?

DR. VON HALLER: Only to an emotion you felt in childhood, and which does not seem to have been very common with you since. Felix was a friend. He was a loving friend, but because of your own disposition, he was very much a thinking, considering friend. Now just as the Shadow makes his appearance in this sort of personal investigation, so does a figure we call the Friend. And because you have worked well and diligently for the last few weeks, when the going cannot have been very pleasant, I am glad to be able to give you good news. The appearance of the Friend in your inner life and in your dreams is a favourable sign. It means that your analysis is going well.

MYSELF: You're quite right. This probing and recollecting hasn't been pleasant. There have been times when I have been annoyed and disgusted with you. There were moments when I wondered if I were really out of my mind to put myself in the hands of anyone who tormented me and thwarted me as you have done.

DR. VON HALLER: Quite so. I was aware of it, of course.

But as we go on you will find that I seem to be many things to you. If you understand me, part of my professional task is to be the bearer of your projections. When the Shadow was under investigation, and so much of your inferior self was coming to light, you found the Shadow in me. Now we seem to have awakened the image of the Friend in your mind, your spirit, your soul—these are not scientific terms but I promised not to deluge you with jargon—and perhaps I shall not now be so intolerable.

MYSELF: I'm delighted. I would truly like to know you better.

DR. VON HALLER: It is yourself you must truly know better. And I should warn you that I shall appear as the Friend only for a limited time. Yes; I have many other parts to play before we are done. And even the Friend is not always benevolent: sometimes friends are truest when they seem unfriendly. It's funny that your Friend is a bear; I mean, the Friend often appears as an animal, but rarely as a savage animal. . . . Now, let me see; we have reached your mother's death, and the moment when Caroline, mischievously but perhaps not untruly, made some suggestions that made you see yourself in a new light. It sounds almost like the end of childhood.

(5)

It was. I was adolescent now. Of course I knew a good deal about what people stupidly call the facts of life, but I had not had much physical experience of what sex meant. Now it began to be very troublesome. I find it odd, now, to read some of the popular books that glorify masturbation; I never thought it would kill me, or anything stupid like that, but I did my best to control it because—well, it seemed such a shabby thing. I suppose I didn't bring much imagination to it.

As I look back now I see that, although I knew a good deal about sex, I had retained an unusual innocence for my age, and I suppose it was my father's money, and the sense of isolation it brought, that made my innocence possible.

I told you what Netty had said about "Anglican guff." She was scornful of what she called "Pancake Christianity" because we ate pancakes at Shrove; she used to snort when my parents had lobster salad on Fridays in Lent and always demanded that meat be sent up to the nursery for herself. She never, I think, quite forgave my parents for leaving the wholesome bosom of evangelistic Protestantism. Church matters—I won't call it religion—played a big part in my growing up. We were attached to St. Simon Zelotes, which had the reputation of being a rich people's church. It wasn't the most fashionable Anglican church in the city, but it had a special cachet. The fashionable one, I suppose, was St. Paul's, but it was Broad Church. I suppose you are familiar with these distinctions? And the High Church was St. Mary Magdalene, but it was poor. St. Simon Zelotes was neither so High as Mary Mag, nor so rich as Paul's. The vicar was Canon Woodiwiss—he later became an Archdeacon and finally Bishop—and he was a gifted apostle to the well-to-do. I don't say that sneeringly. There always seems to be a notion that the rich can't be devout and that God doesn't like them as much as He likes the poor. There are lots of Christians who are all pity and charity for the miserable and the outcast, but who think it a spiritual duty to give the rich a good snubbing whenever they can. So Woodiwiss was a real find for a church like Simon Zelotes.

He soaked the rich for money, which was fair enough. At least once a year he preached his famous sermon about "it is easier for a camel to go through the eye of a needle than for a rich man to enter into the kingdom of God." He would explain that the Needle's Eye was the name of a gate to Jerusalem which was so narrow that a heavily laden camel had to be relieved of some of its burden to get through, and that custom demanded that whatever was taken from the camel became the property of the Temple. So the obvious course for a rich man was to divest himself of some of his wealth for the church and thereby take a step toward salvation. I believe that in terms of history and theology this is all moonshine and Woodiwiss may even have invented it himself, but it worked like a charm. Because, as he said, following on from his text, "with God all things are possible." So he persuaded his rich camels to strip off a few bales of this world's goods and leave the negotiation of the needle's eye in his capable hands.

I didn't see much of the Canon, though I heard many of his wonder-working sermons. He had the gift of the gab as few parsons do. But I came much under the influence of one of his curates, who was named Gervase Knopwood.

Father Knopwood, as he liked us to call him, had an extraordinary way with boys, though on the face of it this seemed unlikely. He was an Englishman with an almost farcically upper-class accent and long front teeth and an appearance of being an elderly schoolboy. He wasn't old; probably he was in his early forties, but his hair was almost white and he had deep furrows in his face. He wasn't a joker or a jolly good fellow, and he played no games, though he was tough enough to have been a missionary in the Canadian West in some very difficult territory. But everybody respected him, and everybody feared him in a special way, for his standards were high, he expected the best from boys, and he had some ideas that to me were original.

For one thing, he didn't pay the usual lip-service to Art, which enjoyed more than sacred status in the kind of society in which we lived. I discovered this one day when I was talking to him in one of the rooms at the back of the church where we met for the Servers' Guild and Confirmation classes and that sort of thing. There was a picture on the wall, a perfectly hideous thing in vivid colours, of a Boy Scout looking the very picture of boyish virtue, and behind him stood the figure of Christ with His hand on the Scout's shoulder. I was making great game of it for the benefit of some other boys when I became aware that Father Knopwood was standing at a little distance, listening carefully.

"You don't think much of it, Davey?"

"Well, Father, could anybody think much of it? I mean, look at the way it's drawn, and the raw colours. And the sentimentality!"

"Tell us about the sentimentality."

"Well—it's obvious. I mean, Our Lord standing with His hand on the fellow's shoulder, and everything."

"I seem to have missed something you have seen. Why is it sentimental to suggest that Christ stands near to anyone, whether it is a boy, or a girl, or an old man, or anyone at all?"

"That's not sentimental, of course. But it's the way it's done. I mean, the concept is so crude."

"Must a concept be sophisticated to be a good one?"

"Well—surely?"

"Must the workmanship always be superior? If something is to be said, must it always be said with eloquence and taste?"

"That's what they teach us in the Art Club. I mean, if it's not well done it's no good, is it?"

"I don't know. I've never been able to make up my mind. A lot of modern artists are impatient of technical skill. It's one of the great puzzles. Why don't you come and see me after the meeting, and we'll talk about it and see what we can find out."

This led to seeing a lot of Father Knopwood. He used to ask

me to meals in his rooms, as he called a bed-sitter with a gas-ring in a cupboard that he had not far from the church. He wasn't poison-poor, but he didn't believe in spending money on himself. He taught me a lot and put some questions I have never been able to answer.

The art thing was one of his pet subjects. He loved art and knew a lot about it, but he was always rather afraid of it as a substitute religion. He was especially down on the idea that art was a thing in itself—that a picture was simply a flat composition of line and pigment, and the fact that it seemed also to be Mona Lisa or The Marriage at Cana was an irrelevance. Every picture, he insisted, was "of" something or "about" something. He was interesting about very modern pictures, and once he took me to a good show of some of the best, and talked about them as manifestations of questing, chaos, and sometimes of despair that artists sensed in the world about them and could not express adequately in any other way. "A real artist never does anything gratuitously or simply to be puzzling," he would say, "and if we don't understand it now, we shall understand it later."

This was not what Mr. Pugliesi said in the Art Club at school. We had a lot of clubs, and the Art Club had rather a cachet, as attracting the more intellectual boys; you were elected to it, you didn't simply join. Mr. Pugliesi was always warning us not to look for messages and meanings but to take heed of the primary thing—the picture as an object—so many square feet of painted canvas. Messages and meanings were what Father Knopwood chiefly sought, so I had to balance my ideas pretty carefully. That was why he got after me for laughing at the Boy Scout picture. He agreed that it was an awful picture, but he thought the meaning redeemed it. Thousands of boys would understand it who would never notice a Raphael reproduction if we put one in its place.

I have never been convinced that he was right, and was shocked by his idea that not everybody needed art to be educated. He saved me from becoming an art snob, and he could be terribly funny about changes in art taste; the sort of fashionable enthusiasm that admires Tissot for thirty years, kicks him out of the door for forty, and then drags him back through the window as an artist of hitherto unappreciated quality. "It's simply the immature business of assuming that one's grandfather must necessarily be a fool, and then getting enough sense to realize that the old gentleman was almost as intelligent as oneself," he said.

This was important to me because another kind of art was coming to the fore at home. Caroline, who had always had lessons on the piano, was beginning to show some talent as a musician. We had both had some musical training and used to go to Mrs. Tattersall's Saturday morning classes, where we sang and played rhythm instruments and learned some basic stuff very pleasantly. But I had no special ability, and Caroline had. By the time she was twelve she had fought through a lot of the donkey-work of learning that extraordinarily difficult instrument that all unmusical parents seem to think their children should play, and she was pretty good. She has never become a first-rate pianist, but she is a much better than average amateur.

When she was twelve, though, she was sure that she was going to be another Myra Hess and worked very hard. She played musically, which is really quite rare, even among people who get paid big fees to do it. Like Father Knopwood, she was interested in content as well as technique, and it was always a puzzle to me how she got to be that way, for nothing at home encouraged it. She played the things young pianists play—Schumann's *The Prophet Bird* and his *Scenes from Childhood,* and of course lots of Bach and Scarlatti and Beethoven. She could wallop out Schumann's *Carnaval* with immense authority for a girl of twelve or thirteen. The mischievous little snip she was in her personal life seemed to disappear, and somebody much more important took her place. I think I liked it best when she played some of the easier things she had learned in earlier years and fully commanded. There is one trifle—I don't suppose it has much musical value—by Stephen Heller, called in English *Curious Story*, which is a very misleading translation of *Kuriose Geschichte;* she really succeeded in making it eerie, not by playing in a false, spooky way, but by a refined, Hans Andersen treatment. I loved listening to her, and though she tormented me horribly at other times, we seemed to be able to reach one another when she was playing and I was listening, and Netty was somewhere else.

Caroline was glad to see me at weekends, because the house was even gloomier than before our mother died. It wasn't neglected; there were still servants, though the staff had been cut down, and they polished and tidied things that never grew dim or untidy because nobody ever touched them; but the life had gone out of the house, and even though its former life had been unhappy, it had been life of a kind. Caroline lived there, supposedly under the care of Netty, and once a week Father's secretary, an extremely efficient woman from Alpha Corporation, called to see that everything was in good order. But this secretary didn't want to be involved personally, and I don't blame her. Caroline was a day-girl at Bishop Cairncross's, so she had friends and a social life there, as I did at Colborne College.

We rarely asked anybody home, and our first attempt to take over the house as our own soon spent itself. Father wrote letters now and then, and I know he asked Dunstan Ramsay to keep an eye on us, but Ramsay had his hands full at the school during those war years, and he didn't trouble us often. I rather think he disliked Carol, so he confined his supervision to questioning me now and then at school.

You might suppose my sister and I were to be pitied, but we rather liked our weekend solitude. We could lighten it whenever we pleased by going out with friends, and people were kind about inviting us both to parties and such things, though during the war they were on a very modest scale. But I didn't want to go out much because I had no money and could get into embarrassing positions; I borrowed all I could from Carol but didn't want to be wholly in her clutch.

What we both liked best were the Saturday evenings when we were together, because it had become the custom for Netty to devote that time to her pestilent brother Maitland and his deserving young family. Carol played the piano, and I looked through books about art which I was able to borrow from the school library. I was determined about this because I didn't want her to think that I had no independent artistic interest of my own, but as I looked at pictures and read about them, I was really listening to her. It was the only time the drawing-room showed any hint of life, but the big empty fireplace—the secretary from Alpha and Netty agreed that it was foolish to light it during wartime, when presumably even cord-wood was involved in our total war effort—was a reminder that the room was merely enduring us, and that as soon as we went to bed a weight of inanition would settle on it again.

I remember one night when Ramsay did drop in, and laughed to see us.

"Music and painting," said he; "the traditional diversions of the third generation of wealthy families. Let us hope you will both become discriminating patrons. God knows they are rare."

We didn't like this, and Carol was particularly offended by his assumption that she would never do anything directly as a musician. But time has proved him right, as it does with so many disagreeable people. Carol and Beesty are now generous patrons of music, and I collect pictures. With both of us, as Father Knopwood feared, it has become the only spiritual life we have, and not a very satisfactory one when life is hard.

Knopwood prepared me for Confirmation, and it was a much more important experience than I believe is usually the case. Most curates, you know, take you through the Catechism and bid you to ask them about anything you don't understand. Of course most people don't understand any of it, but they are content to let sleeping dogs lie. Most curates gives you a vaguely worded talk about keeping yourself pure, without any real hope that you will.

Knopwood was very different. He expounded the Creed in tough terms, very much in the C. S. Lewis manner. Christianity was serious and demanding, but worth any amount of trouble. God is here, and Christ is now. That was his line. And when it came to the talk about purity, he got down to brass tacks better than anybody I have ever known.

He didn't expect you to chalk up a hundred per cent score, but he expected you to try, and if you sinned, he expected you to know what you had done and why it was sin. If you knew that, you were better armed next time. This appealed to me. I liked dogma, for the same reason that I grew to like law. It made sense, it told you where you stood, and it had been tested by long precedent.

He was very good about sex. It was pleasure: yes. It could be a duty: yes. But it wasn't divorced from the rest of life, and what you did sexually was of a piece with what you did in your friendships and in your duty to other people in your public life. An adulterer and a burglar were bad men for similar reasons. A seducer and a sneak-thief were the same kind of man. Sex was not a toy. The great sin—quite possibly the Sin against the

Holy Ghost—was to use yourself or someone else contemptu-
ously, as an object of convenience. I saw the lógic of that and
agreed.

There were problems. Not everybody fitted all rules. If you
found yourself in that situation you had to do the best you
could, but you had to bear in mind that the Sin against the
Holy Ghost would not be forgiven you, and the retribution
would be in this world.

The brighter members of Knoppy's Confirmation classes
knew what he was talking about at this point. It was clear
enough that he was himself a homosexual and knew it, and
that his work with boys was his way of coping with it. But he
never played favourites, he was a dear and thoroughly masculine friend, and there was never any monkey-business when he
asked you to his rooms. I suppose there are hundreds like me
who remember him with lasting affection and count having
known him as a great experience. He stood by me during my
early love-affair in a way I can never forget and which nothing
I could do would possibly repay.

I wish we could have remained friends.

(6)

People jeer at first love, and in ridiculous people it is certainly
ridiculous. But I have seen how hot its flame can be in people
of passionate nature, and how selfless it is in people who are
inclined to be idealistic. It does not demand to be requited, and
it can be a force where it is obviously hopeless. The worst fight
I saw in my schooldays was caused when a boy said something
derogatory about Loretta Young; another boy, who cherished a
passion for the actress, whom he had seen only in films, hit this
fellow in the mouth, and in an instant they were on the

ground, the lover trying to murder the loudmouth. Our gym master parted them and insisted that they fight it out in the ring, but it was hopeless: the lover ignored all rules, kicked and bit and seemed like a madman. Of course nobody could explain to the master what the trouble was, but all of us supposed it was a fight about love. What I know now was that it was really a fight about honour and idealism—what Dr. von Haller calls a projection—and that it was a necessary part of the spiritual development of the lover. It may also have done something for the fellow who was so free with the name of Miss Young.

I fell in love, with a crash and at first sight, on a Friday night in early December of 1944. I had been in love before, but trivially. Many boys, I think, are in love from the time they are able to walk, and I had cherished my hidden fancies and had had my conquests, of whom Toad Wilson was by no means the best example. Those were childish affairs, with shallow roots in Vanity. But now I was sixteen, serious and lonely, and in three hours Judith Wolff became the central, absorbing element in my life.

Caroline's school, named for a Bishop Cairncross who had been a dominant figure in the nineteenth-century life of our Canadian province, had a reputation for its plays and its music. Every school needs to be known for something other than good teaching, and its Christmas play was its speciality. In the year when I was sixteen the school decided to combine music and drama and get up a piece by Walter de la Mare called *Crossings*. I heard a good deal about it because it had a lot of music and four songs in it, and Caroline was to play the piano offstage. She practised at home and talked about the play as if it were the biggest musical show since Verdi wrote *Aida* for the Khedive of Egypt.

I read the playbook she had to work from, and I did not

think much of it. It was certainly not in the Plain Style, and I was now much under the influence of Ramsay's enthusiasm for unadorned prose. It was not a Broadway kind of play, and I am not certain it is even a good play, but it is unmistakably a poet's play, and I was the most deeply enchanted of an audience that seemed, in a variety of ways suitable to their age and state of mind and relationship to the players or the school, to be delighted by it.

It is about some children who are left to their own devices because of a legacy. They have an aunt who has strict educational theories and expects them to get into hopeless messes without her guidance; instead they have some fine adventures with strange people, including fairy people. The oldest child is a girl called Sally, and that was Judith Wolff.

Sally is very much a de la Mare girl, and I don't think I ever saw Judith except through de la Mare eyes. The curtain went up (or rather, was drawn apart with a wiry hiss) and there she sat, at a piano, precisely as the poet describes her in the stage directions—slim, dark, of mobile face, speaking in a low clear voice as if out of her thoughts. She had a song almost at once. The illusion that she was playing the piano was not successful, because the sound was plainly coming from Caroline backstage, and her pretence to be playing was no better than it usually is. But her voice made shortcomings of that sort irrelevant. I suppose it was just a charming girl's voice, but I shall never know. It was a voice that seemed to be for me only in all the world. I was engulfed in love, and I suppose I have been in love with Judith ever since. Not as she is now. I see her from time to time, by chance; a woman of my own age, still gravely beautiful. But she is a Mrs. Julius Meyer, whose husband is an admired professor of chemistry, and I know that she has three clever children and is an important figure on the committee of the Jewish hospital. Mrs. Julius Meyer is not

Judith Wolff to me, but her ghost, and when I see her I get away as fast as possible. The David Staunton who fell in love still lives in me, but Judith Wolff—the girl of the de la Mare play—lives only in my memories.

Judith had two songs in *Crossings*. She acted as she sang, with a grave natural charm, and was much, much, much the best of the girls in the play.

There were people who thought differently. As always at these affairs, there were people who thought the girls who played masculine parts were wildly funny, and I suppose that when they turned their whiskered, carefully made-up faces away, and we saw their girl-shaped bottoms, it was funny if that is where you find your fun. There was much applause for a small blonde who played the Queen of the Fairies; she acted with a sweetness which I thought painfully overdone. There was a ballet of fairies, very pretty as they danced through a snow-scene, holding little lanterns; there were plenty of parents with eyes only for a special fairy. But I saw nothing clearly but Judith, and in justice to the audience generally I must say that they thought that she was—always excepting their own child—the best. For the curtain call the stage was filled with the whole cast, and also the inevitable clown assembly of mistresses in sensible shoes who had helped in some way, looking as such helpers always do, too big and too clumsy to have had anything to do with creating an illusion. Judith stood in the centre of the first line, and it seemed to me that she was aware of her popularity and was blushing at it.

I applauded uproariously, and I noticed some parents looking approvingly at me. I suppose they thought I was clapping for Caroline and was a loyal brother. Caroline was on the stage, certainly, holding the score of the music so people would know what she had done, but I had no eyes for her. After the party for the cast and friends—school coffee and school cookies—I took Caroline home and tried to find out something about Judith Wolff. She had been surrounded by some foreign-looking people whom I supposed to be her parents and their friends, and I had not been able to get a good look at her. But Caroline was full of herself, as always, and demanded again and again that I reassure her that the music had been suitably audible, yet not too loud, and had supported the weaker singers without seeming to dominate them, and had really carried the ballet, who were just little girls and had no more sense of rhythm than so many donkeys, and had indeed been fully orchestral in effect. This was egotistical nonsense, but I had to put up with it in order to bring the conversation around to what I wanted to know.

Weren't they lucky to get such a good girl for the part of Sally? Who was she?

Oh—Judy Wolff. Nice voice, but dark. Brought it too much from the back of her throat. Needed some lessons in production.

Perhaps. Good for that part, though.

Possibly. A bit of a cow at rehearsal. Hard to stir her up.

I considered killing Caroline and leaving her battered body on the lawn of one of the houses we were passing.

Caroline knew I wouldn't have noticed, because it was a fine point not many people would get, but in Sally's *Lullaby* in Act Two, at "Leap fox, hoot owl, wail warbler sweet," Judy was all over the place, and as Caroline had a very tricky succession of chromatic chords to play there was nothing she could do to drag Judy back, and she just hoped it would be better tomorrow night.

You cannot have a sister like Caroline without picking up a few tricks. I asked if there was any chance that I could see the play again on Saturday night?

"So you can go and moon at Judy again?" she said. In another age Caroline would have been burnt as a witch; she could smell what you were thinking, especially when you wanted to conceal it. I set aside plans for burning her then and there.

"Judy who? Oh, the Sally girl. Don't be silly. No, I just thought it was good, and I'd like to see it again. And I was thinking you didn't really get the recognition you deserved to-night. If I came tomorrow night, I could send you a bouquet, and it could be handed up over the footlights at the end, and people would know what you were worth."

"Not a bad idea, but where would you get any money to send a bouquet? You're broke."

"I'd wondered if you could possibly see your way to making me a small loan. As it's really for you, anyhow."

"What's the need? Why can't I just send myself a bouquet? That would cut out the middleman."

"Because it's ridiculous and undignified and cheap and gen-erally two-bit and no-account, and if Netty heard of it, as she would from me, she would make your life a burden. Whereas if the bouquet comes from me, nobody need know, and if they find out they'll think what a sweet brother I am. But I'll put a big ticket on it with 'Homage to those eloquent fingers, from Arturo Toscanini' if you like."

It worked. I thought it would be a cheap dollar bouquet, but I had underrated Caroline's vanity, and she handed over a nice, resounding five bucks as a tribute to herself. This was splendid because I had craftily decided to sequester some portion of whatever I got from Caroline, and use it to send another bou-quet to Judy Wolff. With five dollars I could do the thing in style.

Florists were more grasping than I had supposed, but after shopping around on Saturday I managed quite a showy tribute for Caroline, of chrysanthemums with plenty of fern to eke them out, for a dollar seventy-five. With the remaining three twenty-five, to which I added fifty cents I ground out of Netty by pretending I had to get a couple of special pencils for making maps, I bought roses for Judy. Not the best roses; I had no money for those; but indubitable roses.

I was playing a dangerous game. I knew it, yet I could not help myself. Caroline would find out about the two bouquets and would take it out of me in some dreadful way, for she was a terrible skinflint. But I was ready to risk anything, so long as Judy Wolff received the tribute that was her due. The thought of the evening sustained me through a nervous, worrisome Saturday.

It worked out quite differently from anything I could have foreseen. In the first place, Netty wanted to go to *Crossings*, and it was assumed that I should take her. There is a special sort of enraged misery that overcomes a young man who is absorbed in his love for an ideal girl and who is thrust into the company of a distasteful, commonplace older woman. Dr. von Haller talks about the concept of the Shadow; how much of my Shadow—of my impatience, my snobbery, my ingratitude —was visited on poor Netty that night! To have to sit beside her, and answer her tomfool questions and listen to her crass assertions, and breathe up her smell of fevered flesh and laundry starch, and be conscious of her garment of state, her sheared mouton coat, among all the minky mothers, was torture to me. Had I been Romeo and she the Nurse, I could have risen above her with aristocratic ease, and everybody would have known she was my retainer; but I was Davey and she was Netty who had washed under my foreskin and threatened to cut my heart out with a whip when I was naughty, and my dread was that the rest of the audience would think she was my mother! But Netty was not sensitive; she was on a spree; she was to witness the triumph of her adored Caroline. I was merely her escort, and she felt kindly toward me and sought to divert me with her Gothic vivacity. How was I to insinuate myself into the moonlight world of Judith Wolff after the play, with this goblin in tow?

Consequently I did not enjoy the play as I had expected to do. I was conscious of faults Caroline had been niggling about all day, and although my worship of Judy was more agonizing than before, it heaved on a sea of irritability and discontentment. And always there was the dread of the moment when the bouquets would be presented.

Here again I had reckoned without Fate, which was disposed to spare me from the consequences of my folly. When the curtain call came, some of the girls who had been serving as ushers rushed to the footlights like Birnam Wood moving to Dunsinane, loaded with bouquets. Judy got my roses and another much finer bunch from another usher. Caroline was handed the measly bundle of chrysanthemums, but also a very grand bunch of yellow roses, which were her favourites; she pretended extreme astonishment, read the card, and gave a little jump of joy! When the applause was over and almost every girl on the stage had been given flowers of some sort, I stumbled out of the hall like one who has, at the last minute, been snatched from in front of the firing-squad.

The party in the school's dining-room was larger and gayer than the night before, though the food was the same. There were so many people that they stood in groups, and not in a single mass. Netty made a bee-line for Caroline, demanding to know who had sent her flowers. Caroline was busy displaying the roses and the card that was with them, on which was printed, in bold script, "From a devoted admirer, who wishes to remain unknown." The chrysanthemums and their rotten little card, on which I had printed "Congratulations and Good Luck," she gave to Netty to hold. She was in tearing high spir-

its and loved all mankind; she seized me by the arm and
rushed me over to Judy Wolff and shrieked, "Judy, I want you
to meet my baby brother; he thinks you're the tops," and left
me gangling. But she immediately showed her roses to Judy,
and made a great affair of wondering who could have sent
them; Judy, like every girl when confronted with an obvious
admirer, ignored me and chattered away to Caroline and tried
to talk about the mystery of her own roses. My roses. Hopeless.
Caroline was not to be distracted. But in time she did go away,
and I was left with Judy, and had opened my mouth to say my
carefully prepared speech—"You sang awfully well; you must
have a marvellous teacher." (Oh, was it too daring? Would
she think I was a pushy nuisance? Would she think it was just
a line I used with all the dozens of girls I knew who sang?
Would she think I was trying to move in on her like some
football tough who—Knopwood, stand by me now!—wanted
to use her as an object of convenience?) But near her were the
same smiling, dark-skinned, big-nosed people I had seen last
night, and they took me over as Judy (what manners, what
aplomb, she must be foreign) introduced me as Caroline's
brother. My father, Dr. Louis Wolff. My mother. My Aunt
Esther. My uncle, Professor Bruno Schwarz.

They were very kind to me, but they all had X-ray eyes, or
extrasensory perception, because they assumed without asking
that it was I who had sent Judy the other bouquet of roses.
And this flummoxed me. There I stood, a declared lover, a role
for which I had no preparation whatever, and which I had
entered on a level of roses, which I was utterly unable to sus-
tain. But what was most remarkable was that they took it for
granted that I should admire Judy and send her flowers as an
entirely suitable way of getting to know her. I gathered that
being Caroline's brother was, to them, a sufficient introduction.
How little they knew Caroline! They understood. They sympa-

thized. Of course they said nothing directly, but their attitude toward me and their conversation made it plain that they supposed I wanted to be accepted as a friend, and were willing that it should be so. I didn't know what to do. The course of true love was, contrary to everything that was right and proper, running smooth, and I was not ready for it.

Friends of mine at school were in love with girls. The parents of these girls were always hilarious nuisances, eager to tar and feather Cupid and make a clown of him; or, if not that, they were unpleasantly ironic and seemed to have forgotten all about love except as something that ailed puppies and calves. The Wolffs took me seriously as a human being. I had hoped for a furtive romance, unknown to anyone else in the world. But here was Mrs. Wolff saying that they were always at home on Sunday afternoons between four and six, and if I liked to look in, they would be delighted to see me. I asked if tomorrow would be too soon. No, tomorrow would do beautifully. They were delighted to meet me. They hoped we would meet often.

During all of this, Judy said very little, and when I shook hands with her at parting—an awful struggle; was this the thing to do, or not; did one shake the hands of girls?—she cast down her eyes.

This was something I had never seen a girl do. Caroline's friends always looked you straight in the eye, especially if they had something disagreeable to say. This dropping of the gaze almost disembowelled me with its modest beauty.

But the publicity of it all! Can I have been so obvious? On the way home even Netty remarked that I certainly seemed to be taken with that dark girl, and when I asked her haughtily what she meant she said she had eyes in her head like anybody else, and I had been lallygagging so nobody could miss it.

Netty was in high good humour. Dunstan Ramsay had been at *Crossings,* invited, I suppose as Headmaster of a neighbouring school. He had paid Netty a good deal of attention. That was like Buggerlugs; he never overlooked anybody, and he seemed to put himself out to be gallant to women nobody else could stand. He had introduced Netty to Miss Gostling, the Headmistress of Bishop Cairncross's, and had said she was the mainstay of the Staunton household while Father had to be away on war business. Miss Gostling had been quite the lady; hadn't put on any airs. But it was a good thing that place was a school and not a hotel, because their coffee would choke a dog.

As we were going to bed, Caroline came to my room to thank me for the flowers. "I must say you did it in style," said she, "and you must have shopped around for quite a while to get yellow roses like that for five dollars. I know what these things cost; this is identical with the bunch Buggerlugs sent Ghastly Gostling, and I'll bet it didn't cost him a cent less than eight."

I was in a mood to dare much. "Who sent you the other flowers?" I asked.

"Scotland Yard suspects Tiger McGregor," she replied. "He's been lurking for a couple of months. Cheap creep! It looks like about a dollar seventy-five"—this with a glint of her pawnbroker's eye—"and he'll probably expect me to go to the Colborne dance with him on the strength of it. Maybe I will, at that. . . . By the way, you and I are invited to tea at Judy Wolff's tomorrow. I worked that for you, so clean yourself up and do me credit."

So Buggerlugs had sent the roses and saved me from God knows what humiliation and servitude to Carol! Could he have known anything? Not possibly. He was just doing right by an old friend's daughter and having a little joke on his card. But he was a friend, whether he knew it or not. Was he more than a friend? . . . Damn Carol!

We went to tea with the Wolffs next day. It was not a social occasion I knew anything about, and I was in a frenzy of nerves. But the Wolff apartment was full of people, and Tiger McGregor was there and kept Caroline out of my way. I had a few words with Judy, and once she gave me a plate of sandwiches to hand around, so obviously she thought I was a trustworthy person and not just somebody who regarded her as an object of convenience. Her parents were charming and kind, and although I had experienced kindness, I was a stranger to charm, so I fell in love with all the Wolffs and Schwarzes in properly respectful degrees, and felt that I had suddenly moved into a new sort of world.

Thus began a love which fed my life and expanded my spirit for a year, before it was destroyed by an act of kindness which was in effect an act of shattering cruelty.

Need we go into details about what I said to Judy? I am no poet, and I suppose what I said was very much what everybody always says, and although I remember her as speaking golden words, I cannot recall precisely anything she said. If love is to be watched and listened to without embarrassment, it must be transmuted into art, and I don't know how to do that, and it is not what I have come to Zürich to learn.

DR. VON HALLER: We must go into it a little, I think. You told her you loved her?

MYSELF: On New Year's Day. I said I would love her always, and I meant it. She said she couldn't be sure about loving me; she would not say it unless she was sure she meant it, and forever. But she would not withhold it, if ever she were sure, and meanwhile the greatest kindness I could show was not to press her.

DR. VON HALLER: And did you?

MYSELF: Yes, quite often. She was always gentle and always said the same thing.

DR. VON HALLER: What was she like? Physically, I mean. Was her appearance characteristically feminine? A well-developed bosom? Was she a clean person?

MYSELF: She was dark. Complexion what is called olive, but with wonderful deep red colour in her cheeks when she blushed. Hair dark brown. Not tall, but not short. She laughed at herself about being fat, but of course she wasn't. Curvy. Those uniforms that schools like Bishop Cairncross's insisted on at that time were extraordinarily revealing. If a girl had breasts, they showed up under those middies, and some girls had positive shelves almost under their chins. And those absurd short blue skirts, showing seemingly miles of leg from ankle to thigh. It was supposed to be a modest outfit, to make them look like children, but a pretty girl dressed like that is a quaint, touching miracle. The sloppy ones and the fatties were pretty spooky, but not a girl like Judy.

DR. VON HALLER: You felt physical desire for her, then?

MYSELF: I most certainly did! There were times when I nearly fried! But I was heedful of what Knopwood said. Of course I talked to Knopwood about it, and he was wonderful. He said it was a very great experience, but I was the man, and the greater responsibility was mine. So—nothing that would harm Judy. He also gave me a hint about Jewish girls; said they were brought up to be modest and that her parents, being Viennese, were probably pretty strict. So—no casual Canadian ways, and never get the parents against me.

DR. VON HALLER: Did you have erotic dreams about her?

MYSELF: Not about her. But wild dreams about women I

couldn't recognize, and sometimes frightful hags, who ravished me. Netty began to look askew and hint about my pyjamas. And of course she had some awful piece of lore from Deptford to bring out. It seems there had been some woman there when she was a little girl who had always been "at it" and had eventually been discovered in a gravel pit, "at it" with a tramp; of course this woman had gone stark, staring mad and had had to be kept in her house, tied up. But I think this tale of lust rebuked was really for Caroline's benefit, because Tiger McGregor was lurking more and more, and Carol was getting silly. I spoke to her about it myself, and she replied with some quotation about showing her the steep and thorny way to heaven, while I was making an ass of myself over Judy Wolff. But I kept my eye on her, just the same.

DR. VON HALLER: Yes? A little more, please.

MYSELF: It's not a part of my life I take pride in. Now and then I would gum-shoe around the house when Tiger was there, just to see that everything was on the level.

DR. VON HALLER: And was it?

MYSELF: No. There was a lot of prolonged kissing, and once I caught them on the sofa, and Carol's skirt was practically over her head, and Tiger was snorting and puffing, and it was what Netty would call a scene.

DR. VON HALLER: Did you intervene?

MYSELF: No. I didn't quite do that, but I was as mad as hell, and went upstairs and walked around over their heads and then took another peep, and they had straightened up.

DR. VON HALLER: Were you jealous of your sister?

MYSELF: She was just a kid. She oughtn't to have known about that kind of thing. And I couldn't trust Tiger to understand that the greater responsibility was his. And Carol was as hot as a Quebec heater anyhow.

DR. VON HALLER: What did you say to Tiger?

MYSELF: That's where the shame of the thing comes in. I didn't say anything to him. I was pretty strong; I got over all that nonsense about being frail by the time I was twelve; but Tiger was a football tough, and he could have killed me.

DR. VON HALLER: Should you not have been prepared to fight for Father Knopwood's principles?

MYSELF: Knopwood prepared Carol for Confirmation; she knew what his principles were as well as I did. But she laughed at him and referred to him as my "ghostly father." And Tiger had no principles, and still hasn't. He's ended up as a public-relations man in one of Father's companies.

DR. VON HALLER: So what was perfectly all right for you and Judy was not all right for Tiger and Carol?

MYSELF: I loved Judy.

DR. VON HALLER: And you had no sofa-scenes?

MYSELF: Yes—but not often. The Wolffs lived in an apartment, you see, and though it was a big one there was always somebody going or coming.

DR. VON HALLER: In fact, they kept their daughter on a short string?

MYSELF: Yes, but you wouldn't think of it that way. They were such charming people. A kind of person I'd never met before. Dr. Wolff was a surgeon, but you'd never know it from his conversation. Art and music and the theatre were his great interests. And politics. He was the first man I ever met who was interested in politics without being a partisan of some kind. He was even cool about Zionism. He actually had good words for Mackenzie King; he admired King's political astuteness. He weighed the war news as nobody else did, that I knew, and even when the Allies were having setbacks near the end, he was perfectly certain the end was near. He and Professor Schwarz, who was his brother-in-law, had seen things clearly enough to leave Austria in 1932. There was a sophistication in that house that was a continual refreshment to me. Not painted on, you know, but rising from within.

DR. VON HALLER: And they kept their daughter on a short string?

MYSELF: I suppose so. But I was never aware of the string.

DR. VON HALLER: And there were some tempestuous scenes between you?

MYSELF: Whenever it was possible, I suppose.

DR. VON HALLER: To which she consented without being sure that she loved you?

MYSELF: But I loved her. She was being kind to me because I loved her.

DR. VON HALLER: Wasn't Carol being kind to Tiger?

MYSELF: Carol was being kind to herself.

DR. VON HALLER: But Judy wasn't being kind to herself?

MYSELF: You won't persuade me that the two things were the same.

DR. VON HALLER: But what would Mr. Justice Staunton say if these two young couples were brought before him? Would he make a distinction? If Father Knopwood were to appear as a special witness, would he make a distinction?

MYSELF: Knopwood was the soul of charity.

DR. VON HALLER: Which you are not? Well, don't answer now. Charity is the last lesson we learn. That is why so much of the charity we show people is retrospective. Think it over and we shall talk about it later. Tell me more about your wonderful year.

It was wonderful because the war was ending. Wonderful because Father was able to get home for a weekend now and then. Wonderful because I found my profession. Wonderful because he raised my allowance, because of Judy.

That began badly. One day he told Caroline he wanted to see her in his office. She thought it was about Tiger, and was in a sweat for fear Netty had squealed. Only Supreme Court cases took place in Father's office. But he just wanted to know why she had been spending so much money. Miss Macmanaway, the secretary, advanced Caroline money as she needed it, without question, but of course she kept an account for Father. Caroline had been advancing me the money I needed to take Judy to films and concerts and plays, and to lunch now and then. I think Caroline thought it kept me quiet about Tiger, and I suppose she was right. But when Father wanted to know how she had been getting through about twenty-five dollars a week, apart from her accounts for clothes and oddments, she lost her nerve and said she had been giving money to me. Why? He takes this girl out, and you know what he's like when he can't have his own way. Carol warned me to look out for storms.

There was no storm. Father was amused, after he had scared me for a few minutes. He liked the idea that I had a girl. Raised my allowance to seven dollars and fifty cents a week, which was a fortune after my miserable weekly dollar for so long. Said he had forgotten I was growing up and had particular needs.

I was so relieved and grateful and charmed by him—because he was really the most charming man I have ever known, in a sunny, open way which was quite different from the Wolffs' complex, baroque charm—that I told him a lot about Judy. Oddly enough, like Knopwood, he warned me about Jewish girls; very strictly guarded on the level of people like the Wolffs. Why didn't I look a little lower down? I didn't understand that. Why would I want a girl who was less than Judy, when not only she, but all her family, had such distinction? I knew Father liked distinguished people. But he didn't make any reply to that.

So things were very much easier, and I was out of Carol's financial clutch.

(7)

Summer came, and the war had ended, in Europe, on May 7.

I went to camp for the last time. Every year Caroline and I were sent to excellent camps, and I liked mine. It was not huge, it had a sensible program instead of one of those fake-Indian nightmares, and we had a fair amount of freedom. I had grown to know a lot of the boys there, and met them from year to year, though not otherwise because few of them were from Colborne College.

There was one fellow who particularly interested me because he was in so many ways unlike myself. He seemed to have extraordinary dash. He never looked ahead and never counted the cost. His name was Bill Unsworth.

I went to camp willingly enough because Judy's parents were taking her to California. Professor Schwarz was going there to give some special lectures at Cal Tech. and other places, and the Wolffs went along to see what was to be seen. Mrs. Wolff said it was time Judy saw something of the world, before she went to Europe to school. I did not grasp the full significance of that, but thought the end of the war must have something to do with it.

Camp was all very well, but I was growing too old for it, and Bill Unsworth was already too old, though he was a little younger than I. When the camp season finished, about the middle of August, he asked me and two other boys to go with him to a summer place his parents owned which was in the same district, for a few days before we returned to Toronto. It was pleasant enough, but we had had all the boating and swimming we wanted for one summer, and we were bored. Bill suggested that we look for some fun.

None of us had any idea what he had in mind, but he was certain we would like it, and enjoyed being mysterious. We drove some distance—twenty miles or so—down country roads, and then he stopped the car and said we would walk the rest of the way.

We struck into some pretty rough country, for this was Muskoka and it is rocky and covered with scrub which is hard to break through. After about half an hour we came to a pretty summer house on a small lake; it was a fussy place, with a little rock garden around it—gardens come hard in Muskoka —and a lot of verandah furniture that looked as if it had been kept in good condition by fussy people.

"Who lives here?" asked Jerry Wood.

"I don't know their names," said Bill. "But I do know they aren't here. Trip to the Maritimes. I heard it at the store."

"Well—did they say we could use the place?"

"No. They didn't say we could use the place."

"It's locked," said Don McQuilly, who was the fourth of our group.

"The kind of locks you open by spitting on them," said Bill Unsworth.

"Are you going to break a lock?"

"Yes, Donny, I am going to break a lock."

"But what for?"

"To get inside. What else?"

"But wait a minute. What do you want to get inside for?"

"To see what they've got in there, and smash it to buggery," said Bill.

"But why?"

"Because that's the way I feel. Haven't you ever wanted to wreck a house?"

"My grandfather's a judge," said McQuilly. "I have to watch my step."

"I don't see your grandfather anywhere around," said Bill, sweeping the landscape with eyes shaded by his hand like a pirate in a movie.

We had an argument about it. McQuilly was against going ahead, but Jerry Wood thought it might be fun to get in and turn a few things upside down. I was divided in my opinion, as usual. I was sick of camp discipline; but I was by nature law-abiding. I had often wondered what it would be like to wreck something; but on the other hand I had a strong conviction that if I did anything wrong I would certainly be caught. But no boy likes to lose face in the eyes of a leader, and Bill Unsworth was a leader, of a sort. His sardonic smile as we haggled was worth pages of wordy argument. In the end we decided to go ahead, I for one feeling that I could put on the brakes any time I liked.

The lock needed rather more than spitting on, but Bill had brought some tools, which surprised and rather shocked us. We got in after a few minutes. The house was even more fussy inside than the outside had promised. It was a holiday place, but everything about it suggested elderly people.

"The first move in a job like this," Bill said, "is to see if they've got any booze."

They had none, and this made them enemies, in Bill's eyes. They must have hidden it, which was sneaky and deserved punishment. He began to turn out cupboards and storage places, pulling everything onto the floor. We others didn't want to seem poor-spirited, so we kicked it around a little. Our lack of zeal angered the leader.

"You make me puke!" he shouted and grabbed a mirror

from the wall. It was round, and had a frame made of that plaster stuff twisted into flowers that used to be called barbola. He lifted it high above his head, and smashed it down on the back of a chair. Shattered glass flew everywhere.

"Hey, look out!" shouted Jerry. "You'll kill somebody."

"I'll kill you all," yelled Bill, and swore for three or four minutes, calling us every dirty name he could think of for being so chicken-hearted. When people talk about "leadership quality" I often think of Bill Unsworth; he had it. And like many people who have it, he could make you do things you didn't want to do by a kind of cunning urgency. We were ashamed before him. Here he was, a bold adventurer, who had put himself out to include us—lily-livered wretches—in a daring, dangerous, highly illegal exploit, and all we could do was worry about being hurt! We plucked up our spirits and swore and shouted filthy words, and set to work to wreck the house.

Our appetite for destruction grew with feeding. I started gingerly, pulling some books out of a case, but soon I was tearing out pages by handfuls and throwing them around. Jerry got a knife and ripped the stuffing out of the mattresses. He threw feathers from sofa cushions. McQuilly, driven by some dark Scottish urge, found a crowbar and reduced wooden things to splinters. And Bill was like a fury, smashing, overturning, and tearing. But I noticed that he kept back some things and put them in a neat heap on the dining-room table, which he forbade us to break. They were photographs.

The old people must have had a large family, and there were pictures of young people and wedding groups and what were clearly grandchildren everywhere. When at last we had done as much damage as we could, the pile on the table was a large one.

"Now for the finishing touch," said Bill. "And this is going to be all mine."

He jumped up on the table, stripped down his trousers, and squatted over the photographs. Clearly he meant to defecate on them, but such things cannot always be commanded, and so for several minutes we stood and stared at him as he grunted and swore and strained and at last managed what he wanted, right on the family photographs.

How long it took I cannot tell, but they were critical moments in my life. For as he struggled, red-faced and pop-eyed, and as he appeared at last with a great stool dangling from his apelike rump, I regained my senses and said to myself, not "What am I doing here?" but "Why is he doing that? The destruction was simply a prelude to this. It is a dirty, animal act of defiance and protest against—well, against what? He doesn't even know who these people are. There is no spite in him against individuals who have injured him. Is he protesting against order, against property, against privacy? No; there is nothing intellectual, nothing rooted in principle—even the principle of anarchy—in what he is doing. So far as I can judge—and I must remember that I am his accomplice in all but this, his final outrage—he is simply being as evil as his strong will and deficient imagination will permit. He is possessed, and what possesses him is Evil."

I was startled out of my reflection by Bill shouting for something with which to wipe himself.

"Wipe on your shirt-tail, you dirty pig," said McQuilly. "It'd be like you."

The room stank, and we left at once, Bill Unsworth last, looking smaller, meaner, and depleted, but certainly not repentant.

We went back to the car in extremely bad temper. Nobody spoke on the way to the Unsworths' place, and the next day Wood, McQuilly, and I took the only train home to Toronto.

We did not speak of what we had done, and have never done so since.

On the long journey from Muskoka back to Toronto I had plenty of time to think, and I made my resolve then to be a lawyer. I was against people like Bill Unsworth, or who were possessed as he was. I was against whatever it was that possessed him, and I thought the law was the best way of making my opposition effective.

(8)

It was a surprise that brought no pleasure when I discovered that I was in love with Dr. von Haller.

For many weeks I had been seeing her on Mondays, Wednesdays, and Fridays and was always aware of changes in my attitude toward her. In the beginning, indifference; she was my physician, and though I was not such a fool as to think she could help me without my co-operation I assumed that there would be limits to that; I would answer questions and provide information to the best of my ability, but I assumed without thinking that some reticences would be left me. Her request for regular reports on my dreams I did not take very seriously, though I did my best to comply and even reached a point where I was likely to wake after a dream and make notes on it before sleeping again. But the idea of dreams as a key to anything very serious in my case or any other was still strange and, I suppose, unwelcome. Netty had set no store by dreams, and the training of a Netty is not quickly set aside.

In time, however, quite a big dossier of dreams accumulated, which the doctor filed, and of which I kept copies. I had taken rooms in Zürich; a small service flat, looking out on a courtyard, did me very well; meals with wine could be taken at the *table d'hôte*, and I found after a time that the wine was enough, with a nightcap of whisky, just so that I should not forget what it tasted like. I was fully occupied, for the doctor gave me plenty of homework. Making up my notes for my next appointment took far more time than I had expected— quite as much as preparing a case for court—because my problem was to get the tone right; with Johanna von Haller I was arguing not for victory, but for truth. It was hard work, and I took to napping after lunch, a thing I had never done before. I walked, and came to know Zürich fairly well—certainly well enough to understand that my knowledge was still that of a visitor and a stranger. I took to the museums; even more, I took to the churches, and sometimes sat for long spells in the Grossmünster, looking at the splendid modern windows. And all the time I was thinking, remembering, reliving; what I was engaged on with Dr. von Haller (which I suppose must be called an analysis, though it was nothing like what I had ever imagined an analysis to be) possessed me utterly.

To what extent should I surrender myself, I asked, and as I asked I was aware that the time for turning back had passed and I no longer had any choice in the matter. I even lost my embarrassment about dreams, and would take a good dream to my appointment as happily as a boy who has prepared a good lesson.

(*The dream dossier I kept in another notebook, and only a few references to its contents appear here. This is not wilful concealment. The dreams of someone undergoing such treatment as mine are numbered in tens and hundreds, and extracting meaning from the mass is slow work, for dreams say their say in series, and only rarely is a single dream revelatory. Reading such a record of dreams is comparable to reading the*

*whole of a business correspondence when preparing a case—
dull panning for gold, with a hundredweight of gravel dis-
carded for every nugget.*)

Indifference gave way to distaste. The doctor seemed to me
to be a commonplace person, not as careful about her appearance as I had at first thought, and sometimes I suspected her of
a covert antipathy toward me. She said things that seemed mild
enough until they were pondered, and then a barb would appear. I began to wonder if she were not like so many people I
have met who can never forgive me for being a rich and privi-
leged person. Envy of the rich is understandable enough in
people whose lives are lived under a sky always darkened by
changing clouds of financial worry and need. They see people
like me as free from the one great circumstance that conditions
their lives, their loves, and the fate of their families—want of
cash. They say, glibly enough, that they do not envy the rich,
who must certainly have many cares; the reality is something
very different. How can they escape envy? They must be especially envious when they see the rich making fools of themselves, squandering big sums on trivialities. What that fellow
has spent on his yacht, they think, would set me up for life.
What they do not understand is that folly is to a great extent a
question of opportunity, and that fools, rich or poor, are always
as foolish as they can manage. But does money change the
essential man? I have been much envied, and I know that
many people who envy me my money are, if they only knew it,
envying me my brains, my character, my appetite for work,
and a quality of toughness that the wealth of an emperor cannot buy.

Did Dr. von Haller, sitting all day in her study listening to
other people's troubles, envy me? And perhaps dislike me? I
felt that it was not impossible.

Our relationship improved after some time. It seemed to me that the doctor was friendlier, less apt to say things that needed careful inspection for hidden criticism. I have always liked women, in spite of my somewhat unusual history with them; I have women friends, and have had a substantial number of women clients whose point of view I pride myself on understanding and setting forward successfully in court.

In this new atmosphere of friendship, I opened up as I had not done before. I lost much of my caution. I felt that I could tell her things that showed me in a poor light without dreading any reprisal. For the first time in my life since I lost Knopwood, I felt the urge to confide. I know what a heavy burden everybody carries of the unconfessed, which sometimes appears to be the unspeakable. Very often such stuff is not disgraceful or criminal; it is merely a sense of not having behaved well or having done something one knew to be contrary to someone else's good; of having snatched when one should have waited decently; of having turned a sharp corner when someone else was thereby left in a difficult situation; of having talked of the first-rate when one was planning to do the second-rate; of having fallen below whatever standards one had set oneself. As a lawyer I heard masses of such confession; a fair amount of what looks like crime has its beginning in some such failure. But I had not myself confided in anybody. For in whom could I confide? And, as a criminal lawyer—comic expression, but the usual one for a man who, like myself, spends much of his time defending people who are, or possibly may be, criminals—I knew how dangerous confession was. The priest, the physician, the lawyer—we all know that their lips are sealed by an oath no torture could compel them to break. Strange, then, how many people's secrets become quite well known. Tell nobody anything, and be closemouthed even about that, had been my watchword for more than twenty of my forty years. Yet was it not urgent need for confession that brought me to Zürich? Here I was, confident that I could confide in this Swiss doctor, and thinking it a luxury to do so.

What happened to my confidences when I had made them? What did I know about Johanna von Haller? Where was she when she was not in her chair in that room which I now knew very well? Whence came the information about the world that often arose in our talks? I took to reading *Die Neue Zürcher Zeitung* to keep abreast of her, and although at first I thought I had never read such an extraordinary paper in my life, my understanding and my German improved, and I decided that I had indeed never read such an extraordinary paper, meaning that in its most complimentary sense.

Did she go to concerts? Did she go to the theatre? Or to films? I went to all of these entertainments, because I had to do something at night. I had made no friends, and wanted none, for my work on my analysis discouraged it, but I enjoyed my solitary entertainments. I took to arriving early at the theatre and staring about at the audience to see if I could find her. My walks began to lead me near her house, in case I should meet her going or coming. Had she any family? Who were her friends? Did she know any men? Was there a husband somewhere? Was she perhaps a Lesbian? These intellectual women —but no, something told me that was unlikely. I had seen a good many collar-and-tie teams in my professional work, and she was neither a collar nor a tie.

Gradually I realized that I was lurking. This is not precisely spying; it is a kind of meaningful loitering, in hopes. Lurking could only mean one thing, but I couldn't believe it of myself. In love with my analyst? Absurd. But why absurd? Was I too old for love? No, I was going on forty-one, and knew the world. She was mature. Youthful, really, for her probable age. I took her to be about thirty-eight, but I had no way of finding

out. Except for the relationship in which we stood to one another, there was nothing in the world against it. And what was
that, after all, but doctor and patient? Didn't doctors and patients fall in love? I have been involved in more than one case
that made it clear they did.

Everything in me that had kept its reason was dismayed.
What could come of such a love? I didn't want to marry; I
didn't want an affair. No, but I wanted to tell Johanna von
Haller that I loved her. It had to be said. Love and a cough
cannot be hid, as Netty told me when I was seventeen.

I dressed with special care for my next appointment, and
told Johanna that before we began, I had something of importance to say. I said it. She did not seem to be as dumbfounded
as I had expected, but after all, she was not a girl.

"So what is to be done?" I said.

"I think we should continue as before," said she. But she
smiled quite beautifully as she said it. "I am not ungrateful, or
indifferent, you know; I am complimented. But you must trust
me to be honest with you, so I must say at once that I am not
surprised. No, no; you must not imagine you have been showing your feelings and I have been noticing. Better be completely frank: it is part of the course of the analysis, you understand. A very pleasant part. But still well within professional
limits."

"You mean I can't even ask you to dinner?"

"You may certainly ask me, but I shall have to say no."

"Do you sit there and tell me it is part of my treatment that
I should fall in love with you?"

"It is one of those things that happens now and then, because I am a woman. But suppose I were a wise old doctor, like
our great Dr. Jung; you would hardly fall in love with me
then, would you? Something quite other would happen; a
strong sense of discipleship. But always there comes this period

of special union with the doctor. This feeling you have—which I understand and respect, believe me—is because we have been talking a great deal about Judy Wolff."

"You are not in the least like Judy Wolff."

"Certainly not—in one way. In another way—let us see. Have you had any dreams since last time?"

"Last night I dreamed of you."

"Tell."

"It was a dream in colour. I found myself in an underground passage, but some light was entering it, because I could see that it was decorated with wall-paintings, in the late Roman manner. The whole atmosphere of the dream was Roman, but the Rome of the decadence; I don't know how I knew that, but I felt it. I was in modern clothes. I was about to walk down the passage when my attention was taken by the first picture on the left-hand side. These pictures, you understand, were large, almost life-size, and in the warm but not reflective colours of Roman frescoes. The first picture—I couldn't see any others—was of you, dressed as a sibyl in a white robe with a blue mantle; you were smiling. On a chain you held a lion, which was staring out of the picture. The lion had a man's face. My face."

"Any other details?"

"The lion's tail ended in a kind of spike, or barb."

"Ah, a manticore!"

"A what?"

"A manticore is a fabulous creature with a lion's body, a man's face, and a sting in his tail."

"I never heard of it."

"No, they are not common, even in myths."

"How can I dream about something I've never heard of?"

"That is a very involved matter, which really belongs to the second part of your analysis. But it is a good sign that this sort of material is making its way into your dreams already. People very often dream of things they don't know. They dream of minotaurs without ever having heard of a minotaur. Thoroughly respectable women who have never heard of Pasiphaë dream that they are a queen who is enjoying sexual congress with a bull. It is because great myths are not invented stories but objectivizations of images and situations that lie very deep in the human spirit; a poet may make a great embodiment of a myth, but it is the mass of humanity that knows the myth to be a spiritual truth, and that is why they cherish his poem. These myths, you know, are very widespread; we may hear them as children, dressed in pretty Greek guises, but they are African, Oriental, Red Indian—all sorts of things."

"I should like to argue that point."

"Yes, I know, but let us take a short cut. What do you suppose this dream means?"

"That I am your creature, under your subjection, kept on a short string."

"Why are you so sure that I am the woman in the sibyl's robe?"

"How can it be anyone else? It looked like you. You are a sibyl. I love you. You have me under your control."

"You must believe me when I tell you that the only person you can be certain of recognizing in a dream is yourself. The woman might be me. Because of what you feel about me— please excuse me if I say what you at present suppose you feel about me—the woman could be me, but if so why do I not appear as myself, in this modern coat and skirt with which I am sure you are becoming wearily familiar."

"Because dreams are fanciful. They go in for fancy dress."

"I assure you that dreams are not fanciful. They always mean exactly what they say, but they do not speak the language of every day. So they need interpretation, and we cannot always be sure we have interpreted all, or interpreted correctly. But we can try. You appear in this dream; you are in two forms, yourself and this creature with your face. What do you make of that?"

"I suppose I am observing my situation. You see, I have learned something about dream interpretation from you. And my situation is that I am under your dominance; willingly so."

"Women have not appeared in your dreams very prominently, or in a flattering light, until recently. But this sibyl has the face of someone you love. Did you think it was the face of someone who loved you?"

"Yes. Or at any rate someone who cared about me. Who was guiding me, obviously. The smile had extraordinary calm beauty. So who could it be but you?"

"But why are you a manticore?"

"I haven't any idea. And as I never heard of a manticore till now, I have no associations with it."

"But we have met a few animals in your dreams before now. What was Felix?"

"We agreed that Felix was a figure who meant some rather kind impulses and some bewilderment that I was not quite willing to accept as my own. We called him the Friend."

"Yes. The Animal-Friend, and because an animal, related to the rather undeveloped instinctual side of your nature. He was one of the characters in your inner life. Like the Shadow. Now, as your sister Caroline used to say, you know my methods, Watson. You know that when the Shadow and the Friend appeared, they had a special vividness. I felt the vividness and I bore the character of Shadow and Friend. That was quite usual; part of my professional task. I told you I should play many roles. This latest dream of yours is vivid, and apparently simple, and clearly important. What about the manticore?"

"Well, as he is an animal, I suppose he is some baser aspect of me. But as he is a lion, he can't be wholly base. And he has a human face, my face, so he can't be wholly animal. Though I must say the expression on the face was fierce and untrustworthy. And there I run out of ideas."

"What side of your nature have we considered as not being so fully developed as it could be?"

"Oh, my feeling. Though I must say once more that I have plenty of feeling, even if I don't understand and use it well."

"So might not your undeveloped feeling turn up in a dream as a noble creature, but possibly dangerous and only human in part?"

"This is the fanciful side of this work that always rouses my resistance."

"We have agreed, have we not, that everything that makes man a great, as opposed to a merely sentient creature, is fanciful when tested by what people call common sense? That common sense often means no more than yesterday's opinions? That every great advance began in the realm of the fanciful? That fantasy is the mother not merely of art, but of science as well? I am sure that when the very first primitives began to think that they were individuals and not creatures of a herd and wholly bound by the ways of the herd, they seemed fanciful to their hairy, low-browed brothers—even though those hairy lowbrows had no concept of fantasy."

"I know. You think the law has eaten me up. But I have lived by reason, and this is unreason."

"I think nothing of the kind. I think you do not understand the law. So far as we can discover, anything like a man that has inhabited this earth lived by some kind of law, however crude. Primitives have law of extraordinary complexity. How did they get it? If they worked it out as a way of living tribally, it must once have been fantasy. If they simply knew what to do from the beginning, it must have been instinct, like the nest-building instinct of birds."

"Very well; if I accept that the lion represents my somewhat undeveloped feeling, what about it?"

"Not a lion; a manticore. Do not forget that stinging tail. The undeveloped feelings are touchy—very defensive. The manticore can be extremely dangerous. Sometimes he is even described as hurling darts from his tail, as people once thought the porcupine did. Not a bad picture of you in court, would you say? Head of a man, brave and dangerous as a lion, capable of wounding with barbs? But not a whole man, or a whole lion, or a merely barbed opponent. A manticore. The Unconscious chooses its symbolism with breath-taking artistic virtuosity."

"All right. Suppose I am the manticore. Why shouldn't you be the sibyl?"

"Because we have come to a part of our work together where a woman, or a variety of women, are very likely to appear in your dreams in just some such special relationship to you as this. Did you notice the chain?"

"I noticed everything, and I can call it up now. It was a handsome gold chain."

"Good. That is much better than if it had been an iron chain, or a chain with spikes. Now, what have we: an image that appears on the left-hand side, which means that it comes from the Unconscious—"

"I haven't completely swallowed the idea of the Unconscious, you know."

"Indeed I do know. 'Fanciful . . . fancy dress . . .' all these scornful words come up whenever we discuss it. But we are at a point where you are going to have to face it, because that is where that blue-mantled sibyl resides. She has emerged from the Unconscious and can be of great help to you, but if you banish her you might as well stop this work now and go home."

"I have never heard you so threatening before."

"There comes a time when one must be strong with rationalists, for they can reduce anything whatever to dust, if they happen not to like the look of it, or if it threatens their deep-buried negativism. I mean of course rationalists like you, who take some little provincial world of their own as the whole of the universe and the seat of all knowledge."

"Little, provincial world . . . I see. Well, what is the name of this lady I am compelled to meet?"

"Oho—irony! How well that must sound in court! The lady's name is Anima."

"Latin for Soul. I gave up the idea of a soul many years ago. Well?"

"She is one of the figures in your psychological make-up, like the Shadow and the Friend, whom you have met and about whom you entertain few doubts. She is not a soul as Christianity conceives it. She is the feminine part of your nature: she is all that you are able to see, and experience, in woman: she is not your mother, or any single one of the women you have loved, but you have seen all of them—at least in part—in terms of her. If you love a woman you project this image upon her, at least at the beginning, and if you hate a woman it is again the Anima at work, because she has a very disagreeable side which is not at all like the smiling sibyl in the blue mantle. She has given rise to some of the world's greatest art and poetry. She is Cleopatra, the enchantress, and she is Faithful Griselda, the patient, enduring woman; she is Beatrice, who glorifies the life of Dante, and she is Nimue, who imprisons Merlin in a thorn-bush. She is the Maiden who is wooed, the Wife who bears the sons, and she is the Hag who lays out her man for his last rest. She is an angel, and she may also be a witch. She is Woman as she appears to every man, and to every man she appears somewhat differently, though essentially the same."

"Quite a nicely practised speech. But what do women do about this fabulous creature?"

"Oh, women have their own deep-lying image of Man, the Lover, the Warrior, the Wizard, and the Child—which may be either the child of a few months who is utterly dependent, or the child of ninety years who is utterly dependent. Men often find it very hard to carry the projection of the Warrior or the Wizard that is put upon them by some woman they may not greatly like. And of course women have to bear the projection of the Anima, and although all women like it to some degree, only rather immature women like that and nothing else."

"Very well. If the Anima is my essential image, or pattern of woman, why does she look like you? Isn't this proof that I love you?"

"No indeed; the Anima must look like somebody. You spoke of dreadful hags who assailed you in sexual dreams when you were a boy. They were the Anima, too. Because your sister and Netty could see you were in love, which I expect was pretty obvious, you projected witchlike aspects of the Anima on their perfectly ordinary heads. But you can never see the Anima pure and simple, because she has no such existence; you will always see her in terms of something or somebody else. Just at present, you see her as me."

"I am not convinced."

"Then think about it. You are good at thinking. Didn't you dislike me when the Shadow was being slowly brought to your notice; do you suppose I didn't see your considering looks as you eyed my rather perfunctory attempts at fashionable dress; do you suppose I was unaware of the criticism and often the contempt in your voice? Don't look alarmed or ashamed. It is part of my professional duty to assume these roles; the treatment would be ineffective without these projections, and I am the one who is nearest and best equipped to carry them. And then when we changed to the Friend, I know very well that my features began to have a look, in your eyes, of Felix's charming bear-expression of puzzled goodwill. And now we have reached the Anima, and I am she; I am as satisfactory casting for the role as I was for the Shadow or the Friend. But I must assure you that there is nothing personal about it.

"And now our hour is finished. We shall go on next day talking more about Judy Wolff. I trust it will be delightful."

"Well, Dr. von Haller, I am sorry to inform you, sibyl though you seem to be, that you are about to be disappointed."

(9)

The autumn that followed the war was wonderful. The world seemed to breathe again, and all sorts of things that had been taut were unfolding. Women's clothes, which had been so skimped during the war, changed to an altogether more pleasing style. When Judy was not in the Bishop Cairncross uniform she was marvellous in pretty blouses and flaring skirts; it was almost the last time that women were allowed by their epicene masters of fashion to wear anything that was unashamedly flattering. I was happy, for I was on top of my world: I had Judy, I was in my last year at Colborne College, and I was a prefect.

How can I describe my relationship with Judy without looking a fool or a child? Things have changed so startlingly in recent years that the idealism with which I surrounded everything about her would seem absurd to a boy and girl of seventeen now. Or would it? I can't tell. But now, when I see girls who have not yet attained their full growth storming the legislatures for abortion on demand, and adolescents pressing their right to freedom to have intercourse whenever and however they please, and read books advising women that anal intercourse is a jolly lark (provided both partners are "squeaky clean"), I wonder what has happened to the Davids and Judys, and if the type is extinct? I think not; it is merely waiting for another age, different from our supernal autumn but also different from this one. And, as I look back, I do not really wish we had greater freedom than was ours; greater freedom is only another kind of servitude. Physical fulfilment satisfies appetite, but does it sharpen perception? What we had of sex was limited; what we had of love seems, in my recollection, to have been illimitable. Judy was certainly kept on a short string, but the free-ranging creature is not always the best of the breed.

That autumn Bishop Cairncross's was shaken by unreasonable ambition; the success of *Crossings* had been so great that the music staff and all the musical girls like Caroline and Judy were mad to do a real opera. Miss Gostling, after the usual Headmistress's doubts about the effect on schoolwork, gave her consent, and it was rumoured that unheard-of sums of money had been set aside for the project—something in the neighbourhood of five hundred dollars, which was a Metropolitan budget for the school.

What opera? Some of the girls were shrieking for Mozart; a rival band, hateful to Caroline, thought Puccini would be more like it, and with five hundred dollars they could not see why *Turandot* would not be the obvious choice. Of course the mistresses made the decision, and the music mistress resurrected, from somewhere, Mendelssohn's *Son and Stranger*. It was not the greatest opera ever written; it contained dialogue, which to purists made it no opera at all; nevertheless, it was just within the range of what schoolgirls could manage. So *Son and Stranger* it was to be, and quite hard enough, when they got down to it.

I heard all about it. Judy told me of its charms because its *gemütlich*, nineteenth-century naïveté appealed strongly to her; either she was innocent in her tastes or else sophisticated in seeing in this humble little work delights and possibilities the other girls missed; I rather think her feeling was a combination of both these elements. Caroline was a bore about its difficulties. She and another girl were to play the overture and accompaniments at two pianos, which is trickier than it seems. In full view, too; no hiding behind the scenes this time. Of course, as always with Caroline, nobody but herself knew just how it ought to be done, and the music mistress, and the mistress who directed the production, and the art mistress who arranged the setting, were all idiots, without a notion of how to manage anything. I even had my own area of agitation and knowing-best; if Miss Gostling were not such a lunatic, insisting that everything about the production be kept within the school, I could have mustered a crew of carpenters and scene-shifters and painters and electricians among the boys at Colborne who would have done all the technical work at lightning speed, with masculine thoroughness and craftsmanship, and guaranteed wondrous result. Both Judy and Carol and most of their friends agreed that this was undoubtedly so, but none of them quite saw her way to suggesting it to Miss Gostling, who was, as we all agreed, the last surviving dinosaur.

Not many people know *Son and Stranger*. Mendelssohn wrote it for private performance, indeed for the twenty-fifth wedding anniversary of his parents, and it is deeply, lumberingly domestic in the nineteenth-century German style. "A nice old bit of Biedermeier," said Dr. Wolff, and lent some useful books to the art mistress for her designs.

The plot is modest; the people of a German village are expecting a recruiting-sergeant who will take their sons away to fight in the Napoleonic wars; a peddler, a handsome charlatan, turns up and pretends to be the sergeant, hoping to win the favours of the Mayor's ward Lisbeth; but he is unmasked by the real sergeant, who proves to be Herrmann, the Mayor's long-lost soldier son, and Lisbeth's true love. The best part is the peddler, and there was the usual wrangle as to whether it should be played by a girl who could act but couldn't sing, or whether a girl who could sing but couldn't act should have it. The acting girl was finally banished to the comic role of the Mayor, who must have been no singer in the original production, for Mendelssohn had given him a part which stayed firmly on one note. Judy was Lisbeth, of course, and had some pretty songs and a bit of acting for which her quiet charm was, or seemed to me, to be exactly right.

At last early December came, *Son and Stranger* was performed for two nights, and of course it was a triumph. What school performance of anything is ever less than a triumph? Judy sang splendidly; Caroline covered herself with honour; even the embarrassing dialogue—rendered from flat-footed German into murderous English, Dr. Wolff assured me—was somehow bathed in the romantic light that enveloped the whole affair.

This year my father was in the audience, and cut a figure because everybody knew him from newspaper pictures and admired the great work he had done during the war years. I took Netty on the Friday and went again with Father on Saturday. He asked me if I really wanted to go twice or was I going just to keep him company; not long after Judy appeared on the stage I felt him looking at me with curiosity, so I suppose I was as bad at concealing my adoration as I had always been. Afterward, at the coffee and school-cake debauch in the dining-room, I introduced him to the Wolffs and the Schwarzes, and to my astonishment Judy curtsied to him—one of those almost imperceptible little bobs that girls used to do long ago in Europe and which some girls of Bishop Cairncross's kept for the Bishop, who was the patron of the school. I knew Father was important, but I had never dreamed of him as the kind of person anybody curtsied to. He liked it; he didn't say anything, but I knew he liked it.

If any greater glory could be added to my love for Judy, Father's approval supplied it. I had been going through hell at intervals ever since Mother's death because of Carol's declaration that I was Dunstan Ramsay's son. I had come to the conclusion that whether or not I was Ramsay's son in the flesh, I was Father's son in the spirit. He had not been at home during the period of my life when boys usually are possessed with admiration for their fathers, and I was having, at seventeen, a belated bout of hero-worship. Sometimes I had found Ramsay's saturnine and ironic eye on me at school, and I had wondered if he were reflecting that I was his child. That seemed less significant now because Father's return had diminished Ramsay's importance; after all, Ramsay was the Acting Headmaster of Colborne, filling in for the war years, but Father was the Chairman of the school's Board of Governors and in a sense Ramsay's boss, as he seemed to be the boss of so many other people. He was a natural boss, a natural leader. I know I tried to copy some of his mannerisms, but they fitted me no better than his hats, which I also tried.

Father's return to Toronto caused a lot of chatter, and some of it came to my ears because the boys with whom I was at school were the sons of the chatterers. He had been remarkable as a Minister of Food, a Cabinet position that had made him even more significant in the countries we were supplying during the war than at home. He had been extraordinary in his ability to get along with Mackenzie King without wrangling and without any obvious sacrifice of his own opinions, which were not often those of the P.M. But there was another reputation that came home with him, a reputation spoken of less freely, with an ambiguity I did not understand or even notice for a time. This was a reputation as something called "a swordsman."

It is a measure of my innocence that I took this word at its face value. It was new then in the connotation it has since acquired, and I was proud of my father being a swordsman. I assumed it meant a gallant, cavalier-like person, a sort of Prince Rupert of the Rhine as opposed to the Cromwellian austerity of Mackenzie King.

When boys at school talked to me about Father, as they did because he was increasingly a public figure, I sometimes said, "You can sum him up pretty much in a word—a swordsman." I now remember with terrible humiliation that I said this to the Wolffs, who received it calmly, though I thought I saw Mrs. Wolff's nostrils pinch and if I had been more sensitive I would surely have noticed a drop in the social temperature. But the word had such a fine savour in my mouth that I think I repeated it; I knew the Wolffs and Schwarzes liked me, but how much better they would like me if they understood that I was the son of a man who was recognized for aristocratic behaviour and a temperament far above that of the upper-bourgeois world in which we lived and which, in Canada, was generally supposed to be the best world there was. Swordsmen were people of a natural distinction, and I was the son of one of them. Would I ever be a swordsman myself? Oh, speed the day!

The Wolffs, like many Jewish people, were going to a resort for Christmas, so I was not dismayed by the thought of any loss of time with Judy when my father asked me to go with him to

Montreal on Boxing Day. He had some business to do there and thought I might like to see the city. So we went, and I greatly enjoyed the day-long journey on the train and putting up at the Ritz when we arrived. Father was a good traveller; everybody heeded him and our progress was princely.

"We're having dinner with Myrrha Martindale," he said; "she's an old friend of mine, and I think you'll like her very much."

She was, it appeared, a singer, and had formerly lived in New York and had been seen—though not in leading roles— in several Broadway musical comedies. A wonderful person. Witty. Belonged to a bigger world. Would have had a remarkable career if she had not sacrificed everything to marriage.

"Was it worth it?" I asked. I was at the age when sacrifice and renunciation were great, terrifying, romantic concepts.

"No, it blew up," said Father. "Jack Martindale simply had no idea what a woman like that is, or needs. He wanted to turn her into a Westmount housewife. Talk about Pegasus chained to the plough!"

Oh, indeed I was anxious to talk about Pegasus chained to the plough. That was just the kind of swordsman thing Father could say; he could see the poetry in daily life. But he didn't want to talk about Myrrha Martindale; he wanted me to meet her and form my own opinion. That was like him, too: not dictating or managing, as so many of my friends' fathers seemed to do.

Mrs. Martindale had an apartment on Côte des Neiges Road with a splendid view over Montreal; I guessed it was costing the banished Jack Martindale plenty, and I thought it was quite right that it should do so, for Mrs. Martindale was indeed a wonderful person. She was beautiful in a mature way, and had a delightful voice, with an actress's way of making things seem much more amusing than they really were. Not that she strove to shine as a wit. She let Father do that, very properly, but her responses to his jokes were witty in themselves—not topping him, but supporting him and setting him off.

"You mustn't expect a real dinner," she said to me. "I thought it would be more fun if we were just by ourselves, the three of us, so I sent my maid out. I hope you won't be disappointed."

Disappointed! It was the most grown-up affair I had ever known. Wonderful food that Myrrha—she insisted I call her Myrrha, because all her friends did—produced herself from under covers and off hot-trays, and splendid wines that were better than anything I had ever tasted. I knew they must be good because they had that real musty aftertaste, like dusty red ink instead of fresh red ink.

"This is terribly good of you, Myrrha," said Father. "It's time Davey learned something about wines. About vintage wines, instead of very new stuff." He raised his glass to Mrs. Martindale, and she blushed and looked down as I had so often seen Judy do, only Mrs. Martindale seemed more in command of herself. I raised my glass to her, too, and she was delighted and gave me her hand, obviously meaning that I should kiss it. I had kissed Judy often enough, though never while eating and seldom on the hand, but I took it as gallantly as I could— surely I was getting to be a swordsman—and kissed it on the tips of the fingers. Father and Mrs. Martindale looked pleased but didn't say anything, and I felt I had done well.

It was a wonderful dinner. It wasn't necessary to be excited, as if I were with people my own age; calmness was the key-note, and I told myself that it was educational in the very best sense and I ought to keep alert and not miss anything. And not drink too much wine. Father talked a lot about wines, and Mrs.

Martindale and I were fascinated. When we had coffee he produced a huge bottle of brandy, which was very hard to get at that time.

"Your Christmas gift, Myrrha dear," he said. "Winston gave it to me last time I saw him, so you can be sure it's good."

It was. I had tasted whisky, but this was a very different thing. Father showed me how to roll it around in the mouth and get it on the sides of the tongue where the tastebuds are, and I rolled and tasted in adoring imitation of him.

How wonderfully good food and drink lull the spirit and bring out one's hidden qualities! I thought something better than just warm agreement with everything that was said was expected of me, and I raked around in my mind for a comment worthy of the occasion. I found it.

> "And much as Wine has played the Infidel,
> And robbed me of my Robe of Honour—Well,
> I wonder often what the Vintners buy
> One half so precious as the stuff they sell,"

said I, looking reflectively at the candles through my glass of brandy, as I felt a swordsman should. Father seemed nonplussed, though I knew that was an absurd idea. Father? Nonplussed? Never!

"Is that your own, Davey?" he said.

I roared with laughter. What a wit Father was! I said I wished it was and then reflected that perhaps a swordsman ought to have said Would that it were, but by then it was too late to change. Myrrha looked at me with the most marvellous combination of amusement and admiration, and I felt that in a modest way I was making a hit.

At half-past nine Father said he must keep another appointment. But I was not to stir. Myrrha too begged me not to think of going. She had known all along that Father would have to leave early, but then she was so grateful that he had been able to spare her a few hours from a busy life. She would love it if I would stay and talk further. She knew Omar Khayyam too, and would match verses with me. Father kissed her and said to me that we would meet at breakfast.

So Father went, and Myrrha talked about Omar, whom she knew a great deal better than I did, and it seemed to me that she brought a weight of understanding to the poem that was far outside my reach. All that disappointment with Martindale, I supposed. She was absolutely splendid about the fleetingness of life and pleasure and the rose that blows where buried Caesar bled, and it seemed to me she was piercing into a world of experience utterly strange to me but which, of course, I respected profoundly.

> "Yet Ah, that Spring should vanish with the Rose!
> That Youth's sweet-scented manuscript should close!
> The Nightingale that in the branches sang,
> Ah, whence, and whither flown again, who knows!"

she recited, thrillingly, and talked about what a glorious thing youth was, and how swift its passing, and the terrible sadness of life which pressed on and on, without anybody being able to halt it, and how wise Omar was to urge us to get on with enjoyment when we could. This was all wonderful to me, for I was new to poetry and had just begun reading some because Professor Schwarz said it was his great alternative to chemistry. If a professor of chemistry thought well of poetry, it must be something better than the stuff we worked through so patiently in Eng. Lit. at school. I had just begun to see that poetry was about life, and not ordinary life but the essence and miraculous underside of life. What a leap my understanding took when I heard Myrrha reciting in her beautiful voice; she was near to tears, and so was I. She mastered herself, and with obvious effort not to break down she continued—

> "Ah Love! could you and I with Him conspire
> To grasp this sorry Scheme of Things entire,
>   Would not we shatter it to bits—and then
> Remold it nearer to the Heart's Desire!"

I could not speak, nor could Myrrha. She rose and left me to myself, and I was full of surging thoughts, recognition of the evanescence of life, and wonder that this glorious understanding woman should have stirred my mind and spirit so profoundly.

I do not know how much time passed until I heard her voice from another room, calling me. She has been crying, I thought, and wants me to comfort her. And so I should. I must try to tell her how tremendous she is, and how she has opened up a new world to me, and perhaps hint that I know something about the disappointment with Martindale. I went through a little passage into what proved to be her bedroom, very pretty and full of nice things and filled with the smell of really good perfume.

Myrrha came in from the bathroom, wearing what it is a joke to call a diaphanous garment, but I don't know how else to name it. I mean, as she stood against the light, you could see she had nothing under it, and its fullness and the way it swished around only made it seem thinner. I suppose I gaped, for she really was beautiful.

"Come here, angel," she said, "and give me a very big kiss."

I did, without an instant of hesitation. I knew a good deal about kissing, and I took her in my arms and kissed her tenderly and long. But I had never kissed a woman in a diaphanous garment before, and it was like Winston Churchill's brandy. I savoured it in the same way.

"Wouldn't you like to take off all those stupid clothes?" she said, and gave me a start by loosening my tie. It is at this point I cease to understand my own actions. I really didn't know where this was going to lead and had no time for thought, because life seemed to be moving so fast, and taking me with it. But I was delighted to be, so to speak, under this life-enlarging authority. I got out of my clothes quickly, dropping them to the floor and kicking them out of the way.

There is a point in a man's undressing when he looks stupid, and nothing in the world can make him into a romantic figure. It is at the moment when he stands in his underwear and socks. I suppose a very calculating man would keep his shirt on to the last, getting rid of his socks and shorts as fast as possible, and then cast off the shirt, revealing himself as an Adonis. But I was a schoolboy undresser, and had never stripped to enchant. When I was in the socks-shorts moment, Myrrha laughed. I whipped off the socks, hurling them toward the dressing-table, and trampled the shorts beneath my feet. I seized her, held her firmly, and kissed her again.

"Darling," said she, breaking away, "not like a cannibal. Come and lie down with me. Now, there's no hurry whatever. So let us just do nice things for a while, shall we, and see what comes of it."

So we did that. But I was a virgin, bursting with partly gratified desire for Judy Wolff, and had no notion of preliminaries; nor, in spite of her words, did Myrrha seem greatly interested in them. I was full of poetry and power.

> Now is she in the very lists of love,
> Her champion mounted for the hot encounter—

thought I when, after some discreet stage-management by Myrrha, I was properly placed and out of danger of committing an unnatural act. It was male vanity. I was seventeen, and it was the first time I had done this; it would have been clear to anyone but me that I was not leading the band. Very quickly it was over, and I was lying by Myrrha, pleased as Punch.

So we did more nice things, and after a while I was conscious that Myrrha was nudging and manœuvring me back into the position of advantage. Good God! I thought; do people do it twice at a time? Well, I was ready to learn, and well prepared for my lesson. Myrrha rather firmly gave the time for this movement of the symphony, and it was a finely rhythmic *andante*, as opposed to the lively *vivace* I had set before. She seemed to like it better, and I began to understand that there was more to this business than I had supposed. It seemed to improve her looks, though it had not occurred to me that they needed improvement. She looked younger, dewier, gentler. I had done that. I was pleased with myself in quite a new way.

More nice things. Quite a lot of talk, this time, and some scraps of Omar from Myrrha, who must have had him by heart. Then again the astonishing act, which took much longer, and this time it was Myrrha who decided that the third movement should be a *scherzo*. When it was over, I was ready for more talk. I liked the talking almost as much as the doing, and I was surprised when Myrrha showed a tendency to fall asleep. I don't know how long she slept, but I may have dozed a little myself. Anyhow, I was in a deep reverie about the strangeness of life in general, when I felt her hand on my thigh. Again? I felt like Casanova, but as I had never read Casanova, and haven't to this day, I suppose I should say I felt as a schoolboy might suppose Casanova to feel. But I was perfectly willing to oblige and soon ready. I have read since that the male creature is at the pinnacle of his sexual power at seventeen, and I was a well-set-up lad in excellent health.

If I am to keep up the similitude of the symphony, this movement was an *allegro con spirito*. Myrrha was a little rough, and I wondered who was the cannibal now? I was even slightly alarmed, because she seemed unaware of my presence just when I was most poignantly aware of being myself, and made noises that I thought out of character. She puffed. She grunted. Once or twice I swear she roared. We brought the symphony to a fine Beethovenian finish with a series of crashing chords. Then Myrrha went to sleep again.

So did I. But not before she did, and I was lost in wonderment.

I do not know how long it was until Myrrha woke, snapped on her bedside light, and said, "Good God, sweetie, it's time you went home." It was in that instant of sudden light that I saw her differently. I had not observed that her skin did not fit quite so tightly as it once had done, and there were some little puckers at the armpits and between the breasts. When she lay on her side her stomach hung down, slightly but perceptibly. And under the light of the lamp, which was so close, her hair had a metallic sheen. As she turned to kiss me, she drew one of her legs across mine, and it was like a rasp. I knew women shaved their legs, for I had seen Carol do it, but I did not know that this sandpaper effect was the result. I kissed her, but without making a big thing of it, dressed myself, and prepared to leave. What was I to say?

"Thanks for a wonderful evening, and everything," I said.

"Bless you, darling," said she, laughing. "Will you turn out the lights in the sitting-room as you go?" and with that she turned over, dragging most of the bed-clothes with her, and prepared to sleep again.

It was not a great distance back to the Ritz, and I walked through the snowy night, thinking deeply. So that was what sex was! I dropped into a little all-night place and had two bacon-and-egg sandwiches, two slices of their hot mince pie, and two cups of chocolate with whipped cream, for I found I was very hungry.

DR. VON HALLER: When did you realize that this ceremony of initiation was arranged between your father and Mrs. Martindale?

MYSELF: Father told me as we went back to Toronto in the train; but I didn't realize it until I had a terrible row with Knopwood. What I mean is, Father didn't say in so many words that it was an arranged thing, but I suppose he was proud of what he had done for me, and he gave some broad hints that I was too stupid to take. He said what a wonderful woman she was and what an accomplished amorist—that was a new word to me—and that if there were such a thing as a female swordsman, certainly Myrrha Martindale was one.

DR. VON HALLER: How did he bring up the subject?

MYSELF: He remarked that I was looking very pleased with myself, and that I must have enjoyed my evening with Myrrha. Well, I knew that you aren't supposed to blab about these things, and anyhow she was Father's friend and perhaps he felt tenderly toward her and might be hurt if he discovered she had fallen for me so quickly. So I simply said I had, and he said she could teach me a great deal, and I said yes, she was very well read, and he laughed and said that she could teach me a good deal that wasn't to be found in books. Things that would be very helpful to me with my little Jewish piece. I was shocked to hear Judy called a "piece" because it isn't a word you use about anybody you love or respect, and I tried to set him right about Judy and how marvellous she was and what very nice people her family were. It was then he became serious about never marrying a girl you met when you were very young. "If you want fruit, take all you want, but don't buy the tree," he said. It hurt me to hear him talk that way when Judy was obviously in his mind, and then when he went on to talk about swordsmen I began to wonder for the first time if I knew everything there was to know about that word.

DR. VON HALLER: But did he say outright that he had arranged your adventure?

MYSELF: Never flatly. Never in so many words. But he talked about the wounding experiences young men often had learning about sex from prostitutes or getting mixed up with virgins, and said that the only good way was with an experienced older woman, and that I would bless Myrrha as long as I lived, and be grateful it had been managed so intelligently and pleasantly. That's the way the French do it, he said.

DR. VON HALLER: Was Myrrha Martindale his mistress?

MYSELF: Oh, I don't imagine so for a minute. Though he did leave some money for her in his will, and I know from things that came out later that he helped her with money from time to time. But if he ever had an affair with her, I'm sure it was because he loved her. It couldn't have been a money thing.

DR. VON HALLER: Why not?

MYSELF: It would be sordid, and Father always had such style.

DR. VON HALLER: Have you ever read Voltaire's *Candide?*

MYSELF: That was what Knopwood asked me. I hadn't, and he explained that Candide was a simpleton who believed everything he was told. Knopwood was furious with Father. But he didn't know Father, you see.

DR. VON HALLER: And you did?

MYSELF: I sometimes think I knew him better than anyone. Do you suggest I didn't?

DR. VON HALLER: That is one of the things we are working to find out. Tell me about your row with Father Knopwood.

I suppose I brought it on because I went to see Knopwood a
few days after returning to Toronto. I was in a confused state
of mind. I didn't regret anything about Myrrha; I was grateful
to her, just as Father had said, though I thought I had noticed
one or two things about her that had escaped him, or that he
didn't care about. Really they only meant that she wasn't as
young as Judy. But I was worried about my feelings toward
Judy. I had gone to see her as soon as I could after returning
from Montreal; she was ill—bad headache or something—and
her father asked me to chat for a while. He was kind, but he
was direct. Said he thought Judy and I should stop seeing each
other so much, because we weren't children any longer, and we
might become involved in a way we would regret. I knew he
meant he was afraid I might seduce her, so I told him I loved
her, and would never do anything to hurt her, and respected
her too much to get her into any kind of mess. Yes, he said, but
there are times when good resolutions weaken, and there are
also hurts that are not hurts of the flesh. Then he said something I could hardly believe; he said that he was not sure Judy
might not weaken at some time when I was also weak, and
then what would our compounded weakness lead to? I had
assumed the man always led in these things, and when I said
that to Dr. Wolff he smiled in what I can only describe as a
Viennese way.

"You and Judy have something that is charming and beautiful," he said, "and I advise you to cherish it as it is, for then it
will always be a delight to you. But if you go on, we shall all
change our roles; I shall have to be unpleasant to you, which I
have no wish to do, and you will begin to hate me, which

would be a pity, and perhaps you and Judy will decide that in order to preserve your self-respect you must deceive me and Judy's mother. That would be painful to us, and I assure you it would also be dangerous to you."

Then he did an extraordinary thing. He quoted Burns to me! Nobody had ever done that except my Cruikshank grandfather, down by the crick in Deptford, and I had always assumed that Burns was a sort of crick person's poet. But here was this Viennese Jew, saying,

> "The sacred lowe of weel-placed love,
>   Luxuriously indulge it;
> But never tempt th' illicit rove
>   Tho' naething should divulge it;
> I waive the quantum of the sin
>   The hazard of concealing;
> But, och! it hardens a' within,
>   And petrifies the feeling.

"You are a particularly gentle boy," he said (and I was startled and resented it); "it would not take many bad experiences to scar your feelings over and make you much less than the man you may otherwise become. If you seduced my daughter, I should be very angry and might hate you; the physical injury is really not very much, if indeed it is anything at all, but the psychological injury—you see I am too much caught up in the modern way of speaking to be quite able to say the spiritual injury—could be serious if we all parted bad friends. There are people, of course, to whom such things are not important, and I fear you have had a bad example, but you and Judy are not such people. So be warned, David, and be our friend always; but you will never be my daughter's husband, and you must understand that now."

"Why are you so determined I should never be Judy's husband?" I asked.

"I am not determined alone," said he. "There are many hundreds of determining factors on both sides. They are called ancestors, and there are some things in which we are wise not to defy them."

"You mean, I'm not a Jew," I said.

"I had begun to wonder if you would get to it," said Dr. Wolff.

"But does that matter in this day and age?" I said.

"You were born in 1928, when it began to matter terribly, and not for the first time in history," said Dr. Wolff. "But set that aside. There is another way it matters which I do not like to mention because I do not want to hurt you and I like you very much. It is a question of pride."

We talked further, but I knew the conversation was over. They were planning to send Judy to school abroad in the spring. They would be happy to see me from time to time until then. But I must understand that the Wolffs had talked to Judy, and though Judy felt very badly, she had seen the point. And that was that.

It was that night I went to Knopwood. I was working up a rage against the Wolffs. A question of pride! Did that mean I wasn't good enough for Judy? And what did all this stuff about being Jews mean from people who gave no obvious external evidence of their Jewishness? If they were such great Jews, where were their side-curls and their funny underwear and their queer food? I had heard of these things as belonging to the bearded Jews in velours hats who lived down behind the Art Gallery. I had assumed the Wolffs and the Schwarzes were trying to be like us; instead I had been told I wasn't good enough for them! Affronted Christianity roiled up inside me. Christ had died for me, I was certain, but I wouldn't take any bets on His having died for the Wolffs and the Schwarzes! Off to Knopwood! He would know.

I was with him all evening, and in the course of an involved conversation everything came out. To my astonishment he sided with Louis Wolff. But worst of all, he attacked Father in terms I had never heard from him, and he was amused, and contemptuous and angry about Myrrha.

"You triple-turned jackass!" he said, "couldn't you see it was an arranged thing? And you thought it was your own attraction that got you into bed with such a scarred old veteran! I don't blame you for going to bed with her; show an ass a peck of oats and he'll eat it, even if the oats is musty. But it is the provincial vulgarity of the whole thing that turns my stomach —the winesmanship and the tatty gallantries and the candlelit frumpery of it! The 'good talk,' the imitations of Churchill by your father, the quotations from *The Rubaiyat*. If I could have my way I'd call in every copy of that twenty-fourth-rate rhymed gospel of hedonism and burn it! How it goes to the hearts of trashy people! So Myrhha matched verses with you, did she? Well, did the literary strumpet quote this—

> " 'Well,' murmured one, 'Let whoso make or buy,
> My Clay with long Oblivion is gone dry:
> But fill me with the old familiar Juice
> Methinks I might recover by and by.'

Did she whisper that in your ear as Absalom went in unto his father's concubine?"

"You don't understand," I said; "this is a thing French families do to see that their sons learn about sex in the right way."

"Yes, I have heard that, but I didn't know they put their cast mistresses to the work, the way you put a child rider on your safe old mare."

"That's enough, Knoppy," I said; "you know a lot about the Church and religion, but I don't think that qualifies you to talk about what it is to be a swordsman."

That made him really furious. He became cold and courteous.

"Help me then," he said. "Tell me what a swordsman is and what lies behind the mystique of the swordsman."

I talked as well as I could about living with style, and not sticking to dowdy people's ways. I managed to work in the word amorist because I thought he might not know it. I talked about the Cavaliers as opposed to the Roundheads, and I dragged in Mackenzie King as a sort of two-bit Cromwell, who had to be resisted. Mr. King had made himself unpopular early in the war by urging the Canadian people to "buckle on the whole armour of God," which when it was interpreted meant watering and rationing whisky without reducing the price. I said that if that was the armour of God, I would back the skill and panache of the swordsman against it any day. As I talked he seemed to be less angry, and when I had finished he was almost laughing.

"My poor Davey," he said, "I have always known you were an innocent boy, but I have hoped your innocence was not just the charming side of a crippling stupidity. And now I am going to try to do something that I had never expected to do, and of which I disapprove, but which I think is necessary if between us we are going to save your soul. I am going to disillusion you about your father."

He didn't, of course. Not wholly. He talked a lot about Father as a great man of business, but that cut no ice with me. I don't mean he suggested Father was anything but honest, because there were never any grounds for that. But he talked about the corrupting power of great wealth and the illusion it created in its possessor that he could manipulate people, and the dreadful truth that there were a great many people whom he undoubtedly could manipulate, so that the illusion was never seriously challenged. He talked about the illusion wealth creates that its possessor is of a different clay from that of common men. He talked about the adulation great wealth attracts from people to whom worldly success is the only measure of worth. Wealth bred and fostered illusion and illusion brought corruption. That was his theme.

I was ready for all of this because Father had talked a great deal to me since he began to be more at home. Father said that a man you could manipulate had to be watched because other people could manipulate him as well. Father had also said that the rich man differed from the ordinary man only in that he had a wider choice, and that one of his dangerous choices was a lightly disguised slavery to the source of his wealth. I even told Knoppy something he had never guessed. It was about what Father called the Pathological Compassion of Big Business, which seems to demand that above a certain executive level a man's incompetence or loss of quality had to be kept from him so that he would not be destroyed in the eyes of his family, his friends, and himself. Father estimated that Corporation Compassion cost him a few hundred thousand every year, and this was charity of a kind St. Paul had never foreseen. Like a lot of people who have no money, Knoppy had some half-baked ideas about people who had it, and the foremost of these was that wealth was achieved, and held, only by people who were essentially base. I accused him of lack of charity, which I knew was a very great matter to him. I accused him of a covert, Christian jealousy, that blinded him to Father's real worth because he could not see beyond his wealth. People strong enough to get wealth are sometimes strong enough to resist illusion. Father was such a man.

"You should do well at the Bar, Davey," he said. "You are already an expert at making the worser seem the better cause.

To be cynical is not the same as avoiding illusion, for cynicism is just another kind of illusion. All formulas for meeting life —even many philosophies—are illusion. Cynicism is a trashy illusion. But a swordsman—shall I tell you what a swordsman is? It is just what the word implies: a swordsman is an expert at sticking something long and thin, or thick and curved, into other people; and always with intent to wound. You've read a lot lately. You've read some D. H. Lawrence. Do you remember what he says about heartless, cold-blooded fucking? That's what a swordsman is good at, as the word is used nowadays by the kind of people who use it of your father. A swordsman is what the Puritans you despise so romantically would call a whoremaster. Didn't you know that? Of course swordsmen don't use the word that way; they use other terms, like amorist, though that usually means somebody like your Myrrha, who is a great proficient at sex without love. Is that what you want? You've told me a great deal about what you feel for Judy Wolff. Now you have had some skilful instruction in the swordsman-and-amorist game. What is it? Nothing but the cheerful trumpet-and-drum of the act of kind. Simple music for simple souls. Is that what you want with Judy? Because that is what her father fears. He doesn't want his daughter's life to be blighted by a whoremaster's son and, as he very shrewdly suspects, a whoremaster's pupil."

This was hitting hard, and though I tried to answer him I knew I was squirming. Because—believe it or not, but I swear it is the truth—I had never understood that was what people meant when they talked about a swordsman, and it suddenly accounted for some of the queer responses I had met with when I applied the word so proudly to Father. I remembered with a chill that I had even used this word about him to the Wolffs, and I was sure they were up to every nuance of speech in three languages. I had made a fool of myself, and of course the realization made me both weak and angry. I lashed out at Knoppy.

"All very well for you to be so pernickety about people's sexual tastes," I said. "But what cap do you wear? Everybody knows what you are. You're a fairy. You're a fairy who's afraid to do anything about it. So what makes you such an authority about real men and women, who have passions you can't begin to share or understand?"

I had hit home. Or so I thought. He seemed to become smaller in his chair, and all the anger had gone out of him.

"Davey, I want you to listen very carefully," he said. "I suppose I am a homosexual, really. Indeed, I know it. I'm a priest, too. By efforts that have not been trivial I have worked for over twenty years to keep myself always in full realization of both facts and to put what I am and the direction in which my nature leads me at the service of my faith and its founder. People wounded much worse than I have been good fighters in that cause. I have not done too badly. I should be stupid and falsely humble if I said otherwise. I have done it gladly, and I shall only say that it has not been easy. But it was my personal sacrifice of what I was to what I loved.

"Now I want you to remember something because I don't think we shall meet again very soon. It is this; however fashionable despair about the world and about people may be at present, and however powerful despair may become in the future, not everybody, or even most people, think and live fashionably; virtue and honour will not be banished from the world, however many popular moralists and panicky journalists say so. Sacrifice will not cease to be because psychiatrists have popularized the idea that there is often some concealed, self-serving element in it; theologians always knew that. Nor do I think love as a high condition of honour will be lost; it is a pattern in the spirit, and people long to make the pattern a reality in their own lives, whatever means they take to do so. In short, Davey, God is not dead. And I can assure you God is not mocked."

(10)

I never saw Knopwood after that. What he meant when he said we would not meet again was soon explained; he had been ordered off to some more missionary work, and he died a few years ago in the West, of tuberculosis, working almost till the end among his Indians. I have never forgiven him for trying to blacken Father. If that is what his Christianity added up to, it wasn't much.

DR. VON HALLER: As you report what Father Knopwood said about Mrs. Martindale, he was abusive and contemptuous; did he know her, by any chance?

MYSELF: No, he just hated her because she was very much a woman, and I have told you what he was. He made up his mind she was a harlot, and that was that.

DR. VON HALLER: You don't think any of it was indignation on your behalf—because she had, so to speak, abused your innocence?

MYSELF: How had she done that? I think that's silly.

DR. VON HALLER: She had been party to a plan to manipulate you in a certain direction. I don't mean your virginity, which is simply physical and technical, but the scheme to introduce you to what Knopwood called the cheerful trumpet-and-drum, the simple music.

MYSELF: One has to meet it somehow, I suppose? Better in such circumstances than many we can imagine. I had forgotten the Swiss were so Puritanical.

DR. VON HALLER: Ah, now you are talking to me as if I were Father Knopwood. True, everybody has to encounter sex, but usually the choice is left to themselves. They find it; it is not offered to them like a tonic when somebody else thinks it would be good for them. May not the individual know the right time better than someone else? Is it not rather patronizing to arrange a first sexual encounter for one's son?

MYSELF: No more patronizing than to send him to any other school, so far as I can see.

DR. VON HALLER: So you are in complete agreement with what was arranged for you. Let me see—did you not say that the last time you had sexual intercourse was on December 26, 1945?—Was Mrs. Martindale the first and the last, then? —Why did you hesitate to put this valuable instruction to fur ther use?—Take all the time you please, Mr. Staunton. If you would like a glass of water there is a carafe beside you.

MYSELF: It was Judy, I suppose.

DR. VON HALLER: Yes. About Judy—do you realize that in what you have been telling me Judy remains very dim? I am getting to know your father, and I have a good idea of Father Knopwood, and you implied much about Mrs. Martindale in a very few words. But I see very little of Judy. A well-bred girl, somewhat foreign to your world, Jewish, who sings. Otherwise you say only that she was kind and delightful and vague words like that which give her no individuality at all. Your sister suggested that she was cowlike; I attach quite a lot of significance to that.

MYSELF: Don't. Carol is very sharp.

DR. VON HALLER: Indeed she is. You have given a sharp picture of her. She is very perceptive. And she said Judy was cowlike. Do you know why?

MYSELF: Spite, obviously. She sensed I loved Judy.

DR. VON HALLER: She sensed Judy was an Anima-figure to you. Now we must be technical for a little while. We talked about the Anima as a general term for a man's idea of all a woman is or may be. Women are very much aware of this figure when it is aroused in men. Carol sensed that Judy had suddenly embodied the Anima for you, and she was irritated. You know how women are always saying, "What does he see in her?" Of course what he sees is the Anima. Furthermore, he is usually only able to describe it in general terms, not in detail. He is in the grip of something that might as well be called an enchantment; the old word is as good as any new one. It is notorious that when one is enchanted, one does not see clearly.

MYSELF: Judy was certainly clear to me.

DR. VON HALLER: Even though you do not seem to remember one thing she said that is not a commonplace? Oh, Mr. Staunton—a pretty, modest girl, whom you saw for the first time in enchanting circumstances, singing—an Anima, if ever I heard of one.

MYSELF: I thought you people weren't supposed to lead your witnesses?

DR. VON HALLER: Not in Mr. Justice Staunton's court, perhaps, but this is my court. Now tell me; after your talk with your father, in which he referred to Judy as "your little Jewish piece," and your talk with her father, when he said you must not think of Judy as a possible partner in your life, and after your talk with that third father, the priest, how did matters stand between you and Judy?

MYSELF: It went sour. Or it lost its gloss. Or anything you like to express a drop in intensity, a loss of power. Of course we met and talked and kissed. But I knew she was an obedient daughter, and when we kissed I knew Louis Wolff was near, though invisible. And try as I would, when we kissed I could hear a voice—it wasn't my father's, so don't think it was—saying "your Jewish piece." And hateful Knopwood seemed always to be near, like Christ in his sentimental picture, with His hand on the Boy Scout's shoulder. I don't know how it would have worked out because I had rather a miserable illness. It would probably be called mononucleosis now, but they didn't know what it was then, and I was out of school for a long time and confined to the house with Netty as my nurse. When Easter came I was still very weak, and Judy went to Lausanne to a school. She sent me a letter, and I meant to keep it, of course, but I'll bet any money Netty took it and burned it.

DR. VON HALLER: But you remember what it said?

MYSELF: I remember some of it. She wrote, "My father is the wisest and best man I know, and I shall do what he says." It seemed extraordinary, for a girl of seventeen.

DR. VON HALLER: How, extraordinary?

MYSELF: Immature. Wouldn't you say so? Oughtn't she to have had more mind of her own?

DR. VON HALLER: But wasn't that precisely your attitude toward your own father?

MYSELF: Not after my illness. Nevertheless, there was a difference. Because my father really was a great man. Dunstan Ramsay once said he was a genius of an unusual, unrecognized kind. Whereas Louis Wolff, though very good of his kind, was just a clever doctor.

DR. VON HALLER: A very sophisticated man; sophisticated in a way your father was not, it appears. And what about Knopwood? You seem to have dismissed him because he was a homosexual.

MYSELF: I see a good many of his kind in court. You can't take them seriously.

DR. VON HALLER: But you take very few people seriously when you have them in court. There are homosexuals we do well to take seriously and you are not likely to meet them in court. You spoke, I recall, of Christian charity?

MYSELF: I am no longer a Christian, and too often I have uncovered pitiable weakness masquerading as charity. Those who talk about charity and forgiveness usually lack the guts to push anything to a logical conclusion. I've never seen charity bring any unquestionable good in its train.

DR. VON HALLER: I see. Very well, let us go on. During your illness I suppose you did a lot of thinking about your situation. That is what these illnesses are for, you know—these mysterious ailments that take us out of life but do not kill us. They are signals that our life is going the wrong way, and intervals for reflection. You were lucky to be able to keep out of a hospital, even if it did return you to the domination of Netty. Now, what answers did you find? For instance, did you think about why you were so ready to believe your mother had been the lover of your father's best friend, whereas you doubted that Mrs. Martindale had been your father's mistress?

MYSELF: I suppose children favour one parent more than the other. I have told you about Mother. And Father used to talk about her sometimes when he visited me when I was ill. Several times he warned me against marrying a boyhood sweetheart.

DR. VON HALLER: Yes, I suppose he knew what was wrong with you. People often do, you know, though nothing would persuade them to bring such knowledge to the surface of their thoughts or admit what they so deeply know. He sensed you were sick for Judy. And he gave you very good advice, really.

MYSELF: But I loved Judy. I really did.

DR. VON HALLER: You loved a projection of your own Anima. You really did. But did you ever know Judy Wolff? You have told me that when you see her now, as a grown woman with a husband and family, you never speak to her.

Why? Because you are protecting your boyhood dream. You don't want to meet this woman who is somebody else. When you go home you had better make an opportunity to meet Mrs. Professor Whoever-It-Is, and lay that ghost forever. It will be quite easy, I assure you. You will see her as she is now, and she will see the famous criminal lawyer. It will all be smooth as silk, and you will be delivered forever. So far as possible, lay your ghosts. . . . But you have not answered my question: why adultery for mother but not for father?

MYSELF: Mother was weak.

DR. VON HALLER: Mother was your father's Anima-figure, whom he had been so unfortunate, or so unwise, as to marry. No wonder she seemed weak, poor woman, with such a load to carry for such a man. And no wonder he turned against her, as you would probably have turned against poor Judy if she had been so unfortunate as to fall into the clutch of such a clever thinker and such a primitive feeler as you are. Oh, men revenge themselves very thoroughly on women they think have enchanted them, when really these poor devils of women are merely destined to be pretty or sing nicely or laugh at the right time.

MYSELF: Don't you think there is any element of enchantment in love, then?

DR. VON HALLER: I know perfectly well that there is, but has anybody ever said that enchantment was a basis for marriage? It will be there at the beginning, probably, but the table must be laid with more solid fare than that if starvation is to be kept at bay for sixty years.

MYSELF: You are unusually dogmatic today.

DR. VON HALLER: You have told me you like dogma. . . . But let us get back to an unanswered question: why did you believe your mother capable of adultery but not your father?

MYSELF: Well—adultery in a woman may be a slip, a peccadillo, but in a man, you see—you see, it's an offense against property. I know it doesn't sound very pretty, but the law makes it plain and public opinion makes it plainer. A deceived husband is merely a cuckold, a figure of fun, whereas a deceived wife is someone who has sustained an injury. Don't ask me why; I simply state the fact as society and the courts see it.

DR. VON HALLER: But this Mrs. Martindale, if I understood you, had left her husband, or he had left her. So what injury could there be?

MYSELF: I am thinking of my mother: Father knew her long before Mother's death. He may have drifted away from Mother, but I can't believe he would do anything that would injure her—that might have played some part in her death. I mean, a swordsman is one thing—a sort of chivalrous concept, which may be romantic but is certainly not squalid. But an adulterer—I've seen a lot of them in court, and none of them was anything but squalid.

DR. VON HALLER: And you could not associate your father with anything you considered squalid? So: you emerged from this illness without your beloved, and without your priest, but with your father still firmly in the saddle?

MYSELF: Not even that. I still adored him, but my adoration was flawed with doubts. That was why I determined not to try to be like him, not to permit myself any thought of rivalling him but to try to find some realm where I could show that I was worthy of him.

DR. VON HALLER: My God, what a fanatic!

MYSELF: That seems a rather unprofessional outburst.

DR. VON HALLER: Not a bit. You are a fanatic. Don't you know what fanaticism is? It is overcompensation for doubt. Well: go on.

Yes, I went on, and what my life lacked in incident it made up for in intensity. I finished school, pretty well but not as well as if I had not had such a long illness, and I was ready for university. Father had always assumed I would go to the University of Toronto, but I wanted to go to Oxford, and he jumped at that. He had never been to a university himself because he was in the First World War—got the D.S.O., too—during what would have been his college years; he had wanted to get on with life and had qualified as a lawyer without taking a degree. You could still do that, then. But he had romantic ideas about universities, and Oxford appealed to him. So I went there, and because Father wanted me to be in a big college, I got into Christ Church.

People are always writing in their memoirs about what Oxford meant to them. I can't pretend the place itself meant extraordinary things to me. Of course it was pleasant, and I liked the interesting buildings; architectural critics are always knocking them, but after Toronto they made my eyes pop. They spoke of an idea of education strange to me; discomfort there was, but no meanness, no hint of edification on the cheap. And I liked the feel of a city of youth, which is what Oxford seems to be, though anybody with eyes in his head can see that it is run by old men. But my Oxford was a post-war Oxford, crammed to the walls and rapidly growing into a big industrial city. And there was much criticism of the privilege it implied, mostly from people who were sitting bang in the middle of the privilege and getting all they could out of it. Oxford was part of my plan to become a special sort of man, and I bent everything that came my way to my single purpose.

I read law, and did well at it. I was very lucky in being assigned Pargetter of Balliol as my tutor. He was a great law don, a blind man who nevertheless managed to be a famous chess-player and such a teacher as I had never known. He was relentless and exacting, which was precisely what I wanted because I was determined to be a first-class lawyer. You see, when I told Father I wanted to be a lawyer, he assumed at once that I wanted law as a preparation for business, which was what he himself had made of it. He was sure I would follow him in Alpha; indeed I don't think any other future for me seemed possible to him. I was perhaps a little bit devious because I did not tell him at once that I had other ideas. I wanted the law because I wanted to master something in which I would know where I stood and which would not be open to the whims and preconceptions of people like Louis Wolff, or Knopwood—or Father. I wanted to be a master of my own craft and I wanted a great craft. Also, I wanted to know a great deal about people, and I wanted a body of knowledge that would go as far as possible to explain people. I wanted to work in a realm that would give me some insight into the spirit that I had seen at work in Bill Unsworth.

I had no notions of being a crusader. One of the things I had arrived at during that wearisome, depleting illness was a determination to be done forever with everything that Father Knopwood stood for. Knoppy, I saw, wanted to manipulate people; he wanted to make them good, and he was sure he knew what was good. For him, God was here and Christ was now. He was prepared to accept himself and impose on others a lot of irrational notions in the interests of his special idea of goodness. He thought God was not mocked. I seemed to see God being mocked, and rewarding the mocker with splendid success, every day of my life.

I wanted to get away from the world of Louis Wolff, who now appeared to me as an extremely shrewd man whose culture was never allowed for an instant to interfere with some age-old ideas that governed him and must also govern his family.

I wanted to get away from Father and save my soul, insofar as I believed in such a thing. I suppose what I meant by my soul was my self-respect or my manhood. I loved him and feared him, but I had spied tiny chinks in his armour. He too was a manipulator and, remembering his own dictum, I did not mean to be a man who could be manipulated. I knew I would always be known as his son and that I would in some ways have to carry the weight of wealth that I had not gained myself in a society where inherited wealth always implies a stigma. But somehow, in some part of the great world, I would be David Staunton, unreachable by Knopwood or Louis Wolff, or Father, because I had outstripped them.

The idea of putting sex aside never entered my head. It just happened, and I was not aware that it had become part of my way of living until it was thoroughly established. Pargetter may have had something to do with it. He was unmarried, and being blind he was insulated against a great part of the charm of women. He seized on me, as he did on all his students, with an eagle's talons, but I think he knew by the end of my first year that I was his in a way that the others, however admiring, were not. If you hope to master the law, he would say, you are a fool, for it has no single masters; but if you hope to master some part of it, you had better put your emotions in cold storage at least until you are thirty. I decided to do that, and did it, and by the time I was thirty I liked the chill. It helped to make people afraid of me, and I liked that, too.

Pargetter must have taken to me, though he was not a man to hint at any such thing. He taught me chess, and although I was never up to his standard I grew to play well. His room never had enough light, because he didn't need it and I think he was a little cranky about making people who had their eyesight use it to the full. We would sit by his insufficient fire in a twilight that could have been dismal, but which he contrived somehow to give a legal quality, and play game after game; he sat fatly in his arm-chair, and I sat by the board and made all the moves; he would call his move, I would place the piece as he directed, and then I would tell him my counter-move. When he had beaten me he would go back over the game and tell me precisely the point at which I had gone wrong. I was awed by such a memory and such a spatial sense in a man who lived in darkness; he was contemptuous of me when I could not remember what I had done six or eight moves back, and of sheer necessity I had to develop the memory-trick myself.

He really was alarming: he had three or four boards set up around his room, on which he played chess by post with friends far away. If I arrived for an early tutorial he would say, "There's a postcard on the table; I expect it's from Johannesburg; read it." I would read a chess move from it and make the move on a board which he had not touched for perhaps a month. When my tutorial was finished he would dictate a counter-move to me, and I would rearrange the board accordingly. He won a surprising number of these long-distance, tortoise-paced games.

He had never learned Braille. He wrote in longhand on paper he fitted into a frame which had guide-wires to keep him on the lines, and he never seemed to forget anything he had written. He had a prodigious knowledge of law books he had never seen, and when he sent me, with exact directions, to his shelves to hunt up a reference, I often found a slip of paper in the book with a note in his careful, printlike hand. He kept up with books and journals by having them read to him, and I felt myself favoured when he began to ask me to read; he would make invaluable comment as he listened, and it was always a master-lesson in how to absorb, weigh, select, and reject.

This was precisely what I wanted and I came almost to worship Pargetter. Exactitude, calm appraisal, close reasoning applied to problems which so often had their beginning in other people's untidy emotions acted like balm on my hurt mind. It was not ordinary legal instruction and it did not result in ordinary legal practice. Many lawyers are beetle-witted ignoramuses, prey to their own emotions and those of their clients; some of them work up big practices because they can fling themselves fiercely into other people's fights. Their indignation is for sale. But Pargetter had honed his mind to a shrewd edge, and I wanted to be like Pargetter. I wanted to know, to see, to sift, and not to be moved. I wanted to get as far as possible from that silly boy who had not realized what a swordsman was when everybody else knew, and who mooned over Judy Wolff and was sent away by her father to play with other toys. I wanted to be melted down, purged of dross, and remoulded in a new and better form; Pargetter was just the man to do it. I had other instructors, of course, and some of them were very good, but Pargetter continues to be my ideal, my father in art.

(11)

I wrote to Father every week and grew aware that my letters were less and less communicative, for I was entering a world where he could not follow. I visited Canada once a year, for as short a time as I could manage, and it was when I was about to enter my third year at Oxford that he took me to dinner one night, and after some havering which I realize now was shyness about what he was going to say, he made what seemed to me to be an odd request.

"I've been wondering about the Stauntons," he said. "Who

do you suppose they could have been? I can't find out anything about Father, though I've wormed out a few facts. He graduated from the medical school here in Toronto in 1887, and the records say he was twenty then, so he must have been born in 1867. They really just gave doctors a lick and a promise then, and I don't suppose he knew much medicine. He was a queer old devil, and as you probably know, we never hit it off. All I know about his background is that he wasn't born in Canada. Mother was, and I've traced her family, and it was easy and dull; farmers culminating in a preacher. But who was Dr. Henry Staunton? I want to know. You see, Davey, though it sounds vain, I have a strong hunch that there must be some good blood somewhere in our background. Your grandfather had a lot of ability as a businessman; more than I could ever persuade him to put to work. His plunge into sugar, when nobody else could see its possibilities, took imagination. I mean, when he was a young man, a lot of people were still rasping their sugar off a loaf with a file, and it all came from the Islands. He had drive and foresight. Of course lots of quite ordinary people have done very well for themselves, but I wonder if he was quite ordinary? When I was in England during the war I wanted to look around and find out anything I could, but the time was wrong and I was very busy with immediate things. But I met two people over there at different times who asked me if I were one of the Warwickshire Stauntons. Well, you know how Englishmen like it when Canadians play simple and rough-hewn, so I always answered that so far as I knew I was one of the Pitt County Stauntons. But I tucked it away in the back of my mind, and it might just be so. Who the Warwickshire Stauntons are I haven't the slightest idea, but they appear to be well known to people who are interested in old families. So, when you go back to Oxford, I'd like you to make some enquiries and let me know what you find. We're probably bastards, or something, but I'd like to know for certain."

I had long known Father was a romantic, and I had once been a romantic myself—two or three years ago—so I said I would do what I could.

How? And what? Go to Warwickshire and find the Stauntons, and ask if they had any knowledge of a physician who had been Pitt County's foremost expert on constipation, and to the end of his days a firm believer in *lignum vitae* sap as a treatment for rheumatism? Not for me, thank you. But one day in the Common Room I was looking through the *Times Literary Supplement,* and my eye fell on a modest advertisement. I can see it now:

> GENEALOGIES erected and pedigrees searched by an Oxonian curiously qualified. Strict confidence exacted and extended.

This was what I wanted. I made a note of the box number, and that night I wrote my letter. I wanted a pedigree searched, I said, and if it proved possible to erect a genealogy on it I should like that, too.

I don't know what I expected, but the advertisement suggested a pedant well past youth and of a sharp temper. I was utterly unprepared for the curiously qualified Oxonian when he arrived in my study two days later. He seemed not to be much older than myself, and had a shy, girlish manner and the softest voice that was compatible with being heard at all. The only elderly or pedantic thing about him was a pair of spectacles of a kind nobody wore then—gold-rimmed and with small oval lenses.

"I thought I'd come round instead of writing, because we are near neighbours," he said, and handed me a cheap visiting-card on which was printed—

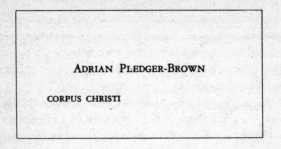

ADRIAN PLEDGER-BROWN

CORPUS CHRISTI

So this was the curiously qualified Oxonian!

"Sit down," I said. "You erect genealogies?"

"Oh, indeed," he breathed. "That is to say, I know precisely how it is done. That is to say, I have examined many scores of pedigrees which have already been erected, and I am sure I could do it myself if I were to be entrusted with such a task. It involves research, you see, of a kind I understand quite well and could undertake with a very fair likelihood of success. I know, you see, where to look, and that is everything. Almost everything."

He smiled such a girlish smile and his eyes swam so unassumingly behind the comic specs that I was tempted to be easy with him. But that was not the Pargetter way. Beware of a witness who appeals to you, he said. Repress any personal response, and if it seems to be gaining the upper hand, go to the other extreme and be severe with the witness. If Ogilvie had remembered that in Cripps-Armstrong *vs.* Clatterbos & Dudley in 1884 he would have won the case, but he let Clatterbos's difficulty with English arouse his compassion; it's a famous instance. So I sprang upon Pledger-Brown, and rent him.

"Am I right in deducing that you have never erected a genealogy independently before?"

"That would be—well, to put it baldly—yes, you might say that."

"Never mind what I might say or might not say. I asked a plain question, and I want a plain answer. Is this your first job?"

"My first professional engagement? Working as an independent investigator? If you wish to put it that way, I suppose the answer must be that it is."

"Aha! You are in a word, a greenhorn."

"Oh, dear, no. I mean, I have studied the subject, and the method, extensively."

"But you have never done a job of this kind before, for a fee. Yes or no?"

"To be completely frank, yes; or rather, no."

"But your advertisement said 'curiously qualified.' Tell me, Mr.—(business of consulting card)—ah, Pledger-Brown, in precisely what direction does your curious qualification lie?"

"I am the godson of Garter."

"Godson of—?"

"Garter."

"I do not understand."

"Quite possibly not. But that is why you need me, you see. I mean, people who want genealogies erected and pedigrees searched don't usually know these things. Americans in particular. I mean that my godfather is the Garter King of Arms."

"What's that?"

"He is the principal officer of the College of Heralds. I hope that one day, with luck, I may be a member of the College myself. But I must make a beginning somewhere, you see."

"Somewhere? What do you imply by somewhere? You regard me as a starting-point, is that it? I would be rough material for your prentice-hand; is that what you mean?"

"Oh, dear me, no. But I must do some independent work before I can hope to get an official appointment, mustn't I?"

"How should I know what you must do? What I want to

know is whether there is any chance that you can undertake the job I want done and do it properly."

"Well, Mr. Staunton, I don't think anybody will do it for you if you go on like this."

"Like this? Like this? I don't understand you. What fault have you to find with the way I have been going on, as you express it?"

Pledger-Brown was all mildness, and his smile was like a Victorian picture of a village maiden.

"Well, I mean playing Serjeant Buzfuz and treating me really quite rudely when I've only come in answer to your letter. You're a law student, of course. I've looked you up, you see. And your father is a prominent Canadian industrialist. I suppose you want some ancestors. Well, perhaps I can find some for you. And I want the work, but not badly enough to be bullied about it. I mean, I am a beginner at genealogy, but I've studied it: you're a beginner at the law, but you've studied it. So why are you so horrid when we are on an even footing?"

So I stopped being horrid, and in quite a short time he had accepted a glass of sherry and was calling me Staunton and I was calling him Pledger-Brown, and we were discussing what might be done.

He was in his third year at Corpus, which I could almost have hit with a stone from my windows, because I was in Canterbury Quad at the rear of Christ Church. He was mad for genealogy and couldn't wait to get at it, so he had advertised while he was still an undergraduate, and his anxiety for strict confidence was because his college would have been unsympathetic if they thought he was conducting any sort of business within their walls. He was obviously poor, but he had an air of breeding, and there was a strain of toughness in him that lay well below his wispy, maidenly ways. I took to him because he was as keen about his profession as I was about mine, and for anything I knew his diffidence may have been the professional manner of his kind. Soon he was cross-examining me.

"This Dr. Henry Staunton who has no known place of birth is a very common figure in genealogical work for people from the New World. But we can usually find the origin of such people, if we sift the parish records, wills, records of Chancery and Exchequer, and Manor Court Rolls. That takes a long time and runs into money. So we start with the obvious, hoping for a lucky hit. Of course, as your father thinks, he may be a Staunton of Longbridge in Warwickshire, but there are also Stauntons of Nottingham, Leicester, Lincolnshire, and Somerset, all of a quality that would please your father. But sometimes we can take a short cut. Was your grandfather an educated man?"

"He was a doctor. I wouldn't call him a man of wide cultivation."

"Good. That's often a help. I mean, such people often retain some individuality under the professional veneer. Perhaps he said some things that stuck in your mind? Used unusual words that might be county dialect words? Do you recall anything like that?"

I pondered. "Once he told my sister, Caroline, she had a tongue sharp enough to shave an urchin. I've repeated it to her often."

"Oh, that's quite helpful. He did use some dialect words then. But urchin as a word for the common hedgehog is very widespread in country districts. Can you think of anything more unusual?"

I was beginning to respect Pledger-Brown. I had always thought an urchin was a boy you didn't like, and could never figure out why Grandfather would want to shave one. I thought further.

"I do just remember that he called some of his old patients who stuck with him, and were valetudinarians, 'my old wallowcrops.' Is that of any use? Could he have made the word up?"

"Few simple people make up words. 'Wallowcrop'; I'll make a note of that and see what I can discover. Meanwhile keep thinking about him, will you? And I'll come again when I have a better idea what to do."

Think about Grandfather Staunton, powerful but dim in my past. A man, it seemed to me now, with a mind like a morgue in which a variety of defunct ideas lay on slabs, kept cold to defer decay. A man who knew nothing about health, but could identify a number of diseases. A man whose medical knowledge belonged to a time when people talked about The System and had spasms and believed in the efficacy of strong, clean smells, such as oil of peppermint, as charms against infection. A man who never doubted that spankings were good for children, and once soundly walloped both Caroline and me because we had put Eno's Fruit Salts in the bottom of Granny's chamber-pot, hoping she would have a fantod when it foamed. A furious teetotaller, malignantly contemptuous of what he called "booze-artists" and never fully reconciled to my father when he discovered that Father drank wines and spirits but had contumaciously failed thereby to become a booze-artist. A man whom I could only recall as gloomy, heavy, and dull, but pleased with his wealth and unaffectedly scornful of those who had not the wit or craft to equal it; preachers were excepted as being a class apart, and sacred, but needing frequent guidance from practical men in the conduct of their churches. In short, a nasty old village moneybags.

A strange conduit through which to convey the good blood Father thought we Stauntons must have. But then, Father had never troubled to pretend that he had much regard for Doc

Staunton. Which was strange in itself, in a way, for Father was very strong on the regard children should have for parents. Not that he ever said so directly, or urged Caroline and me to honour our father and mother. But I recall that he was down on H. G. Wells, because in his *Experiment in Autobiography* Wells had said frankly that his parents weren't up to much and that escape from them was his first step toward a good life. Father was not consistent. But Doc Staunton had been consistent, and what had consistency made of him?

The hunt was up, and Doc Staunton was the fox.

Notes from Pledger-Brown punctuated the year that followed. He wrote an elegant Italic hand, as became a genealogist, and scraps of intelligence would arrive by the college messenger service: *"Wallowcrop* Cumberland dialect word. Am following up this clue. A.P-B." And, "Sorry to say nothing comes of enquiries in Cumberland. Am casting about in Lincoln." Or, "Tally-ho! A Henry Staunton born 1866 in Somerset!" followed a week later by, "False scent; Somerset Henry died aged 3 mos." Clearly he was having a wonderful adventure, but I had little time to think about it. I was up to my eyes in Jurisprudence, that formal science of positive law, and in addition to formal studies Pargetter was making me read Kelly's *Famous Advocates and Their Speeches* and *British Forensic Eloquence* aloud to him, dissecting the rhetoric of notable counsel and trying to make some progress in that line myself. Pargetter was determined that I should not be what he called an ignorant pettifogger, and he made it clear that as a Canadian I started well behind scratch in the journey toward professional literacy and elegance.

" 'The law, besides being a profession, is one of the humanities,' " he said to me one day, and I knew from the way he spoke he was quoting. "Who said that?" I didn't know. "Then never forget that it was one of your countrymen, your present

Prime Minister, Louis St. Laurent," he said, punching me sharply in the side, as he often did when he wanted to make a point. "It's been said before, but it's never been said better. Be proud it was a Canadian who said it." And he went on to belabour me, as he had often done before, with Sir Walter Scott's low opinion of lawyers who knew nothing of history or literature; from these studies, said he, I would learn what people were and how they might be expected to behave. "But wouldn't I learn that from clients?" I asked, to try him. "Clients!" he said, and I would not have believed anyone could make a two-syllable word stretch out so long; "you'll learn precious little from clients except folly and duplicity and greed. You've got to stand above that."

Working as I was under the English system I had to be a member of one of the Inns of Court and go to London at intervals to eat dinners in its Hall; I was enrolled in the Middle Temple, and reverently chewed through the thirty-six obligatory meals. I liked it. I liked the ceremony and solemnity of the law, not only as safeguards against trivializing of the law but as pleasant observances in themselves. I visited the courts, studied the conduct and courtesy of their workings, and venerated judges who seemed able to carry a mass of detail in their heads and boil it down and serve it up in a kind of strong judicial consommé for the jury when all the pleading and testimony were over. I liked the romance of it, the star personalities of the great advocates, the swishing of gowns and flourishing of impractical but traditional blue bags full of papers. I was delighted that although most people seemed to use more modern instruments, everybody had access to quill pens, and could doubtless have called for sand to do their blotting, with full confidence that sand would have been forthcoming. I loved wigs, which established a hierarchy that was palpable and turned unremarkable faces into the faces of priests serving a great purpose. What if all this silk and bombazine and horsehair awed and even frightened the simple people who came to court for justice? It would do them no harm to be a little frightened. Everybody in court, except the occasional accused creature in the dock, seemed calmed, reft from the concerns of everyday; those who were speaking on oath seemed to me, very often, to be revealing an aspect of their best selves. The juries took their duties seriously, like good citizens. It was an arena in which gladiators struggled, but the end for which they struggled was that right, so far as right could be determined, should be done.

I was not naïve. That is how I think of courts still. I am one of the very few lawyers I know who keeps his gown beautifully clean, whose collar and bands and cuffs are almost foppishly starched, whose striped trousers are properly pressed, whose shoes gleam. I am proud that the newspapers often say I cut an elegant figure in court. The law deserves that. The law is elegant. Pargetter took good care that I should not be foolishly romantic about the law, but he knew that there was a measure of romance in my attitude toward it, and if he had thought it should be rooted out, he would have done so. One day he paid me a walloping great compliment.

"I think you'll make an advocate," said he. "You have the two necessities, ability and imagination. A good advocate is his client's *alter ego;* his task is to say what his client would say for himself if he had the knowledge and the power. Ability goes hand in hand with the knowledge: the power is dependent on imagination. But when I say imagination I mean capacity to see all sides of a subject and weigh all possibilities; I don't mean fantasy and poetry and moonshine; imagination is a good horse to carry you over the ground, not a flying carpet to set you free from probability."

I think I grew a foot, spiritually, that day.

DR. VON HALLER: So you might. And how lucky you were. Not everybody encounters a Pargetter. He is a very important addition to your cast of characters.

MYSELF: I don't think I follow you. What I am telling you is history, not invention.

DR. VON HALLER: Oh, quite. But even history has characters, and a personal history like yours must include a few people whom it would be stupid to call stock characters, even though they appear in almost all complete personal histories. Or let us put it differently. You remember the little poem by Ibsen that I quoted to you during one of our early meetings?

MYSELF: Only vaguely. Something about self-judgement.

DR. VON HALLER: No, no; self-judgement comes later. Now pay attention, please:

> To *live* is to battle with trolls
> in the vaults of heart and brain.
> To *write:* that is to sit
> in judgement over one's self.

MYSELF: But I have been writing constantly; everything I have told you has been based on careful notes; I have tried to be as clear as possible, to follow Ramsay's Plain Style. I have raked up some stuff I have never told to another living soul. Isn't this self-judgement?

DR. VON HALLER: Not at all. This has been the history of your battle with the trolls.

MYSELF: Another of your elaborate metaphors?

DR. VON HALLER: If you like. I use metaphor to spare you jargon. Now consider: what figures have we met so far in our exploration of your life? Your Shadow; there was no difficulty about that, I believe, and we shall certainly meet him again. The Friend: Felix was the first to play that part, and you may yet come to recognize Knopwood as a very special friend, though I know you are still bitter against him. The Anima; you are very rich there, for of course there were your mother and Caroline and Netty, who all demonstrate various aspects of the feminine side of life, and finally Judy. This figure has been in eclipse for some years, at least in its positive aspect; I think we must count your stepmother as an Anima-figure, but not a friendly one; we may still find that she is not so black as you paint her. But there are happy signs that the eclipse is almost over, because of your dream—let us be romantic and call it The Maiden and the Manticore—in which you were sure you recognized me. Perfectly in order. I have played all of these roles at various stages of our talks. Necessarily so: an analysis like this is certainly not emotion recollected in tranquillity. You may call these figures many things. You might call them the Comedy Company of the Psyche, but that would be flippant and not do justice to the cruel blows you have had from some of them. In my profession we call them archetypes, which means that they represent and body forth patterns toward which human behaviour seems to be disposed; patterns which repeat themselves endlessly, but never in precisely the same way. And you have just been telling me about one of the most powerful of all, which we may call the Magus, or the Wizard, or the Guru, or anything that signifies a powerful formative influence toward the development of the total personality. Pargetter appears to have been a very fine Magus indeed: a blind genius who accepts you as an apprentice in his art! But he has just turned up, which is unusual though not seriously so. I had expected him earlier. Knopwood looked rather like a Magus for a time, but we shall have to see if any of his influence lasted. But the other man, the possible father, the man you call Old Buggerlugs—I had expected rather more from him. Have you been keeping anything back?

MYSELF: No. And yet . . . there was always something about him that held the imagination. He was an oddity, as I've said. But a man who never seemed to come to anything. He wrote some books, and Father said some of them sold well, but they were queer stuff, about the nature of faith and the necessity of faith—not Christian faith, but some kind of faith, and now and then in classes he would point at us and say, "Be sure you choose what you believe and know why you believe it, because if you don't choose your beliefs, you may be certain that some belief, and probably not a very creditable one, will choose you." Then he would go on about people whose belief was in Youth, or Money, or Power, or something like that, and who had found that these things were false gods. We liked to hear him rave, and some of his demonstrations from history were very amusing, but we didn't take it seriously. I have always looked on him as a man who missed his way in life. Father liked him. They came from the same village.

DR. VON HALLER: But you never felt any urge to learn from him?

MYSELF: What could he have taught me, except history and the Plain Style?

DR. VON HALLER: Yes, I see. It seemed to me for a time that he had something of the quality of a Magus.

MYSELF: In your Comedy Company, or Cabinet of Archetypes, you don't seem to have any figure that might correspond to my father.

DR. VON HALLER: Oh, do not be impatient. These are the common figures. You may depend on it that your father will not be forgotten. Indeed, it seems to me that he has been very much present ever since we began. We talk of him all the time. He may prove to be your Great Troll. . . .

MYSELF: Why do you talk of trolls? It seems to me that you Jungians sometimes go out of your way to make yourselves absurd.

DR. VON HALLER: Trolls are not Jungian; they are just part of my promise not to annoy you with jargon. What is a troll?

MYSELF: A kind of Scandinavian spook, isn't it?

DR. VON HALLER: Yes, spook is a very good word for it—another Scandinavian word. Sometimes a troublesome goblin, sometimes a huge, embracing lubberfiend, sometimes an ugly animal creature, sometimes a helper and server, even a lovely enchantress, a true Princess from Far Away: but never a full or complete human being. And the battle with trolls that Ibsen wrote about is a good metaphor to describe the wrestling and wrangling we go through when the archetypes we carry in ourselves seem to be embodied in people we have to deal with in daily life.

MYSELF: But people are people, not trolls or archetypes.

DR. VON HALLER: Yes, and our great task is to see people as people and not clouded by archetypes we carry about with us, looking for a peg to hang them on.

MYSELF: Is that the task we are working at here?

DR. VON HALLER: Part of it. We take a good look at your life, and we try to lift the archetypes off the pegs and see the people who have been obscured by them.

MYSELF: And what do I get out of that?

DR. VON HALLER: That depends on you. For one thing, you will probably learn to recognize a spook when you see one, and keep trolls in good order. And you will recover all these projections which you have visited on other people like a magic lantern projecting a slide on a screen. When you stop doing that you are stronger, more independent. You have more mental energy. Think about·it. And now go on about the genealogist.

(12)

I didn't pay much attention to him, because as I told Dr. von Haller, I was greatly taken up with my final year of law studies. Pargetter expected me to get a First, and I wanted it even more than he. The notes kept arriving with reports of nothing achieved in spite of impressive activity. I had written to Father that I had a good man on the job, and had his permission to advance money as it was needed. Pledger-Brown's accounts were a source of great delight to me; I felt like Diogenes, humbled in the presence of an honest man. Sometimes in the vacations he went off hunting Stauntons and sent me bills detailing third-class tickets, sixpenny rides on buses, shillings spent on beer for old men who might know something, and cups of tea and buns for himself. There was never any charge for his time or his knowledge, and when I asked about that he replied that we would agree on a fee when he produced his results. I foresaw that he would starve on that principle, but I cherished him as an innocent. Indeed, I grew to be very fond of him, and we were Adrian and Davey when we talked. His besotted enthusiasm for the practise of heraldry refreshed me; I knew nothing about it, and couldn't see the use of it, and wondered why anybody bothered with it, but in time he brought me to see that it had once been necessary and was still a pleasant personal indulgence, and—this was important—that using somebody else's armorial bearings was no different in spirit from using his name; it was impersonation. It was, in legal terms, no different from imitating a trade-mark, and I knew what that meant. Undoubtedly Pledger-Brown was the best friend I made at Oxford, and I keep up with him still. He got into the College of Heralds, by the way, and is now Clarencieux King of Arms and looks exceedingly peculiar on ceremonial occasions in a tabard and a hat with a feather.

What finally bound us into the kind of friendship that does not fade was complicity in a secret.

Early in the spring term of my third year, when I was deep in work for my Final Schools, a message arrived: "I have found Henry Staunton. A.P.B." I had a mountain of reading to do and had planned to spend all afternoon at the Codrington, but this called for something special, so I got hold of Adrian and took him to lunch. He was as nearly triumphant as his diffident nature would allow.

"I was just about to offer you a non-grandfather," said he; "there was a connection of the Stauntons of Warwickshire— not a Longbridge Staunton but a cousin—who cannot be accounted for and might perhaps have gone to Canada at the age of eighteen or so. By a very long shot he might have been your grandfather; without better evidence it would be guesswork to say he was. But then during the Easter vacation I had a flash. You otiose ass, Pledger-Brown, I said to myself, you've never thought of Staunton as a place-name. It is an elementary rule in this work, you know, to check place-names. There is Staunton Harold in Leicestershire and two or three Stantons, and of course I had quite overlooked Staunton in Gloucestershire. So off I went and checked parish records. And there he was in Gloucestershire: Albert Henry Staunton, born April 4, 1866, son of Maria Ann Dymock, and if you can find a better West Country name than Dymock, I'd be glad to hear it."

"What kind of Staunton is he?" I asked.

"He's an extraordinarily rum Staunton," said Pledger-Brown, "but that's the best of it. You get not only a grandfather but a good story as well. You know, so many of these forbears that people ferret out are nothing at all; I mean, perfectly good and reputable, but no personal history of any interest. But Albert Henry is a conversation-piece. Now listen.

"Staunton is a hamlet about ten miles north-west of Gloucester, bearing over toward Herefordshire. In the middle of the last century it had only one public house, called the Angel, and by rights it ought to have been near a church named for the Annunciation, but it isn't. That doesn't matter. What is important is that in the 1860s there was an attractive girl working at the Angel who was called Maria Ann Dymock, and she must have been a local Helen, because she was known as Mary Dymock the Angel."

"A barmaid?" I asked, wondering how Father was going to take to the idea of a barmaid.

"No, no," said Adrian; "barmaids are a bee in the American bonnet. A country pub of that time would be served by its landlord. Maria Ann Dymock was undoubtedly a domestic servant. But she became pregnant, and she said the child's father was George Applesquire, who was the landlord of the Angel. He denied it and said it could have been several other men. Indeed, he said that all Staunton could claim to be the child's father, and he would have nothing to do with it. He or his wife turned Maria Ann out of the Angel.

"Now, the cream of the story is this. Maria Ann Dymock must have been a girl of some character, for she bore the child in the local workhouse and in due time marched off to church to have it christened. 'What shall I name the child?' said parson. 'Albert Henry,' said Maria Ann. So it was done. 'And the father's name?' said parson; 'shall I say Dymock?' 'No,' said Maria Ann, 'say Staunton, because it's said by landlord the whole place could be his father, and I want him to carry his father's name.' I get all this out of the county archaeological society's records, which include quite an interesting diary of the clergyman in question, whose name was the Reverend Theophilus Mynors, by the way. Mynors must have been a sport, and probably he thought the girl had been badly used by Applesquire, because he put down the name as Albert Henry Staunton in the parish record.

"It caused a scandal, of course. But Maria Ann stuck it out, and when Applesquire's cronies threatened to make things too hot for her to stay in the parish, she walked the village street with a collecting bag, saying, 'If you want me out of Staunton, give me something for my journey.' She must have been a Tartar. She didn't get much, but the Rev. Theophilus admits that he gave her five pounds on the quiet, and there were one or two other contributors who admired her pluck, and soon she had enough to go abroad. You could still get a passage to Quebec for under five pounds in those days if you supplied your own food, and infants travelled free. So off went Maria Ann in late May of 1866, and undoubtedly she was your great-grandmother."

We were eating in one of those Oxford restaurants that spring up and sink down again because they are run by amateurs, and we had arrived at the stage of eating a charlotte russe made of stale cake, tired jelly, and chemicals; I can still remember its taste because it is associated with my bleak wonder as to what I was going to report to Father. I explained to Pledger-Brown.

"But my dear Davey, you're missing the marvel of it," he said; "what a story! Think of Maria Ann's resource and courage! Did she slink away and hide herself in London with her bastard child, gradually sinking to the basest forms of prostitution while little Albert Henry became a thief and a pimp? No! She was of the stuff of which the great New World has been forged! She stood up on her feet and demanded to be recog-

nized as an individual, with inalienable rights! She braved the
vicar, and George Applesquire, and all of public opinion. And
then she went off to carve out a glorious life in what were
then, my dear chap, still the colonies and not the great self-
governing sisterhood of the Commonwealth! She was there
when Canada became a Dominion! She may have been among
the cheering crowds who hailed that moment in Montreal or
Ottawa or wherever it was! You're not grasping the thing at
all."

I was grasping it. I was thinking of Father.

"I confess that I've been meddling," said Adrian, turning
very red; "Garter would be as mad as hops if he knew I'd been
playing with my paint-box like this. But after all, this is my
first shot at tracing a forbear independently, and I can't help it.
So I beg you, as a friend, to accept this trifle of *anitergium*
from me."

He handed me a cardboard roll, and when I had pried the
metal cap off one end, I found a scroll inside it. I folded it out
on the table where the medical charlotte russe had given place
to some coffee—a Borgia speciality of the place—and it was a
coat-of-arms.

"Just a very rough shot at something the College of Heralds
would laugh at, but I couldn't help myself," he said. "The description in our lingo would be 'Gules within a bordure wavy
or, the Angel of the Annunciation bearing in her dexter hand
a sailing-ship of three masts and in her sinister an apple.' In
other words, there's Mary the Angel with the ship she went to
Canada on, and a good old Gloucester cider apple, on a red
background with a wiggly golden border around the shield.
Sorry about the wavy border; it means bastardy, but you don't
have to tell everybody. Then here's the crest: 'a fox statant
guardant within his jaws a sugar cane, all proper.' It's the
Staunton crest, but slightly changed for your purposes, and the

sugar cane says where you got your lolly from, which good heraldry often does. The motto, you see is *De forte egressa est dulcedo*—'Out of the strong came forth sweetness'—from the Book of Judges, and couldn't be neater, really. And look here —you see I've given the fox rather a saucy privy member, just as a hint at your father's prowess in that direction. How do you like it?"

"You called it something," said I; "a trifle of something?"

"Oh, *anitergium*," said Adrian. "It's just one of those Middle Latin terms I like to use for fun. It means a trifle, a sketch, something disposable. Well, actually the monks used it for the throw-outs from the scriptorium which they used for bum-wipe."

I hated to hurt his feelings, but Pargetter always said that hard things should be said as briefly as possible.

"It's bum-wipe, all right," I said. "Father won't have that."

"Oh, most certainly not. I never meant that he should. The College of Heralds would have to prepare you legitimate arms, and I don't suppose it would be anything like this."

"I don't mean the *anitergium*," I said. "I mean the whole story."

"But Davey! You told me yourself your father said you were probably bastards. He must have a sturdy sense of humour."

"He has," I said, "but I doubt if it extends to this. However, I'll try it."

I did. And I was right. His letter in reply was cold and brief. "People talk jokingly about being bastards, but the reality is something different. Remember that I am in politics now and you can imagine the fun my opponents would have. Let us drop the whole thing. Pay off Pledger-Brown and tell him to keep his trap shut."

And that, for a while, was that.

(13)

I suppose nobody nowadays gets through a university without some flirtation with politics, and quite a few lasting marriages result. I had my spell of socialism, but it was measles rather than scarlet fever, and I soon recovered; as a student of law, I was aware that in our time whatever a man's political convictions may be he lives under a socialist system. Furthermore, I knew that my concern for mankind disposed me toward individuals rather than masses, and as Pargetter was pushing me toward work in the courts, and especially toward criminal law, I was increasingly interested in a class of society for which no political party has any use. There was, Pargetter said, somewhat less than five per cent of society which could fittingly be called the criminal class. That five per cent were my constituents.

I got my First Class in law at Oxford, and was in time called to the Bar in London, but I had always intended to practise in Canada, and this involved me in three more years of work. Canadian law, though rooted in English law, is not precisely the same, and the differences, and a certain amount of professional protectionism, made it necessary for me to qualify all over again. It was not hard. I was already pretty good and was able to do the Canadian work with time to spare for other reading. Like many well-qualified professional men I knew very little but my job, and Pargetter was very severe on that kind of ignorance. " 'If practice be the whole that he is taught, practice must also be the whole that he will ever know,' " he would quote from Blackstone. So I read a lot of history, as my schoolwork with Ramsay had given me a turn in that direction, and quite a few great classical works which have formed the minds of men for generations, and of which I retain nothing but a vague sense of how long they were and how clever people must be who liked them. What I really liked was poetry, and I read a lot of it.

It was during this time, too, that I became financially independent of my father. He had been making a man of me, so far as a tight check on my expenditures would do it; his training was effective, too, for I am a close man with money to this day, and have never come near to spending my income, or that part of it taxation allows me to keep. My personal fortune began quite unexpectedly when I was twenty-one.

Grandfather Staunton had not approved of Father, who had become what the old man called a "high-flyer," and although he left him a part of his estate, he left half of it to Caroline, in trust. To me he left what Father regarded as a joke legacy, in the form of five hundred acres of land in Northern Ontario, which he had bought as a speculation when it was rumoured that there was coal up there. Coal there may have been, but as there was no economically sane way of getting it down to places where it could be sold, the land lay idle. Nobody had ever seen it, and it was assumed that it was a wilderness of rock and scrub trees. Grandfather's executor, which was a large trust company, did nothing about this land until my majority, and then suggested that I sell it to a company which had offered to buy it for a hundred dollars an acre; there was fifty thousand dollars to be picked up for nothing, so to speak, and they advised me to take it.

I was stubborn. If the land was worthless, why did anyone want to pay a hundred dollars an acre for it? I had a hunch that I might as well see it before parting with it, so I set off to look at my inheritance. I am no woodsman, and it was a miserable journey from the nearest train-stop to my property, but I did it by canoe, in the company of a morose guide, and was frightened out of my wits by the desolation, the dangers of canoeing in some very rough water, and the apparent untrustworthiness of my companion. But after a couple of days we were on my land, and as I tramped around it I found that there were other people on it, too, and that they were unmistakably drilling for minerals. They were embarrassed, and I became thoughtful, for they had no authority to be doing what they were doing. Back in Toronto I made a fuss with the trust company, who knew nothing about the drillers, and I made something more than a fuss to the mining company. So after some legal huffing and puffing, and giving them the Pargetter treatment, I disposed of my northern land at a thousand dollars an acre, which would have been dirt cheap if there had been a mine. But there was nothing there, or not enough. I emerged from this adventure with half a million dollars. A nice, round sum, surely never foreseen by Grandfather Staunton.

Father was not pleased, because the trust company who had been so casual about my affairs was one of which he was a director, and at one point I had threatened to sue them for mismanagement, which he considered unfilial. But I stuck to my guns, and when it was all over asked him if he would like me to move out of the family house. But he urged me to stay. It was large, and he was lonely when his political career allowed him to be there, and so I stayed where I was and thus came once again under the eye of Netty.

Netty was the survivor of an endless train of servants. She had never been given the title of housekeeper, but she was the Black Pope of the domestic staff, never frankly tattling but always hinting or wearing the unmistakable air of someone who could say a great deal if asked. With no children to look after, she had become almost a valet to Father, cleaning his clothes and washing and ironing his shirts, which she declared nobody else could do to his complete satisfaction.

When I had finished my Canadian legal studies I gave offence to Father once again, for he had always assumed that I would be content to have him find a place for me in the Alpha Corporation. But that was not at all my plan; I wanted to practise as a criminal lawyer. Pargetter, with whom I kept in constant touch (though he never raised me to the level of one of his long-distance chess opponents) urged me to get some general practice first, and preferably in a small place. "You will see more of human nature, and get a greater variety of experience, in three years in a country town than you will get in five years with a big firm in a city," he wrote. So once again I returned, not to Deptford, but to the nearby county town, a place of about sixty thousand people, called Pittstown. I easily got a place in the law office of Diarmuid Mahaffey, whose father had once been the lawyer in Deptford and with whom there was a family connection.

Diarmuid was very good to me and saw that I got a little work of every kind, including a few of those mad clients all lawyers seem to have if their practice extends into the country. I don't suggest that city lawyers have no madmen on their books, but I honestly believe the countryside breeds finer examples of the *paranoia querulans,* the connoisseurs of litigation. He bore in mind that I wanted to work in the courts and put me in the way of getting some of those cases on which most young lawyers cut their teeth; some indigent or incompetent accused person needs a lawyer, and the court appoints a lawyer, usually a young man, to act for him.

I learned a valuable lesson from my first case of this kind. A Maltese labourer was charged with indecent assault; it was not a very serious matter, because the aspiring rapist had trouble with his buttons, and the woman, who was considerably bigger than he, hit him with her handbag and ran away. "You must tell me honestly," said I, "did you do it? I'll do my best to get you off, but I must know the truth." "Meester Stown," said he, with tears in his eyes, "I swear to you on the grave of my dead mother, I never did no such dirty thing. Spit in my mouth if I even touch this woman!" So I gave the court a fine harangue, and the judge gave my client two years. My client was delighted. "That judge, he's very clever man," he said to me afterward; "he knew all the time I done it." Then he shook my hand and trotted off with the warder, pleased to have been punished by such an expert in human nature. I decided then that the kind of people with whom I had chosen to associate myself were not to be trusted, or at least not taken literally.

My next serious case was a far bigger thing, nothing less than a murderess. Poor woman, she had shot her husband. He was a farmer, known far and wide to be no good and brutal to her and his livestock, but he was decisively dead; she had poked a shotgun through the back window of the privy while he was perched on the seat and blown his head off. She made no denial, and was indeed silent and resigned through all the preliminaries. But they still hanged women in those days, and it was my job to save her from the gallows if I could.

I spent a good deal of time with her and thought so much about the case that Diarmuid began to call me Sir Edward, in reference to Marshall Hall. But one night I had a bright idea, and the next day I put a question to my client and got the answer I expected. When at last the case came to trial I spoke of extenuating circumstances, and at the right moment said that the murdered man had repeatedly beaten his wife in order to make her perform *fellatio*.

"Know your judge" was one of Diarmuid's favourite maxims; of course no barrister knows a judge overtly, but most of the Bar know him before he is elevated to the Bench and have some estimate of his temperament. Obviously you don't take a particularly messy divorce before a Catholic judge, or a drunk who has caused an accident before a teetotal judge, if you can help it. I was lucky in this case because our assize judge that season was Orley Mickley, known to be a first-rate man of the law, but in his private life a pillar of rectitude and a great deplorer of sexual sin. As judges often are, he was innocent of things that lesser people know, and the word *fellatio* had not come his way.

"I assume that is a medical term, Mr. Staunton," said he; "will you be good enough to explain it to the court."

"May I ask your lordship to order the court cleared?" said I; "or if your lordship would call a recess I should be glad to explain the term in your chambers. It is not something that any of us would take pleasure in hearing."

I was playing it up for all it would stand, and I had an intimation—Dr. von Haller says I have a good measure of intuition—that I was riding the crest of a wave.

The judge cleared the court and asked me to explain to him and the jury what *fellatio* was. I dragged it out. Oral and lingual caress of the erect male organ until ejaculation is brought about was the way I put it. The jury knew simpler terms for this business, and my delicacy struck them solemn. I did not need to labour the fact that the dead man had been notably dirty: the jury had all seen him. Usually performed by the woman on her knees, I added, and two women jurors straightened up in their chairs. A gross indignity exacted by force; a perversion for which some American states exacted severe penalties; a grim servitude no woman with a spark of self-respect could be expected to endure without cracking.

It worked like a charm. The judge's charge to the jury was a marvel of controlled indignation; they must find the woman guilty but unless they added a recommendation of clemency his faith in mankind would be shattered. And of course they did so, and the judge gave her a sentence which, with good conduct, would not be more than two or three years. I suppose the poor soul ate better and slept better in the penitentiary than she had ever done in her life.

"That was a smart bit of business," said Diarmuid to me afterward, "and I don't know how you guessed what the trouble was. But you did, and that's what matters. B'God, I think old Mickley would have hung the corpse, if it'd had a scrap of neck left to put in a rope."

This case gained me a disproportionate reputation as a brilliant young advocate filled with compassion for the wretched. The result was that a terrible band of scoundrels who thought themselves misunderstood or ill used shouted for my services when they got into well-deserved trouble. And thus I gained my first client to go to the gallows.

Up to this time I had delighted unashamedly in the law. Many lawyers do, and Diarmuid was one of them. "If lawyers allowed their sense of humour free play, b'God they wouldn't be able to work for laughing," he once said to me. But the trial and hanging of Jimmy Veale showed me another aspect of the law. What I suppose Dr. von Haller would call its Shadow.

Not that Jimmy didn't have a fair trial. Not that I didn't exert myself to the full on his behalf. But his guilt was clear, and all I could do was try to find explanations for what he had done, and try to arouse pity for a man who had no pity for anyone else.

Jimmy had a bad reputation and had twice been in jail for petty thievery. He was only twenty-two, but he was a thorough-going crook of an unsophisticated kind. When I met him the provincial police had run him down, hiding in the woods about thirty miles north of Pittstown, with sixty-five dollars in his pocket. He had entered the house of an old woman who lived alone in a rural area, demanded her money, and when she would not yield he sat her on her own stove to make her talk. Which she did, of course, but when Jimmy found the money and left, she appeared to be dead. However, she was not quite dead, and when a neighbour found her in the morning she lived long enough to describe Jimmy and assure the neighbour that he had repeatedly sworn that he would kill her if she didn't speak up. In this evidence the neighbour was not to be shaken.

Jimmy's mother, who thought him wild but not bad, engaged me to defend him, and I did what I could by pleading insanity. It is a widespread idea that people who are unusually cruel must be insane, though the corollary of that would be that anybody who is unusually compassionate must be insane. But the Crown Attorney applied the McNaghton Rule to Jimmy, and I well recall the moment when he said to the jury, "Would the prisoner have acted as he did if a policeman had been standing at his elbow?" Jimmy, lounging in the prisoner's dock, laughed and cried out, "Jeeze, d'you think I'm crazy?" After which it did not take the court long to send him to the gallows.

I decided that I had better be present when Jimmy was hanged. It is a common complaint against the courts that they condemn people to punishments of which the legal profession have no direct knowledge. It is a justifiable reproach when it is true, but it is true less often than tender-hearted people think. There are people who shrink from the whole idea of a court, and there are the There-But-for-the-Grace-of-Godders who seem to think it is only by a narrow squeak that they have kept out of the prisoner's dock themselves; they are bird-brains to whom God's grace and good luck mean the same thing. There are the democrats of justice, who seem to believe that every judge should begin his career as a prisoner at the bar and work his way up to the Bench. Tender-minded people, all of them, but they don't know criminals. I wanted to know criminals, and I made my serious start with Jimmy.

I was sorry for his mother, who was a fool but punished for it with unusual severity; she had not spoiled Jimmy more than countless mothers spoil boys who turn out to be sources of pride. Jimmy had been exposed to all the supposed benefits of a democratic state; he had the best schooling that could be managed for as long as he cared to take it—which was no longer than the law demanded; his childhood had been embowered in a complexity of protective laws, and his needs had been guaranteed by Mackenzie King's Baby Bonus. But Jimmy was a foul-mouthed crook who had burned an old woman to death, and never, in all the months I knew him, expressed one single word of regret.

He was proud of being a condemned man. While awaiting trial he acquired from somewhere a jail vocabulary. Within a day of his imprisonment he would greet the trusty who brought him his food with "Hiya, shit-heel!" that being the term the hardened prisoners used for those who co-operated with the warden. After his trial, when the chaplain tried to talk to him he was derisive, shouting, "Listen, I'm gonna piss when I can't whistle, and that's all there is to it, so don't give me none of your shit." He regarded me with some favour, for I qualified as a supporting player in his personal drama; I was his "mouthpiece." He wanted me to arrange for him to sell his story to a newspaper, but I would have nothing to do with that. I saw Jimmy at least twice a week while he was waiting for execution, and I never heard a word from him that did not make me think the world would be better off without him. None of his former friends tried to see him, and when his mother visited him he was sullen and abusive.

When the time for his hanging came, I spent a dismal night with the sheriff and the chaplain in the office of the warden of the jail. None of them had ever managed a hanging, and they were nervous and haggled about details, such as whether a flag should be flown to show that justice had been done upon Jimmy; it was a foolish question, for a flag would have to be flown at seven o'clock anyway, and that was the official hour for Jimmy's execution; in fact he was to be hanged at six, before the other prisoners were awakened. Whether they were sleeping or not I do not know, but certainly there was none of that outcry or beating on cell-bars which is such a feature of romantic drama on this subject. The hangman was busy about concerns of his own. I had seen him; a short, stout, unremarkable man who looked like a carpenter dressed for a funeral, which I suppose is what he was. The chaplain went to Jimmy and soon returned. The doctor came at five, and with him two or three newspaper reporters. In all, there were about a dozen of us at last, of whom only the hangman had ever been present at such an affair before.

As we waited, the misery which had been palpable in the small office became almost stifling, and I went out with one of the reporters to walk in the corridor. As six o'clock drew near we moved into the execution chamber, a room like an elevator shaft, though larger, and stuffy from long disuse. There was a platform about nine feet high of unpainted new wood, and under it hung some curtains of unbleached cotton that were crumpled and looked as if they had been used before and travelled far; above the platform, from the roof, was suspended a heavily braced steel beam, painted the usual dirty red, and from this hung the rope, with its foot-long knot which would, if all was well, dislocate Jimmy's cervical vertebrae and break his spinal cord. To my surprise, it was almost white; I do not know what I expected, but certainly not a white rope. The hangman in his tight black suit was bustling about trying the lever that worked the trap. Nobody spoke. When everything was to his liking, the hangman nodded, and two warders brought Jimmy in.

He had been given something by the doctor beforehand, and needed help as he walked. I had seen him the day before, in his cell where the lights always burned and where he had spent so many days without a belt, or braces, or even laces in his shoes—deprivations which seemed to rob him of full humanity, so that he appeared to be ill or insane. Now his surly look was gone, and he had to be pushed up the ladder that led to the platform. The hangman, whom he never saw, manœuvred Jimmy gently to the right spot, then put the noose over his head and adjusted it with great care—in other circumstances one might say with loving care. Then he slid down the ladder—literally, for he put his feet on the outsides of the supports and slipped down it like a fireman—and immediately pulled the lever. Jimmy dropped out of sight behind the curtains, with a loud thump, as the cord stretched tight.

The silence, which had been so thick before, was now broken as Jimmy swung to and fro and the rope banged against the sides of the trap. Worse than that, we heard gurgling and gagging, and the curtains bulged and stirred as Jimmy swung within them. The hanging, as is sometimes the case, had not gone well, and Jimmy was fighting for life.

The doctor had told us that unconsciousness was immediate, but that the cessation of Jimmy's heartbeat might take from three to five minutes. If Jimmy were unconscious, why am I sure that I heard him cry out—curses, of course, for these had always been Jimmy's eloquence? But I did hear him, and so did the others, and one of the reporters was violently sick. We looked at one another in terror. What was to be done? The hangman knew. He darted inside the curtains, and beneath them we saw a great shuffling of feet, and soon the violent swinging stopped, and the sighs and murmurings were still. The hangman came out again, flustered and angry, and mopped his brow. None of us met his eye. When five minutes had passed the doctor, not liking his work, went inside the curtains with his stethoscope ready, came out again almost at once, and nodded to the sheriff. And so it was over.

Not quite over for me. I had promised Jimmy's mother that I would see him before he was buried, and I did. He was laid on a table in a neighbouring room, and I looked him right in the face, which took some resolution in the doing. But I noticed also a damp stain on the front of his prison trousers, and looked enquiringly at the doctor.

"An emission of semen," he said; "they say it always happens. I don't know."

So that was what Jimmy meant when he said he'd piss when he couldn't whistle. Where could he have picked up such a jaunty, ugly, grotesque idea of death by hanging? But that was Jimmy; he had a flair for whatever was brutal and macabre and such knowledge sought him out because he was eager for it.

I had seen a hanging. Worse things happen in wars and in great catastrophes, but they are not directly planned and ordered. This had been the will of Jimmy's fellow-countrymen, as expressed through the legal machinery devised to deal with such people as he. But it was unquestionably a squalid business, an evil deed, and we had all of us, from the hangman down to the reporters, been drawn into it and fouled by it. If Jimmy had to be got rid of—and I fully believe that was all that could have been done with such a man, unless he were to be kept as a caged, expensive nuisance for another fifty years— why did it have to be like this? I do not speak of hanging alone; the executioner's sword, the guillotine, the electric chair are all dreadful and involve the public through its legal surrogates in a revolting act. The Greeks seem to have known a better way than these.

Jimmy's evil had infected us all—had indeed spread far beyond his prison until something of it touched everybody in his country. The law had been tainted by evil, though its great import was for good, or at least for order and just dealing. But it would be absurd to attribute so much power to Jimmy, who was no more than a fool whose folly had become the conduit by which evil had poured into so many lives. When I visited Jimmy in prison I had sometimes seen on his face a look I knew, the look I had seen on the face of Bill Unsworth as he squatted obscenely over a pile of photographs. It was the look of one who has laid himself open to a force that is inimical to man, and whose power to loose that force upon the world is limited only by his imagination, his opportunities, and his daring. And it seemed to me then that it was with such people I had cast my lot, for I was devoting my best abilities to their defence.

I changed my mind about that later. The law gives every accused man his chance, and there must be those who do for him what he cannot do for himself; I was one of these. But I was always aware that I stood very near to the power of evil when I undertook the cases that brought me the greatest part of my reputation. I was a highly skilled, highly paid, and cunning mercenary in a fight which was as old as man and greater than man. I have consciously played the Devil's Advocate and I must say I have enjoyed it. I like the struggle, and I had better admit that I like the moral danger. I am like a man who has built his house on the lip of a volcano. Until the volcano claims me I live, in a sense, heroically.

DR. VON HALLER: Good. I was wondering when he would make his appearance.

MYSELF: Whom are we talking about now?

DR. VON HALLER: The hero who lives on the lip of the volcano. We have talked of many aspects of your inner life, and we have identified them by such names as Shadow, Anima, and so on. But one has been seen only in a negative aspect, and he is the man you show to the outer world, the man in whose character you appear in court and before your acquaintances. He has a name, too. We call him the Persona, which means, as you know, the actor's mask. This man on the edge of the volcano, this saturnine lawyer-wizard who snatches people out of the jaws of destruction, is your Persona. You must enjoy playing the role very much.

MYSELF: I do.

DR. VON HALLER: Good. You would not have admitted that a few months ago, when you first sat in that chair. Then you were all for imposing him on me as your truest self.

MYSELF: I'm not sure that he isn't.

DR. VON HALLER: Oh, come. We all create an outward self with which to face the world, and some people come to believe that is what they truly are. So they people the world with doctors who are nothing outside the consulting-room, and judges who are nothing when they are not in court, and businessmen who wither with boredom when they have to retire from business, and teachers who are forever teaching. That is why they are such poor specimens when they are caught without their masks on. They have lived chiefly through the Persona. But you are not such a fool, or you would not be here. Everybody needs his mask, and the only intentional impostors are those whose mask is one of a man with nothing to conceal. We all have much to conceal, and we must conceal it for our soul's good. Even your Wizard, your mighty Pargetter, was not all Wizard. Did you ever find some chink in his armour?

MYSELF: Yes, and it was a shock. He died without a will.

A lawyer who dies without a will is one of the jokes of the profession.

DR. VON HALLER: Ah, but making a will is not part of a Persona; it is, for most of us, an hour when we look our mortality directly in the face. If he did not want to do that, it is sad, but do you really think it diminishes Pargetter? It lessens him as the perfect lawyer, certainly, but he must have been something more than that, and a portion of that something else had a natural, pathetic fear of death. He had built his Persona so carefully and so handsomely that you took it for the whole man; and it must be said that you might not have learned so much from him if you had seen him more fully; young people love such absolutes. But your own Persona seems to be a very fine one. Surely it was built as a work of art?

MYSELF: Of art, and of necessity. The pressures under which I came to live were such that I needed something to keep people at bay. And so I built what I must say I have always thought of as my public character, my professional manner, but which you want me to call a Persona. I needed armour. You see—this is not an easy thing for me to say, even to someone who listens professionally to what is usually unspeakable—women began to throw out their lures for me. I would have been a good catch. I came of a well-known family; I had money; I was at the start of a career of a kind that some women find as attractive as that of a film actor.

DR. VON HALLER: And why were you so unresponsive? Anything to do with Myrrha Martindale?

MYSELF: That wore off, after a time. I had come to hate the fact that I had been initiated into the world of physical sex in something Father had stage-managed. It wasn't sex itself, but Father's proprietorial way with it, and with me. I was young and neither physically cold nor morally austere, but even when the urge and the opportunity were greatest I wanted no more of it. It seemed like following in the swordsman's footsteps, and I wanted none of that. But I might have married if Father had not gone before me, even there.

DR. VON HALLER: This was the second marriage, to Denyse?

MYSELF: Yes, when I was twenty-nine. I had passed my third year in Pittstown with Diarmuid, and was thinking it was time to be moving, for one does not become a first-rank criminal lawyer in a town where criminals are few and of modest ambition. One day a letter came from Father; would I meet Caroline for dinner at the family house in Toronto, as he had something of great importance to tell us? Since getting into politics Father had not dwindled in self-esteem, I can assure you, and this was in what painters call his later manner. So up to Toronto I went on the appointed day, and the other guests at dinner were Caroline and Beesty. Caroline had married Beeston Bastable the year before, and it had done her a lot of good; he was no Adonis, running rather to fat, but he was a fellow of what I can only call a sweet disposition, and after Caroline had tormented and jeered at him long enough she discovered she loved him, and that was that. But Father was not there. Only a letter, to be read while we were having coffee. I wondered what it could be, and so did Beesty, but Caroline jumped to it at once, and of course she was right. The letter was rather a floundering and pompous piece of work, but it boiled down to the fact that he was going to marry again and hoped we would approve and love the lady as much as he did, and as much as she deserved. There was a tribute in it to Mother, rather stiffly worded. Stuff about how he could never be happy in this new marriage unless we approved. And, finally, the name of the lady herself. It was Denyse Hornick.

Of course we knew who she was. She ran a good-sized travel agency of her own, and was prominent in politics, on the women's side.

DR. VON HALLER: A women's liberationist?

MYSELF: Not in any extreme way. An intelligent, moderate, but determined and successful advocate of equality for women under the law, and in business and professional life. We knew she had attached herself to Father's personal group of supporters during his not very fortunate post-war political career. None of us had ever met her. But we met her that night because Father brought her home at about half-past nine to introduce her. It wasn't an easy situation.

DR. VON HALLER: He seems to have managed it rather heavy-handedly.

MYSELF: Yes, and I suppose it was immature of me, but it galled me to see him so youthful and gallant toward her when they came in, like a boy bringing his girl home to run the gauntlet of the family. After all, he was sixty. And she was modest and sweet and deferential like a girl of seventeen, though she was in fact a hefty forty-one. I don't mean fat-hefty, but a psychological heavy-weight, a woman of obvious self-confidence and importance in her sphere, so that these milkmaid airs were a grotesque fancy dress. Of course we did the decent thing, and Beesty bustled around and prepared drinks with the modesty proper to an in-law at a somewhat tense family affair, and eventually everybody had kissed Denyse and the farce of seeking our approval had been played out. An hour later Denyse had so far thrown aside her role as milkmaid that when I showed some signs of getting drunk she said, "Now only one more tiny one, baa-lamb, or you'll hate yourself in the morning." I knew at that moment I couldn't stand Denyse, and that one more very serious thing had come between me and Father.

DR. VON HALLER: You were never reconciled to her?

MYSELF: You doubtless have some family, Doctor. You must know of the currents that run through families? I'll tell you of one that astonished me. It was Caroline who told Netty about the approaching marriage, and Netty broke into a fit of sobs—she had no tears, apparently—and said, "And after what I've done for him!" Caroline dropped on that at once, for it could have been proof of her favourite theory that Netty killed Mother, or at least put her in the way of dying. Surely those words couldn't have simply referred to those shirts she'd ironed so beautifully? But with her notion of "her place" it wouldn't be like Netty to think that years of service gave her a romantic claim on Father. Caroline couldn't get Netty to admit, in so many words, that she had put Mother out of the way because she was an embarrassment to Father. Nevertheless, there was something fishy there. If I could have Netty in the witness-box for half an hour, I bet I could break her down! What do you think of that? This isn't some family in the mythic drama of Greece I'm telling you about; it is a family of the twentieth century, and a Canadian family at that, supposedly the quintessence of everything that is emotionally dowdy and unaware.

DR. VON HALLER: Mythic pattern is common enough in contemporary life. But of course few people know the myths, and fewer still can see a pattern under a mass of detail. What was your response to this woman who was so soon proprietorial in her manner toward you?

MYSELF: Derision tending toward hatred; with Caroline it was just derision. Every family knows how to make the newcomer feel uncomfortable, and we did what we dared. And I did more than spar with her when we met. I found out everything I could about her through enquiries from credit agencies and by public records; I also had some enquiries made through underworld characters who had reason to want to please me—

DR. VON HALLER: You spied on her?

MYSELF: Yes.

DR. VON HALLER: You have no doubts about the propriety of that?

MYSELF: None. After all, she was marrying considerably over a hundred million dollars. I wanted to know who she was.

DR. VON HALLER: And who was she?

MYSELF: There was nothing against her. She had married a serviceman when she was in the W.R.N.S. and divorced him as soon as the war was over. That was where Lorene came from.

DR. VON HALLER: The retarded daughter?

MYSELF: An embarrassing nuisance, Denyse's problem. But Denyse liked problems and wanted to add me to her list.

DR. VON HALLER: Because of your drinking. When did that begin?

MYSELF: In Pittstown it began to be serious. It is very lonely living in a small town where you are anxious to seem quite ordinary but everybody knows that there is a great fortune, as they put it, "behind you." How far behind, or whether you really have anything more than a romantic claim on it, nobody knows or cares. More than once I would hear some Pittstown worthy whisper of me, "He doesn't have to work, you know; his father's Boy Staunton." But I did work; I tried to command my profession. I lived in the best hotel in town, which, God knows, was a dismal hole with wretched food; I confined my living to a hundred and twenty-five dollars a week, which was about what a rising young lawyer might be expected to have. I wanted no favours and if it had been practical to take another name I would have done it. Nobody understood, except Diarmuid, and I didn't care whether they understood or not. But it was lonely, and while I was hammering out the character of David Staunton the rising criminal lawyer, I also created the character of David Staunton who drank too much. The two went well together in the eyes of many romantic people, who like a brilliant man to have some large, obvious flaw in his character.

DR. VON HALLER: This was the character you took with you to Toronto, where I suppose you embroidered it.

MYSELF: Embroidered it richly. I achieved a certain courtroom notoriety; in a lively case I drew a good many spectators because they wanted to see me win. They also had the occasional thrill of seeing me stagger. There were rumours, too, that I had extensive connections in the underworld, though that was nonsense. Still, it provided a whiff of sulphur for the mob.

DR. VON HALLER: In fact, you created a romantic Persona that successfully rivalled that of the rich, sexually adventurous Boy Staunton without ever challenging him on his own ground?

MYSELF: You might equally well say that I established myself as a man of significance in my own right without in any way wearing my father's cut-down clothes.

DR. VON HALLER: And when did the clash come?

MYSELF: The——?

DR. VON HALLER: The inevitable clash between your father and yourself. The clash that gave so much edge to the guilt and remorse you felt when he died, or was killed, or whichever it was.

MYSELF: I suppose it really came into the light when Denyse made it clear that her ambition was to see Father appointed Lieutenant-Governor of Ontario. She made it very clear to me that what she insisted on calling my "image"—she had a walletful of smart terms for everything—would not fit very well with my position as son of a man who was the Queen's representative.

DR. VON HALLER: In effect she wanted to reclaim you and make you into your father's son again.

MYSELF: Yes, and what a father! She is a great maker of images, is Denyse! It disgusted and grieved me to see Father being filed and pumiced down to meet that inordinate woman's idea of a fit candidate for ceremonial office. Before, he had style—his personal style: she made him into what she would have been if she had been born a man. He became an unimaginative woman's creation. Delilah had shorn his locks and assured him he looked much neater and cooler without them. He gave her his soul, and she transformed it into a cabbage. She reopened the whole business of the Staunton arms because he would need something of the sort in an official position and it looked better to take the position with all the necessary trappings than to cobble them up during his first months in office. Father had never told her about Maria Ann Dymock, and she wrote boldly to the College of Arms, and I gather she pretty much demanded that the arms of the Warwickshire Stauntons, with some appropriate differences, be officially granted to Father.

DR. VON HALLER: What did your father think about it?

MYSELF: Oh, he laughed it off. Said Denyse would manage it if anyone could. Didn't want to talk about it. But it never happened. The College took a long time answering letters and asked for information that was hard to provide. I knew all about it because by this time my old friend Pledger-Brown was one of the pursuivants, and we had always written to each other at least once a year. One of his letters said, as I remember it, "This can never be, you know; not even your

stepdame's New World determination can make you Stauntons of Longbridge. My colleague in charge of the matter is
trying to persuade her to apply for new arms, which your father might legitimately have, for after all bags of gold are a
very fair earnest of gentility, and always have been. But she is
resolute, and nothing will do but a long and very respectable
descent. It is one of the touching aspects of our work here in
the College that so many of you New World people, up to the
eyebrows in all the delights of republicanism, hanker after a
link with what is ancient and rubbed by time to a fine sheen.
It's more than snobbery; more than romanticism; it's a desire
for an ancestry that somehow postulates a posterity and for an
existence in the past that is a covert guarantee of immortality
in the future. You talk about individualism; what you truly
want is to be links in a long unbroken chain. But you, with our
secret about Maria Ann and the child whose father might have
been all Staunton, know of a truth which is every bit as good
in its way, even though you use it only as food for your sullen
absalonism."

DR. VON HALLER: Absalonism; I do not know that word.
Explain it, please.

MYSELF: It was one of Adrian's revivals of old words. It
refers to Absalom, the son of King David, who resisted and
revolted against his father.

DR. VON HALLER: A good word. I shall remember it.

(14)

The time was drawing near to Christmas, when I knew that
Dr. von Haller would make some break in my series of appointments. But I was not prepared for what she said when
next we met.

"Well, Mr. Staunton, we seem to have come to the end of your *anamnesis*. Now it is necessary to make a decision about what you are going to do next."

"The end? But I have a sheaf of notes still! I have all sorts of questions to ask."

"Doubtless. It is possible to go on as we have been doing for several years. But you have been at this work for a little more than one year, and although we could haggle over fine points and probe sore places for at least another year, I think that for you that is unnecessary. Ask your questions of yourself. You are now in a position to answer them."

"But if I give wrong answers?"

"You will soon know that they are wrong. We have canvassed the main points in the story of your life; you are equipped to attend to details."

"I don't feel it. I'm not nearly through with what I have to say."

"Have you anything to say that seems to you extraordinary?"

"But surely I have been having the most remarkable spiritual—well, anyhow, psychological—adventures?"

"By no means, Mr. Staunton. Remarkable in your personal experience, which is what counts, but—forgive me—not at all remarkable in mine."

"Then you mean this is the end of my work with you?"

"Not if you decide otherwise. But it is the end of this work —this reassessment of some personal, profound experience. But what is most personal is not what is most profound. If you want to continue—and you must not be in a hurry to say you will—we shall proceed quite differently. We shall examine the archetypes with which you are already superficially familiar, and we shall go beyond what is personal about them. I assure you that is very close and psychologically demanding work. It

cannot be undertaken if you are always craving to be back in
Toronto, putting Alpha and Castor and all those things into
good order. But you are drinking quite moderately now, aren't
you? The symptom you complained of has been corrected.
Wasn't that what you wanted?"

"Yes, though I had almost forgotten that was what I came
for."

"Your general health is much improved? You sleep better?"

"Yes."

"And you will not be surprised or angry when I say you are
a much pleasanter, easier person?"

"But if I go on—what then?"

"I cannot tell you, because I don't know, and in this sort of
work we give no promises."

"Yes, but you have experience of other people. What happens to them?"

"They finish their work, or that part of it that can be done
here, with a markedly improved understanding of themselves,
and that means of much that goes beyond self. They are in
better command of their abilities. They are more fully themselves."

"Happier, in fact."

"I do not promise happiness, and I don't know what it is.
You New World people are, what is the word, hipped on the
idea of happiness, as if it were a constant and measurable
thing, and settled and excused everything. If it is anything at
all it is a by-product of other conditions of life, and some
people whose lives do not appear to be at all enviable, or indeed admirable, are happy. Forget about happiness."

"Then you can't or won't, tell me what I would be working
for?"

"No, because the answer lies in you, not in me. I can help, of
course. I can put the questions in such a way as to draw forth

your answer, but I do not know what your answer will be. Let me put it this way: the work you have been doing here during the past year has told you *who* you are; further work would aim at showing you *what* you are."

"More mystification. I thought we had got past all that. For weeks it seems to me that we have been talking nothing but common sense."

"Oh, my dear Mr. Staunton, that is unworthy of you! Are you still scampering back to that primitive state of mind where you suppose psychology must be divorced from common sense? Well—let me see what I can do. Your dreams—We have worked through some dozens of your dreams, and I think you are now convinced that they are not just incomprehensible gases that get into your head during sleep. Recall your dream of the night before you first came to me. What was that enclosed, private place where you commanded such respect, from which you walked out into strange country? Who was the woman you met, who talked in an unknown language? Now don't say it was me, because you had never met me then, and though dreams may reflect deep concerns and thus may hint at the future, they are not second sight. After some exploration, you came to the top of a staircase that led downward, and some commonplace people discouraged you from going down, though you sensed there was treasure there. Your decision now is whether or not you are going to descend the staircase and find the treasure."

"How do I know it will be a treasure?"

"Because your other recurrent dream, where you are the little prince in the tower, shows you as the guardian of a treasure. And you manage to keep your treasure. But who are all those frightening figures who menace it? We should certainly encounter them. And why are you a prince, and a child? — Tell me, did you dream last night?"

"Yes. A very odd dream. It reminded me of Knopwood because it was Biblical in style. I dreamed I was standing on a plain, talking with my father. I was aware it was Father, though his face was turned away. He was very affectionate and simple in his manner, as I don't think I ever knew him to be in his life. The odd thing was that I couldn't really see his face. He wore an ordinary business suit. Then suddenly he turned from me and flew up into the air, and the astonishing thing was that as he rose, his trousers came down, and I saw his naked backside."

"And what are your associations?"

"Well, obviously it's the passage in Exodus where God promises Moses that he shall see Him, but must not see His face; and what Moses sees is God's back parts. As a child I always thought it funny for God to show His rump. Funny, but also terribly real and true. Like those extraordinary people in the Bible who swore a solemn oath clutching one another's testicles. But does it mean that I have seen the weakness, the shameful part of my father's nature because he gave so much of himself into the keeping of Denyse and because Denyse was so unworthy to treat him properly? I've done what I can with it, but nothing rings true."

"Of course not, because you have neglected one of the chief principles of what I have been able to tell you about the significance of dreams. That again is understandable, for when the dream is important and has something new to tell us, we often forget temporarily what we know to be true. But we have always agreed, haven't we, that figures in dreams, whoever or whatever they may look like, are aspects of the dreamer? So who is this father with the obscured face and the naked buttocks?"

"I suppose he is my idea of a father—of my own father?"

"He is something we would have to talk about if you decided to go on to a deeper stage in the investigation of yourself. Because your real father, your historical father, the man whom you last saw lying so pitiably on the dock with his face obscured in filth, and then so dishevelled in his coffin with his face destroyed by your stepmother's ambitious meddling, is by no means the same thing as the archetype of fatherhood you carry in the depths of your being, and which comes from— well, for the present we won't attempt to say where. Now tell me, have you had any of those demanding, humiliating sessions in Mr. Justice Staunton's court during the past few weeks? You haven't mentioned them."

"No. They don't seem to have been necessary recently."

"I thought that might be so. Well, my friend, you know now how very peculiar dreams are, and you know that they are not liars. But I don't believe you have found out yet that they sometimes like a little joke. And this is one. I believe that you have, in a literal sense, seen the end of Mr. Justice Staunton. The old Troll King has lost his trappings. No court, no robes, a sense of kindliness and concern, a revelation of that part of his anatomy he keeps nearest to the honoured Bench, and which nobody has ever attempted to invest with awe or dignity, and then—gone! If he should come again, as he well may, at least you have advanced so far that you have seen him with his trousers down. . . . Our hour is finished. If you wish to arrange further appointments, will you let me know sometime in the week between Christmas and the New Year? I wish you a very happy holiday."

· III ·

My Sorgenfrei Diary

»»»» ««««

DEC. 17, Wed.: Wretched letter from Netty this morn. Was feeling particularly well because of Dr. Johanna's saying on Monday that I had finished my *anamnesis* so far as she thought it necessary to go; extraordinary flood of energy and cheerfulness. Now this.

Seven pages of her big script, like tangled barbed wire, the upshot of which is that Meritorious Matey has at last done what I always expected him to do—revealed himself as a two-bit crook and opportunist. Has fiddled trust funds which somehow lay in his clutch; she doesn't say how and probably doesn't know. But she is certain he has been wronged. Of course he is her brother and the apple of her eye and Netty is nothing if not loyal, as the Staunton family knows to its cost—and also, I suppose, to its extraordinary benefit. One must be fair.

But how can I be fair to Matey? He has always been the deserving, hard-working fellow with his own way to make, while I have hardly been able to swallow for the weight of the silver spoon in my mouth. Certainly this is how Netty has put it to me, and when Father refused to take Matey into Alpha and wouldn't let Matey's firm handle the audit of Castor, she thought we were bowelless ingrates and oppressors. But Father smelled Matey as no good, and so did I, because of the way he sponged on Netty when he had no need. And now Netty begs me to return to Canada as soon as possible and undertake Matey's defence. "You have spent your talents on many a scoundrel, and you ought to be ready to see that a wronged honest boy is righted before the world"; that is how she puts it. And: "I've never asked you or the family for a thing and God knows what I've done for the Stauntons through thick and thin, and some things will never be known, but now I'm begging you on my bended knees."

There is a simple way of handling this, and I have done the simple thing already. Cabled Huddleston to look into it and let me know: he can do whatever can be done fully as well as I. Do I now write Netty and say I am unwell, and the doctor forbids, etc., and Frederick Huddleston, Q.C., will take over? But Netty doesn't believe there is anything wrong with me. She has let Caroline know that she is sure I am in some fancy European home for booze-artists, having a good time and reading books, which I was always too ready to do anyhow. She will think I am dodging. And in part she will be right.

Dr. Johanna has freed me from many a bogey, but she has also sharpened my already razorlike ethical sense. In her terms I have always projected the Shadow onto Matey; I have seen in him the worst of myself. I have been a heel in too many ways to count. Spying on Carol; spying on Denyse; making wisecracks to poor slobbering Lorene that she wasn't able to understand and which would have hurt her if she had understood; being miserable to Knopwood; miserable to Louis Wolff;

worst of all, miserable to Father about things where he was vulnerable and I was strong. The account is long and disgusting.

I have accepted all that; it is part of what I am and unless I know it, grasp it, and acknowledge it as my own, there can be no freedom for me and no hope of being less a miserable stinker in future.

Before I came to my present very modest condition of self-recognition I was a clever lad at projecting my own faults onto other people, and I could see them all and many more in Maitland Quelch, C.A. Of course he had his own quiverful of perfectly real faults; one does not project one's Shadow on a man of gleaming virtue. But I detested Matey more than was admissible, for he never put a stone in my way, and in his damp-handed, grinning fashion he tried to be my friend. He was not a very nice fellow, and now I know that it was my covert spiritual kinship with him that made me hate him.

So when I refuse to go back to Canada and try to get Matey off, what is my ethical position? The legal position is perfectly clear; if Matey is in trouble with the Securities Commission there is good reason for it, and the most I could do would be to try to hoodwink the court into thinking he didn't know what he was doing, which would make him look like a fool if slightly less a crook. But if I refuse to budge and hand him over even to such a good man as Huddleston, am I still following a course that I am trying, in the middle of my life, to change?

Oh Matey, you bastard, why couldn't you have kept your nose clean and spared me this problem at a time when I am what I suppose must be called a psychic convalescent?

»»»» ««««

DEC. 18, Thurs.: Must get away. Might have stayed in Zürich over Xmas if it were not for this Matey thing, but Netty will try to get me on the telephone, and if I talk with her I will·be lost. . . . What did she mean by "some things will never be known"? Could it possibly be that Carol was right? That Netty put Mother in the way of dying (much too steep to say she killed her) because she thought Mother had been unfaithful to Father and Father would be happier without her? If Netty is like that, why hasn't she put rat-poison in Denyse's martinis? She hates Denyse, and it would be just like Netty to think that her opinion in such a matter was completely objective and beyond dispute.

Thinking of Netty puts me in mind of Pargetter's warning about the witnesses, or clients, whose creed is *esse in re;* to such people the world is absolutely clear because they cannot understand that our personal point of view colours what we perceive; they think everything seems exactly the same to everyone as it does to themselves. After all, they say, the world is utterly objective; it is plain before our eyes; therefore what the ordinary intelligent man (this is always themselves) sees is all there is to be seen, and anyone who sees differently is mad, or malign, or just plain stupid. An astonishing number of judges seem to belong in this category. . . .

Netty was certainly one of those, and I never really knew why I was always at odds with her (while really loving the old girl, I must confess) till Pargetter rebuked me for being an equally wrong-headed, though more complex and amusing creature, whose creed is *esse in intellectu solo.* "You think the world is your idea," he said one November day at a tutorial when I had been offering him some fancy theorizing, "and if you don't understand that and check it now it will make your whole life a gigantic hallucination." Which, in spite of my success, is pretty much what happened, and my extended experiments as a booze-artist were chiefly directed to checking any incursions of unwelcome truth into my illusion.

But what am I headed for? Where has Dr. Johanna been taking me? I suspect toward a new ground of belief that wouldn't have occurred to Pargetter, which might be called *esse in anima:* I am beginning to recognize the objectivity of the world, while knowing also that because I am who and what I am, I both perceive the world in terms of who and what I am and project onto the world a great deal of who and what I am. If I know this, I ought to be able to escape the stupider kinds of illusion. The absolute nature of things is independent of my senses (which are all I have to perceive with), and what I perceive is an image in my own psyche.

All very fine. Not too hard to formulate and accept intellectually. But to *know* it; to bring it into daily life—that's the problem. And it would be real humility, not just the mock-modesty that generally passes for humility. Doubtless that is what Dr. Johanna has up her sleeve for me when we begin our sessions after Christmas.

Meanwhile I must go away for Christmas. Netty will get at me somehow if I stay here. . . . Think I shall go to St. Gall. Not far off and I could hire ski stuff if I wanted it. It is said to have lots to see besides the scenery.

»»»» ««««

DEC. 19, Fri.: Arrive St. Gall early p.m. Larger than I expected; about 70,000, which was the size of Pittstown, but this place has an unmistakable atmosphere of consequence. Reputedly the highest city in Europe, and the air is thin and clean. Settle into a good hotel (Walhalla—why?) and walk out to get my bearings. Not much snow, but everything is decorated for Christmas very prettily; not in our N. American whorehouse style. Find the Klosterhof square, and admire it, but leave the Cathedral till tomorrow. Dinner at a very good restaurant (Metropole) and to the Stadtheater. It has been rebuilt in the Brutalist-Modern manner, and everything is rough cement and skew-whiff instead of right-angled or curved, so it is an odd setting for Lehar's *Paganini,* which is tonight's piece. Music prettily Viennese. How simple, loud, and potent love always is in these operettas! If I understood the thing, Napoleon would not permit Pag to have his countess because he was not noble: once I could not have the girl I loved because I was not a Jew. But Pag made a lot of eloquent noise about it, whereas I merely went sour. . . . Did I love Judy? Or just something of myself in her as Dr. Johanna implies? Does it matter, now? Yes, it matters to me.

»»»» ««««

DEC. 20, Sat.: Always the methodical sight-seer, I am off to the Cathedral by 9:30. Knew it was Baroque, but had not been prepared for something *so* Baroque; breath-taking enormities of spiritual excess everywhere, but no effect of clutter or gim-crackery. Purposely took no guide-book; wanted to get a first impression before fussing about detail.

Then to the Abbey library, which is next door, and gape at some very odd old paintings and the wonders of their Baroque room. Keep my coat on as there is no heating in any serious sense; the woman who sells tickets directs me to put on huge felt overshoes to protect the parquet. Superb library to look at, and there are two or three men of priestly appearance actually reading and writing in a neighbouring room, so it must also be more than a spectacle. I gape reverently at some splendid MSS, including a venerable *Nibelungenlied* and a *Parsifal,* and wonder what a frowsy old mummy, with what appear to be its

own teeth, is doing there. I suppose in an earlier and less spe-
cialized time libraries were also repositories for curiosities.
Hovered over a drawing of Christ's head, done entirely in cal-
ligraphy; dated "nach 1650." Some painstaking penman had
found a way of writing the Scripture account of the Passion
with such a multitude of eloquent squiggles and crinkum-
crankum that he had produced a monument of pious ingenu-
ity, if not a work of art.

At last the cold becomes too much, and I scuttle out into
the sunshine, and look for a bookshop where I can buy a guide,
and turn myself thereby into a serious tourist. Find a fine shop,
get what I want, and am poking about among the shelves
when my eye is taken by two figures; a man in an engulfing
fur coat over what was obviously one of those thick Harris-
tweed suits is talking loudly to a woman who is very smartly and
expensively dressed, but who is the nearest thing to an ogress I
have ever beheld.

Her skull was immense, and the bones must have been
monstrously enlarged, for she had a gigantic jaw, and her eyes
peered out of positive caverns. She had made no modest con-
cessions to her ugliness, for her iron-gray hair was fashionably
dressed, and she wore a lot of make-up. They spoke in German, but there was something decidedly un-German and un-
Swiss about the man and the more I stared (over the top of a
book) the more familiar his back appeared. Then he moved,
with a limp that could only belong to one man in the world. It
was Dunstan Ramsay. Old Buggerlugs, as I live and breathe!
But why in St. Gall, and who could his dreadful companion
be? Someone of consequence, unquestionably, for the manag-
eress of the shop was very attentive. . . . Now: was I to
claim acquaintance, or sneak away and preserve the quiet of
my holiday? As so often in these cases, the decision was not
with me. Buggerlugs had spotted me.

—Davey! How nice to see you.

—Good-morning, sir. A pleasant surprise.

—The last person I would have expected. I haven't seen you since poor Boy's funeral. What brings you here?

—Just a holiday.

—Have you been here long?

—Since yesterday.

—How is everyone at home? Carol well? Denyse is well, undoubtedly. What about Netty? Still your dragon?

—All well, so far as I know.

—Liesl, this is my lifelong friend—his life long, that's to say—David Staunton. David, this is Fraulein Doktor Liselotte Naegeli, whose guest I am.

The ogress gave me a smile which was extraordinarily charming, considering what it had to work against. When she spoke her voice was low and positively beautiful. It seemed to have a faintly familiar ring, but that is impossible. Amazing what distinguished femininity the monster had. More chat, and they asked me to lunch.

The upshot of that was that my St. Gall holiday took an entirely new turn. I had counted on being solitary, but like many people who seek solitude I am not quite so fond of it as I imagine, and when Liesl—in no time I was asked to call her Liesl—asked me to join them at her country home for Christmas, I had said yes before I knew what I was doing. The woman is a spellbinder, without seeming to exert much effort, and Buggerlugs has changed amazingly. I have never fully liked him, as I told Dr. Johanna, but age and a heart attack he said he had had shortly after Father's death seem to have improved him out of all recognition. He was just as inquisitorial and ironic as ever, but there was a new geniality about him. I gather he has been convalescing with the ogress, whom I suppose to be a medico. She took an odd line with him.

—Wasn't I lucky, Davey, to persuade Ramsay to come to live with me? Such an amusing companion. Was he an amusing schoolmaster? I don't suppose so. But he is a dear man.

—Liesl, you will make Davey think we are lovers. I am here for Liesl's company, certainly, but almost as much because this climate suits my health.

—Let us hope it suits Davey's health, too. You can see he has been seriously unwell. But is your cure coming along nicely, Davey? Don't pretend you aren't working toward a cure.

—How can you tell that, Liesl? He looks better than when I last saw him, and no wonder. But what makes you think he is taking a cure?

—Well, look at him, Ramsay. Do you think I've lived near Zürich so long and can't recognize the "analysand look"? He is obviously working with one of the Jungians, probing his soul and remaking himself. Which doctor do you go to, Davey? I know several of them.

—I can't guess how you know, but there's no use pretending, I suppose. I've been a little more than a year with Fraulein Doktor Johanna von Haller.

—Jo von Haller! I have known her since she was a child. Not friends, really, but we know each other. Well, have you fallen in love with her yet? All her male patients do. It's supposed to be part of the cure. But she is very ethical and never encourages them. I suppose with her successful lawyer husband and her two almost grown-up sons it mightn't do. Oh, yes; she is Frau Doktor, you know. But I suppose you spoke in English and it never came up. Well, after a year with Jo, you need something more lively. I wish we could promise you a really gay Christmas at Sorgenfrei, but it is certain to be dull.

—Don't believe it, Davey. Sorgenfrei is an enchanted castle.

—Nothing of the sort, but it should at least be a little more friendly than a hotel in St. Gall. Can you come back with us now?

And so it was. An hour after finishing lunch I had picked up my things and was sitting beside Liesl in a beautiful sports car, with Ramsay and his wooden leg crammed into the back with the luggage, dashing eastward from St. Gall on the road to Konstanz, and Sorgenfrei—whatever it might be. One of those private clinics, perhaps, that are so frequent in Switzerland? We were mounting all the time, and at last, after half a mile or so through pine woods we emerged onto a shelf on a mountainside, with a breath-taking view—really breath-taking, for the air was very cold and thinner than at St. Gall—and Sorgenfrei commanding it.

Sorgenfrei is like Liesl, a fascinating monstrosity. In England it would be called Gothic Revival; I don't know the European equivalent. Turrets, mullioned windows, a squat tower for an entrance and somewhere at the back a much taller, thinner tower like a lead-pencil rising very high. But bearing everywhere the unmistakable double signature of the nineteenth century and a great deal of money. Inside, it is filled with bearskin rugs, gigantic pieces of furniture on which every surface has been carved within an inch of its life with fruits, flowers, birds, hares, and even, on one thing which seems to be an altar to greed but is more probably a sideboard, full-sized hounds; six of them with real bronze chains on their collars. This is the dream castle of some magnate of 150 years ago, conceived in terms of the civilization which has given the world, among a host of better things, the music box and the cuckoo clock.

We arrived at about five p.m., and I was taken to this room, which is as big as the board-room of Castor, and where I am seizing my chance to bring my diary up to the minute. This is exhilarating. Is it the air, or Liesl's company? I am glad I came.

Later: Am I still glad I came? It is after midnight and I have had the most demanding evening since I left Canada.

This house troubles me and I can't yet say why. Magnificent houses, palaces, beautiful country houses, comfortable houses —I know all these either as a guest or a tourist. But this house, which seems at first appearances to be rather a joke, is positively the damnedest house I have ever entered. One might think the architect had gained all his previous experience illustrating Grimm's fairy stories, for the place is full of fantasy— but spooky, early-nineteenth-century fantasy, not the feeble Disney stuff. Yet, on second glance, it seems all to be meant seriously, and the architect was obviously a man of gifts, for though the house is big, it is still a house for people to live in and not a folly. Nor is it a clinic. It is Liesl's home, I gather.

Sorgenfrei. Free of care. Sans Souci. The sort of name someone of limited imagination might give to a country retreat. But there is something here that utterly contradicts the suggestion of the rich bourgeoisie resting from their money-making.

When I went down to dinner I found Ramsay in the library. That is to say, in an English country-house it would have been the library, comfortable and pleasant, but at Sorgenfrei it is too oppressively literary; bookshelves rise to a high, painted ceiling, on which is written in decorative Gothic script what I can just make out to be the Ten Commandments. There is a huge terrestrial globe, balanced by an equally huge celestial one. A big telescope, not much less than a century old, I judged, is mounted at one of the windows that look out on the mountains. On a low table sits a very modern object, which I discovered was five chess-boards mounted one above another in a brass frame; there are chessmen on each board, arranged as for five different games in progress; the boards are made of transparent lucite or some such material, so that it is possible to look down through them from above and see the position of every man. There was a good fire, and Ramsay was warming his legs, one flesh and one artificial, in front of it. He caught my mood at once.

—Extraordinary house, isn't it?

—Very. Is this where you live now?

—I'm a sort of permanent guest. My position is rather in the eighteenth-century mode. You know—people of intellectual tastes kept a philosopher or a scholar around the place. Liesl likes my conversation. I like hers. Funny way for a Canadian schoolmaster to end up, don't you think?

—You were never an ordinary schoolmaster, sir.

—Don't call me sir, Davey. We're old friends. Your father was my oldest friend; if friends is what we were, which I sometimes doubted. But you're not a lad now. You're a notable criminal lawyer; what used to be called "an eminent silk." Of course the problem is that I haven't any name by which all my friends call me. What did you call me at school? Was it Corky? Corky Ramsay? Stupid name, really. Artificial legs haven't been made of cork in a very long time.

—If you really want to know, we called you Buggerlugs. Because of your habit of digging in your ear with your little finger, you know.

—Really? Well, I don't think I like that much. You'd better call me Ramsay, like Liesl.

—I notice she generally calls you "dear Ramsay."

—Yes; we're rather close friends. More than that, for a while. Does that surprise you?

—You've just said I'm an experienced criminal lawyer; nothing surprises me.

—Never say that, Davey. Never, never say that. Especially not at Sorgenfrei.

—You yourself just said it was an extraordinary house.

—Oh, quite so. Rather a marvel, in its peculiar style. But that wasn't precisely what I meant.

We were interrupted by Liesl, who appeared through a door which I had not noticed because it is one of those nineteenth-century affairs, fitted close into the bookshelves and covered with false book-backs, so that it can hardly be seen. She was wearing something very like a man's evening suit, made in dark velvet, and looked remarkably elegant. I was beginning not to notice her Gorgon face. Ramsay turned to her rather anxiously, I thought.

—Is himself joining us at dinner tonight?

—I think so. Why do you ask?

—I just wondered when Davey would meet him.

—Don't fuss, dear Ramsay. It's a sign of age, and you are not old. Look, Davey, have you ever seen a chess-board like this?

Liesl began to explain the rules of playing what is, in effect, a single game of chess, but on five boards at once and with five sets of men. The first necessity, it appears, is to dismiss all ideas of the normal game, and to school oneself to think both horizontally and laterally at the same time. I, who could play chess pretty well but had never beaten Pargetter, was baffled—so much so that I did not notice anyone else entering the room, and I started when a voice behind me said:

—When am I to be introduced to Mr. Staunton?

The man who spoke was surprising enough in himself, for he was a most elegant little man with a magnificent head of curling silver hair, and the evening dress he wore ended not in trousers, but in satin knee-breeches and silk stockings. But I knew him at once as Eisengrim, the conjuror, the illusionist, whom I had twice seen in Toronto at the Royal Alexandra Theatre, the last time when I was drunk and distraught, and shouted at the Brazen Head, "Who killed Boy Staunton?" Social custom is ground into our bones, and I put out my hand to shake his. He spoke:

—I see you recognize me. Well, are the police still trying to involve me in the murder of your father? They were very persistent. They even traced me to Copenhagen. But they had nothing to go on. Except that I seemed to know rather more about it than they did, and they put all sorts of fanciful interpretations on some improvised words of Liesl's. How pleasant to meet you. We must talk the whole thing over.

No point in reporting in detail what followed. How right Ramsay was! Never say you can't be surprised. But what was I to do? I was confronted by a man whom I had despised and even hated when last I saw him, and his opening remarks to me were designed to be disconcerting if not downright quarrel-picking. But I was not the same man who shouted his question in the theatre; after a year with Dr. Johanna I was a very different fellow. If Eisingrim was cool, I would be cooler. I have delicately slain and devoured many an impudent witness in the courts, and I am not to be bamboozled by a mountebank. I think my behaviour was a credit to Dr. Johanna, and to Pargetter; I saw admiration in Ramsay's face, and Liesl made no attempt to conceal her pleasure at a situation that seemed to be entirely to her taste.

We went in to dinner, which was an excellent meal and not at all in the excessive style of the house. There was plenty of good wine, and cognac afterward, but I knew myself well enough to be sparing with it, and once again I could see that Ramsay and Liesl were watching me closely and pleased by what I did. There was none of that English pretence that serious things should not be discussed while eating, and we talked of nothing but my father's murder and what followed it, his will and what sprang from that, and what Denyse, and Carol, and Netty and the world in general—so far as the world in general paid any attention—had thought and said about it.

It was a trial and a triumph for me, because since I came to Zürich I have spoken to nobody of these things except Dr. Johanna, and then in the most subjective terms possible. But tonight I found myself able to be comparatively objective, even when Liesl snorted with rude laughter at Denyse's antics with the death-mask. Ramsay was sympathetic, but he laughed when I said that Father had left some money for my non-existent children. His comment was:

—I don't believe you ever knew what a sore touch it was with Boy that you were such a Joseph about women. He felt it put him in the wrong. He always felt that the best possible favour you could do a woman was to push her into bed. He simply could not understand that there are men for whom sex is not the greatest of indoor and outdoor sports, hobbies, arts, sciences, and food for reverie. I always felt that his preoccupation with women was an extension of his miraculous touch with sugar and sweetstuffs. Women were the most delightful confectioneries he knew, and he couldn't understand anybody who hadn't a sweet tooth.

—I wonder what your father would have made of a woman like Jo von Haller?

—Women of that kind never came into Boy's ken, Liesl. Or women like you, for that matter. His notion of an intelligent woman was Denyse.

I found it still pained me to hear Father talked of in this objective strain, so I tried to turn the conversation.

—I suppose all but a tiny part of life lies outside anybody's ken, and we all get shocks and starts, now and then. For instance, who would have supposed that after such a long diversion through Dr. von Haller's consulting-room I should meet you three by chance? There's a coincidence, if you like.

But Ramsay wouldn't allow that to pass.

—As an historian, I simply don't believe in coincidence. Only very rigid minds do. Rationalists talk about a pattern they can see and approve as logical; any pattern they can't see and wouldn't approve they dismiss as coincidental. I suppose you had to meet us, for some reason. A good one, I hope.

Eisengrim was interested but supercilious; after dinner he and Liesl played the complex chess game. I watched for a while, but I could make nothing of what they were doing, so I sat by the fire and talked with Ramsay. Of course I was dying to know how he came to be part of this queer household, but Dr. von Haller has made me more discreet than I used to be about cross-examining in private life. That suggestion that he and Liesl had once been lovers—could it be? I probed, very, very gently. But I had once been Buggerlugs' pupil, and I still feel he can see right through me. Obviously he did, but he was in a mood to reveal, and like a man throwing crumbs to a bird he let me know:

1. That he had known Eisengrim from childhood.
2. That Eisengrim came from the same village as Father and himself, and Mother—my Deptford.
3. That Eisengrim's mother had been a dominant figure in his own life. He spoke of her as "saintly," which puzzles me. Wouldn't Netty have mentioned somebody like that?
4. That he met Liesl travelling with Eisengrim in Mexico and that they had discovered an "affinity" (his funny, old-fashioned word) which existed still.
5. When we veered back to the coincidence of my meeting

them in St. Gall, he laughed and quoted G. K. Chesterton: "Coincidences are a spiritual sort of puns."

He has, it appears, come to Switzerland to recuperate himself after his heart attack, and seems likely to stay here. He is working on another book—something about faith as it relates to myth, which is his old subject—and appears perfectly content. This is not a bad haul, and gives me encouragement for further fishing.

Eisengrim affects royal airs. Everything suggests that this is Liesl's house, but he seems to regard himself as the regulator of manners in it. After they adjourned their game (I gather it takes days to complete), he rose, and I was astonished to see that Liesl and Ramsay rose as well, so I followed suit. He shook us all by the hand, and bade us good-night with the style of a crowned head taking leave of courtiers. He had an air of You-people-are-welcome-to-sit-up-as-long-as-you-please-but-We-are-retiring, and it was pretty obvious he thought the tone of the gathering would drop when he left the room.

Not so. We all seemed much easier. The huge library, where the curtains had now been drawn to shut out the night sky and the mountaintops and the few lights that shone far below us, was made almost cosy by his going. Liesl produced whisky, and I thought I might allow myself one good drink. It was she who brought up what was foremost in my mind.

—I assure you, Davey, there is nothing premeditated about this. Of course when we met in the bookshop I knew you must be the son of the man who died so spectacularly when Eisengrim was last in Toronto, but I had no notion of the circumstances.

—Were you in Toronto with him?

—Certainly. We have been business partners and artistic

associates for a long time. I am his manager or impresario or whatever you want to call it. On the programs I use another name, but I assure you I am very much present. I am the voice of the Brazen Head.

—Then it was you who gave that extraordinary answer to my question?

—What question are you talking about?

—Don't you recall that Saturday night in the theatre when somebody called out, "Who killed Boy Staunton?"

—I remember it very clearly. It was a challenge, you may suppose, coming suddenly like that. We usually had warning of the questions the Head might have to answer. But was it you who asked the question?

—Yes, but I didn't hear all of your answer.

—No; there was confusion. Poor Ramsay here was standing at the back of an upstairs box, and that was when he had his heart attack. And I think a great many people were startled when he fell forward into sight. Of course there were others who thought it was part of the show. It was a memorable night.

—But do you remember what you said?

—Perfectly. I said: "He was killed by the usual cabal: by himself, first of all; by the woman he knew; by the woman he did not know; by the man who granted his inmost wish; and by the inevitable fifth, who was keeper of his conscience and keeper of the stone."

—I don't suppose it is unreasonable of me to ask for an explanation of that rigmarole?

—Not unreasonable at all, and I hope you get an answer that satisfies you. But not tonight. Dear Ramsay is looking a little pale, and I think I should see him to bed. But there is plenty of time. I know you will take care that we talk of this again.

And with that I have to be contented at least until tomorrow.

»»»» ««««

DEC. 21, Sun.: This morn. Liesl took me on a tour of the house, which was apparently built in 1824 by some forbear who had made money in the watch-and-clock business. The entrance hall is dominated by what I suppose was his masterpiece, for it has dials to show seconds, days of the week, days of the months, the months, the seasons, the signs of the zodiac, the time at Sorgenfrei and the time at Greenwich, and the phases of the moon. It has a chime of thirty-seven bells, which play a variety of tunes, and is ornamented with figures of Day and Night, the Seasons, two heads of Time, and God knows what else, all in fine *verd-antique.* Monstrous but fascinating, like Liesl, and she seems to love it. As we wandered through the house and climbed unexpected staircases and looked at the bewildering views from cunningly placed windows, I did my best to bring the conversation to the strange words of the Brazen Head about Father's death, but Liesl knows every trick of evasion, and in her own house I could not nail her down as I might in court. But she did say one or two things:

—You must not interpret too closely. Remember that I, speaking for the Head, had no time—not even ten seconds—to reflect. So I gave a perfectly ordinary answer, like any experienced fortune-teller. You know there are always things that fit almost any enquirer: you say those things and they will do the interpreting. "The woman he knew—the woman he did not know." . . . From what I know now, which is only what Ramsay has told me at one time or another, I would have said the woman he knew was your mother, and the woman he did not know was your stepmother. He felt guilty about your mother, and the second time he married a woman who was far stronger than he had understood. But I gather from the terrible fuss your stepmother made that she thought she must be the woman he knew, and was very angry at the idea that she had any part in bringing about his death. . . . I really can't tell you any more than that about why I spoke as I did. I have a tiny gift in this sort of thing; that was why Eisengrim trusted me to speak for the Head; maybe I sensed something—because one does, you know, if one permits it. But don't brood on it and try to make too much of it. Let it go.

—My training has not been to let things go.

—But Davey, your training and the way you have used yourself have brought you at last to Zürich for an analysis. I'm sure Jo von Haller, who is really excellent, though not at all my style, has made you see that. Are you going to do more work with her?

—That's a decision I must make.

—Well, don't be in a hurry to say you will.

Went for a long walk alone this afternoon, and thought about Liesl's advice.

This eve. after dinner Eisengrim showed us some home-movies of himself doing things with coins and cards. New illusions, it seems, for a tour they begin early in January. He is superb, and knows it. What an egotist! And only a conjuror, after all. Who gives a damn? Who needs conjurors? Yet I am unpleasantly conscious of a link between Eisengrim and myself. He wants people to be in awe of him, and at a distance: so do I.

»»»» ««««

DEC. 22, Mon.: I suppose Eisengrim sensed my boredom and disgust last night, because he hunted me up after breakfast and took me to see his workrooms, which are the old stables of Sorgenfrei; full of the paraphernalia of his illusions, and with very fine workbenches, at one of which Liesl was busy with a jeweller's magnifying-glass stuck in her eye. . . . "You didn't know I had the family knack of clockwork, did you?" she said. But Eisengrim wanted to talk himself:

—You don't think much of me, Staunton? Don't deny it; it is part of my profession to sniff people's thoughts. Well, fair enough. But I like you, and I should like you to like me. I am an egotist, of course. Indeed, I am a great egotist and a very unusual one, because I know what I am and I like it. Why not? If you knew my history, you would understand, I think. But you see that is just what I don't want, or ask for. So many people twitter through life crying, "Understand me! Oh, please understand me! To know all is to forgive all!" But you see I don't care about being understood, and I don't ask to be forgiven. Have you read the book about me?

(I have read it, because it is the only book in my bedroom, and so obviously laid out on the bedside table that it seems an obligation of the household to read the thing. I had seen it before; Father bought a copy for Lorene the first time we went to see Eisengrim, on her birthday. *Phantasmata: the Life and Adventures of Magnus Eisengrim.* Shortish; about 120 pages. But what a fairy-tale! Strange birth to distinguished Lithuanian parents, political exiles from Poland; infancy in the Arctic, where father was working on a secret scientific project (for Russia, it was implied, but because of his high lineage the Russians did not want to acknowledge the association); recognition of little Magnus by an Eskimo shaman as a child of strange gifts; little Magnus, between the ages of four and eight, learns arts of divination and hypnosis from the shaman and his colleagues. Father's Arctic work completed and he goes off to do something similar in the dead centre of Australia (because it is implied that father, the Lithuanian genius, is some sort of extremely advanced meteorological expert) and there little Magnus is taught by a tutor who is a great savant, who has to keep away from civilization for a while because he has done something dreadfully naughty. Little Magnus, after puberty, is irresistible to women, but he is obliged to be careful about this as the shaman had warned him women would disagree with his delicately balanced nerves. Nevertheless, great romances are hinted at; a generous gobbet of sadism spiced with pornography here. Having sipped, and rejected with contumely the learning of several great universities, Magnus Eisengrim determines to devote his life to the noble, misunderstood science which he first encountered in the Arctic, and which claimed him for its own. . . . And this is supposed to explain why he is travelling around with a magic show. A very good magic show, but still—a travelling showman.)

—Is one expected to take it seriously?

—I think it deserves to be taken more seriously than most biographies and autobiographies. You know what they are. The polished surface of a life. What the Zürich analysts call the Persona—the mask. Now, *Phantasmata* says what it is quite frankly in its title; it is an illusion, a vision. Which is what I am, and because I am such a thoroughly satisfactory illusion, and because I satisfy a hunger that almost everybody has for marvels, the book is a far truer account of me than ordinary biographies, which do not admit that their intent is to deceive and are woefully lacking in poetry. The book is extremely well written, don't you think?

—Yes. I was surprised. Did you write it?

—Ramsay wrote it. He has written so much about saints and marvels, Liesl and I thought he was the ideal man to provide the right sort of life for me.

—But you admit it is a pack of lies?

—It is not a police-court record. But as I have already said, it is truer to the essence of my life than the dowdy facts could ever be. Do you understand? I am what I have made myself— the greatest illusionist since Moses and Aaron. Do the facts suggest or explain what I am? No: but Ramsay's book does. I am truly Magnus Eisengrim. The illusion, the lie, is a Canadian called Paul Dempster. If you want to know his story, ask Ramsay. He knows, and he might tell. Or he might not.

—Thank you for being frank. Are you any more ready than Liesl to throw some light on the answer of the Brazen Head?

—Let me see. Yes, I am certainly "the man who granted his inmost wish." You would never guess what it was. But he told me. People do tell me things. When I met him, which was on the night of his death, he offered me a lift back to my hotel in his car. As we drove he said—and as you know this was at one of the peaks of his career, when he was about to realize a dream which he, or your stepmother, had long cherished—he said, "You know, sometimes I wish I could step on the gas and drive right away from all of this, all the obligations, the jealousies, the nuisances, and the relentlessly demanding people." I said, "Do you mean that? I could arrange it." He said, "Could you?" I replied, "Nothing easier." His face became very soft, like a child's, and he said, "Very well. I'd be greatly obliged to you." So I arranged it. You may be sure he knew no pain. Only the realization of his wish.

—But the stone? The stone in his mouth?

—Ah, well, that is not my story. You must ask the keeper of the stone. But I will tell you something Liesl doesn't know, unless Ramsay has told her: "the woman he did not know" was my mother. Yes, she had some part in it.

With that I had to be contented because Liesl and a workman wanted to talk with him. But somehow I found myself liking him. Even more strange, I found myself believing him.

But he was a hypnotist of great powers; I had seen him demonstrate that on the stage. Had he hypnotized Father and sent him to his death? And if so, why?

Later: That was how I put the question to Ramsay when I cornered him this afternoon in the room he uses for his writing. Pargetter's advice: always go to a man in *his* room, for then he has no place to escape to, whereas you may leave when you please. What did he say?

—Davey, you are behaving like the amateur sleuth in a detective story. The reality of your father's death is much more complex than anything you can uncover that way. First, you must understand that nobody—not Eisengrim or anyone—can make a man do something under hypnotism that he has not some genuine inclination to do. So: Who killed Boy Staunton? Didn't the Head say, "Himself, first of all?" We all do it, you know, unless we are taken off by some unaccountable accident. We determine the time of our death, and perhaps the means. As for the "usual cabal" I myself think "the woman he knew and the woman he did not know" were the same person—your mother. He never had any serious appraisal of her weakness or her strength. She had strength, you know, that he never wanted or called on. She was Ben Cruikshank's daughter, and don't suppose that was nothing just because Ben wasn't a village grandee like Doc Staunton. Boy never had any use for your mother as a grown-up woman, and she kept herself childish in the hope of pleasing him. When we have linked our destiny with somebody, we neglect them at our peril. But Boy never knew that. He was so well graced, so gifted, such a genius in his money-spinning way, that he never sensed the reality of other people. Her weakness galled him, but her occasional shows of strength shamed him.

—You loved Mother, didn't you?

—I thought I did when I was a boy. But the women we

really love are the women who complete us, who have the qualities we can borrow and so become something nearer to whole men. Just as we complete them, of course; it's not a one-way thing. Leola and I, when romance was stripped away, were too much alike; our strengths and weaknesses were too nearly the same. Together we would have doubled our gains and our losses, but that isn't what love is.

—Did you sleep with her?

—I know times have changed, Davey, but isn't that rather a rum question to put to an old friend about your mother?

—Carol used to insist that you were my father.

—Then Carol is a mischief-making bitch. I'll tell you this, however: your mother once asked me to make love to her, and I refused. In spite of one very great example I had in my life I couldn't rise to love as an act of charity. The failure was mine, and a bitter one. Now I'm not going to say the conventional thing and tell you I wish you were my son. I have plenty of sons—good men I've taught, who will carry something of me into places I would never reach. Listen, Davey, you great clamorous baby-detective, there is something you ought to know at your age: every man who amounts to a damn has several fathers, and the man who begat him in lust or drink or for a bet or even in the sweetness of honest love may not be the most important father. The fathers you choose for yourself are the significant ones. But you didn't choose Boy, and you never knew him. No; no man knows his father. If Hamlet had known his father he would never have made such an almighty fuss about a man who was fool enough to marry Gertrude. Don't you be a two-bit Hamlet, clinging to your father's ghost until you are destroyed. Boy is dead; dead of his own will, if not wholly of his own doing. Take my advice and get on with your own concerns.

—My concerns are my father's concerns and I can't escape

that. Alpha is waiting for me. And Castor.

—Not your father's concerns. Your kingdoms. Go and reign, even if he has done a typical Boy trick by leaving you a gavel where he used a golden sceptre.

—I see you won't talk honestly with me. But I must ask one more question; who was "the inevitable fifth, who was keeper of his conscience and keeper of the stone?"

—I was. And as keeper of his conscience, and as one who has a high regard for you, I will say nothing about it.

—But the stone? The stone that was found in his mouth when they rescued his body from the water? Look, Ramsay, I have it here. Can you look at it and say nothing?

—It was my paperweight for over fifty years. Your father gave it to me, very much in his own way. He threw it at me, wrapped up in a snowball. The rock-in-the-snowball man was part of the father you never knew, or never recognized.

—But why was it in his mouth?

—I suppose he put it there himself. Look at it; a piece of that pink granite we see everywhere in Canada. A geologist who saw it on my desk told me that they now reckon that type of stone to be something like a thousand million years old. Where has it been, before there were any men to throw it, and where will it be when you and I are not even a pinch of dust? Don't cling to it as if you owned it. I did that. I harboured it for sixty years, and perhaps my hope was for revenge. But at last I lost it, and Boy got it back, and he lost it, and certainly you will lose it. None of us counts for much in the long, voiceless, inert history of the stone. . . . Now I am going to claim the privilege of an invalid and ask you to leave me.

—There's nothing more to be said?

—Oh, volumes more, but what does all this saying amount to? Boy is dead. What lives is a notion, a fantasy, a whim-wham in your head that you call Father, but which never had anything seriously to do with the man you attached it to.

—Before I go: who was Eisengrim's mother?

—I spent decades trying to answer that. But I never fully knew.

Later: Found out a little more about the super-chess game this eve. Each player plays both black and white. If the player who draws white at the beginning plays white on boards one, three, and five, he must play black on boards two and four. I said to Liesl that this must make the game impossibly complicated, as it is not five games played consecutively, but one game.

—Not half so complicated as the game we all play for seventy or eighty years. Didn't Jo von Haller show you that you can't play the white pieces on all the boards? Only people who play on one, flat board can do that, and then they are in agonies trying to figure out what black's next move will be. Far better to know what you are doing, and play from both sides.

»»»» ««««

DEC. 23, Tues.: Liesl has the ability to an extraordinary extent to worm things out of me. My temperament and professional training make me a man to whom things are told; somehow she makes me into a teller. I ran into her—better be honest, I sought her out—this morning in her workshop, where she sat with a jeweller's magnifying glass in her eye and tinkered with a tiny bit of mechanism, and in five minutes had me caught in a conversation of a kind I don't like but can't resist when Liesl creates it.

—So you must give Jo a decision about more analysis? What is it to be?

—I'm torn about it. I'm seriously needed at home. But the work with Dr. von Haller holds out the promise of a kind of satisfaction I've never known before. I suppose I want to have it both ways.

—Well, why not? Jo has set you on your path; do you need her to take you on a tour of your inner labyrinth? Why not go by yourself?

—I've never thought of it—I wouldn't know how.

—Then find out. Finding out is half the value. Jo is very good. I say nothing against her. But these analyses, Davey—they are duets between the analyst and the analysand, and you will never be able to sing louder or higher than your analyst.

—She has certainly done great things for me in the past year.

—Undoubtedly. And she never pushed you too far, or frightened you, did she? Jo is like a boiled egg—a wonder, a miracle, very easy to take—but even with a good sprinkling of salt she is invalid food, don't you find?

—I understand she is one of the best in Zürich.

—Oh, certainly. Analysis with a great analyst is an adventure in self-exploration. But how many analysts are great? Did I ever tell you I knew Freud slightly? A giant, and it would be apocalyptic to talk to such a giant about oneself. I never met Adler, whom everybody forgets, but he was certainly another giant. I once went to a seminar Jung gave in Zürich, and it was unforgettable. But one must remember that they were all men with systems. Freud, monumentally hipped on sex (for which he personally had little use) and almost ignorant of Nature: Adler, reducing almost everything to the will to power: and Jung, certainly the most humane and gentlest of them, and possibly the greatest, but nevertheless the descendant of parsons and professors, and himself a super-parson and a super-professor. All men of extraordinary character, and they devised systems that are forever stamped with that character. . . . Davey, did you ever think that these three men who were so splendid at understanding others had first to understand themselves? It was from their self-knowledge they spoke. They did not go trustingly to some doctor and follow his lead because they were too lazy or too scared to make the inward journey alone. They dared heroically. And it should never be forgotten that they made the inward journey while they were working like galley-slaves at their daily tasks, considering other people's troubles, raising families, living full lives. They were heroes, in a sense that no space-explorer can be a hero, because they went into the unknown absolutely alone. Was their heroism simply meant to raise a whole new crop of invalids? Why don't you go home and shoulder your yoke, and be a hero too?

—I'm no hero, Liesl.

—Oh, how modest and rueful that sounds! And you expect me to think, isn't he splendid to accept his limitations so manfully. But I don't think that. All that personal modesty is part of the cop-out personality of our time. You don't know whether or not you are a hero, and you're bloody well determined not to find out, because you're scared of the burden if you are and scared of the certainty if you're not.

—Just a minute. Dr. von Haller, of whom you think so little, once suggested that I was rather inclined toward heroic measures in dealing with myself.

—Good for Jo! But she didn't encourage you in it, did she? Ramsay says you are very much the hero in court—voice of the mute, hope of the hopeless, last resort of those society has condemned. But of course that's a public personality. Why do you put yourself on this footing with a lot of riff-raff, by the way?

—I told Dr. von Haller that I liked living on the lip of a volcano.

—A good, romantic answer. But do you know the name of the volcano? That's what you have to find out.

—What are you suggesting? That I go home and take up

my practice and Alpha and Castor and see what I can do to
wriggle crooks like Matey Quelch off the hooks on which they
have been caught? And at night, sit down quietly and try to
think my way out of all my problems, and try to make some
sort of sense of my life?

—Think your way out. . . . Davey, what did Jo say was
wrong with you? Obviously you have a screw loose somewhere; everybody has. What did she find at the root of most of
your trouble?

—Why should I tell you?

—Because I've asked, and I truly want to know. I'm not just
a gossip or a chatterer, and I like you very much. So tell me.

—It's nothing dreadful. She just kept coming back to the
point that I am rather strongly developed in Thinking, and
seem to be a bit weak in Feeling.

—I guessed that was it.

—But honestly I don't know what's wrong with thinking.
Surely it's what everybody is trying to do?

—Oh yes; very fine work, thinking. But it is also the greatest bolt-hole and escape-hatch of our time. It's supposed to excuse everything. . . . "I think this . . . I thought that. . . .
You haven't really thought about it. . . . Think, for God's
sake. . . . The thinking of the meeting (or the committee, or
God help us, the symposium) was that. . . ." But so much of
this thinking is just mental masturbation, not intended to
beget anything. . . . So you are weak in feeling, eh? I wonder
why?

—Because of Dr. von Haller, I can tell you. In my life feeling has not been very handsomely rewarded. It has hurt like
hell.

—Nothing unusual in that. It always does. But you could
try. Do you remember the fairy-tale about the boy who

couldn't shudder and was so proud of it? Nobody much likes shuddering, but it's better than existing without it, I can assure you.

—I seem to have a natural disposition to think rather than feel, and Dr. von Haller has helped me a good deal there. But I am not ambitious to be a great feeler. Wouldn't suit my style of life at all, Liesl.

—If you don't feel, how are you going to discover whether or not you are a hero?

—I don't want to be a hero.

—So? It isn't everybody who is triumphantly the hero of his own romance, and when we meet one he is likely to be a fascinating monster, like my dear Eisengrim. But just because you are not a roaring egotist, you needn't fall for the fashionable modern twaddle of the anti-hero and the mini-soul. That is what we might call the Shadow of democracy; it makes it so laudable, so cosy and right and easy to be a spiritual runt and lean on all the other runts for support and applause in a splendid apotheosis of runtdom. Thinking runts, of course—oh, yes, thinking away as hard as a runt can without getting into danger. But there are heroes, still. The modern hero is the man who conquers in the inner struggle. How do you know you aren't that kind of hero?

—You are as uncomfortable company as an old friend of mine who asked for spiritual heroism in another way. "God is here and Christ is now," he would say, and ask you to live as if it were true.

—It is true. But it's equally true to say "Odin is here and Loki is now." The heroic world is all around us, waiting to be known.

—But we don't live like that, now.

—Who says so? A few do. Be the hero of your own epic. If

others will not, are you to blame? One of the great follies of our time is this belief in some levelling of Destiny, some democracy of *Wyrd*.

—And you think I should go it alone?

—I don't think: I feel that you ought at least to consider the possibility, and not cling to Jo like a sailor clinging to a lifebelt.

—I wouldn't know how to start.

—Perhaps if you felt something powerfully enough it would set you on the path.

—But what?

—Awe is a very unfashionable, powerful feeling. When did you last feel awe in the presence of anything?

—God, I can't remember ever feeling what I suppose you mean by awe.

—Poor Davey! How you have starved! A real little workhouse boy, an Oliver Twist of the spirit! Well, you're rather old to begin.

—Dr. von Haller says not. I can begin the second part of this exploration with her, if I choose. But what is it? Do you know, Liesl?

—Yes, but it isn't easily explained. It's a thing one experiences—feels, if you like. It's learning to know oneself as fully human. A kind of rebirth.

—I was told a lot about that in my boyhood days, when I thought I was a Christian. I never understood it.

—Christians seem to have got it mixed up, somehow. It's certainly not crawling back into your mother's womb; it's more a re-entry and return from the womb of mankind. A fuller comprehension of one's humanity.

—That doesn't convey much to me.

—I suppose not. It's not a thinker's thing.

—Yet you suggest I go it alone?

—I don't know. I'm not as sure as I was. You might manage it. Perhaps some large experience, or even a good, sharp shock, might put you on the track. Perhaps you are wrong even to listen to me.

—Then why do you talk so much, and throw out so many dangerous suggestions?

—It's my métier. You thinkers drive me to shake you up. Maddening woman!

»»»» ««««

DEC. 24, Wed. and Christmas Eve: Was this the worst day of my life, or the best? Both.

Liesl insisted this morning that I go on an expedition with her. You will see the mountains at their best, she said; it is too cold for the tourists with their sandwiches, and there is not enough snow for skiers. So we drove for about half an hour, uphill all the way, and at last came to one of those cable-car affairs and swayed and joggled dizzily through the air toward the far-off shoulder of a mountain. When we got out of it at last, I found I was panting.

—We are about seven thousand feet up now. Does it bother you? You'll soon get used to it. Come on. I want to show you something.

—Surely the view elsewhere is the same as it is here?

—Lazy! What I want to show you isn't a view.

It was a cave; large, extremely cold as soon as we penetrated a few yards out of the range of the sun, but not damp. I couldn't see much of it, and although it is the first cave I have ever visited it convinced me that I don't like caves. But Liesl was enthusiastic, because it is apparently quite famous since somebody, whose name I did not catch, proved conclusively in the 'nineties that primitive men had lived here. All the sharp-

ened flints, bits of carbon, and other evidence had been removed, but there were a few scratches on the walls which appear to be very significant, though they looked like nothing
more than scratches to me.

—Can't you imagine them, crouching here in the cold as the
sun sank, with nothing to warm them but a small fire and a
few skins? But enduring, enduring, enduring! They were
heroes, Davey.

—I don't suppose they conceived of anything better. They
can't have been much more than animals.

—They were our ancestors. They were more like us than
they were like any animal.

—Physically, perhaps. But what kind of brains had they?
What sort of mind?

—A herd-mind, probably. But they may have known a few
things we have lost on the long journey from the cave to—
well, to the law-courts.

—I don't see any good in romanticizing savages. They knew
how to get a wretched living and hang on to life for twenty-
five or thirty years. But surely anything human, any sort of
culture or civilized feeling or whatever you want to call it,
came ages later?

—No, no; not at all. I can prove it to you now. It's a little
bit dangerous, so follow me, and be careful.

She went to the very back of the cave, which may have been
two hundred feet deep, and I was not happy to follow her,
because it grew darker at every step, and though she had a big
electric torch it seemed feeble in that blackness. But when we
had gone as far as seemed possible, she turned to me and said,
"This is where it begins to be difficult, so follow me very
closely, close enough to touch me at all times, and don't lose
your nerve." Then she stepped behind an outcropping of rock
which looked like solid cave wall and scrambled up into a hole

about four feet above the cave floor.

I followed, very much alarmed, but too craven to beg off. In the hole, through which it was just possible to move on hands and knees, I crept after the torch, which flickered intermittently because every time Liesl lifted her back she obscured its light. And then, after perhaps a dozen yards of this creeping progress over rough stone, we began what was to me a horrible descent.

Liesl never spoke or called to me. As the hole grew smaller she dropped from her knees and crawled on her belly, and there was nothing for me but to do the same. I was as frightened as I have ever been in my life, but there was nothing for me to do but follow, because I had no idea of how I could retreat. Nor did I speak to her; her silence kept me quiet. I would have loved to hear her speak, and say something in reply, but all I heard was the shuffling as she crawled and wriggled, and now and then one of her boots kicked against my head. I have heard of people whose sport it is to crawl into these mountain holes, and read about some of them who had stuck and died. I was in terror, but somehow I kept on wriggling forward. I have not wriggled on my belly since I was a child, and it hurt; my shoulders and neck began to ache torturingly, and at every hunch forward my chest, privates, and knees were scraped unpleasantly on the stone floor. Liesl had outfitted me in some winter clothes she had borrowed from one of the workmen at Sorgenfrei, and though they were thick, they were certainly not much protection from the bruises of this sort of work.

How far we wriggled I had no idea. Later Liesl, who had made the journey several times, said it was just under a quarter of a mile, but to me it might have been ten miles. At last I heard her say, Here we are, and as I crawled out of the hole and stood up—very gingerly because for some reason she did not use her electric torch and the darkness was complete and I had no idea how high the roof might be—there was the flash of a match, and soon a larger flame that came from a torch she had lit.

—This is a pine-torch; I think it the most appropriate light for this place. Electricity is a blasphemy here. The first time I came, which was about three years ago, there were remains of pine torches still by the entry, so that was how they must have lit this place.

—Who are you talking about?

—The people of the caves. Our ancestors. Here, hold this torch while I light another. It takes some time for the torches to give much light. Stand where you are and let it unfold before you.

I thought she must mean that we had entered one of those caves, of which I have vaguely heard, which are magnificently decorated with primitive paintings. I asked her if that were it, but all she would say was, "Very much earlier than that," and stood with her torch held high.

Slowly, in the flickering light, the cave revealed itself. It was about the size of a modest chapel; I suppose it might have held fifty people; and it was high, for the roof was above the reach of the light from our torches. It was bitter cold but there was no ice on the walls; there must have been lumps of quartz, because they twinkled eerily. Liesl was in a mood that I had never seen in her before; all her irony and amusement were gone and her eyes were wide with awe.

—I discovered this about three years ago. The outer cave is quite famous, but nobody had noticed the entrance to this one. When I found it I truly believe I was the first person to enter it in—how long would you guess, Davey?

—I can't possibly say. How can you tell?

—By what is here. Haven't you noticed it yet?

—It just seems to be a cave. And brutally cold. Do you suppose somebody used it for something?

—Those people. The ancestors. Look here.

She led me toward the farthest wall from where we had entered, and we came to a little enclosure, formed by a barrier made of heaped up stones; in the cave wall, above the barrier, were seven niches, and I could just make out something of bone in each of these little cupboards; old, dark brown bone, which I gradually made out to be skulls of animals.

—They are bears. The ancestors worshipped bears. Look, in this one bones have been pushed into the eyeholes. And here, you see, the leg-bones have been carefully piled under the chin of the skull.

—Do you suppose the bears lived in here?

—No cave-bear could come through the passage. No; they brought the bones here, and the skins, and set up this place of worship. Perhaps someone pulled on the bear skin, and there was a ceremony of killing.

—That was their culture, was it? Playing bears in here?

—Flippant fool! Yes, that was their culture.

—Well, don't snap at me. I can't pretend it means much to me.

—You don't know enough for it to mean anything to you. Worse for you, you don't feel enough for it to mean anything to you.

—Liesl, are we going to go over all that again in the depths of this mountain? I want to get out. If you want to know, I'm scared. Now look: I'm sorry I haven't been respectful enough about your discovery. I'm sure it means a lot in the world of archaeology, or ethnology, or whatever it may be. The men around here worshipped bears. Good. Now let's go.

—Not just the men around here. The men of a great part of the world. There are such caves as this all over Europe and

Asia, and they have found some in America. How far is Hudson Bay from where you live?

—A thousand miles, more or less.

—They worshipped the bear there, between the great ice ages.

—Does it matter, now?

—Yes, I think it matters now. What do we worship today?

—Is this the place or the time to go into that?

—Where better? We share the great mysteries with these people. We stand where men once came to terms with the facts of death and mortality and continuance. How long ago, do you suppose?

—I haven't any idea.

—It was certainly not less than seventy-five thousand years ago; possibly much, much more. They worshipped the bear and felt themselves better and greater because they had done so. Compared with this place the Sistine Chapel is of yesterday. But the purpose of both places is the same. Men sacrificed and ate of the noblest thing they could conceive, hoping to share in its virtue.

—Yes, yes: I read *The Golden Bough* when I was young.

—Yes, yes; and you misunderstood what you read because you accepted its rationalist tone instead of understanding its facts. Does this place give you no sense of the greatness and indomitability and spiritual splendour of man? Man is a noble animal, Davey. Not a good animal; a noble animal.

—You distinguish between the two?

—Yes, you—you lawyer, I do.

—Liesl, we mustn't quarrel. Not here. Let's get out and I'll argue all you please. If you want to split morality—some sort of accepted code—off from the highest values we have, I'll promise you a long wrangle. I am, as you say, a lawyer. But for the love of God let's get back to the light.

—For the love of God? Is not God to be found in the darkness? Well, you mighty lover of the light and the law, away we go.

But then, to my astonishment, Liesl flung herself on the ground, face down before the skulls of the bears, and for perhaps three minutes I stood in the discomfort we always feel when somebody nearby is praying and we are not. But what form could her prayers be taking? This was worse—much worse—than Dr. Johanna's Comedy Company of the Psyche. What sort of people had I fallen among on this Swiss journey?

When she rose she was grinning and the charm I had learned to see in her terrible face was quite gone.

—Back to the light, my child of light. You must be reborn into the sun you love so much, so let us lose no time. Leave your torch, here, by the way out.

She dowsed her own torch by stubbing it on the ground and I did so too. As the light diminished to a few sparks I heard a mechanical clicking, and I knew she was snapping the switch of her electric torch, but no light came.

—Something is wrong. The batteries or the bulb. It won't light.

—But how are we to get back without light?

—You can't miss the path. Just keep crawling. You'd better go first.

—Liesl, am I to go into that tunnel without a glimmer of light?

—Yes, unless you wish to stay here in the dark. I'm going, certainly. If you are wise you will go first. And don't change your mind on the way, because if anything happens to you, Davey, I can't turn back, or wriggle backward. It's up and out for both of us, or death for both of us. . . . Don't think about it any longer. Go on!

She gave me a shove toward the hole of the tunnel, and I hit

my head hard against the upper side of it. But I was cowed by
the danger and afraid of Liesl, who had become such a demon
in the cave, and I felt my way into the entrance and began to
wriggle.

What had been horrible coming in, because it was done
head downward, was more difficult than anything I have ever
attempted until I began the outward journey; but now I had to
wriggle upward at an angle that seemed never less than forty-
five degrees. It was like climbing a chimney, a matter of knees
and elbows, and frequent cracks on the skull. I know I kicked
Liesl in the face more than once, but she made no sound except
for the grunting and panting without which no progress was
possible. I had worn myself out going in; going out I had to
find strength from new and unguessed-at sources. I did not
think; I endured, and endurance took on a new character, not
of passive suffering but of anguished, fearful striving. Was it
only yesterday I had been called the boy who could not shudder?

Suddenly, out of the darkness just before me, came a roar so
loud, so immediate, so fearful in suggestion that I knew in that
instant the sharpness of death. I did not lose consciousness.
Instead I knew with a shame that came back in full force from
childhood that my bowels had turned to water and gushed out
into my pants, and the terrible stench that filled the tunnel was
my own. I was at the lowest ebb, frightened, filthy, seemingly
powerless, because when I heard Liesl's voice—"Go on, you
dirty brute, go on"—I couldn't go on, dragging with me that
mess which, from being hot as porridge, was cooling quickly in
the chill of the tunnel.

—It's only a trick of the wind. Did you think it was the bear-
god coming to claim you? Go on. You have another two hundred yards at least. Do you think I want to hang about here
with your stink? Go on!

—I can't, Liesl. I'm done.

—You must.

—How?

—What gives you strength? Have you no God? No, I suppose not. Your kind have neither God nor Devil. Have you no ancestors?

Ancestors? Why, in this terrible need, would I want such ornaments? Then I thought of Maria Dymock, staunch in the street of Staunton, demanding money from the passers-by to get herself and her bastard to Canada. Maria Dymock, whom Doc Staunton had suppressed, and about whom my father would hear nothing after that first, unhappy letter. (What had Pledger-Brown said? "Too bad, Davey; he wanted blood and all we could offer was guts.") Would Maria Dymock see me through? In my weakened, terrified, humiliated condition I suppose I must have called upon Maria Dymock and something—but it's absurd to think it could have been she!—gave me the power I needed to wriggle that last two hundred yards, until an air that was sweeter but no less cold told me that the outer cave was near.

Out of the darkness into the gloom. Out of the gloom into sunshine, and the extraordinary realization that it was about three o'clock on a fine Christmas Eve, and that I was seven thousand feet above the sea on a Swiss mountain. An uncomfortable, messy walk back to the cable-railway and the discovery—God bless the Swiss!—that the little station had a good men's toilet with lots of paper towels. A dizzy, light-headed journey downward on one of the swaying cars, during which Liesl said nothing but sulked like some offended shaman from the days of her bear-civilization. We drove home in silence; even when she indicated that she wished me to sit on a copy of the *Neue Zürcher Zeitung* that was in the car, so as not to soil her upholstery, she said nothing. But when we drove into the stable-yard which led to the garages at Sorgenfrei, I spoke.

—Liesl, I am very, very sorry. Not for being afraid, or messing my pants, or any of that. But for falling short of what you expected. You thought me worthy to see the shrine of the bears, and I was too small a person to know what you meant. But I think I have a glimmering of something better, and I beg you not to shut me out of your friendship.

Another woman might have smiled, or taken my hand, or kissed me, but not Liesl. She glared into my eyes.

—Apology is the cheapest coin on earth, and I don't value it. But I think you have learned something, and if that is so, I'll do more than be your friend. I'll love you, Davey. I'll take you into my heart, and you shall take me into yours. I don't mean bed-love, though that might happen, if it seemed the right thing. I mean the love that gives all and takes all and knows no bargains.

I was bathed and in bed by five o'clock, dead beat. But so miraculous is the human spirit, I was up and about and able to eat a good dinner and watch a Christmas broadcast from Lausanne with Ramsay and Eisengrim and Liesl, renewed—yes, and it seemed to me reborn, by the terror of the cave and the great promise she had made to me a few hours before.

»»»» ««««

DEC. 25, Thurs. and Christmas Day: Woke feeling better than I have done in years. To breakfast very hungry (why does happiness make us hungry?) and found Ramsay alone at the table.

—Merry Christmas, Davey. Do you recall once telling me you hated Christmas more than any day in the year?

—That was long ago. Merry Christmas, Dunny. That was what Father used to call you, wasn't it?

—Yes, and I always hated it. I think I'd almost rather be called Buggerlugs.

Eisengrim came in and put a small pouch beside my plate. Obviously he meant me to open it, so I did, and out fell a fine pair of ivory dice. I rolled them a few times, without much luck. Then he took them.

—What would you like to come up?

—Double sixes, surely?

He cast the dice, and sure enough, there they were.

—Loaded?

—Nothing so coarse. They are quite innocent, but inside they have a little secret. I'll show you how it works later.

Ramsay laughed.

—You don't suppose an eminent silk would use such things, Magnus? He'd be thrown out of all his clubs.

—I don't know what an eminent silk might do with dice but I know very well what he does in court. Are you a lucky man? To be lucky is always to play with—well, with dice like these. You might like to keep them in your pocket, Davey, just as a reminder of—well, of what our friend Ramsay calls the variability and mutability and general rumness of things.

Liesl had come in, and now she handed me a watch.

—From the Brazen Head.

It was a handsome piece, and on the back was engraved, "Time is . . . Time was . . . Time is past," which is perfectly reasonable if you like inscribed watches, and of course these were the words she and Eisengrim used to introduce their Brazen Head illusion. I knew that, between us, it meant the mystery and immemorial age of the cave. I was embarrassed.

—I had no idea there was to be an exchange of gifts. I'm terribly sorry, but I haven't anything for anyone.

—Don't think of it. It is just as one feels. You see, dear Ramsay has not worried about gifts either.

—But I have. I have my gifts here. I wanted to wait till everyone was present before giving mine.

Ramsay produced a paper bag from under the table and solemnly handed us each a large gingerbread bear. They were handsome bears, standing on their hindlegs and each holding a log of wood.

—These are the real St. Gall bears; the shops are full of them at this time of year.

Eisengrim nibbled at his bear experimentally.

—Yes, they are made like the bear which is the city crest, or totem, aren't they?

—Indeed, they are images of the veritable bear of St. Gall himself. You know the legend. Early in the seventh century an Irish monk, Gallus, came to this part of the world to convert the wild mountaineers. They were bear-worshippers, I believe. He made his hermitage in a cave near where the present city stands, and preached and prayed. But he was so very much a holy man, and so far above merely creatural considerations, that he needed a servant or a friend to help him. Where would he find one? Now it so happened that Gallus's cave had another inhabitant, a large bear. And Gallus, who was extremely long-headed, made a deal with the bear. If the bear would bring him wood for his fire, he would give the bear bread to eat. And so it was. And this excellent gingerbread—I hope I may say it is excellent without seeming to praise my own gift —reminds us even today that if we are really wise, we will make a working arrangement with the bear that lives with us, because otherwise we shall starve or perhaps be eaten by the bear. You see, like every tale of a saint it has a moral, and the moral is my Christmas gift to you, Davey, you poor Canadian bear-choker, and to you, Magnus, you enchanting fraud, and to you, my dearest Liesl, though you don't need it: cherish your bear, and your bear will feed your fire.

Later: For a walk with Ramsay. It was not long after three o'clock, but already in the mountains sunset was well advanced. He cannot walk far with his game leg, but we went a few hundred yards, toward a precipice; a low stone wall warned us not to go too near, for the drop was steep toward a valley and some little farmsteads. Talked to him about the decision Liesl wants me to make and asked his advice.

—Liesl likes pushing people to extremes. Are you a man for extremes, Davey? I don't think I can help you. Or can I? You still have that stone. . . . You know, the one that was found in Boy's mouth?

I took it out of my pocket and handed it to him.

—I can do this for you, anyhow, Davey.

He raised his arm high, and with a snap of the wrist threw it far down into the valley. In that instant it was possible to see that he had once been a boy. We both watched until the little speck could no longer be seen against the valley dusk.

—There. At least that's that. Pray God it didn't hit anybody.

We turned back toward Sorgenfrei, walking in companionable silence. My thoughts were on the dream I dreamed the night before I first confronted Dr. von Haller. It was splendidly clear in my recollection. I had left my enclosed, ordered, respected life. Yes. And I had ventured into unknown country, where archaeological digging was in progress. Yes. I had attempted to go down the circular staircase inside the strange, deceptive hut—so wretched on the outside and so rich within—and my desire had been thwarted by trivial fellows who behaved as if I had no right there. Yes. But as I thought about it, the dream changed; the two young men were no longer at the stairhead, and I was free to go down if I pleased. And I did please, for I sensed that there was treasure down there. I was filled with happiness, and I knew this was what I wanted most.

I was walking with Ramsay, I was fully aware of everything

about me, and yet it was the dream that was most real to me. The strange woman, the gypsy who spoke so compellingly, yet incomprehensibly—where was she? In my waking dream I looked out of the door of the hut, and there she was, walking toward me; to join me, I knew. Who was she? "Every country gets the foreigners it deserves." The words which I had thought so foolish still lingered in my mind. They meant something more important than I could yet understand, and I struggled for an explanation. Was I going down the staircase to a strange land? Was I, then, to be a stranger there? But how could I be foreign in the place where my treasure lay? Surely I was native there, however long I had been absent?

Across the uneven ground the woman came, with a light step. Nearer and nearer, but still I could not see whether her face was that of Liesl or Johanna.

Then Ramsay spoke, and the dream, or vision or whatever it was, lost its compelling quality. But I know that not later than tomorrow I must know what face the woman wore, and which woman is to be my guide to the treasure that is mine.